USA TODAY BESTSELLING AUTHOR
L E X   M A R T I N

Copy editing by RJ Locksley

Proofreading by Alison Evans-Maxwell, Becky Grover, and Jerica MacMillan

Cover by Najla Qamber Designs

Model Photographs by Perrywinkle Photography

February 2018 paperback edition

ISBN 978-0-9975139-0-5

ABOUT THE NOVEL

Tori...

For the record, I'm not going to hook up with my boss.

I'm a lot of things—a screwup, a basket case, a flunky. But when I take a nanny job to be near my pregnant sister, I swear to myself I'll walk the straight and narrow, which means I cannot fall for my insanely hot boss.

I don't want to be tempted by that rugged rancher. By his chiseled muscles or southern charm or the way he snuggles his kids at bedtime. Ethan Carter won't get the key to my heart, no matter how much I want him.

Ethan...

Between us, she's the last thing I need as I finalize my hellish divorce.

What sane man trying to rebuild his life wants a hot nanny with long, sexy hair, curves for miles, and a smart mouth? A perfectly kissable, pouty mouth that I shouldn't notice.

My focus is on my kids and my ranch, not the insufferable siren who sleeps in the room next to mine. It doesn't matter that she wins over my kids in a heartbeat or runs my life better than I do. Tori Duran is the one woman I can't have and shouldn't want, no matter how much I crave her.

~

Reckless is a standalone companion novel to the *USA Today* bestseller *Shameless*. Each book features a different couple.

To Matt & my little bears

"Being deeply loved by someone gives you strength, while loving someone deeply gives you courage."

- Lao Tzu

PROLOGUE

Tori

A BLUSH CREEPS UP MY SKIN AS I GUN MY CAR THROUGH THE quiet neighborhood intersection, my clunker's obnoxious rattle garnering a dirty look from a suburban mom.

Whatever, lady.

I can't afford to fix that problem now, especially not after I bought my boyfriend's birthday present.

If it weren't so hot inside my deathtrap of a car, I'd be jumping out of my skin with excitement to see Jamie. But I'm trying to conserve my energy for our horizontal activities. Although he's not supposed to be home until tomorrow, I overheard my boss, who's friends with Jamie, mention that my guy might be back today, and I thought I'd surprise him. It's his birthday after all, and I have the perfect gift, something I've been saving up for weeks to afford.

When I see Jamie's Bronco parked in the driveway of his

house, I slow my beater and pull up to the duplex across the street.

My legs are stuck to my seat, and I slide my hands down my bare thighs below my cutoffs to dry the sweat. As soon as I open the door, a blast of cool air hits me, and I sigh with relief. Austin in early May is still relatively cool and breezy. Thank God, because my car windows don't roll down, and the air conditioning died long before I got this junker.

Reaching into my messenger bag, I grab Jamie's present—two tickets to see the Texas Rangers play next month. He's always traveling to Dallas on business, and I thought it might be fun for us to go together.

I wrestle the balloons out of the back seat and skip up the pristine walkway to his two-story colonial.

Pride fills me as I take stock of how much he did to the property. This place was an eyesore when he bought it a few months ago, but after replacing the roof, stripping the interior to the studs, and replacing the appliances, it looks brand spanking new. I don't know how he parts with these investment properties because it would break my heart to sell this gorgeous house.

An image of me and Jamie flashes behind my eyes. A vision of us starting a family. Of kids and more birthdays and barbecues in the back yard. I mean, I haven't decided how many children I want or their names, but I'm pretty sure I want them with Jamie.

Two months ago, I'd laughed off his suggestion that we should get married because we were both drunk, but I can't lie—I want the white picket fence with him someday.

Yeah, he's a little older than me, but what's an eight-year

difference in the grand scheme of things? Besides, he's not all judgy about me struggling with school.

I want to get serious about figuring out my life, which is why I need to keep my shit together long enough to graduate from the University of Texas in a few weeks. Most of my friends seem to know where they're going and what they're going to do. Me? I've operated on the party-now, plan-later mindset, but that only got me an academic warning, mandatory tutoring sessions, and a run-in with law enforcement.

So I'm trying to buckle down. Do the smart thing. Study and whatnot. God knows school is not my thing, but I'm almost done, thank fuck.

When I ring the doorbell, I'm beaming the biggest, brightest smile, but a second later when he opens the door, he frowns, his dark hair falling into his deep brown eyes.

"Happy birthday, babe!" Ignoring whatever weirdness is going on, I throw my arms around his neck. "I missed you." He smells so good. Like spicy cologne and man.

"Tori." His arm comes around my back in a stiff hold. I wait for the passionate kiss. For him to rip off my clothes like he usually does.

Except he just stands there.

What's going on?

I lean back and look at him. He's still frowning.

And then he glances down at his watch.

"Late for something?"

You'd think he hadn't been gone for two weeks. I know we've only been dating for six months, but he's given me jewelry—real jewelry, not that costume crap—and says he wants to marry me someday. Hello, he spoons me after sex sometimes. That has to mean something, right? And he usually makes me come. He's probably batting in the high .400s, and my trigger does not go off easily, so I'd say these are good signs.

But before I can ask him why he's being weird, he ushers me into the house. I turn and find him peering down the driveway, his dark eyes shifting from one side of the street to the other.

He clears his throat and closes the door. A muscle twitches in his jaw. "Sorry, hot stuff. I'm meeting a contractor in a bit. Wasn't expecting you."

Relief washes through me. "No worries. Thought I'd stop by on my way to work. I have an hour."

I waggle my eyebrows at him, and he nods, glancing at his watch again. "That should be enough time."

For me to rock your world? Oh, yeah.

By the time my back hits his mattress, all thoughts of his birthday and the unopened present sitting in the living room fly right out the window. I don't care that we're skipping straight to the main course. I don't even care that he hasn't told me he missed me. It's his birthday. He can do this any way he wants.

So he didn't call me much while he was away. I know work has kept him busy. He owns property all over Texas and commutes often between Dallas and Austin to manage a new housing development he and his family are building. I love that he's motivated and on top of his shit. At least one of us is.

Jamie peels off his t-shirt, putting those gorgeous muscles on display. A sigh escapes me as he wedges himself between my thighs. His rough jeans scrape my skin, but I don't care.

In the two point two seconds we've been in his bedroom, he's managed to strip me of most of my clothes, except for my black lace bra and thong, which he eyes appreciatively before he presses himself against me.

"Missed you, sugar plum," he whispers against my neck.

Warm fuzzies fill my chest. *Of course he missed me.* I knew he did.

The moment his lips touch mine, we're in a frenzy to get closer, and the Jamie who makes me come undone is back. His hand fists my hair, and he's sucking on my neck and grinding his cock against me.

I'm lost in a haze of lust until something slams down the hall. *Was... was that the front door?*

His whole body goes rigid.

"Jamie!" a female voice yells out. "I'm home, baby!"

It's my turn to frown, especially when I see the expression on his face.

"Fuck," he grunts. "Get up. Put your shit on." He leaps off the bed like an Olympic runner at the sound of the starting gun and tosses my shorts and tank top in my face.

I'm still processing what's happening when he closes the bedroom door, but yells, "I'm coming. Be there in a sec!"

"Who is that?" I didn't hear the doorbell, and I doubt a contractor would waltz in like that.

Plus, it's a woman.

He ignores me and yanks on his t-shirt.

With dread slicing through my veins, I open and close my mouth like a beached fish. "Are you...are you seeing someone else?" *Holy shit. Is he dating that other waitress I saw him talking to last month? Is he cheating on me?*

He buttons his jeans and motions for me to move off the bed. I stand up and slide on my shorts, my mouth still agape as I watch him smooth down the comforter. "Seriously, Jamie. Are you fucking someone else?"

Pushing his hands through his hair, he growls, "Not now, Tori. Just fucking get dressed."

I wrestle with my tank top. "Please tell me that's a relative in the other room, and that you're not screwing around behind my back," I plead, my voice low. Why I whisper, I have no clue. If he's cheating on me, I should be screaming in his face and breaking out the crazy.

Footsteps sound down the hall, and a look of panic registers in his eyes.

And then he's pushing me back along the far end of the room.

Back behind the dresser.

Back behind the teal ottoman.

All the way back to the walk-in closet, where he shoves me into the shadows and tells me to wait.

"What's going on?" I ask, horrified. Why is he hiding me in the fucking closet?

His eyes clench, and he shakes his head. "I'm sorry, okay? Just wait here and be quiet. I'll explain everything later. *Please* do this for me. I promise to make it up to you."

But I don't have time to respond before he shuts the closet door in my face just seconds before that woman squeals with delight and launches herself in his arms. How can I tell? Because he slammed the closet so hard the sliding door bounced open, and there's a one-inch gap.

And I can see *everything*. Her gorgeous black hair and designer clothes. Her lithe body and perfect tan. Those expensive black and red heels with the French name I can't pronounce.

Then the kissing starts. She's moaning and telling him how much she missed him. Telling him how she never wants to spend that much time apart again. Saying how much she loves their new house. How she's going to make it their home.

Does she mean this house? Is this their *house?*

Nausea overrides my senses, and suddenly, I'm suffocating. Cold sweat breaks out on my body, and I swallow—hard —so I don't throw up in that asshole's new Nikes, which are sitting at my feet.

"Are those balloons in the living room for me?" the woman asks excitedly in between attacking his face.

No, bitch. They're not.

"You know it," the liar says.

"And the Ranger tickets too?"

He laughs awkwardly, and his body turns toward the closet where he can probably feel me holding up my two middle fingers. Because he knows I don't have any money, but I spent what little I did on him. To make today special. Because I, Tori Duran, am a dumbass.

At least he has the decency to look sheepish.

He coughs. "Yeah, honey. They're for you. Thought we should enjoy a game together for once."

I wipe away the hot tears spilling down my cheeks.

She "awws," and I want to stab them both with her expensive heels.

"I can't believe you got me presents on *your* birthday. We'll get a babysitter and make a night of it!"

He's seeing a woman with kids?

Except my horror isn't over yet. No, it's when she chirps, "I tell my friends that I have the best husband in the whole world!"

Jesus Christ.

It starts to sink in, and my world tilts on its axis.

Because she's not the other woman.

I am.

My stomach rolls, and acid lurches up the back of my throat. I slide to my knees and brace myself against the wall, but I can't tear my eyes away from the nightmare unfolding in front of me.

She pushes him down onto the bed and nestles herself over his body, and he moans the same way he did a few minutes ago when he was touching me.

Except now?

Now he's fucking his wife.

1

TORI

One year later

THERE ARE A LOT OF *SHOULDS* IN THIS WORLD.

Like...

I *should* clean this pigsty of an apartment.

I *should* eat at least one vegetable this week.

I *should* look for a better paying job.

But my least favorite is the one my older sister mutters. "Tori, you should finish school."

Ugh. Tell me something I don't know.

I suck on the generic popsicle that tastes like diluted grape juice and slouch deeper on my ratty couch. Kat, on the other hand, sits as close to the edge of the recliner as humanly possible.

After I take another lick, I wave my purple ice pop at her. "You don't look comfortable like that."

She gives me a look. "I'm six and a half months pregnant. If I lean back, I'm never getting up again. Wait until you're the size of a small buffalo and you can't see your feet and your boobs are stretched like water balloons."

I choke back a laugh. "One, that's never gonna happen because I'm never having kids. Two, you've barely gained any weight." So yeah, I'm lying a smidge, but she's my sister, and I want her to feel good about herself. "And three, what's going on with your boobs?" Aside from them being humongo. What I really want to know is if she's *sure* she's only having *one* baby. Brady's a big guy—tall and muscular—but are his offspring really the size of a bison?

My sister sighs and rubs her belly. "Here's something no one ever tells you in those pregnancy books. Your nipples, um, they get larger. It's the hormones, I guess."

Internally, I'm asking, *What the fuck?* But I keep my shit together because if I freak out, she'll freak out, which sucks because she's usually the picture of calm, and I'm the spaz. "So...they get longer?" *Ew, please say no.*

She shakes her head. "The areola expands."

God, that's just as bad. I try to keep my expression neutral. "And this grosses you out?"

She gives me the face, the one that says, *What do you think, dumbass?* Fine, she doesn't ever call me dumbass, but I know she wants to sometimes. "And since when don't you want kids? You're great with Izzy."

Izzy is her seven-year-old adopted daughter, who is so precious, I want to gobble her up. But let's get real—most kids are a pain in the ass, and patience isn't one of my virtues. At least not these days.

I shrug, not wanting to rehash the whole Jamie fiasco, which was what finally got me to be realistic about my chances of finding someone I'd want to have a family with. I never gave my sister all the gory details about my breakup with Jamie, and ripping off that Band-Aid now would start the blood gushing again.

Besides, me? Have a family? I feel sorry for those hypothetical offspring already. I can't even balance my checkbook, not that I have much to balance.

I don't totally understand what's going on in my head, because when it comes to doing something for my sister or family, I'd gladly crawl over broken glass, but when I have to do something for myself, I can't seem to care.

"Kat, you're lucky, you know that? Brady is perfect. Maybe if I found a guy I didn't want to eviscerate within two minutes, I'd have a change of heart." I don't explain how the last year flying solo has given me a new perspective.

She gets that lovesick grin on her face that almost five years of marriage hasn't dimmed. "Brady is pretty amazing." Her head tilts forward, and she drops her voice. "I feel bad for him, though. With my morning sickness, which I seem to have constantly, not just in the morning, we never get to...*you know.*"

"Bang?"

She laughs. "Yeah. Bang."

"So none of this?" I slurp my melting popsicle loudly before pretending to fellate it.

A snort escapes her. "Oh, my God. Stop that." But she's laughing, so I know I haven't offended her.

Kat is seven years older and everything I could never hope to be. She graduated at the top of her class—all of them, from high school through college. She and her husband run a wildly successful lavender farm and beauty product company.

My sister and I are night and day. Our personalities. What we like. What we wear. How we talk. The only thing we really have in common is that when she's not about to explode with an alien in her belly, we look similar with long, brown hair and hazel eyes.

She nudges her swollen foot against my ankle. "Don't think I didn't see what you did here, changing the subject." Lowering her voice, she asks, "Do you need some money? Brady and I want to pay for half of your credits so you can graduate."

I look down, hating that I should take her up on that offer. "Nah. I'll get by."

Thankfully, she's never asked what classes I failed, and who wants to tell her Hispanic family she failed Spanish? Not me. But I didn't grow up speaking fluently like Kat did. Still, it shames me.

Kat's eyes flit around the apartment, and I know what she sees. The ripped carpet. Pizza boxes piled in the trash. Crumbs and empty soda cans forgotten on the warped coffee table. I'm not a total slob, but my roommates are. I might not be great at making my bed or folding laundry, but I've always tried to keep the rest of this place clean since I'm the one named on the lease. These last few weeks, though, I've sort of given up. I've gotten tired of trying to organize when no one else around here gives a shit.

It sucks having four roommates, but I can't afford to move out on my own, not with my school loans and credit cards. Isn't that the biggest kick in the head? I didn't graduate so I can't use that degree to get a better job than waiting tables and bartending, but I still have the loans.

Kat reaches up and twirls a long lock of her hair. That's her tell.

I sit back and wait for her to spit it out. There has to be a good reason she drove an hour through Austin traffic to see me.

"*Manita*, I actually stopped by to give you a proposition."

Here we go. When she breaks out the Spanish terms of endearment, I know I'm in trouble. "I haven't resorted to stripping yet, so if that's your concern, you should tell Mom and Dad they can stop lighting candles at church." Not that I haven't considered it.

"Brady has a friend—"

"You're trying to set me up on a date? I already told you I'm not dating right now." Because I, Victoria Duran, have sworn off sex, hot douchebags, and general debauchery for the foreseeable future. But my man-free diet only works because I do my best to avoid temptation.

"No, Tori, not a date. Brady's friend Ethan Carter raises cutting horses down the road from us. He needs a nanny this summer for his two kids."

I consider it for three seconds. "No."

"What? Why?" She pouts.

"I don't like kids." It's not entirely a lie. Kids remind me of what I wanted with Jamie, and Jamie reminds me that I'm a fool. And since that whole hit-and-run he played on my heart last year, kids sound shriller. Whinier. Like bigger pains than they're probably worth.

"Not true! You love kids! I've seen you with our cousins and Izzy. You're great with kids."

"They're family. I'm obligated to love those miscreants."

Look at me with the big words. I didn't sleep through *every* class in college.

She fiddles with the hem of her blouse. "Think of it as a way to stay on the straight and narrow. You're always so responsible and on your best behavior around children."

This is about her thinking I'm still a party girl.

That's the thing about a reputation. It's hard to break and even harder to reinvent.

She shifts into her no-nonsense parental voice. "I really think you should consider it."

"No."

"Victoria."

"Katherine."

"I realize you're in the middle of some kind of crisis that's making you doubt all of your amazing qualities, but you and I both know you're one of the few people I trust to babysit Izzy." Kat is crazy protective of that child. I can't say I blame her. "And she's really only learned a few curse words from you over the years."

I have a big mouth. I can't help it.

My sister waves her hand at me. "You haven't heard the best part. You'll get free room and board, so you can save up and finish your coursework in the fall."

"You want me to live on a farm? Are you out of your mind? That's the middle of bumblefuck. How am I supposed to keep my bartending job at Wingman's?"

"It's called driving. You should try it." She sighs. "Think of how much we'll be able to hang out, and you won't have to live in this hell hole with whatever random people your roommates bring home."

That part is tempting. Except... "My car isn't working

right now." The damn rustbucket coughed its last breath last week.

"You can borrow my truck."

She knows that's not a good idea.

"What about my lease?" I counter. "I can't bail."

"Sublet it. Get one more roommate to take your place. Please! This will be so awesome!" My sister juts out her lower lip. God, she really wants this.

"Stop with the puppy dog eyes."

"You'd be doing Brady and me such a huge favor if we could work this out."

I lift an eyebrow. "How do you figure?"

"The doctor said I'm high-risk because of my blood pressure, and this way you'll be close by in case I need you."

Every cell in my body stills.

"Why didn't you tell me you were having health problems? Jesus, you're here for an hour and you're just now telling me?" I'm always the last person to know anything in this family.

"I didn't want to freak you out. I'm fine. Really. But it would give me great comfort to have you nearby. Just think! You could come for dinner all the time, and we could have a girls' night once a week. Izzy would be ecstatic to see you so often."

"Aren't you laying this on kinda thick?"

"Are you considering the job?"

It's my turn to roll my eyes. "As if I have a choice."

She claps and does this weird pregnant wobble on the edge of her seat. It's her version of jumping for joy, I think.

"Careful, Humpty Dumpty." I hold my hand out to steady her. "Don't want you to impair my niece or nephew." I barely contain my own eye roll because Kat refuses to find out the sex of this child.

My sister grins at me. "I knew you loved kids."

"I love *your* kids." Pointing out this difference doesn't seem to deter my sister's exuberance. "But what if this guy's kids hate me? Or what if they're brats? What if they like to eat their boogers? You know I can't handle creepy booger-eaters."

"Trust me when I say you're going to fall in love with the kids, their dad—the whole family. I promise. Plus, you love horses. I'm sure Ethan can teach you how to ride. And..." My sister pauses to giggle and fiddle with her hair. "Well, you'll figure out the rest for yourself."

What does that mean?

Before I can tell my sister this is a bad idea, that I'm probably not the wholesome individual some guy wants to raise his kids, she leans close and clasps my hand. "I can't tell you how much this means to me." Her eyes water, and she blinks quickly. "I know we spent a lot of time apart as kids, so having you close like this—"

She waves her hand in her face, a poor attempt to contain the emotion, but it's too late because I've joined her in this walk down memory lane. My eyes sting, and all the shit I've crammed into my internal lockbox threatens to bust through.

"Fine. Let's do this," I choke out. "But if these kids are little assholes, I'm blaming you."

A laugh escapes her, as do a few tears, and I realize I'd do anything to make my sister happy. Even if it means enduring the summer in the middle of nowhere with some stranger and his two annoying booger-eaters.

2

ETHAN

"AND SHE HAS EXPERIENCE WITH YOUNG CHILDREN?" I ASK AS I wedge the phone between my ear and shoulder while attempting to find the water bill in the mountain of paperwork on my desk.

"She does, worrywart," my brother Logan grumbles.

I rub the scruff on my jaw. "What's Tori doing now? Why does she want the job?" I'm not about to let just anyone babysit my kids.

"Christ, Ethan. Probably to pay her bills? How the hell should I know why she wants the job? Look, Kat raved about her sister, and you know how responsible Kat and Brady are. I can't imagine they'd hook you up with a criminal."

"I'm not excited to hire someone through friends. What if it doesn't work out? Brady is one of the few guys in the area I can tolerate. If I fire his sister-in-law, he'll be pissed, and then who will we get to fill his spot on poker night?"

"So don't fire her, asshole. It's only two or three months, not a lifelong commitment. If you don't like her, just make sure she's good with the kids and feeds them, doesn't let them turn into hooligans, and then go do your own thing." He laughs under his breath. "And everyone says you're the smart one."

I smirk. "That's 'cause I am, little brother." I'm four years older than Logan, but we've always been close. Even if he is a pain in the ass.

Sometimes I forget he doesn't live with me since he's always crawling up my ass about something. He and our mom live in a small house on the other side of our property, but they're both here almost daily.

Although my mom initially inherited Carter Cutting Horses when my dad died, she didn't want the responsibility of the ranch, especially since Logan and I ended up overseeing the day-to-day operations, so she transferred it to us. Which was great until my wife decided to divorce me and untangle our assets.

Logan cocks an eyebrow. "Think of it this way. With a live-in nanny, maybe you'll leave the ranch for once. Go out and have a good time. Laugh again. Hell, maybe get laid. For real this time. Because we're not counting your hand or the pocket pussy I gave you for Christmas."

"I threw that thing out. Like I really want to have a sex toy lying around so Mila or Cody could find it." Besides, it was too narrow. "And I laugh plenty."

He snorts. "Bullshit. You used to be a fun guy. Now you only grunt at everyone."

Barely holding back a grunt, I shrug. *I guess he has a point.*

Shuffling through another pile of mail, I finally spot the envelope I'm looking for. "You know what I really need? Another trainer. Bill hurt his back, and there's no way we'll be ready for the fall auction if I can't get someone to work with the new colts. While we're at it, I need someone to organize my desk before I miss something important. *That's* what I really need. Not pussy."

Although I probably wouldn't turn it away. Being a single dad and running this ranch is stressful as fuck. I could use a release. But dating? Relationships? Commitment? No, thanks. Been there, done that. I'm still recovering from that grenade. Every time I run across the divorce papers I got served this spring, it still fucking hurts. Doesn't matter that we separated over a year ago. When you watch your dreams for your family go up in flames, it kills something inside you can't get back.

The door creaks open, and Mila pokes her head in and rubs her sleepy eyes. Shit, I hope she didn't overhear me talking about a sex toy.

"Hey, honeybunch. Whatcha doing up?"

"Can't sleep," she whispers.

I lean back in my leather chair and pat my lap while I tell my brother I gotta go.

"Think about what I said," he mumbles in my ear. "Because you can't do the work of two trainers, take care of your kids, and deal with all the office paperwork. And if you meet Kat's sister, try not to scare her off with your asshole ways."

That's my brother, telling me shit I already know.

"Yeah, yeah." I hang up and reach for my daughter, who curls up against me and burrows against my neck. "Bad dream?" She nods, I tighten my arms around her. "Need some big hugs, huh?"

I get another nod, and I kiss the top of her head. Mila is five and has been having nightmares on and off since her mother and I split up last year. The counselor says it's natural for her to be experiencing anxiety from the dramatic shift in our family situation. Because she went from being with her mom all day, every day to only seeing her every other weekend, if she's lucky.

I try to breathe through the anxiousness I feel for my kids. Breathe through the lingering sense of abandonment. If I feel it, I know they do. I still don't understand how Allison could leave us. How did she go from being a wife and a mother to being single again and moving two goddamn hours away? If she doesn't love me anymore, fine. Although it hurts, I understand needing some space. But what about the kids? They didn't do anything wrong.

Here's the thing no one ever tells you about love. It turns to hate pretty fucking fast when the object of your affection hurts your kids.

No one forced Allison to move to San Antonio. So those promises she made to Mila and Cody that she would be here at a moment's notice if they needed her? Gone faster than the dust behind her car as it drove down our driveway.

My mom's been helping as much as she can, but between her arthritis and how the kids stress her out, I need to find another solution. I won't let her cancel her plans to help her sister in Chicago this summer because I know she needs a break, which means shit's getting real if I don't find a babysitter in the next week.

Kat's a sweetheart. If her sister is as lovely and patient as she is, we'll be golden.

Here's the problem—I've never left my kids with anyone but family, and I'm not thrilled to start. Especially when you hear about the horrible shit on the news. Whoever I hire is gonna get fingerprinted and background-checked. Hell, if I could, I'd ask to see her SAT scores, psychological profile, and college transcripts. I don't think you can ever know too much about the folks you have around your children. The ranch hands on the property are bad enough, but at least they've been around for years, so I know them and their families. And they know that *I* know how to use a motherfucking shotgun.

Mila's breath steadies against me, and before long, she's asleep. Careful not to jostle her, I head down the hall and gently set her down in bed. I'm reaching for the blanket when something shiny by her pillow catches my eye.

An ache spreads through my chest when I realize it's a framed photo from the mantel in the living room.

In it, Allison and I are arm-in-arm. She's holding a newborn Cody, and Mila is wrapped around my neck like a spider monkey. We look so damn happy. Hell, I *was* happy.

I thought my wife was happy too. Turns out I was wrong.

Because Allison *said* this was what she wanted—life on the ranch, kids, barbecues with our families on the weekend when we weren't working. A simple life with love and laughter.

Except she pawned off the kids to my mother or brother whenever she could, and she hated the horses. I don't know how you hate horses, but she did.

I'm not a bastard. I realize all that domestic stuff is hard. I did as much as I could while working twelve-hour days with the horses and trying to keep this place afloat. But I'm not wealthy like her family, so I couldn't afford the luxuries she grew up with. Butlers? Maids? Drivers? *Sorry, not happening.*

The best I could do was updating the house to make it more comfortable for her.

Sadness washes over me as I look at our faces in the photo. At the hope in my eyes. I thought I could have it all.

Stupid motherfucker.

I'll never make that mistake again.

It happened so fast. One day we were sitting down to dinner and making plans for the weekend, and the next she was packing her bags and leveling me with those four deadly words: *I want a divorce.*

Rubbing a hand over my face, I half wonder if she ever loved me and the life we built together, or if she was always full of shit.

I'll probably never know because that would require clear communication, and we've only been having screaming matches lately. I can't decide if that's better than when she gives me the silent treatment. Isn't there a happy medium where we talk like adults?

But the thing that keeps me up at night, the thorn I can't quite dig out of my side? If I woke up tomorrow and found her on my front steps, admitting that she still loved me and begging to be a family again? I'd probably take her back.

At least then I wouldn't have to hear my kids cry at night while they clutch old photos because they miss their momma. I can live without love, but I'm not sure that they can.

3

ETHAN

"Morning, gorgeous," I whisper, my voice raspy since I've only been in the company of horses for the last several hours. "Keeping these boys in line?" The mare whinnies as I brush out her mane.

The colts in the stalls on either side of her glare at me. I swear they know I'm busting their balls. Horses are smarter than people give them credit for.

I yank back my baseball cap and wipe the sweat away. It's not even seven in the morning, but the air is already thick and humid. It'll be a scorcher.

On days like today, I try to get to the stables along the back of my property as early as possible, usually around four in the morning, because around ten or eleven, it'll be too hot to go riding. I'll have to wait until early evening to attempt it, but that's Texas in the summer for you.

All morning, I think about that conversation with my brother last night and wonder how I'm supposed to find someone who'll love and nurture my kids half as much as my mom. It feels like an insurmountable task.

By the time my nine o'clock lesson shows up, I'm a grumpy fuck.

Eyeing the BMW that pulls up the drive, I groan. Mallory Mathers is richer than God and pays an obscene amount of money for me to board and train her filly and give her lessons, but it's a tradeoff in my sanity for several reasons. One, she's my wife's friend *and* our families go way back. Two, she always hits on me. I can only convey my disinterest so many ways before I lose my patience. Three, I need the business right now, so I can't be a dick.

"How's my girl doing, Ethan?" she coos when she enters the barn, flicking her red hair over her shoulder.

I don't have to force the smile since we're talking horses. "Doing awesome. She's a natural." Baby Got Back is young, so we're still taking it easy, but between her pedigree and her own natural athleticism and cow sense, I'd say Mallory has herself a winner.

There's a lot of money to be won in cutting events. Even though I could use some of those winnings now, it's the competition I've always loved. But the thought of getting back in the arena is bittersweet, so I push it out of my mind and focus on the sorrel filly in front of me.

It takes a special kind of animal to go toe-to-toe with a six-hundred-pound cow and "cut it" from the herd. A cutting horse has to be agile and lightning-fast to stop, turn, and juke the cow, keeping it away from the herd. Not only will Baby be excellent in the ring, she'd make an incredible work horse if that was what her owner needed.

Judging by my client's designer duds, though, work is not what Mallory has in mind. While she knows her horses, Mallory's probably better suited for an equestrian ring than cutting, but who am I to judge?

"You bring a change of clothes? Gonna get those nice threads dirty if you go riding."

A smile tilts her over-painted lips. "These old things?" She laughs, and Baby jerks in her stall, startled. "I don't mind getting a little dirty when I *ride*." Her hand drifts across my shoulder, and I roll my eyes, grateful she can't see my face.

I should probably appreciate that an attractive woman is paying attention to me. Looking down at the mud on my boots and the grime on my hands, all I see is a filthy rancher who trains other people to win.

What's the old adage—those who can't do, teach? That's me.

But no amount of self-pity will get me interested in someone from Allison's circle of friends.

Mallory scratches Baby's ear. "Think I can ride her soon?"

"Nope." The woman whines like my five-year-old, and it's all I can do to not throw her out of my facility. "You wanna teach her some bad habits? Maybe get thrown off 'cause neither of you are ready? Then be my guest. Otherwise you'll be learning on one of my horses until Baby can handle you."

After a staredown, she huffs, "Your daddy was nicer."

No shit. "Well, he ain't here, so buck up, buttercup."

The mention of my father darkens my mood. Pops was a champion cutting horse rider and loved by everyone who trained here. He would've charmed Mallory into thinking it was her idea to ride one of our other horses.

I don't have time for charm.

"Come on. Let's get this over with."

Mallory rolls her eyes, but gathers her equipment so we can get started.

Once her lesson's done and she's out of my hair, I hurry to ride one more horse before it gets too hot. By the time I'm finished, my face is burning from the searing heat. Stomping over to the faucet on the side of the barn, I bend over to splash some cold water on my face, but it comes out warm.

"Damn it." I wipe my face again and tell my two ranch hands that I'm headed to the house for a few minutes and they should take their lunch. I wish I could say we're calling it a day, that I can pick up the rest of my workload this evening when it's cooler, but that's not an option if I want to get my kids fed, bathed, and tucked into bed before a potential buyer swings by tonight to look at one of our yearlings.

My shoes kick up dirt as I trudge across our expansive yard, but I love this walk. A deep pride wells up in me as I approach my home through the field of dandelions and this-tle. I inherited this house from my parents, and I've worked my ass off to take care of it. Some day, I hope to give it to my kids so they can have the same leg up in this world that my folks gave me and Logan.

My brother also inherited a house on the other side of the property, which we share for the sake of the business. Since Allison left, I've wondered if it would be easier to have my mom move back in with me and the kids instead of having her live with Logan, but I'm afraid that would make my dependence on her worse. The woman needs a break, which she won't get here.

Mila comes tearing by me when I open the back door, and Cody toddles after her. "No running in the house."

Mila slows to a halt until Cody plows into her legs, and then she starts power-walking around the corner. My mom lumbers about ten paces behind.

"You doing okay, Ma?"

She rolls her eyes. "Of course I'm okay, but those little punks are getting faster."

"Don't you dare run after them."

"Their mischief and mayhem know no bounds, so until you find that babysitter, don't tell me what to do."

I snicker at her snippy attitude. "I'm on it. I'm on it. Soon, you'll be sipping mimosas with Aunt Hazel, missing your rugrats."

"Ain't it the truth." She pats my cheek like I'm a boy and shuffles off to track down my children.

Turning, I make my way to the kitchen, my least favorite part of the house. Everything about this room reminds me of my wife. The track lighting and the professional range oven. The dark marble counters and fancy cookware. All shit she wanted but never used or appreciated.

At least now I can bathe in the enormous double sink without her bitching about it.

Stripping off my sweat-soaked t-shirt, I duck under the cold faucet in the kitchen, get my head and neck wet, and hope to God the sudden change in temperature doesn't make me stroke out.

This is when Allison would complain I was raised in a barn, which isn't far from the truth.

I'm twisting the faucet when I hear a familiar voice.

"E, you back here?" my brother calls out.

"Yeah. Kitchen."

Footsteps sound down the hall as I reach out for a dry dishtowel. My eyes are stinging with sweat, so it takes me a few tries to find the right drawer.

Finally, I wrap my hands around a towel and bring it to my face just as a throat clears behind me.

By the time I dry my face and open my eyes, I come face to face with Logan, who looks like a cat prowling a cage of canaries. Then I see why.

He's not alone.

"Thought I'd bring Kat and her sister so you could chat."

He smirks as I take in the two women by his side.

"Hey, Kat." I motion with my head.

"Hi, neighbor." She gives me a sweet smile as she rubs her swollen stomach. Then she nudges the woman next to her. "This is my younger sister Tori."

That's when I finally get a good look at the sister. *Fucking Logan.*

My eyes dart back to my brother, who's grinning so wide, I can count his molars. I glare at him, knowing full well what he's doing right now. My brother is worse than my mother when it comes to matchmaking. Because if his expression is any indication, this is about more than finding a babysitter.

Some men are all about tits. Others like a girl's ass. Me, I'm a hair man. So it sucked when Allison chopped hers off right after we got married and kept it short.

With a resigned sigh, I finally turn my full attention to Tori, whose long, dark mane tumbles over her shoulders like she's some kind of mermaid. Dressed in a white tank top, cutoffs, and some weathered shitkickers, she looks ready to star in a dirty cowboy fantasy. Long legs. Curves for miles. So much bare skin. I barely hold in a groan.

Big, luminous hazel eyes blink back at me as she unabashedly studies my face, my chest, my tats... I look down, realizing I'm standing here only sporting jeans and dripping water and barn funk all over the kitchen floor.

I clear my throat. "Ladies, excuse me. Was out with the horses this morning. Had I *known* you were coming by..."

My brother laughs. "The horses are the only ones around here who can tolerate Ethan, since hospitality isn't his strong suit, but he can make a damn fine barbecue."

Kat frowns and turns to Logan. "I thought you said you scheduled this with him."

Yeah, right. I would've told him to do this another day.

Logan runs his hands through his hair. "I mentioned you might be stopping by. He must've forgotten."

"Don't be an ass. You know you didn't tell me," I grumble, more and more pissed by the minute to be blindsided. Turning to the women, I sigh. "I'm gonna go change. Give me five minutes, and ignore everything that comes outta his mouth. Seriously, Logan, I have other shit I need to do right now." A potential buyer from Dallas is stopping by tonight, and my to-do list is obscene. This isn't the day I want to interview Ariel the Mermaid. And yes, I know every damn Disney character. "Next time warn a guy."

Kat's daughter Izzy peeks out from behind her mom's flowing dress and waves. "Hi, Mr. Ethan."

Shit. I shouldn't be cursing in front of her. "Hey, little darlin'. Didn't see you there." She's a couple of years older than my daughter.

Izzy giggles and waves some more, and I twiddle my fingers at her like a lame ass.

Kat tries to hide her smile, but Tori doesn't look amused. In fact, she looks as pissed off as I feel. Hopefully this interview will go fast. Because clearly this isn't gonna work out. And in my experience, there's never a good reason to jam a square peg in a round hole.

4

TORI

This guy's rude. My skin prickles with irritation. And *Kat could've mentioned he looks like a Hemsworth.*

I set my palm on my stomach to calm my nerves. It's bad enough living with a stranger, but a sexy one? Rugged and tatted up, someone who looks like he wrestles bears in his spare time? He's definitely not on my diet plan.

Ethan tosses a legal pad on the island like it has personally offended him—it lands with a loud smack—and then he motions for me to grab a seat on one of the bar stools.

Damn it, I wish Kat hadn't gone to play with the kids, because now I'm alone with Mr. I-Have-a-Six-Pack-and-a-Bad-Attitude. If he didn't want me here, he should've simply asked me to leave.

"How old are you?" he asks without preamble.

Nice to meet you too. Why is it that gorgeous men always treat women like shit? Yeah, he's gorgeous. Probably in his late twenties. Tall with shaggy blond hair and a scruffy face from not shaving. Electric blue eyes that would have me doing a double take if he were a guy in my bar. And those abs he flashed me a few minutes ago? With water dripping over every dip and curve? Totally droolworthy. But if memory serves me, a pretty package means trouble every time.

"I'm twenty-three."

He makes a face. "Let's cut to the chase," he says, leaning one hand on the counter. "Whoever I hire is gonna have to get a background check and fingerprints done, so if there's anything shady in your past, you should tell me now."

Heat rises in my cheeks. "Aren't you a ray of sunshine?" I glare back at him. My sister is high off her ass if she thinks this will work out. And for a live-in position! He and I would annihilate each other. She knows I don't play nice with over-bearing assholes. Those baby hormones must have deteriorated her brain to make her think this would work. "I'm pretty sure I won't pass your precious background check since I did get arrested that one time for snorting coke off a hooker's tits," I snark.

He rolls his eyes.

My glare intensifies. "I'm not even sure I like kids. I'm doing this so I can be near my sister because she has a high-risk pregnancy. But I'll be honest—your attitude sucks. If you didn't want us here, you should've said so instead of being a dick about it." Am I being dramatic? Maybe. Except now I'm worked up, and there's no stopping the crazy train. "You know what? Just forget it. I can't imagine having to live here and deal with you twenty-four seven."

"Why don't you tell me how you really feel?" He chuckles and then rubs his jaw, but then says, "You sound just like my ex-wife," under his breath.

We stare at each other, and I lift my eyebrows, feeling the

awkwardness of the moment pierce my anger. Any mention of wives, ex-wives, or ex-girlfriends gives me the hives.

Clearing his throat, he asks, "What's wrong with Kat? Thought everything was going okay."

"High blood pressure."

He motions to the other room where Kat and Izzy are hanging out with Logan. "That's pretty common. She looks good, though. I'm sure she'll be okay."

I nod, counting the seconds until I can get out of here.

Self-consciously, I survey my outfit, eying the cutoffs and the old boots my sophomore-year roommate gave me. When my sister asked me to come home with her for a few days, I didn't think she'd drag me to an interview the first chance she had. I brought clothes so I could hang out on her farm and do her laundry, maybe cook for her, not sit in front of a firing squad. In this gorgeous, sprawling house no less.

I hate this, not planning ahead and always being the lowly person in need of something. Not being good enough. Story of my life.

Shit.

My eyes sting, and I blink back the heat. I will *not* cry in front of this guy.

When I pull in a breath, I sniffle. Damn it.

"Hey. I'm sorry," he says gruffly. "I don't mean to be an asshole."

"Yeah, you do." I shake my head, not wanting to look at him. "But no worries. I'm gonna go." I sniffle again. "Sorry we messed up your afternoon."

Jumping off the stool, I quickly wipe my eyes and stalk off to find my sister, who is sitting on the living room floor with

Izzy and two other kids jumping around her. Why in the world is she down there?

"Tori!" the little girl screams.

This must be Mila, Ethan's daughter. What a cutie.

She looks familiar. I probably met these kids at one of the festivals my sister hosts at her farm. Mila runs toward me and launches herself into my body. I reach out and try to steady myself before we both topple over, but a strong arm grabs me before I completely lose my footing.

My breath catches and goose bumps break out all over my body when I look up into those intense blue eyes. Immediately, I shake off Ethan's grip and direct my attention to his daughter.

Kneeling, I smile at her. Another sniffle escapes me. "Hey, Mila. Long time no see! How have you been, honey?"

She wraps her arms around my neck in a tight hug. "Did you come to play dress-up with me?" *Oh, my God. What a sweet kid.* "Kat said you like to play dress-up. Remember when you painted my face? Can we do that again? I liked that." Vaguely, I remember a younger Mila asking me to draw a butterfly on her cheek. When she pulls back, she worries her bottom lip. "Or did you come to talk to my mom? She doesn't live here anymore. She's 'posed to come this weekend, but I don't know..." Big tears well in her eyes. "Sometimes she doesn't come."

Oh, shitshitshit.

"Know what? I'd love to play dress-up. I bet you have the best clothes. Maybe even a tiara?"

She blinks real fast and nods like a bobblehead doll. "I do! My daddy got it for me. It's *sooo* pretty!"

"Coolness. Listen, I need to go in a few minutes, but

maybe we could put your tiara on first?" She bobbleheads again, and I laugh. "Hurry and grab it."

As soon as she darts out of the room, I realize there's another woman here sitting next to Logan on the couch. She has short grayish-blonde hair and a friendly face.

Standing, I wave. "Hi, I'm Tori, Kat's sister." I muster a smile, keenly aware that Ethan is watching my every move.

The woman grins as she reaches over to pull a toddler onto her lap. That must be Cody. *Would've been nice if my sister had mentioned that one of the kids is still in diapers.*

The woman returns my wave. "I'm Beverly, the grandma."

"Oh, man. So these two guys are yours?" I motion between Logan and Ethan and blow out a breath. "I'm so sorry."

She barks out a laugh. "I like this one."

Mila trots back in, this time wearing a fluffy, hot pink boa. She waves her tiara at me. "Here."

"I love your boa. Every girl should have one of these." A twinge of sadness settles over me at an old memory of Jamie and that time he made love to me one night while all I wore was my red boa and heels. Despite his promises, I've realized he only wanted me for sex. The thought hardens my heart, which I welcome. No sense in letting anyone do that to me again.

Bending down, I fix Mila's long blonde hair behind her ears before I slide on her tiara. "Voilà! What a perfect princess you are!"

She grins and gently pats her costume jewelry.

I whisper in her ear. "I bet your daddy would love to take a selfie with you while you're dressed up."

Her smile widens as she turns to her father, whose attention is drilled on me. Seriously, why is he staring? I motion my head toward his kid. *Look alive, dude.*

His eyes shift to Mila, and I'm taken aback by the love that floods his expression. She asks him to take a photo with her, and he nods and scoops her into his arms, presses a kiss to her forehead, and reaches for the cell in his back pocket.

I look away, not needing to see some sentimental moment between these two.

Even though Ethan seems to have a stick up his ass, the living room is welcoming with cozy, overstuffed couches and a big flatscreen TV. Along the far wall is a stone fireplace with a mantel full of photos and horse trophies.

When we pulled up to the ranch, my sister said this property has been in Ethan's family for three generations.

"Your house is gorgeous, ma'am," I tell Beverly.

Her face lights up. "Ethan did all the renovations."

He sets down Mila and shoves his hands in his pockets. "Ma, you know I had some help."

I ignore the shiver that runs through me from the sound of his deep voice.

Beverly points down the hall. "He installed those beautiful counters in the kitchen, expanded the house, knocked down walls, added the bedrooms along the East side—the whole shebang. He really is very handy."

Too bad he's a dick. I smile awkwardly and nod, turning my back so I don't have to look at Ethan and his throat-punching presence.

My sister tries to scoot off the floor, and I roll my eyes and rush to help her up.

"No more sitting on the floor," I groan as I steady my sister.

When Izzy grabs her mom's hand, I finally let go of her.

"I told her to sit on the couch," Logan says, rubbing his jaw the same way his brother does.

Logan gives me a shrug and a wink, and I can't resist smiling back. He's a carbon copy of his brother except his eyes are lighter, and he's leaner. *Not to mention nicer.* Ethan is all brawn with hard muscles, tattoos, and a roughness I can't really explain.

It's crystal-clear the Carter brothers are total lady-killers.

That means it's time to go.

Because I've had my fill of these kind of guys for at least a lifetime.

5

ETHAN

My mother stirs the pot on the stove and hums in the back of her throat. "Isn't Tori a peach?"

"Stop it, Ma."

"What? Ethan, she's adorable. Did you see the way Mila lights up around her? I feel better about going to Chicago already."

Propping my hands on my hips, I drop my head back with a sigh. "I'm not hiring her." Even though it kinda kills me not to.

I don't exactly have a string of available babysitters on call, and I'm not dumb enough to think I can take care of the kids on my own when my mom leaves. Why did I have to be such an asshole to Tori this afternoon?

"That girl is exactly what we need around here. She's sweet as pie with the kids and doesn't put up with your malarkey."

"What are you talking about?"

"I heard what you said to her. All that bark, like you were

trying to scare her away, and she just dished it right back. Not like Allison, who told you what you wanted to hear until she lost her noodle over something silly."

That's because Allison never let anyone see the real her. In private, she nitpicked me to death. Nothing was ever good enough or nice enough. To everyone else, though, she pretended things were fine because she wanted them to think she was perfect.

"Has anyone ever told you it's not polite to eavesdrop? And anyway, Tori told me she doesn't like children. That she'd fail a background check. Who says that?"

Though she obviously has a way with kids. Mila hasn't stopped talking about her this evening.

My mom laughs under her breath. "Sounds like you were both lying to each other. You know, in my day, we called that foreplay."

I pinch the bridge of my nose. "Please, *please* stop talking."

She stirs the pot like she hasn't just grossed me the fuck out. "I never thought Allison was right for you." Here we go again. "She never had any spark. Boring as a dishrag."

"She wasn't boring." I groan as I rub the ache in my chest. For some reason, I feel the need to defend her. "We grew apart. When we were at A&M, things were different. Our relationship was easier." Of course shit's easier before you have kids.

I guess I always knew Allison wasn't exactly wired to be home all the time. To be so domestic. She liked hanging with her circle of rich friends. Being social. Being seen.

Rubbing that spot again, I shake my head. "I don't think she realized how hard it was gonna be living out here in the middle of nowhere."

I thought we'd be a team and help each other. Sure, it's my parents' ranch, but I was putting in long days for our family. For her and our kids. Not for shits and giggles.

My mom waves a wooden spoon at me. "Don't be dramatic. Austin is forty minutes away, and there's a Walmart down the road. We're not total hicks."

I chuckle. Beverly Carter is as feisty as they come. "You know what I mean. Being isolated on the ranch. I think she needed to be around more people. And it's not like she was prepared to have a baby so soon." Ain't no way to prepare for a baby when you're a senior in college.

"What she needs is to take care of her kids and be a good mother. What she needs is to be a woman of her word and live up to her marriage vows."

That ache grows, and I open the fridge to grab a beer. "It is what it is. Nothing I can do about it now." Trust me, I've tried.

"Good riddance. At least this way, I know Allison won't be taking off with my jewelry when I die."

"Ma, c'mon." I reach for this teeny woman who somehow birthed me and my brother. Kissing the top of her head, I laugh. "No more talk about dying, okay?"

"Ethan?"

"Yeah."

She puts her hand on my shoulder and looks up at me. "Your daddy would be proud of you. So proud of everything you've done here."

I swallow the lump in my throat and nod. "Thanks. I try." Filling my dad's shoes when he passed six years ago was something none of us expected I'd have to do so soon. He was young and healthy. I thought I'd have more time. More time to travel with Allison. More time to enjoy being young. More time to learn from my father.

"I know it, son. I'm proud of you too. The last few years have been tough, but you hang in there. You're a damn good father and a damn good rancher." She presses her lips together. "I'm sorry your wife didn't appreciate you."

Blowing out a breath, I hug her tight and let her go before we both start crying like little girls. "What's for dinner? I need something with beef before I waste away."

She chuckles and pats my gut. "I got just the thing."

The next morning, I skim my emails and am surprised to see a message from Kat. All it says is, "My sister may seem crabby, but she's a sweetheart under that tough shell, and she's wonderful with kids. Thought you might need this if she hasn't scared you away." When I open the attachment, Tori's driver's license pops up on the screen.

Yes, I was a dick to Tori yesterday. Yes, I deserved her animosity. But I wasn't prepared to like her smart mouth and all that sass. In fact, I haven't stopped thinking about it—about her—since.

Of course, she's beautiful in this photo. Hazel eyes twinkling with mischief. Plump lips smiling. All that fucking hair.

Hair that would feel damn good dragging along my chest while she rode me.

Scrubbing my face, I groan. Jesus, the last thing I need is to be thinking about her like this.

"Why so forlorn, bro?" Logan plops down into the chair on the other side of my desk with a smirk and a shrug like he's footloose and fancy-free.

I love my brother, but I really want to kick his ass for springing Tori on me. "That stunt you pulled yesterday was hysterical. Thanks for that."

"No problemo. Thought you needed a nudge."

"No more fucking nudges. I'll do this when I'm damn well ready." The sound of his snicker makes me lift my eyes. "You're wearing down my last nerve."

"What? I'm a problem-solver. I solved your problem."

"You're a pain in the ass."

He grabs his chest and pretends he's hurt, but then that smirk returns. "You'll thank me some day for hiring Tori. The kids love her, Kat vouches for her, and Tori's hot. It'll be nice to have some eye candy around here for a change. I'd rather stare at her gorgeous ass than your plumber's crack."

My hands automatically clench. "You are not fucking my babysitter." I don't bother reminding him that I haven't hired her yet.

Delight stretches across on his face like it's Christmas morning and I just plunked one of his Instagram crushes on his lap. "Gee, bro. Why not? Are you jealous?"

I ignore the question, even though I'm oddly aware that I might be. Not sure why. I don't even know the girl. Except for that crazy-sexy hair, she's not my type. "And I don't walk around with my crack hanging out, moron."

Reaching over my desk, he grabs a pencil and twirls it on the counter. Silence settles over us as I watch him spin that number two. Finally, he says, "Remember that time I almost got arrested for mooning Charles DeWitt's daughter? Dad was so pissed. How was I supposed to know her family was in the car with her? I thought she was driving her friends back from the football game."

"What was that? Your senior year of high school?" He nods, and I laugh. "I got the highlights when Dad called me that weekend. Your antics made up the bulk of our phone calls when I was at A&M." Chuckling, I point at him with my cup of coffee before I take a sip. "And everyone says you have a way with women. I bet showing Casey DeWitt your hairy balls won her over fast."

"I'll have you know I nailed Casey in her daddy's barn two weeks after the mooning incident. She didn't seem to mind my hairy balls one bit. That girl teabags like a champ."

"Jesus, bro." I shake my head and tuck my hair back in my baseball cap. "TMI." Logan has always been a player with a capital P. I wasn't a monk growing up, but I didn't fuck everything with two legs either.

Reaching for a pen so I can pay some bills, I glance over when he doesn't respond.

Shoulders tight, eyebrows cinched, he shakes his head. "I was so busy raising hell in high school, I didn't notice the signs that Dad was working too hard."

Aw, hell.

The familiar rush of guilt for not being here when it happened makes my stomach clench. Dad died that spring. Right before Allison told me she was pregnant. While my friends were partying and going off to start their lives, I was burying my father and worrying my girlfriend might abort our baby.

Of course, I told her I'd support her decision, stand by her, whatever it was. I might be old-fashioned in a lot of ways, but I'm not arrogant enough to think I have any say over what a woman does with her body. But I'd also be lying if I said I didn't want her to have Mila. Even if I wasn't in any way prepared to be a parent, I always wanted my daughter.

It seemed like the right thing to do. To marry Allison and support her and our child.

I knew Allison and I didn't have amazing chemistry, but we had fun together, and I thought that could turn into love. Besides, I always abide by my commitments, and I wasn't gonna let her go through a situation like that by herself. Her parents were less than thrilled with her marrying some guy from the sticks, even though they knew my folks since they were horse enthusiasts.

I would've done anything to get my dad's advice in those days.

Ignoring the sting in my eyes, I clear my throat. "Those were rough times, but you're not a fortune-teller, Logan. No way for you to know Dad's ticker wasn't healthy. The doctor said that kind of thing takes out high-school kids when they're playing football. The right tackle, the right hit, and lights out." Our mom made us both get echocardiograms to make sure we hadn't inherited the condition.

I wait until Logan looks up and wipes his eyes. "No, you kept Dad young. Kept him on his toes. Not every man in this county can say his son mooned Charles DeWitt and lived to talk about it. I tend to think Dad was proud of his progeny on most days."

Logan laughs, and relief settles over me to see him smile. "Why you always gotta use such big words, huh?"

"'Cause I'm what you'd call edumacated." Regret eats at me since Logan never got a chance to go to college. He wanted to stay here to help me. He swears he doesn't care, that school was never his thing, but it still bothers me he had to buckle down so soon.

My brother's smile fades and he stares at me a long, awkward minute before his expression hardens. "Okay, you educated bastard, do yourself a favor and hire Tori before you die of a heart attack out there, trying to do everything on your own. If you're so damn smart, get some help before you work yourself to death. Think about Mila and Cody. They need you to grow old and fat and lose your hair."

A lump rises in my throat. Logan leans forward, his eyes somber, as he waits for the answer he wants to hear. One I reluctantly give him.

"Fine, I'll hire Tori if it'll get you off my ass." I snatch the baseball hat off my head and toss it at him. "And ain't no one losing his hair around here, asshole."

Logan leans back in his chair, the smile on his face telling me he loves me, the sappy twerp. Thing is? I know I can't do this by myself. And maybe Tori is exactly what I need. If we don't strangle each other first.

"Glad to hear it." He gets up and smacks me on the back. "Because I bought Mom's ticket to Chicago. She leaves on Monday."

6

TORI

THE THICK SMELL OF CUMIN AND CHILI POWDER WAFTS through the air, making my stomach growl. After one more stir, I tap the wooden spoon on the lip of the Dutch oven and place it in the "I love my spicy Mexican" spoon rest. That dumb thing still cracks me up, years after Brady gave it to my sister.

Cooking is the one thing I'm decent at, but only because I've had a shitty social life this last year. Though having a man-free diet made me turn to the next best alternative— actual food. While my friends were out partying, I was watching the Cooking Channel, doing my best to whip up those recipes, and trying not to feel like a loser.

I peer over my shoulder at Kat, who's sitting at the kitchen table. "*Hermana*, are you sure you want it this spicy? I thought you had a lot of heartburn."

Her lips tighten briefly and she blinks, once, twice. Miss Poker Face has the audacity to smile and shrug like she hasn't a clue what I'm talking about.

She's obviously hiding something.

Whatever. She's been acting weird the whole day. Maybe I should chalk it up to a hormonal imbalance. If her feet weren't so swollen, she'd insist on making dinner, but I talked her into kicking back and relaxing even though she's going to be a back seat driver.

"Did you put in the Ro-Tel tomatoes?" she asks, eyeing the pot suspiciously.

See. Backseat driver. "Yeah, and when you're hanging over the toilet later tonight, puking your little heart out, don't blame me."

She gives me that strange smile, the one that tells me she's keeping a secret and thinks I'm clueless.

The front door slams shut and the stomp of boots coming through the living room echoes closer. Izzy comes racing around the corner with her arms open wide.

Three, two, one.

I turn back toward the stove as the sound of her feet stop, which tells me she's gone airborne, followed by a grunt as she throws herself at her father. She might be seven, but she's a total Daddy's Girl.

"There's my angel." His voice rings out in the small kitchen. "And here's my other angel."

A minute later, the sound of smacking makes me smile and shake my head. Without looking, I know Brady has Izzy in his arms, and he's leaning down to plant a wet one on Kat.

"Too much kissing," Izzy jokes, and I snicker to myself. That kid is my mini-me, much to the chagrin of my sister.

Stirring the pot again, I give them a moment to be lovey-dovey. It makes me strangely emotional to be around them. They're this perfect family unit. Every day, their house is filled with warmth and love. Even though I try to tell myself I don't want this, that I don't want a husband or kids because I know I'm a fuck-up, when I'm around Brady and Kat and little Izzy, I do want the happily ever after so much it makes my chest ache.

Damn Jamie for making me think that was possible.

I clench my jaw.

When I think the love fest is over, I turn around.

"Something smells good," Brady says, setting his daughter down. "Ethan still coming over for dinner?"

"Mr. Ethan's coming over?" Izzy grins.

What the... What?

My sister cringes and laughs awkwardly.

Crossing my arms, I squint. "Something you want to tell me, Katherine?"

We never discussed what happened at Ethan's two days ago. What was the point? It was clear from everyone's expressions in the living room they heard my argument with Ethan —his mom, his brother, my sister, the kids.

Although, to be honest, I'm not sure what we argued about. It was more about how Ethan made me feel. Like I wasn't good enough. Like I was putting him out with my very existence. Like he took one glance at me and found me lacking.

The part of me that's always screwing up wonders if I was being overly sensitive. That maybe Ethan's just a crabby ass in general, and I was reading into things that weren't there. Wouldn't be the first time.

I know Kat was disappointed in me for how I reacted to Ethan. She gets quiet when she thinks I'm being a dick. Like I'm in timeout and she wants me to think about what I've done. It's annoying as hell. And for the last two days, she's been *really* quiet around me. I'm typically not one to shy away from saying what's on my mind, but I have to be careful with my sister. She's so hormonal that she'll start crying if I'm too blunt, and I'm never prepared for her tears.

Kat waits until I drag myself to the kitchen table to level me with an innocent smile. "Did I forget to mention that Ethan is joining us for dinner? Must've slipped my mind."

My brother-in-law chuckles and kisses the top of her head. "I'll get Izzy cleaned up for dinner while you guys work this out."

"I'm clean, Dad. I wasn't rolling around in the barn or anything." She huffs out a breath, but runs off wash her hands in the bathroom.

Motioning toward his wife, he gives me a crooked grin. "Don't be too hard on her."

I roll my eyes, and he laughs.

Once Kat and I are alone, my shoulders slump. "What are you doing? You know Ethan and I are like oil and vinegar." Really, I can't explain why I felt so defensive around him. It didn't help that he was so handsome. Muscular and rugged from working on the ranch. Tatted up and shirtless with his Levi's hanging low on his hips. Dripping wet with water and temptation.

All the more reason to stay away.

"Oil and vinegar are a great combo on salads." When I give her a blank stare, she holds up her hands. "Just give him a chance to say his piece, okay? You don't have to agree to work for him if you're still not feeling it after dinner, but I think it would be nice to clear the air."

"I get that you're in this nesting period and want everyone

to hold hands and sing campfire songs while you gestate, so I understand why you want this. But why does *he* need to clear the air? It's obvious I'm not who he wants taking care of his kids."

Tilting her head, she shrugs. "Maybe he was having a bad day. Everyone has them. I just know you shouldn't write him off because he was grouchy. He's a single dad doing it all by himself, Tor. He has a lot on his plate, but if you give him a chance, you'll see he's a good guy. That he's trying his best."

Fuck. When she says it like that.

My sister. Always the peacekeeper.

"Fine. But just because I don't stab him at dinner with the blunt edge of my fork doesn't mean I'm agreeing to this, so don't get your hopes up."

"You know me," she chirps. "Zero expectations."

For some reason, that doesn't make me feel better.

7

ETHAN

A SMOKY ORANGE SUN FILTERS THROUGH THE TREES, WASHING the horizon in the waning daylight. My truck bumps along the gravel driveway until I pull to a stop behind two Ford F150s.

Brady's farmhouse isn't tricked out like mine, but his is far more charming. More welcoming. From the warm glow of the living room behind that picture window to the porch swing, everything about this place says home.

Making my way to the porch, I recognize the improvements he and Kat have made over the years. New siding. Pretty planter boxes. A brand-new playset, complete with a winding slide and monkey bars for their daughter. And rows and rows of lavender bushes that stretch into the distance.

When I reach the front door, I look down to make sure I'm respectable. Jeans. T-shirt. Boots. Sure, maybe I could've tried a little harder, dressed up more, but this isn't a date.

Before I can think too long and hard about why I'm nervous, I wipe my sweaty palms down the front of my jeans.

Yes, this is fucking weird.

Just gotta be nice to Tori, see if we can have a civil conversation. At least I can tell my brother I tried to make this work.

I balance the six-pack of beer in my arm while I knock. Brady said he felt like Corona tonight when I texted to ask what I could bring. Good thing I checked because I was about to get him some Sam Adams, since he's from Boston and that's usually what he orders when we hang out.

When Brady opens the door, the smell of chili and baked things I can't begin to understand how to make waft out.

"Hey, man. Come in. Everyone's in the kitchen."

"Whatever you're making smells amazing." I hand him the beer and slap him on the back.

"I'd say thank you, but I didn't have anything to do with it."

We pass through the living room and into the modest kitchen. I wave to Kat and Izzy, who are sitting at the table, even though my attention immediately zones in on Tori, who is standing at the stove. Her dark brown hair hangs down her back in long waves, and she's wearing cutoffs that make her ass look like a juicy peach.

My palms itch to feel those sweet curves.

The thought is alarming.

Kat waves me into the room. "Hey, Ethan! I'd get up to hug you, but my baby keeps bumping my kidneys, and I'd rather not jostle the little kickboxer right now."

I nod and take off my baseball cap. "Good to see you. Thanks for the invitation to dinner."

Brady holds up the six-pack. "Hey, Tor. Look what Ethan brought. Your favorite beer."

I'll be damned. Guess the beer isn't for him after all.

Finally, the mermaid turns around.

Maybe it's the way the evening sun shines through the kitchen window, making Tori glow in a dreamy light. Maybe it's the fact that I was baking like a catfish in the hot sun all day and probably have heat stroke. Or maybe it's because I'm so hungry I could eat an entire Black Angus by myself. But Tori Duran looks like the most beautiful creature I've ever seen. No makeup or fuss. Just that thick, dark mane and those golden-green eyes staring back. Wary and cautious. Guarded.

Of course she's guarded, asshole. You were a dick to her the other day.

I do that thing with my face where I try to smile. "Hey, Tori. Nice to see you again."

The girl laughs humorlessly. "Did you really bring me that beer or did Brady tell you it was for him?"

Rubbing my jaw, I consider how to answer. Lying isn't my strong suit. Never lied to my wife. Tried not to lie to my parents growing up. What was the point when they could always sniff out the truth anyway? So it doesn't make sense why I want to now except I don't want to hurt Tori's feelings. Plus, something twisted in me suddenly wants to please this girl.

Taking a few steps closer and leaning in, so I don't curse in front of Izzy, I whisper, "If I admit I got it for your brother-in-law, am I back on your shit list?"

Although I expect my answer to piss her off, the corner of her mouth tilts up like she's amused. "You haven't worked your way off it." Her eyes squint playfully. "But honesty is a start."

When I smile at her—a real one because I'm genuinely glad to see her—her lips part and she sucks in a breath.

I give her a wink. "I just need one chance, darlin'."

8

TORI

Dinner passes in a whirlwind of pleasantries between Brady, Kat, and Ethan. I watch them and push the food around on my plate and contemplate why this guy is being nice to me when he seemed to loathe my existence two days ago. And I wonder why, when he aims that smile at me, I feel the singe of a live wire, my skin heating and burning under his scrutiny.

Why I can't seem to catch my breath.

Almost as if...

Almost as if I like him.

Sweat breaks out on my back, and I sink back in my seat.

This is completely unacceptable.

I can't like a man, especially *this* man. I will not be charmed by Ethan Carter or his big blue eyes and rough edges.

See, I can do this. I am a strong, independent woman who doesn't need a man, and that's how it's going to stay.

I straighten my shoulders, proud of my internal pep talk.

"Isn't that great, Tor?" My sister nudges me with her elbow.

"I'm sorry, what?"

Her eyes widen like I need to pay attention, and I shrug, willing myself not to feel embarrassed.

"Ethan was saying how if you took the nanny position, you could borrow his truck to bartend at night. Since you had mentioned wanting to pick up some shifts somewhere."

Ugh. Like I really want him to know I don't have a car. That I don't have near enough money to fix my old clunker.

When I look up, my eyes connect with his across the table. "That's... nice of you. Though I'm not sure I have anything worked out yet. No one seems to be hiring around here."

"Have you tried the Yellow Rose? Just opened up off the access road. I know the guy who runs the place." He scoops the last spoonful of chili into his mouth, makes a growly noise, and points to the empty bowl. "That was fantastic."

"Tori made it. She's a great cook." Kat rambles on about my "eclectic cuisine" like I studied with Gordon Ramsay or something instead of the truth—that I like to veg out to cooking shows, and I have a big Mexican family that demands ten million tamales at Christmas.

Ethan tips his Corona at me. "Well, dinner was delicious. Chili is one of my favorites."

"You don't say." My eyes shift to my sister, who eats her second helping of cornbread and salad, not daring to touch the chili. "*Interesting.* My sister said she was *really* in the mood for chili, and yet she hasn't eaten one bite."

Kat shrugs, her lips tilting up. "I started thinking you were right. That I shouldn't eat anything that spicy."

"Go figure."

Izzy yawns over her plate of half-eaten chicken nuggets, and Kat motions for Brady to help her up.

"We're going to get Izzy ready for bed. You two chat. There's a fresh pot of coffee brewing and a cheesecake in the freezer, so help yourselves."

When did she make coffee? I honestly can't tell if she wants me to work for Ethan or marry the man.

Brady picks up his daughter, and a second later, Ethan and I are alone.

He chuckles and takes a long pull of his beer. His dirty blond hair is disheveled and pointing in ten different directions, but Lord help me, it looks good.

He's still smiling when I level him with a stare. "Why are you being nice to me? What do you want?" I've been around the block enough times to know when something is off. "I'm not going to sleep with you, if that's what you think you're getting by having me move in."

The smile slides off his face. "Jesus, Tori. Do you accuse every potential employer of lechery?"

My face burns, but I'm not ashamed of asking what I need to know. "Because I won't have sex with you. Not even if you're the last guy on the planet."

An annoying smirk quirks his lips. "No one said I was asking, darlin'. Besides"—his eyes pass over me—"you're not my type."

For some reason, that irritates me more. "Well, good."

"Good." He rubs a rough hand over the stubble on his square jaw. "So we're clear about that? No sex. Not even if I'm the last man on the planet."

"Not even then," I whisper.

We stare at each other, his amused blue eyes studying my face like he's seeing me for the first time.

His eyebrows lift, and then—I can't help it—I laugh. We both do.

Before things get any weirder, I get up and start clearing the plates with a sigh. "I'm not good at job interviews."

"You don't say."

"Shocking, I know." I'm not fool enough to think I had that one law firm internship because of my amazing people skills or grades. No, that came compliments of my sweet sister and her impressive Austin connections. She took me getting fired remarkably well back then, but she wasn't pregnant when I called her crying because I had gotten axed for telling off one of the partners.

Truth be told, I don't want to disappoint Kat. It's one thing to disappoint my parents. They're used to it. But Kat? For some reason, she seems to think I have potential. It cuts me to the core to think of letting her down. Again.

The only thing that freaks me out more than truly displeasing my sister is a face-to-face encounter with a spider.

Don't laugh. They're evil.

I shiver at the thought.

A minute later, Ethan's by my side at the sink. He grabs the bowls out of my hands and scrubs them down before handing them to me to rinse.

He's big. Way bigger than I am. Broad and tall and rugged.

Standing so close to him at the sink reminds me of the first time I saw him, shirtless and dripping wet. With all those muscles and that angry ink etched into his golden skin.

The kind of guy to make a girl ache in just the right ways, if he were another guy and I another girl.

This close, I can smell his shower gel. Something manly and crisp. He must've showered right before he came over.

I clear my throat. "Would you need me to cook or clean your house too?"

"I'm not hiring you to be my maid. Just to take care of Mila and Cody. I'll do my best to make them dinner, clean the house, do our laundry. Those aren't your jobs, and I never want you to feel like they are. If you don't care that I smell like a barn animal, I can probably come in to make them a quick breakfast if you want. Then you'd only have to make them lunch."

Something about that image softens me. Ethan slaving away in the heat and stopping to take care of his kids. I'm starting to get what my sister said about this guy doing it all on his own.

"I can handle breakfast and lunch. That's not a big deal." I shift to get a quick glance at him and am overwhelmed by his presence when he reaches across me to turn off the faucet.

His voice is low and gravelly. "Listen, I really am sorry for being such an asshole to you the other day. I'd love nothing more than for you to take care of my kids. I promise to stay out of your way and not annoy you too much."

He dries his hands on his shirt and turns to me, but he's looking at the ground. "You asked why I'm being nice." Those big blue eyes shift up until they sear into mine. "Well, I'm a nice guy. No one seems to think that, but I am. I've just... I've had a rough few years." As though he's flipping through a memory book, he frowns and glances away. "I'm going through an ugly divorce, and my mom, who's been keeping my household together since my wife left, is headed to Chicago on Monday to help her sister. I can't keep the business afloat and take care of my children by myself. It kills me to admit that, but it's true. So I guess you could say I need you. I need your help."

I don't like how those words, *I need you*, make me feel soft and squishy, like a piece of bittersweet chocolate left out in the sun. "Why not call one of those nanny agencies? Get someone who's fingerprinted and meets your qualifications."

"I'm on some waiting lists, but they're not sure they'll find someone willing to live out here." His eyes turn up to mine, a playfulness brightening his expression. "Should I be worried? Do you have a criminal record for all the coke and hookers?"

I laugh, remembering what I told him the other day. "Not exactly, but—"

"Then it's fine. Don't let my kids cook meth or play with sharp objects, and we should be good."

9

ETHAN

The house feels different with Tori in it. Perhaps because nothing's really settled. After some begging and eating crow on my part at dinner the other night, Tori agreed to help me for the next two weeks. Long enough to see if she can get someone to sublet her apartment and for me to explore whether an agency can better handle my situation.

It seemed prudent to contact an agency in case Tori and I ended up clashing again. The fact we didn't at dinner was a pleasant surprise, and if it taught me anything, it's that I want us to get along in the meantime. I want her to know I'll treat her well. That I'm not really an asshole.

As for my unbidden attraction to her? I figure it'll pass. I haven't been around a beautiful woman in a long time. Living on a ranch doesn't make socializing easy. I don't count Mallory Mathers or the like, because hooking up with one of my wife's friends seems about as smart as jamming a wet finger in a light socket.

It's been ages since I've been with anyone. Not since Allison, and that intimacy ended during her pregnancy with Cody. His second birthday later this summer is a reminder that she shut me out a long time ago. Two years is a long damn time to go without sex. I'm twenty-eight, not eighty.

Maybe my brother is right and I need to get out more. Start dating or something to take the edge off. Especially since Tori made it abundantly clear I'm not the kind of guy she goes for. That we would *never* have sex.

I chuckle, thinking about the fire in her eyes as the little tornado told me off again. All that passion oozing from her pores.

But she doesn't have anything to worry about. I'd never take advantage of a woman.

As for her not being my type, well, that's mostly true.

I've always gone for the polite and polished kind of woman. *And a little high-maintenance.* Not sure why since Allison has been anything but polite in the last few years.

Tori has a wildness about her, a level of honesty I'm not used to. At least not from a perfect stranger.

I think I like it.

I just can't like it too much.

After so much time out of the dating game, it's weird to think about diving back in. It's even weirder to consider dating when my divorce isn't final yet, but I know from mutual friends that Allison has already been out with other men. The thought makes my chest feel heavy with too many emotions to name.

A soft knock on the office door makes me look up.

"I'm packed and ready to go, son."

The sight of my mother dressed for the airport shoots a bolt of fear through me.

She starts talking like it's not a big deal she's going to another state. "I told Tori where to find Cody's hiding places. How to get the kids to brush their teeth. Where the emergency numbers are. Their daily schedule. Everything's gonna be fine."

I was never a momma's boy growing up. That was Logan. But I'll admit I'm a little torn up seeing her go. Probably 'cause we relied so heavily on each other after my father died.

We head into the living room where Tori is on the floor, dressed like a princess, compliments of my daughter's styling efforts. Cody is hanging off Tori's neck, and Mila is debating which bauble would look best on her new babysitter.

"Give your grandma a hug goodbye." I motion for the kids to get up.

Mila takes one look at my mother, sees the suitcase behind her, and immediately starts bawling. Rushing into her grandmother's arms, she cries so hard, she starts hiccupping.

Mom coos in her ear. "Honey, calm down. I'm only going for a month or two. I'll be back soon."

"But wha-wha-what if you don't come back? Wha-wha-what if you stay away like Mommy? What if you don't want us anymore?"

I close my eyes, my daughter's words a cattle brand on my heart.

Does this ever get easier?

"Sweetie, I'm always, *always* gonna want you and your brother, and your momma wants you guys too." Her voice is thick with emotion. "She's just going through a rough time is all." Smoothing down my daughter's hair, my mom whispers, "I'm only a phone call away. Call me any time, night or day." She pulls out of my daughter's hug and holds her shoulders.

"Hey, look at me." Mila's tear-stricken face cuts me to the core. "I need you to be a big girl and take care of your daddy and brother. Two men in a house by themselves need a good woman to look after them."

Mila nods and wipes away snot. "I can make Daddy Pop Tarts for breakfast so he's not hungry."

"Thatta girl. And you remember how he likes his coffee, right? Two sugars and a good helping of milk. Don't use half-and half even though he likes it because he should watch those trans fats now while he's young."

Hearing the two most important girls in my life worry about me makes my chest ache.

I'm wondering how I'm gonna get Mila out of my mom's arms when Tori approaches them and whispers in Mila's ear. Not sure what she says, but Mila starts laughing, and Tori picks her up and swings her around so she's on her back, clinging to her neck.

"Have a great trip, Beverly," Tori says cheerfully, like my whole family isn't on the brink of an apocalypse. "Mila and I are going to have a big surprise for you when you get back, aren't we, Mila?"

My daughter wipes her eyes and nods and smiles at my mom. "Big, big, big surprise!"

I stand there, a little dumbfounded that this train wreck has turned around, until Tori mouths, "It's okay. Go." She turns her back so she and Mila are facing the other way.

As I'm walking my mom out, I pause in the doorway to look at my kids, who are playing with Tori like nothing happened.

Only one thought comes to mind—thank God she's here.

~

It's dark when I get back, much later than I thought I'd be. Austin traffic sucked, as always, and Mom's flight was delayed. That was when I realized I didn't have Tori's cell number, and she didn't have mine. I was thinking I was the worst parent ever when I remembered my mom had shown Tori the emergency numbers.

My brother's sprawled on a couch, flipping through baseball channels, when I stride into the house.

"Thanks for coming over."

When I realized I couldn't call Tori's cell and she wasn't picking up the office phone—why would she?—I called Logan and asked him to check on the kids and let Tori know I was running late.

"No problemo. Wasn't like I had plans." His brow lifts meaningfully.

"On a Monday night?"

"Yeah, with this hot-as-fuck waitress I met last week. Thanks for cockblocking, by the way."

I roll my eyes. God forbid my brother doesn't get laid regularly.

He waves the remote in my direction without taking his eyes off the TV. "Do you need Joey to babysit for you this weekend? She says to call or text if you do."

"Yeah, I might need an extra pair of hands." I told Tori she could have the weekends off, and I don't want to break that promise.

Joey is my brother's best friend. She's a couple of years younger than Logan and has helped my mom with the kids once or twice, but the girl has her hands full at home. Even though I thought to ask her about babysitting full-time, I know she'd never be able to.

"Where is everyone?" The house is quiet. Too quiet.

"Asleep, I guess."

"Tori got Mila and Cody to bed?"

"Yuuuuup." He keeps clicking channels. "No thanks required, bro. Don't even mention how I found a Disney princess to be your nanny. I don't need a pat on the back or anything."

I roll my eyes and kick off my boots so my shoes don't wake up the kids.

If Tori were a princess, she'd definitely be Ariel the Mermaid. Only with thick, brown hair and a rounder, bitable ass.

The back hallway is dark, and I tiptoe into Cody's room. Sure enough, he's nestled in bed and zonked out to the world.

Leaning down to give him a kiss, I realize Tori must've given him a bath because he smells like clean little boy instead of the stinker I handed her this afternoon. I check the kids' bathroom, certain it must look like a hurricane blew through it because my kidlets are hellions in the tub, but everything is neat and clean.

I'm half-ready to thank my lucky stars for our new nanny when I get to Mila's room and find her bed empty.

Panic builds in my gut as I fly down the hall to Tori's room. The door is open and the bedside lamp is on, and there, in the middle of the bed, are Tori and Mila, curled up on the comforter, sound asleep, with a copy of *Bedtime for Francis* next to them.

Seeing my daughter, safe and sound, makes me feel foolish for freaking out.

Reaching down to scoop up Mila, I gently move Tori's arm, and her lids flutter open.

"Hey," she whispers.

I hold up one finger to tell her to hang on while I pick up my daughter. Mila's like a sack of potatoes in my arms. After I tuck her into her own bed, I stop back in Tori's doorway.

My eyes widen when I realize how intimate this is. Tori on her bed in a tiny black tank top and sleep shorts. Her gorgeous hair tumbling over her shoulders. The quiet house and soft lighting.

Taking a step back, I look away to give her some privacy.

"Did they wear you out?" I ask, realizing she must be as tired as my kids. "Sorry I woke you. Didn't think you'd want Mila kicking your face in the middle of the night. She sleeps like a starfish."

"No worries," she says as she yawns. "I tried to follow your mom's directions on that sheet. Got them fed and bathed and in bed on time, but I have to confess they ate pizza for dinner with nary a vegetable in sight."

I chuckle and pull off my baseball cap to push my hair back. Reversing the bill, I pull the hat on backwards. "If that's the worst crime, I think you did as well as I could've." It's true. Given how upset Mila was this afternoon, the fact that the rest of the day went smoothly is nothing short of a miracle. "Thanks for taking care of dinner and their bedtime routine. Usually, I can do that so you have your evenings free."

Thinking back to my crisis earlier today and not being able to reach her, I tap on her doorframe. "Before I forget, I need your cell number."

Her lips tug up in one corner as she stretches like a cat. "No sexting, remember?"

My eyes shoot up to hers. At first, I can't tell if she's joking or if she really thinks I'm the dick who sends out, well, pics of my dick. Or dirty messages. Can't say I've ever done either of those with a girl, even in college. Would Allison have been into that sort of thing? Hell, I never thought to test those waters.

She laughs. "Just messin' with you. But you should see the look on your face."

She calls out her digits, and I tap out her number on my cell, shaking my head the whole time.

When I'm done, I slip my phone in my back pocket. "Ya know, you're kind of a menace when you're not playing Mary Poppins."

As soon as the words are out of my mouth, I'm worried I offended her, but the smile she gives me is brilliant and wide and more than a little mischievous. "Don't think I don't know this."

Shaking my head again, I start to close the door. "Night, Tasmanian Devil."

She snickers. "Night, Wolverine."

10

TORI

Lying in bed, I wonder why I flirted with him tonight. In the moment, I didn't think it was *that* flirty. I've said worse things to my friends.

But Ethan isn't a friend.

He's my employer, and sexting is not what you discuss with an employer. *I guess I am an HR nightmare.*

I was half asleep, and he looked so damn cute with his baseball cap on backwards and that sweet expression he gets when he's talking about his kids. And the way his t-shirt stretched across his broad chest, showcasing his tattoos, made my mouth water.

I can't explain why, but I wanted to yank his chain and see how he took it.

Yank his chain. Ha. *I'd definitely love to yank that.*

Wait. *Noooooo.*

Hell, no.

I squeeze my eyes shut to get him out of my head.

I cannot get a thing for this guy. No way. Is he even divorced yet? And didn't I throw down the gauntlet the other day with the "no sex ever" conversation? Not to mention I'm not his type.

Is there an AA meeting for this sort of thing, attraction to unavailable men? Because I definitely should look into attending.

After my breakup with Jamie, I researched a woman's sex drive and found an interesting article that said the more you fed your libido, the more you craved sex, so I figured if I starved the damn thing, the need might disappear. Abstaining from sex sounded reasonable at the time. But now, a year into this endeavor? Now I want to be touched and cuddled and fucked until I can't walk straight.

This is worse than that dumb carb-free fast I tried in high school, which resulted with me stuffing my face with every biscuit, muffin, and tortilla I could get my hands on for three days straight when I finally caved.

With a groan, I kick off the covers, flip on the bedside lamp, and look around my room. Most of my stuff is still in my apartment in Austin, so I don't even have the one, no-frills vibrator I didn't throw out last summer. *If I acquaint myself with the deluxe shower head I noticed in my bathroom, will I wake everyone up?*

Ugh. Not worth it.

Stay strong, Victoria.

Whimpering, I flop back on the bed and cross my arm over my face. At least when I was waiting tables and bartending, I had daily—hell, hourly—reminders of how hot guys were dirtbags. But here, stranded with Mr. Sexy-As-Fuck Farm Boy, I sense the thrill of the chase toying with my resistance, especially now that I'm seeing Ethan's not the giant asshole I assumed he was when we first met.

I mentally flip through this last year where I really only did two things to keep my mind off Jamie—I worked and cooked. Maybe I can use that as an outlet here. Not only is cooking for the kids something I'll enjoy, more elaborate meals wear me out, so I shouldn't have an ounce of extra energy to lust after their dad.

The buzz of an incoming call interrupts my wallowing, but when I see the name on my cell screen, I groan. I love my best friend Vivian, but not the way we always seem to get in trouble when we're together.

An all-girl Catholic high school did nothing to tame the two of us. If anything, it made Viv and me rebel more when we were younger, and college only made us wilder. But we haven't hung out in ages, and I'm starting to feel guilty about it.

"Why aren't you at my party?" she asks, without preamble. A thumping bass punctuates every other word. She must head into a quiet room, because the music fades to a low roar.

"I didn't know you were back from South Padre." I don't bother explaining that some of us have to work for a living. She "works" for her father, but he's always letting her set her own hours.

Yawning, I try to follow what she's saying.

"Wait. Were you asleep? At nine p.m.?"

"Got a new job. Sort of." Everything with Ethan is so up in the air, I don't know if he really plans for me to be here the entire summer. Or if *I* want to be here that long. Except there's no other way I can be as close to Kat if this doesn't work out.

I give Viv a brief rundown of how I came to be the newest employee at Carter Cutting Horses.

"Have you fucked him yet?" She chews ice in my ear.

"Fucked who?"

"The dad. He sounds hot, and you've always had a thing for assholes."

"Of course I haven't fucked him. He's my boss." *And he's not really an asshole.*

"Never stopped you before."

I sigh, feeling the exhaustion of my past bulldoze over me. "I never slept with any of my bosses." People only think I have because I run with friends like Val. Sure, I've had plenty of hookups, and yes, I love sex, but I have a morality clause—no bosses or guys who've dated my friends. As soon as you bang someone's ex, you're headed for crazy town, and I have enough of that in my life without chumming the water.

"Really?" She sounds disappointed.

"I swear."

"Jamie wasn't your boss?"

The sound of his name makes me wince. "No, he wasn't my boss. He was my boss's friend, which was bad enough."

Because one, my boss Kevin never bothered to tell me my boyfriend was fucking *married*, and two, when Jamie and I unceremoniously broke up that fateful day, I had to quit my bartending job or face the very real possibility of seeing him because he frequented that restaurant.

And there was no way I was ever talking to that scumbag again. I changed my number, switched my job, and eventually moved when he kept stalking my place and sending me flowers. Nothing says, "Hey, sorry I didn't tell you I was a cheating douchebag" like bouquets of carnations. Who apologizes with the cheapest flower in the state of Texas? Even after I trashed them, they left behind that sickeningly sweet scent that reminded me of my grandmother's funeral.

"Are you still on that man diet thing?"

"No dicks for me." Figuratively or literally.

"That's a shame. I have a friend—"

"No."

"He's super hot."

"Then *you* date him, and I'll live vicariously through your escapades."

She laughs maniacally. "No one said *date* him. Just let him bang your brains out so you can get over your aversion to attractive men and see that you need to move back to Austin. Then we can party the whole summer. Come on. You haven't been the same since Jamie. Where's the BFF I know and love?"

"Girlfriend, I have to work. I have bills to pay. Daddy ain't gonna cover my rent."

I can almost hear her rolling her eyes. "George doesn't pay my rent." She calls her parents by their first names. My mother would smack me with her *chancla* if I ever did that. "I have a salary, thank you very much."

A salary Daddy pays even when you don't show up to work.

But when she doesn't stop badgering me, I promise to go out with her. I might need a break from Ethan Carter *pronto* anyway.

"Yay!" she yells into the phone. "We'll have a blast! One night of partying never hurt anyone."

I don't bother pointing out how we both know that's not true.

One night is all it takes for everything to go wrong.

∽

When I wake up the next morning, a precious face grins at me over the edge of the bed.

"Hey, Mila."

What time is it? Ethan didn't specify what time he wanted me to get the kids up, only that they ate around eight, and it's not quite seven fifteen.

"Sorry I woke you. Did I wake you?" She bounces up and down on her toes.

This kid is like sunshine on crack. I smile at her even though it pains me to be so cheerful this early in the day without a shot of coffee injected straight into my jugular.

Baby babble sounds through a tiny speaker on the bedside table. Ethan must've put the baby monitor there this morning before he headed out to work with the horses. Cody isn't quite two, so of course his dad still has a monitor for him. I feel dumb for not thinking about that sooner.

"Mila, can you do me a favor and keep your brother company for a few minutes while I brush my teeth? I'll be right out."

"I can do that!" She leaps into action, a blur of little girl racing out the door.

My laughter turns into a groan as I try to roll out of bed. When I bartend, I usually go to bed around three or four. Sometimes later. So getting up with the cows is not something my body knows how to do. I haven't gotten up this early since that internship fired me.

A few minutes later, when I get to Cody's room, his big smile perks me up. These kids are so freaking happy, I don't know what to do with myself. I grin at him and snuggle his warm body to me.

"Did you sleep well, munchkin?" He nuzzles closer. I close my eyes, loving his sweet baby scent. "Are you hungry?"

His grumbling tummy answers the question, and I hurry to get him changed so I can feed him. It takes a few minutes to wrestle him out of his pajamas, and when I get to his diaper, his smile widens.

"Poopies!" He kicks his chubby legs. "Poopies!"

"Okay, buddy. Thanks for the warning."

Except for the toxic diaper, the morning goes smoothly, but by lunch time, Mila's not wearing that bright smile anymore.

This little girl who never stops moving is staring out the back window, completely frozen.

I kneel down next to her. "What's wrong, honey? You look worried."

Her lips twist in her cherubic face. She waves me closer to whisper in my ear. "Can we make my daddy something to eat?"

I almost laugh, except the serious expression on her face tells me I shouldn't. "What does he usually do for lunch?"

"My grandma makes him food."

Ethan expressly told me I shouldn't make him any meals, but that's kind of weird if he's used to coming into the house to eat. What *is* he doing for lunch?

Movement catches my eye in the back yard, and I look

across the expansive field to the beautiful red barn where Ethan leads a horse to his stall.

Returning my attention to Mila, I give her a hug. "How about we make some extra food in case he comes in for lunch?"

She looks down, still frowning, and nods. Clearly, that wasn't the answer she wants to hear.

"Mila, what would you like to do for your dad? What would make you happy?"

"Can we make him lunch and take it to him?"

This kid is too sweet.

"Of course we can." And if he doesn't want it? Too damn bad because I'm not sure I can tell her no.

11

ETHAN

Logan and I toil side by side the entire morning, grooming horse after horse. I should be shitting rainbows after seeing how well the kids have taken to Tori, but the phone call I got from my lawyer this morning put me on edge again.

My brother takes a swig of his water bottle and wipes the sweat off his brow. "So it's set then? When you guys go before the judge in a few weeks, it'll be a done deal? You'll be divorced?"

I grunt, hating the looming court date.

That word. *Divorce.* Sounds so final. I guess it is.

The misery of the last two years weighs on my heart, the failure of it reverberating through my bones. This isn't what I wanted for my kids. Splitting time between two houses. Me worrying if they left their clothes or toys behind. Wondering what they're doing. Hating that I'm not with them. I may work a lot now, but I can check on them a dozen times throughout the day and hear their laughter when they're playing in the yard.

"You want me to come with you to court?" Logan chugs another drink and then douses his face. "I could tag along."

He's acting like we're talking about grabbing a beer instead of ending my marriage. I could use his support, though. "Yeah. Thanks."

As I brush out the mare, it settles in—how out of reach my dream of riding cutting horses competitively has become. I'll never be able to do it again, at least not when the financial future of the ranch is so uncertain. And definitely not while I'm still figuring out how to be a single parent.

What tears at my conscience is how much my father wanted me to get back in the arena, but I don't see how I can make that happen with all of the responsibilities I'm dealing with right now.

With a grimace, I pinch the bridge of my nose. *I can't even drown my sorrows with a good bottle of whiskey 'cause I have so much shit to do.*

We wash down one more mare before Logan breaks the silence. "Sandra keeps asking about you."

I have no idea who he's talking about, but he ignores my foul mood and keeps talking. "She's that cute realtor we met at the Lone Star. The one who got divorced last year?" He sighs. "The one with the son?"

It takes me a minute but then I remember, mostly because I heard her ex was abusive, which pisses me off. I don't understand how a man can hurt a woman.

Logan nods at me. "Want me to set you up? You've been a monk for too long, and this court date gives us the perfect reason to celebrate." Using the words "celebrate" and "court date" in the same sentence make me cringe, but I know he's pissed at Allison on my behalf. "Come on, bro. One beer. Maybe an appetizer. That's it. Sandra's a cutie, but if you're not ready to 'wham, bam, thank you, ma'am,' I'm sure you could keep it casual."

My brother, the romantic.

He nudges my arm, and I shrug him off. "Fine. One beer. Whatever it takes to get you to shut up."

"Or even better, we could go to the coast for the weekend. Maybe when Allison is watching the kids."

With everything I have to do around here, taking a weekend to act like I'm young and carefree is impractical. "How in the world would I pull that off?"

The words are barely out of my mouth when a little voice shouts, "Daddy! We brought you lunch!"

A huge smile lifts my lips before I'm done turning around. Standing in the open gate, with sunlight streaming behind them, are Mila, Cody, and Tori. Mila's carrying a huge picnic basket, one my mother stores over the kitchen cabinets, while Tori bounces Cody on her hip and waves.

It's such a rare treat to see the kids back here that I instantly feel the sadness from a minute ago start to lift.

Tori hoists my son higher in her arms. "Sorry to bother you, but Mila wanted to make you lunch."

"It's no bother. I'll never turn away food."

I kneel down to Mila's eye level, and she throws herself in my arms like she hasn't seen me in a week. Worry fills my heart, and my eyes connect with Tori, who gives me a look of understanding.

Her voice is soft. Comforting. "She's having a good afternoon. She just misses you."

Rubbing Mila's back, I realize how hard this must be for her. Having my mom leave and a new babysitter take over the very next second. I should've planned this better and overlapped them more.

"Hey," I whisper into my daughter's hair. "You totally made my day."

"Yeah?" When she pulls back, she wipes her eyes, but even though she's emotional, she's smiling.

"Yup. I was having a crummy morning, but then my favorite people stopped by."

She looks up at Tori and leans toward me to whisper, "Tori made the food, but I helped."

"I'm sure it's delicious," I say, watching how Tori averts her eyes when I look at her. "What'd ya make?"

Mila jumps up and down. "Sandwiches and salad."

I'll be starving again in an hour, but this sweet delivery fills me up in other ways. "Sure was thoughtful of you." I wait until Tori looks at me to say those words to my daughter, so Tori knows they're meant for her too.

I tell my ranch hands to take a break and corral my brood into the corner stall that's been outfitted into a small office with an extra table.

Tori hands Cody to me, and I kiss his chubby belly and make him laugh while the girls set out the food. And holy shit, my daughter's simple description of the meal doesn't do it justice. Because Tori didn't *just* make sandwiches and salad.

My mouth waters when I see the thick, succulent pieces of meat wedged between the lightly toasted slices of bread.

"You made a roast? And homemade potato salad?" My mom left a roast to thaw in the fridge before she left, and I guess there must've been a sack of potatoes somewhere in the pantry.

I'm almost tempted to say Tori looks embarrassed at the spread.

She tucks her hands in the back pockets of her cutoffs and nods. "That okay?" She glances up at me, her hair tumbling over her shoulders and hiding half of her face. "I probably should've asked first. There's more than enough for you guys for dinner. If you don't mind eating the same thing later."

"This is amazing." I get my daughter seated next to me and prop Cody on my lap while I dig in. Flavor explodes on my tongue with the perfect spices and just the right amount of mayo. The meat practically melts in my mouth.

I'm two bites in and halfway through a whole sandwich when Logan strolls up to our impromptu lunch.

"Did ya bring enough for me too?" he asks Tori, who is standing between me and Cody, helping him dig into a Tupperware of food that's been cut into toddler-sized pieces. *Shit. I should be doing that.*

She tucks a long strand of hair behind her ear. "We brought plenty. I wasn't sure how hungry Ethan would be, so if he doesn't mind sharing..."

I'm tempted to growl and keep this for myself, except my brother has been busting his ass all day.

Nodding toward the empty chair across from me, I don't bother to stop devouring my lunch.

He takes one look at the spread and wraps an arm around Tori and kisses the top of her head. "This fu— freaking rocks. You're amazing." Squeezing her harder, he looks at me. "Isn't she amazing?"

Tori gives him a self-depreciating smile, and her cheeks heat.

I pause mid-bite, frozen with the very real desire to peel Logan off Tori with my fist. "Stop mauling the woman and sit your butt down and eat." My attention darts back to Tori. "Yes, she's amazing."

She averts her eyes, like she's at a loss for words. *Interesting.*

"You gonna join us?" I peek in the basket and notice the last of the oatmeal cookies my mom made this weekend.

"No. I, um, I lose my appetite when I cook. From smelling the food all that time, I guess." She turns to Mila and unwraps her sandwich carefully so the thick chunks of meat don't fall out.

"Make sure you eat at some point so my kids don't run you ragged. I can watch them for a bit if you need a break. I didn't intend for you to do a marathon cooking session while you babysat. Thought they could eat some chicken nuggets or mac and cheese or something easy for lunch."

Shrugging, she turns those big hazel eyes up to mine. "It's not a big deal. I like to cook, and your kitchen is amazing, so that makes it really fun. I don't mind. But if you have any requests, let me know ahead of time so I can make sure you have all of the ingredients."

Logan leans forward in his seat. "You take requests?"

I toss my napkin at his face. "Not from you."

He chuckles and winks at Tori, and I force myself not to clench my fists. Not sure why that bothers me, but it does. Logan's a flirt. That's who he is, but watching him fawn over Tori gets under my skin.

When we're done eating, I head out into the main part of

the barn. My kids are hanging off my brother when I notice Tori reaching up to pet one of our buckskin quarter horses, who's leaning his head out of his stall and enjoying the attention. Can't say I blame him.

Her slender arms wrap around his neck, and she nuzzles him with her face. The moment is such a sweet one that it draws me closer. Allison never came back here. Never cared about the horses. Makes me wonder if things would've been different if she had. It's not like I never invited her to see what I did. Would've loved to have her appreciate what my family and I spent our whole lives building.

"What's his name?" Tori asks, her eyes full of wonder and appreciation for the magnificent animal in her arms.

Reaching behind his ear, I give him a good scratch. "Moves Like Mick Jagger, but I call him Mick."

"That's a crazy name." She slides her hands over him, a beautiful smile on her face.

"You ride?" I'm wildly curious now given how comfortable she is petting Mick.

"Nope."

Hmm. "Wanna learn?"

Her bright eyes shift to mine. "Really?"

"Sure. Why not?"

She bites that full lower lip. "You spend so much time with these guys. Why would you want to work more to show me how to ride?"

The words come without thinking. "Because this doesn't feel like work." I'm not sure if I mean raising horses or the idea of teaching her what I do, but the answer is the same regardless.

I don't mean to check her out, but it's hard not to notice

her beauty or her warm amber eyes. Those rosy, flushed cheeks. Her teasing smile.

Tori twists her long hair up into a top knot, and I can't help appreciating her graceful neck.

Which has me looking down her body, my pulse quickening from the generous curves of her breasts beneath the maddeningly snug tank top.

I look away, not wanting to be *that* guy.

A moment later, her voice draws my attention back to her.

"Must be nice to have something you love so much." A cool breeze blows through the barn, and she tilts her head and closes her eyes. "To have something that's so a part of you, you feel it all the way down to the soles of your shoes."

"It's fulfilling, for sure, and there's nothing like teaching someone who loves horses how to ride." It's true. It'd be a damn delight to show her the ropes if she's as interested in these guys as I think she is. Peeling off my baseball cap, I wipe the sweat off my forehead and put my baseball cap on backwards, so I can feel more of that breeze on my face. I lower my voice, so my children don't overhear. "But I'd be lying if I said it wasn't stressful. Being here, doing this for my family, it's a lot of pressure. As much as I love the ranch, I wish I could spend more time with my kids."

She studies my face, and those crazy golden eyes turn wistful. "You're a good guy, Ethan Carter."

Her praise washes over me, and I'm almost speechless from the compliment. I open my mouth, but a shrill female voice interrupts.

"Ethan, honey. Yoo-hoo!" Mallory struts through my barn even though I don't have her down for a lesson today.

The sweet, dreamy gaze in Tori's eyes shutters faster than my brother drops his drawers on a Friday night.

Mallory flutters up to us. "And who is this?" She eyeballs Tori up and down, but Tori gives her a small smile.

"I'm nobody. Just the nanny. I'll get out of your hair so you guys can work." With a quick wave, she wrangles the kids and is out the door before Mallory's claws fully extend.

After I get my client out of my hair, I'm still thinking about Tori and how she made us lunch. Apparently, my brother is too.

He elbows me when I reach for the leftover cookies in my desk.

"Maybe you don't need to head out to find yourself a little hookup." He wiggles his fingers around his head. "Because the sparks were flying around here earlier with you and your new employee."

"Shut the fuck up," I grunt. "You and I both know I have too much on my plate right now to entertain anything like that."

But sometimes, I wish I didn't.

12

TORI

Even with my bedroom door closed, I can hear the kids in the kitchen. The way their dad talks sweetly to them. His deep voice. Their laughter.

Part of me—a *big* part of me—wants to go out there and enjoy dinner with them, but after we had lunch in the barn with Ethan and his brother, I don't need more opportunities to see Ethan with his children. To see how much he adores them. How hard he works to provide for them. How much he wants to spend time with them.

Lucky kids.

Wish I could've seen my dad in the middle of the day like that. Laughed with my sister so easily when we were young. The thought makes my stomach ache.

I'm not sure who that woman in the barn was, but she gazed at Ethan like he was a prized stallion she wanted to mount, with or without the audience. I'm surprised she didn't lean over and lick him to show ownership.

No amount of sexy ruggedness is enough to get me interested in a guy who might be involved elsewhere.

Never mind that he's still married.

Yeah, complicated.

I'll stick to my single lifestyle, thank you very much.

The best distraction just so happens to live a few miles down the road.

I pick up my phone and call my sister. Ten minutes later, I jump in Kat's truck, and we head to her house.

"Hey, preggo. How's your baby bun?" She can barely fit behind the wheel. How does she still have two months left to go? My vag hurts when I think about that delivery.

"Kickin' up a storm. I almost peed my pants earlier today, and my back hurts like a mother."

"Ooooh. Look at you almost curse." I love teasing my sister. She's always such a saint. *Saint Katherine.* I almost snort at my old nickname for her.

"Are you settling in at the ranch? How's your room?"

I think about the pale blue paint with white trim and the neat bookshelf that's been alphabetized. The lovely curtains that were obviously sewed with love and care, and the colorful quilt that covers the cushy queen-sized bed.

"It's perfect." I avoid telling her about the corner of my room where my shit explodes out of my suitcase. "Like the rest of the house. Spacious."

Stunning. A dream house, really. A wrap-around porch with a swing and potted plants. Five bedrooms and three and a half baths. A fantastic kitchen with tons of gleaming counter space and every appliance imaginable. Big, comfy couches that make me itch to have a Netflix marathon.

My sister motions to me. "Ethan added a whole addition.

Did a ton of work himself. Well, him and his brother. The east side of the house, I think."

Pregnancy has made her spacey, because she was there when Beverly told us that Ethan had done those renovations. "Yeah, I've heard those Carter boys are good with their hands."

I'm looking forward to something breaking around the house so I can watch Ethan fix it. Hopefully while shirtless.

She glances at me. "Don't keep me in suspense. How are things going? Is Ethan still getting on your nerves?"

My sister knows I can be a snarky bitch sometimes.

"No, Ethan's a great guy." Too great maybe. I fill my lungs with a deep breath and decide to come clean. "Actually, I'm trying *not* to like him."

"Oh." A beat passes. *"Oh!* Well, what's wrong with that? He's single and has his act together."

Unlike me.

She looks thrilled at this prospect.

"No, he's not single. He's in the middle of a divorce. His words, not mine." I fiddle with a loose thread on my tank top. "Plus, he has 'rebound' stamped all over him."

If that experience with Jamie taught me anything, it's that guys like Ethan don't settle down with girls like me. I'm a fun fuck. A good time. A way to burn off steam or sow some wild oats. Not a forever girl. Not someone you keep.

Regret weighs in my heart. How I wish I hadn't invested so much of myself in that relationship.

Ripping off the loose thread, I suddenly wish I could go back to Austin. "Ethan needs to play the field, get laid, get over his wife, and I don't want to be just a hookup. I'm not in the mood to be the rebound."

It doesn't escape me that Ethan has photos of his wife everywhere. I wish I could say Allison is ugly, but she's not. She has a button nose and one of those cute pixie haircuts, which makes her gorgeous blonde hair look feather-soft. I toy with the ends of my hair, lamenting the split ends, but a haircut requires money I don't have.

Kat rubs her belly. "I think all those rosaries Mom says for you are paying off. Listen to you, wanting something more substantial."

I roll my eyes as she laughs, but I'm glad she doesn't pick up on my glum mood. I'm here to soak up her happiness. I'm here to mask the fact that I wish I were at dinner with Ethan and his kids. I'm here because I don't want to think about how he looked at me in the barn when we were standing so close or the fact that Miss Prissy Pants earlier is probably riding him in his free time.

It's easy for me to think Ethan looked disappointed when I told him I wasn't joining him and the kids this evening.

Except I know that's my head playing tricks on me.

Because guys like him don't do long-term with girls like me.

I might as well get used to that idea.

13

ETHAN

EVERY DAY, I LISTEN TO THE DELIGHTED SOUNDS OF MY children playing in the backyard, squealing and laughing as they buzz around Tori. Her laugh carries too, a note or two below theirs, but just as dazzling.

But the moment I'm cleaned up after work and head into the kitchen, Tori quiets and scurries off to her room, leaving me with a piping-hot dinner on the stove and the table set for three.

And my kids? All they do is talk about Tori. How fun she is. How she colors with them and plays pretend. How she gives them little tasks while she's cooking so they stay busy. *Snap the peas. Wash the carrots. Organize the Tupperware.* And they love it. They love feeling useful. Mila tells me that Cody attaches himself to Tori's leg half the time while she's in the kitchen, and she lets him. Talks to him. Explains what she's doing, and the kid listens—or tries to. It's like she's a goddamn baby whisperer.

Don't get me started about her meals. They're delicious.

I feel guilty as hell for enjoying them without her.

It's maddening. It shouldn't be. I shouldn't care what she does with her evenings. In fact, I told her she was free to do as she pleased when I was done working each day, but it bothers me that she seems to be going out of her way to avoid me.

We haven't had lunch together again either. Just that first day. Now she packs the food and sends Mila in with the picnic basket to drop it off while she waits at the entrance of the barn with Cody. Or the kids come to eat with me while she starts dinner.

All week. She avoids me *all week.*

By Friday, I've had enough. After I get the kids to bed, I knock on her bedroom door.

"Come in."

She's sprawled across the bed with her arm over her face. Her hair is wet and she's wearing those tiny sleep shorts and another tank top. She does one of those cat-like stretches, and I ignore the throb in my groin when the fabric of her shirt pulls up to display the taut skin on her smooth stomach.

You're not here to ogle her, douchebag. I make a point to focus on her face.

"Hey. Wanted to thank you for dinner. Best brisket I've had in ages, but don't tell my mom your food is better than hers."

Tori sits up slowly and gives me a hesitant smile. "No prob."

Those bright eyes study me. At least she's not looking away.

Say something.

"It's Friday night. No big plans?"

She hums. "I'm not really in the mood to beg any of my

friends to drive this far to pick me up for a night of cheap beer and loud music."

"You can borrow my truck anytime."

A shadow passes over her, but in a flash, it's gone. "I'd feel weird asking."

"I don't mind."

Her slender shoulders shrug. "Still."

Leaning against her doorframe, I cross my arms. "You always this stubborn?"

That smile returns, and it hits me in the sternum. "Yeah. Get used to it."

There it is. There's the fire she hosed me down with the first time we met.

I chuckle and slip my hands into my pockets. "Since you're too good to drive my truck and too cool to eat dinner with us, how about keeping me company while I watch the end of the Rangers game? You like baseball? I have two pints of Ben & Jerry's, and I'm willing to share in exchange for conversation with someone who isn't my sibling or child."

Her eyes lower. "I shouldn't, but thanks for the offer."

Here we go again. "Can I ask you something? Did I offend you?" Those golden eyes, wide and surprised, meet mine. "Because you've been doing your damnedest to avoid me since lunch earlier this week."

After a long pause, she sighs. "I'm doing you a favor."

"How do you figure?"

She doesn't answer right away, until I give her an exasperated look, and she sighs again. "I'm staying out of your way. This is your house, and I know you're not used to having a stranger around."

I frown. "You're not a stranger. Well, not anymore. And I

feel like a giant ass enjoying your cooking without you joining us. I mean, it's fine if you're sick of me and my kids and need some space—"

"I'm not sick of your kids. Not at all."

It pains me to think of what she's not saying. "Okay, so then... just sick of me?" I dig deep for the next words. "Do you still think I'm a dick? I know I'm not always the nicest guy or the most patient, but—"

"Shut up. I'm not sick of you either. And you're not a dick, okay?" Rolling her eyes, she gets up in a huff and stomps over. Without shoes, she's tiny, barely coming up to my shoulders. I'm thinking Tinkerbell's gonna shove me out of her room and slam the door in my face when she grabs my arms and turns me. "I'll watch anything with you but the Rangers, okay?"

I smile as she manhandles me out of her room. "How about the Cubs? They're playing the Dodgers." This close, I can smell the coconut fragrance of her shampoo.

"Fine."

After I find the game on TV, I collect the ice cream and two spoons, drop down next to Tori on the couch, and hand her a spoon. "Chocolate Cherry Garcia or Chocolate Chip Cookie Dough?"

"Chocolate Cherry, please."

"Here ya go, m'lady."

I adjust the volume on my flatscreen and settle in. I'm about to pat myself on the back for getting her to relax when she moans, and my dick sits up and takes notice.

Reflexively, I turn toward her and immediately wish I hadn't.

93

The look on her face is pure ecstasy. Her eyes are closed as she wraps her lips around the spoon and moans. Again.

Throb. Throb. Throb.

Fuck.

Reaching down, I yank my jeans at the knees to make more room and stretch the hem of my t-shirt out before I strategically place the ice cream over my erection.

What the fuck? I glare down at my lap, wondering how the hell I'm sporting spontaneous wood when I've barely noticed a woman in the last two years, much less popped a boner around one like a horny teenager.

"This," she mumbles around a bite, "is sooo good. Thank you."

"Welcome." I muster a grunt.

We eat in silence while the Cubs get their asses kicked. *C'mon, guys.*

The tension in my shoulders finally starts to ease, which is when I remember the phone call this afternoon.

"I heard from the babysitting agency this afternoon."

"Oh?" She stills next to me.

"They told me I was shit outta luck. That no one wants to come out this far, but they'll keep me posted if something changes."

"They did not say you were 'shit outta luck.'" She makes this little sound in the back of her throat.

Laughing, I shrug. "No, but you get the gist." I look over at her hesitantly. "So what do you say? Think you could stay on longer? I know we initially said we'd start with two weeks to see how things went, but I honestly don't know what I'd do without you right now."

Her eyes soften, and she gazes into her ice cream like it holds all the answers. *Please say yes.*

"I might have someone interested in subletting my place, so... maybe?"

"Maybe is better than no, so I'll take maybe. What if I promise unlimited Ben & Jerry's?"

She gives me a shy smile. "Giving me the hard sell, huh?"

I try not to think about all the hard things I'd love to give her. "Just keep me posted about your apartment situation. I'd hate to lose you."

See, I can keep things professional.

The room quiets as we return to the baseball game. She keeps making those eager noises as she eats her ice cream. I can't decide if giving her Ben & Jerry's is the best idea I've ever had or the worst as I try to ignore how much those sounds remind me of sex.

Christ. Maybe I do need to get out more, but I'd rather endure my mother's henpecking knitting circle than go on a blind date.

A few minutes later, Tori closes up the pint and relaxes back. "I practically ate the whole thing. Guess I didn't realize I was that hungry."

"What'd you eat for dinner?" I know she made *me* brisket, but what did she eat?

She shrugs and doesn't answer.

"Tori." I wait until she looks at me. "What did you eat?" I study her again, realizing she looks thinner than she did last week. If she's on some dumb diet when she's already a beautiful woman, we're gonna have words.

"PB and J."

That's not the answer I want to hear. "Why didn't you

have a real dinner? Some brisket? You made enough to feed an army." Roasted corn and summer squash. Fresh-baked rolls. Homemade cookies. It was ridiculous. Ridiculously delicious. But the leftovers barely fit in my fridge.

She shakes her head—at me, at herself, I'm not sure. "I'm going to my sister's this weekend."

"Okay."

Her cheeks redden and her voice drops down to a whisper. "I wanted to make sure you and the kids and Logan had enough to eat while I was gone."

Well, damn.

I don't think. I just react, pulling her into a side hug. "That's about the nicest thing anyone's done for me in a long time, darlin'. Thank you."

Her hand looks small on my chest, her body tiny nestled against mine. She's still for a second and then she hugs me back, and I can feel her smile against me. "You're welcome." God, she's cute. And fuck, she smells good, like summer and sunshine and coconuts.

I lean away and give her a stern look. "No more skipping meals or eating sandwiches on my account. If you want something else to eat, then go for it, but your wellbeing is just as important as my family's, okay? Don't skimp at dinner so we can eat the next day. That's unacceptable. And Logan can get his own damn meals over the weekend. He doesn't even live here."

"Yes, sir."

Chuckling, I let her go, immediately wishing I could hold her again.

"Please don't exhaust yourself on our account. If you're

too tired to make dinner, we'll order pizza or the kids can deal with my mac and cheese."

When she agrees, I nudge her with my elbow, and she nudges me back, and I try not to think about how much I like having her here next to me. The fact that the woman worried enough about me and my kids to cook up a small feast proves how wrong I was about her when we first met. God, I was such a cock. This girl is amazing. Thoughtful. Sweet with my kids.

Sexy as hell.

As we watch the game, I mull over the reason she says she didn't eat tonight. It doesn't explain the rest of the week or why she darts off to her room in the evenings, but I think I've pushed her enough for now.

When I get up for a beer a little later, I make a couple of brisket sandwiches and place one on the coffee table in front of her.

I park myself on the couch and nudge her again. "This babe I know makes me the best food. You really should try her brisket."

Tori laughs and shakes her head. To my delight, she eats the sandwich.

14

———

ETHAN

Not even forty-eight hours later, I find myself looking out the window, glancing at the front door, listening for signs of a car or truck along the driveway.

Logan kicks me under the table while we eat dinner with the kids. "Don't look so eager."

My brother, his best friend Joey, my kids, and I are having dinner in the kitchen.

"What are you talking about?" I shove a bite of Tori's shredded beef in my mouth and barely contain a groan because it's so good.

He leans closer and lowers his voice. "The whole trick is to not let women know you want them."

I wait until Joey washes the kids' hands to respond. "You do realize I was having sex when you were still in Little League, right? Besides, I'm not making a play for Tori."

There's no way I'll forget the way she threw down the gauntlet at her sister's house. *No sex. Ever.* That hasn't helped the dreams I started having two nights ago after the ice cream incident. I woke up with my hand in my boxer briefs like a damn fifteen-year-old.

"No?" His eyebrow curves up. "Not gonna bang the hot nanny?"

Smacking him in the chest, I give him a look. "No. And neither are you. In case you were wondering."

He grins like an idiot.

The front doorbell rings, and my heart leaps in my chest. Joey offers to answer it.

Groaning, I drop my face in my hands. *Am I seriously nervous over this woman? A woman who has sworn nothing is gonna happen between us?* Fucking figures. Not that I need this kind of complication with the court date for my divorce two weeks away. That's the best reminder that I suck at relationships.

Fuck. I did not just use the R-word right now.

I'm not in a good place to have one yet, not with the truckload of baggage weighing me down at the moment.

This gives me pause because I've always been a one-woman kind of guy. Sleeping around with random chicks does nothing for me. If given a choice, I'd always pick something special with one girl over meaningless sex with many.

But is this really something I should be exploring with my kids' nanny?

Damn. I know how to get myself in messed-up situations.

Female voices come down the hall, and the second I see Tori, I smile. She looks more relaxed, and her face brightens when the kids go barreling into her for a hug.

I open my mouth to say hi, but my brother beats me to it.

"Hey, gorgeous. How's your sister?"

I bristle at his term of endearment, and he smirks at me.

Asshole. But she is gorgeous, even in cutoffs and an old t-shirt. It's the affection in her eyes for my kids, though, that really hits me. I love how she gives them all her attention.

Tori's laughing at Cody's sloppy kisses. "Good. I swear Kat's giving birth to a giant. Her baby is enormous, but don't tell her that."

Logan shivers like he's about to have a seizure. "Pregnant women scare me. Too many hormones."

Joey rolls her eyes.

I point to my brother's best friend. "Tori, this is Josephine. She went to school with Logan and somehow manages to put up with this lazy bag of bones. She helped me out today with the kids so I could get some work done."

Tori gives her a sweet smile. "I love your hair. It's beautiful."

Joey touches her blue locks. "Thanks. *Someone* told me I look like a deranged Smurf." She punches my brother, and he puts her in a headlock with one arm while he scrolls through his phone on the other. She's still hanging halfway upside down when she points to Tori. "But your hair is, *wow*. It's so pretty."

"Thank you. It needs a trim."

"I could do it."

Motioning toward Joey, I explain that she does hair.

"Yeah?" Tori perks up. "How much do you charge? Just to trim the dead ends?"

Joey wiggles her way out of my brother's choke hold and strokes Tori's hair gently, taking a moment to study the ends. "I'd do it for free. You know, the friends and family discount."

"No way. My hair is a pain in the ass. Your arm will fall off by the time you're done. I have to pay you something."

"Um." Joey tilts her head. "How about we trade? You show me how to make this recipe"—she points to her half-eaten plate of dinner—"and I'll cut your hair."

Tori leans over to see which leftovers we ate. "You want to learn how to make *carne guisada*? Sure. It's super easy."

"Dinner was dope, Tor," my brother says, not looking up from his phone. "I can't believe you made enough leftovers for the weekend. I think I love you."

Tori laughs and stoops down to look at a painting Mila made for her. A few minutes later, Tori starts to lug her bag from the hall.

Logan stops her to pick it up. "You pack more than Joey does for two days."

"I needed to do some laundry, but I didn't get a chance. That's okay. I'll do it next weekend."

What is she talking about? I get up and take the bag from my brother, whose eyebrows lift. I motion toward the kids, and he smirks again, offering to get them ready for bed. I watch as he and Joey take them down the hall before I return my attention to Tori.

I stand right in front of her until she looks at me. "Tori, why would you need to wait until you go to your sister's to do your laundry? Are you too good for my washer and dryer too?"

She laughs and shakes her head. I like her laugh. I want to hear it again.

"No? Then why are you saving it for your sister's?"

Her lips twist as she tries to contain that smile.

"That's what I thought. C'mon." I take her hand and drag her down the hall. "I didn't think you needed a personal invitation to use all the amenities in this house, but apparently you do."

Stopping in the laundry room, I hoist her enormous duffle bag onto the counter. "Here's the washer and dryer. Now, it might not be as nice as your sister's, but you should use it."

She opens her mouth to respond, but I pull her into the adjacent office. "This place is a mess because I only have two hands and twenty-four hours a day, but this is my office." I don't think she's been in here. "If you ever need to print anything or use my laptop, feel free. Or if you want to watch TV and we're hogging the one in the living room, you can watch in here."

"Thanks, but I don't—"

Ignoring whatever she's saying, I maneuver her back out and across the house. When I open my bedroom door, she falters. I turn around. "It's okay. I'm not abducting you. Just wanna show you my tub. It has these fancy jets and all kinds of functions I haven't even figured out yet. I thought you might want to use it after a long day watching my rugrats. You know, when you're busy avoiding me at dinner."

She looks embarrassed. "Ethan, I—"

I don't wait for her to finish. Taking her hand, I tug her into my huge bathroom and flip on the lights. It's beautiful. All custom marble and shit I don't care about but my ex-wife did.

"Please, take a bath. I never do, and the guilt is killing me for spending that kind of money on something no one uses."

Her eyes are huge as she takes in the bathroom.

Reaching for the cabinet, I present the wide array of bath products my ex left behind. Bottles and bottles of crap

Allison never bothered to use herself. Of course, I threw out the shit that smelled like her when I realized she wasn't coming back. I have enough reminders of her in this house without smelling her lotions. "Go to town. Use everything. I don't care."

Before Tori can say anything, I resume the tour. Past the kids' bedrooms, past the kids' bathroom and Tori's bedroom. I stop in front of the last room. Flipping on the lights, I motion for her to step inside.

"I don't know if you like crafts or sewing, but my mom has a ton of stuff stored here, and I know she'd love for you to use whatever you want. For yourself or for the kids."

Tori takes a small step forward and lightly touches the bolts of fabrics that are arranged along the wall. "This is amazing." She frowns and retracts her hand. "Are you sure she'd be okay with me messing with her things?"

"I promise. Go for it." Sighing, I run my hand over my chin. "Sorry I never gave you the grand tour. I realize now that I kinda threw you into our lives, and maybe you haven't felt a hundred percent welcome, but I want you to know you are. My kids love you, and for all of my bitching at you the first time we met, I have to admit I'm pretty fond of you too." Her eyes shoot up to mine, and I give her a stupid smile. "Even when you are a little feisty, but if I'm being honest, I like that side of you the best."

She laughs that sexy, raspy laugh, and my blood heats with the playfulness in her eyes. "Why, Ethan Carter, are you saying you want the uncensored version of me?" She tsks. "I'm not entirely sure you can handle that."

I take a step closer and tug on a strand of her hair. "Try me."

15

TORI

Tiny hands tangle in my hair, and I smile down at Mila. This girl loves playing with my hair almost as much as Cody does.

"Once upon a time..."

In the soft light of her bedroom, I read as quietly as I can to lull her to sleep. Page after page, I watch her snuggle deeper into her cozy bed. Even though I hate these stories, the kind where the woman is beholden to the man for rescuing her, a teeny part of me loves the romance.

"And the prince saved the princess from the dangerous dragon, and they lived happily ever after. The end."

Her eyes are closed, and she's breathing so deeply, I'm thinking I can sneak out of here when she crinkles her nose and whispers, "Why couldn't the princess climb outta the castle by herself? Why'd the prince hafta climb in to save her?"

I smile, loving her inquisitive mind. "Because if the prince had stayed outside of the castle any longer, the dragon would've gotten him. This way, the princess is really saving him."

My crazy answer seems to satisfy her, and she nods into her pillow with a deep sigh.

When I close her bedroom door, Ethan is tiptoeing out of Cody's room too.

"Sorry you needed to do double duty today," he says softly as we head toward the living room.

"No worries. I'm glad Cody settled down."

Usually, Ethan manages to get both kids to bed on his own, but for some reason, Cody was restless tonight and wanted extra snuggle time with his dad. I was happy to help and read to Mila.

Ethan hands me a bag of popcorn when we get settled in front of the TV. He makes a quick call to his mom, and I stifle a laugh when he makes a face at me and says, "Yes, Ma, your pot roast is better," while he's shaking his head no.

When he hangs up, I ask how Beverly's doing.

"She misses the kids, but she's long overdue for this trip to see her sister." He reaches across my lap for some popcorn. "She wanted to know how you like your room. If you have everything you need."

I nod, feeling oddly pleased his mom asked about me. "Tell her the amenities are lovely and that I am so delighted someone introduced me to the washer and dryer."

"Smartass." He chuckles and adjusts the volume on the remote.

Even though the couch is enormous, he's sitting right next to me, so close I can feel the heat from his body.

I shove a huge bite of popcorn into my mouth to distract me from the clean, masculine scent of his body wash. Being around Ethan fresh out of the shower every evening after work is the hardest part of my day. Seeing him barefoot around his house in jeans and old t-shirts suggests a certain intimacy I don't really have with him.

"Mmm. I love kettle corn," I say around a mouthful. Despite how nervous he makes me sometimes, I force myself to act like I would around my friends in Austin, which means my inner tomboy is at full throttle. Thus, I'm stuffing my face.

He dips his hand into the bag. "Me too. Between our desserts and your dinners, I'm gonna weigh two tons by the end of the summer."

"As if. You must burn four thousand calories a day." It's true. Ethan works like a dog, slaving from sun-up until sun-down in the sweltering barn. Sometimes after the kids are in bed, he ties the long-range baby monitor to his belt and toils some more. The man has a remarkable work ethic.

And I'm guessing remarkable stamina.

I mean, I can only imagine.

When a commercial comes on for a concert, I smile at the memories. "Ryan Hunter was so good live."

Ethan turns to me with a nod. "Saw him and his band a few years ago. They kicked ass."

"I didn't peg you as an alternative music fan." Ryan Hunter is known for his acoustic style, original songwriting, and his hot AF face and bod.

Though, now that I'm sitting next to Ethan, I'd say my number one celebrity crush has some competition.

Ethan shrugs. "Brady got me into his music, strangely enough."

I push him playfully. "He got me into Ryan's music too. I

was in my senior year of high school, and Brady wouldn't shut up about this band he knew from Boston."

He gives me a sexy smirk. "I forget you're still a baby."

I roll my eyes, but I'm laughing. "Whatever. You can't help that you're old."

It's weird how natural it feels to give him a hard time. It's even weirder to figure out we were both at the same Ryan Hunter concert all those years ago.

With us shooting the shit, I can't help but let down my defenses because, after a week of hanging out, this vibe between us seems natural.

Despite my better judgment, I find myself liking Ethan more than I should. But if the only way I'm going to *not* like him is to avoid him altogether, then I'll just have to deal with this puppy crush. Because disappearing in the evenings only hurt his feelings, which I won't do again.

I've also learned that the beautiful redhead I saw last week is a client, and judging from the comments I've overheard from Logan, she's not someone whose attention Ethan welcomes.

Still.

I need to tread carefully.

I figure it's only two months, and then I'll go back to Austin. The thought saddens me, but it's not like I'm a permanent member of this family. Even though I sort of wish I was. Unlike when I was dating Jamie, however, I don't let myself fantasize.

It would be so easy to daydream. To wonder what it would be like if Ethan and I were together. Like right now? I'd sit closer to him and lean into his broad chest. He'd band one of his big arms around me and kiss the top of my head, and

I'd sigh happily and let my hand meander over his stomach and appreciate every one of those ridges. Maybe I'd nuzzle against him. Smell his sexy scent. Lick and nibble my way up his neck until I straddled his lap and felt his thick, hard length through his jeans.

Yes, please.

The benefit to living with this man is seeing him in all manner of dress. My favorite happens to be those thin nylon sweatpants that show exactly how much he's packing.

More than a mouthful.

The sound of baseball fills the room, snapping my attention to the TV.

"You didn't check the MLB app, did you?" he asks.

His voice is so sexy. Deep and masculine. Commanding.

"No." I shake my head to get out of whatever loony place it had gone a moment ago. *Is it hot in here?* "I would never cheat and see who won." Squeezing my thighs together, I realize I might need a *verrrrry* cold shower later.

"Good girl."

"But I *might've* seen that someone hit a grand slam." I cringe playfully and wait for him to freak out. The goofball DVRed the Astros game since they played earlier today. He's very serious about not seeing spoilers before he can watch.

His eyebrows furrow, and he holds his chest. "You're breaking my heart, Victoria. No ice cream for you this week."

"What? That's not fair, you big bully." I push him, and he yanks me closer and tickles me. Popcorn goes flying.

I yelp, and instantly, his giant paw covers my mouth, and he laughs in my ear. "Shh. Don't wake up the kids."

Wiggling as hard as I can, I try to tickle him back, but he's so big, I'm like a rag doll in his arms. I'm cackling and squealing and kicking my legs. And Jesus Christ, I'm turned on. The harder I fight against him, the stronger that throb between my legs pulses.

He shifts, leans sideways, and the next thing I know, we're horizontal on the couch. I'm huffing and puffing into his palm and laughing so fucking hard when his amused eyes meet mine.

"Say, 'Ethan is the tickle master of the universe,' and I'll let you go."

I squint but nod slowly. When he removes his hand, I smirk. "Ethan fights like a little girl!"

Those taunting words are barely out when he covers my mouth with his palm and starts tickling me again.

"Okay!" I scream into his hand. It comes out muffled. "Okay, okay!" I'm practically hyperventilating.

He props himself up, straddling my legs, and hauls my arms over my head. "I'm sorry. What were you saying? Something about how I'm the strongest man you know? How my muscles are so big and impressive?"

I shake my head, smiling, gasping and trying to catch my breath when his gaze travels over my chest. I look down and realize my nipples are rock hard and happily pointing straight at him, my sheer bra and white tank top doing little to mask how turned on I am right now.

His hand tightens on my wrists, and my pulse beats out of control. I love when a guy takes control. And I want Ethan to control this.

When those cobalt-blue eyes brimming with need meet mine, I practically melt into the couch.

Panting, I realize he's leaning closer, and I let out a small gasp when he lowers himself to me. I'm overwhelmed by his heat. By his weight. By his erection, hard and insistent on my hip. *Fuck, yes.*

He licks his lips as one hand slowly moves down my arm where goosebumps erupt. And just when I can feel his breath on my skin, just when I start to close my eyes and arch up and give into the desire detonating inside me, a disgruntled baby voice cries, "Daa-dee!" from the monitor.

Like teenagers getting busted for making out, we scramble away from each other.

Ethan rubs his face and takes a deep breath before he turns slowly to me. I can't read his expression, but now's not the time to chat.

"It's okay. Go." I motion toward the hall. With as much calm as I can muster, I give him a steady smile. "I'll pause the game."

Then I wait.

And wait.

And wait some more.

An hour later, when he still isn't back, I poke my head into Cody's room and see the two of them passed out.

Disappointment washes over me, but also relief. Maybe that interruption was a blessing in disguise. I don't want to mess this up, and sex or whatever Ethan and I were about to do on the couch definitely would've wreaked havoc on our delicate ecosystem here.

He and his son look so sweet together. Cody is nestled in the crook of Ethan's big arm. My sappy heart pitter-patters in my chest at the sight, but I know I can't grow attached.

As I watch them, the reality of what almost happened settles in.

I almost broke my year-long fast with a man who is not available.

My shoulders slump when I think about it like this. I've heard him and his brother talking about a court date later this month, but Ethan hasn't exactly explained what that means.

Don't guys going through a divorce bitch about it? Complain about their exes? Ethan never brings up Allison. Only that one time during my interview almost two weeks ago and then a few days later when he came to my sister's house for dinner. Allison hasn't had the kids yet, so I haven't seen how they act around each other to judge for myself whether he's still in love with her.

Turning, I see a photo of him and his *wife* on the dresser. Ethan doesn't seem the type of guy who would jerk me around if he wanted to reconcile with Allison, but Jamie didn't seem like the kind of guy who lived a double life either.

See, this is why I instituted the diet. Because I can't fucking figure out men!

When I'm in my room, I close the door quietly and drop my forehead against it. *I don't want to repeat the same mistakes. I refuse to get my heart detonated by another guy.*

I might be jumping the gun, but I know myself, and I could totally fall for someone like Ethan. It scares me. Right now, this is only a crush, but what happens if I sleep with him? We already see each other every day. We have dinner together *every day*. We watch TV together—alone—almost *every night*. How long would it take before I was totally in love with him?

Rubbing my temples, I think back to that photo of him and Allison. If they've been separated for over a year and things were really over, why did they wait so long to file for divorce?

The questions won't stop bombarding me. When I slip between my sheets, all I do is toss and turn. Sleep is elusive, and eventually I head to my en-suite shower, crank up the hot water, and hope the sound of the water doesn't wake everyone up.

I *should* take a cold shower. I should stop feeding the hunger I have for this man when I know we can't happen, but I can't seem to get a hold of myself.

Steam billows up, and I close my eyes and give in, blindly reaching for the shower head. I fumble with the settings until it's the perfect pulsing tempo and then aim it between my legs.

A gasp escapes me, and I lean against the cold tiles. The tension builds quickly, everything in me begging for relief. I haven't gotten off once since I've been here. I didn't want to spark something in me that I couldn't contain, but tonight I can't seem to care about my good intentions. I just need some relief.

With my eyes clenched shut, I let my thoughts wander. Let myself think about what it would be like with Ethan. How he'd kiss me if he'd had the chance tonight. How he'd move against me. In me. That gorgeous mouth sucking and biting my skin. His huge hands gripping my breasts. His thick cock stroking me in all the right places.

With a muffled cry, I come, my orgasm hitting me so hard, my knees almost buckle.

Exhaustion weighs my limbs down like lead. With as much energy as I can muster, I rinse off and reach for a towel. When I'm back in bed, for some reason my thoughts go to my grandmother, who always believed in signs. She used to tell me if I paid attention to what life told me, I'd always know what to do.

I'm afraid to think about what tonight's interruption was trying to tell me.

It probably means I'm right, and that Ethan and I will never happen.

Or worse, that we shouldn't happen.

16

ETHAN

THE SECOND I WAKE UP IN CODY'S ROOM, I KNOW I'VE SCREWED up. The house is dark and still, the TV is off in the living room, and Tori's door is closed.

Goddammit.

I want to knock on her door, but to say what? That I'm sorry for Cody interrupting? That I'm pissed but also relieved because I have no idea what I'm doing?

Collapsing on my own bed, I groan. Leave it to me to screw up everything.

I stayed with Cody after he'd fallen asleep so I could make sense of what had happened on the couch, but I hadn't meant to knock out.

Tori and I have been having fun this week. Hanging out after dinner while we watched baseball. When she smarted off about the game tonight, I simply reacted, tickling her. Wrestling her down to the couch. She was laughing, and God, it sounded so good. She felt amazing in my arms, and her bright smile made me crave more. Before I realized it, I found myself hovering over her.

I didn't mean for it to turn sexual. Didn't mean to check her out, but one second we were joking around and the next we weren't.

When I pinned her arms above her head and she stretched out below me, my eyes wandered down her beautiful face, down her bare shoulders with those tiny tank top straps and the lacy bra beneath.

Those delicate pink bra straps short-circuited my brain, and I found myself studying the way the gauzy pattern led under her thin shirt. Until I realized I was staring at her chest.

The way her breath caught when she saw me checking out her gorgeous tits, taut and pointing sky-high through the sheer fabric, had me instantly hard. As I tightened my grip on her wrists, she let out that little moan, and I wanted to strip her bare to see if she was as stunning without her clothes as she was with them. But the way her eyes dilated when I pressed myself to her body, the way she nodded, slowly, almost to herself, like she wanted this as much as I did? Coulda made me come right then and there.

Speaking of coming. I adjust myself with a wince before I get up for a drink of water.

After I fill the glass, I turn off the faucet, but the sound of water continues. I look down at the sink, confused. But the sound is coming from Tori's bathroom, which shares a wall with my master bathroom.

I stare at the tile, wishing I had knocked on her door earlier because Tori is taking a shower. *She was awake, and I was in here when I should've been in there. At least to talk about what happened tonight.*

I'm about to turn off the lights and go to bed when a soft moan makes me freeze.

It takes a second for me to get what's happening. What I'm hearing.

Another muffled groan from the adjacent bathroom has me unbuttoning my jeans.

Fuck. That's hot.

The idea of Tori getting off in there after we almost messed around has me hoping she's thinking of me. Thinking about how we felt pressed together. Thinking about doing it again but with fewer clothes.

With one hand on the vanity, I close my eyes and release my cock, the heavy length springing forward into my waiting palm.

Images of Tori on the couch flash in my mind as I stroke my eager erection. Her lithe body spread out for me. Her sexy, round ass in those damn sleep shorts. That playful smirk she gives me when she's teasing.

But more than anything—I really want to kiss her. To see if she tastes as sweet as I think she does.

With that thought in mind, I squeeze my base and give myself a long, slow tug before I pick up the pace.

I'd lick those plump lips first. Devour them. Make her moan before I work my way down her body. Before I spread those tan legs and hike them over my shoulders. Before I taste her slick heat.

It's that image, of me leaning over her and delving into the most delicate part of her, that has me going off.

Gasping, trying to catch my breath, I realize I'm in over my head. Because if I'm misreading this thing with Tori, I'm in for a long summer.

17

TORI

EVERYONE LOVES FRIDAYS, BUT TODAY IT REMINDS ME THAT I'M headed to my sister's tomorrow morning and won't be back until Sunday night.

When I reach into the kitchen pantry, I pause to stare out the back window, to try to sneak a peek at Ethan, but there's only that picturesque red barn and two whinnying horses trotting along the back field.

I don't know how long I stand there, but when the front door opens, I snap back into action, slicing apples for the kids, who are coloring at the table.

"Morning!"

Logan strolls in looking awfully perky. He must've gotten laid last night. *At least someone did.*

"Hey. What's up?" I try to muster some enthusiasm, but I'm exhausted from worrying about the conversation Ethan and I obviously need to have. I mean, I guess I need to talk to him. That sounds like the kind of thing my sister would do—be an adult and talk through things even though I want to hide under my bed and pretend nothing happened last night. Pretend that I didn't rub one out the first chance I had while I thought about him.

Sighing, I rub my forehead. I have no idea when I became such a wallflower. A year ago I would've marched into the barn, kissed the hell out of that man, and saved all of my questions for after he shoved his hand down my shorts.

Maybe that was your problem, Tori. You ran head-first into lust without thinking.

Logan gives me one of those Carter smiles. "I know you must be tired after cooking all week. I have a surprise for my brother, so you don't need to make anything this evening. I packed a few sandwiches for lunch, and I'm taking everyone to the Lone Star Station for dinner, you included. My treat."

While I love going out to eat, I'm almost disappointed not to have something to cook this afternoon to keep me occupied.

Hmm. *I know. I'll bake some cookies.*

"Sounds great. Want some coffee before you head to the barn?"

"No, I'm good, but thanks."

"You think Ethan would like a cup?" I ask before I realize I shouldn't. *I'm so out of practice.* I used to have nonchalant on lockdown after I hooked up with a guy, but I can't find that happy place where I don't care.

"We have a busy day, so I'm sure he would."

Nodding, I grab a to-go mug and fix it the way Ethan likes it. When I hand it to his brother, Logan squishes me into a side hug. "You're awesome, Tor. We love having you here. Don't we, kids?"

Cody responds by trying to eat his crayon, which I replace

with an apple slice, but Mila brushes her blonde hair out of her face and nods. "I love-a-dub-dub Tori!"

I smile and reach over to pull Mila's hair into a ponytail so it's out of her way.

Watching her buoyant reaction, seeing how easily she gives her whole heart to those around her, twists something inside of me.

It would be so easy to love this family.

A strange melancholy settles in my chest that makes me want to call my parents. It doesn't escape me that I've been living with total strangers for two weeks, and my parents haven't called me once. When Kat moved in with Brady to help him with baby Izzy, back when they first met, my dad called her practically every day. I try not to feel hurt. I know my parents care in their own way, but I wish they'd try to show it more.

By lunchtime, my stomach is knotted like fishing wire. I'm dying to see Ethan and gauge where he's at. Because if he acts like nothing happened, like he doesn't care, then I'm more than happy to follow suit.

Shut up. You know that would hurt your feelings, you little liar.

Twisting my hands, I debate what to say and hope I don't flub this.

I'd hate for things to be awkward when I was starting to think working here this summer might work out. Especially since I'm getting the hang of things. I enjoy taking care of the kids and cooking for the family. This might not be my dream job, but I'm feeling like I'm actually good at this, and it's been so damn long since I've felt useful or good at anything.

Plus, I can't exactly slack off. Sure, I want to work hard

and keep this job so I don't have to explain to my sister that I've failed at something else, but I really and truly want to help Ethan and his family.

Today, though, I'm not doing a great job of achieving that goal. In fact, the whole afternoon I'm so distracted that I burn the first batch of oatmeal raisin cookies and have to toss them in the trash.

Eventually, I give up on following any kind of recipe since I'm feeling like a space cadet and end up playing with the kids. We're building a fort in the living room when the guys finally come in from the barn. Ethan beelines it for his bedroom to shower, which is his typical routine, while Logan ducks into the kids' bathroom to clean off.

With Logan's surprise dinner tonight, I'm starting to worry I won't get a chance to talk to Ethan alone before I head for my sister's in the morning. Not if he and his brother hang out after dinner, like I heard Logan suggest.

I'm staring off in space when Mila crawls into my lap and wraps her arms around my neck.

"Hey, bugaboo." I stroke her silky hair. Her sigh makes me frown, and I pull back to see worry etched all over her delicate face. "What's wrong?"

Those big baby-blue eyes turn up to me. "How do you know somethin's wrong?"

I rub the furrow in her brow. "Because of this. You get all crinkly here." She doesn't laugh the way I expect her to. Instead, she sighs again. "Want to tell me about it?"

She rests her head on my chest. "Momma's supposed to come tomorrow. She said she'd take us to the zoo."

"I bet you're excited to see her, huh? The zoo sounds so fun!" Two weeks is a long time to go without seeing your mom at that age. Thinking back to the long stretches without seeing mine when I was a kid makes me want to squeeze the stuffing out of Mila.

But instead of agreeing, she shrugs. "What if she doesn't come? What if she forgets again?"

Man, shoot me now. This poor kid. I've never met Allison, but how could she not adore Mila and Cody and move heaven and earth to see them?

"Oh, honey. Did she forget once?"

A sniffle escapes her as she nods. "A few times."

The psycho part of me wants to punch that woman in the ovaries for making her kid feel like shit.

Nibbling my lip, I rush to think of something to explain Allison's behavior. "Sometimes, when life gets crazy, people lose track of time. Like how I burned those cookies today when I forgot to set the timer. Or it's possible she misremembered. Wrote down the wrong dates or got confused." I hope to hell she didn't deliberately blow off her kids.

Mila sniffles and looks up at me. "Yeah?"

"Totally. But that doesn't mean your momma doesn't want to see you and your brother. As I get older, I'm starting to understand that parents aren't perfect. They try really hard. Like when you were trying to do that cartwheel the other day. Even though you didn't quite nail it, you gave it your whole heart, right?"

Nodding, she sniffles again, but her eyes don't look quite so downcast anymore.

"So we have to cut our parents some slack. Give them a break sometimes because everyone makes mistakes."

"Okay."

I run my hand gently across her back, wanting to soothe

her. "But if you ever need to talk about this again, you can always talk to me or your daddy. He loves you so much, and I know your momma does too."

She nods against me, and I kiss the top of her head.

Someone clears his throat, and I look up to see Ethan leaning in the doorway, his solemn expression telling me he heard the conversation I had with his daughter.

I stare at him while I whisper to Mila. "I think your daddy could use a hug. What do you think?"

Her head whips around, and a second later, she's bounding into his arms. He's so sweet with her, so tender and reassuring that the sight of him snuggling her close makes my breath catch.

I start to wonder, if he's that gentle with his daughter, maybe he's the type of man who could be gentle with my heart too.

The five of us head for Ethan's enormous four-door truck. Logan yells "shotgun" and grabs the passenger seat, but Ethan smacks him with a baseball cap. "Where are your manners? You should let Tori sit up front."

Logan nods and starts to get out.

"It's okay," I yell from the other side of the cab. "Really. I'll sit between the kids. It's easier for me to fit back here anyway."

Once Cody is all buckled in, I'm debating how the hell I'm getting into this huge vehicle myself when a hand on my hip makes me turn. I'm finally face-to-face with Ethan after this crazy day where I've been making myself nuts debating what's going on between us.

He gently pulls me away from the truck and half-closes the door behind me. "Just wanted to thank you for what you told Mila earlier."

"No problem."

There are so many things I want to say, but with his family waiting for us a foot away, now's not really the time. Instead, I stare at his broad chest, at the tats that extend down both arms, and I shiver when I remember how it felt when he touched me.

I kick the ground between us, feeling too awkward to look him in the eyes. "You know, the Astros lost despite that grand slam."

He hums in the back of his throat. "I have a feeling they're not the only ones who lost out last night." His rough palm slides up my arm. That sexy voice drops to a whisper. "Let's talk later, okay? I think I need to apologize."

That makes me pause.

Does he want to apologize for things that almost happened or for letting things get that far?

Does he want to apologize for not coming back out to the living room?

Or worse, am I all wrong about him finalizing his divorce and maybe he's getting back together with Allison so he feels guilty for flirting?

The younger version of me would blurt out that this whole thing is fucking confusing me. That I know I shouldn't be so wrapped up in whatever we're doing, but I can't help it. That this is the very reason why I shouldn't do relationships.

But I can't ask the questions burning my lips because the

kids are within earshot, and it would be irresponsible to freak out in front of them.

Biting my tongue, I nod and tuck my hands into the back pockets of my jeans and hope I'm not headed for a repeat of last summer.

18

ETHAN

THE WHOLE DRIVE, ALL I CAN THINK IS I MUST'VE SAID THE wrong thing, because I meant to show Tori that I genuinely like her and want to spend time with her outside of whatever family things we do with my kids. Sure, I'm just finalizing my divorce, so I can't get too serious, but we're two consenting adults who have to spend a lot of time together. Why not enjoy that time and see what comes of it?

But the second those words were out of my mouth, that we needed to talk and I wanted to apologize, her shoulders got stiff. She gave me a curt nod and jumped in the truck, and once again, I realize I'm sorely out of practice with women.

I glance at my rearview mirror and catch her eyes briefly before they flit away, and she focuses her attention out the window.

Yeah, great job there, Ethan. You weirded her out.

The tires of my truck crunch the gravel in the parking lot when we pull up to the diner. Not sure what has Logan so excited to grab a bite here, since we frequent the Lone Star, but I'm grateful to give Tori a break from preparing dinner. That's another thing bothering me. She's working far more than I'm paying her to do. It's odd that my first impression of her was that she might be a slacker because she's been nothing but a damn hard worker.

The smell of country food, the kind slathered in gravy and served with a side of biscuits, makes my mouth water when we walk through the front door. It's a busy night, but after greeting a few neighbors, we crowd around a table.

Tori situates Cody in a high chair at the end and smooths back his wavy tufts of blond hair before she sits next to him. Reaching into the diaper bag, she pulls out a toy truck for my son to play with, which he snatches up gleefully to make zoom-zoom noises. Cody's sweet nature seems to relax her, as though her happiness somehow hinges on his.

It's hard to ignore how easygoing she is with my kids. How readily they've taken to her. Even when they're running around like monsters, she seems to take it in stride.

Nothing bothered me more than Allison's perpetual irritation with our children. She acted like they were going out of their way to personally offend her with their rambunctiousness. Even after a weekend away at that spa in Austin, she never seemed relaxed around our family.

The darkness that always sweeps through me when I think of my wife hovers like a shadow in my peripheral vision, but I don't want to go down that road tonight. I've spent too much time sick over the failure of my marriage. Sitting next to my daughter and watching her vibrant smile, hearing Cody's wild laughter when Tori tickles him, makes me realize I have a lot to be grateful for.

That's what the last two weeks have made me realize.

Seeing my kids laugh like they mean it, seeing how carefree they're becoming again—that's my bullseye and that's what I want to focus on. Moving forward, not living in the past.

After we get our drinks, Logan slaps a notepad on the table I hadn't realized he'd brought, and with a flick of a finger, he slides it to me.

"Wanna finish telling you the plan for the weekend." Logan turns to Tori. "You mind if we chat about the ranch? We need to talk through the logistics for those two new horses we're boarding."

Anxiety riddles its way through my shoulders as though Allison can sense we're talking about work at the dinner table. *Old habits die hard.*

But Tori gives him a sweet smile. "I don't mind at all. I'd like to hear what you guys do."

Logan ticks off item after item, and I jot everything down before I forget. Shit's easy to forget when you have two kids and a barn full of horses to look after.

"So they're not all yours?" Tori asks, looking between me and Logan. "The horses, I mean."

I open my mouth, but my brother is already explaining. "Eight are ours, and six are boarders, and we're adding two more to the tally."

Tori draws her finger through the condensation on her glass of iced tea. "This is going to sound crazy, but I like the smell of the barn. I don't know if it's the leather from the saddles, the bales of hay, or the horses themselves. It's this great earthy scent. I can't explain it."

My lips pull into a smile as I look away. I love that smell too. It's one of my earliest memories. Playing in the barn with my dad, racing from one end to the other with my arms spread out wide. Breathing in the warmth that you can only find when you're surrounded by these incredible animals.

Makes me miss my father so damn much.

Across from me, Logan laughs. "Honey, you are welcome to shovel that *smell* whenever you're in the mood. Just let me know."

A growl revs low in my chest. Leave it to my brother to reduce everything to a pile of manure. "She's not shoveling shit, Logan." Mila giggles at my dirty word, but I'm too tired to care that I've cursed in front of my kids. "Tori does enough for us already."

"Take it easy, bro." He holds his hands up. "I was joking. Mostly."

"Yeah, well, I'm not."

Before I can descend into a foul mood, our waitress slides giant plates of steaming chicken fried steak across the table. *Thank you, Jesus.*

I turn to prepare a serving for the baby, but Tori's already cutting up Cody's meal into toddler-sized bites.

"Want to swap seats with me?" I ask her. "That way I can feed him. Sorry, I hadn't really thought through the seating arrangement."

She helps him take a bite. "I don't mind feeding the little man."

Watching her take care of my son floods me with warmth. As we fall into easy conversation, I can't help but sneak glances at her from time to time.

Dinner is delicious, and I'm ready to fall into a food coma when two familiar faces pop up over Tori's shoulder.

"Hey, guys." I wave to Brady and Kat.

Tori's head whips around, and the smile that breaks out

on her face when she sees her sister is ridiculously sweet. She hops out of her chair and gives her sister and brother-in-law quick hugs. "What are y'all doing here? I thought you were barbecuing tonight. I'm glad to see you, though, because I forgot my phone at Ethan's, and you said to call you this evening."

I smile. *Tori remembered to pack a bag of toys and diapers and crayons for the kids but forgot her phone.*

Brady drops an arm over his wife's shoulders. "We did barbecue, but Kat wanted some pie, so we decided to make a pit stop."

"I shouldn't be eating pie. Trust me, I know this," Kat says self-deprecatingly.

Brady kisses the top of her head. "You're perfect, and if my wife and kid want pie, I'm buying them pie."

She rubs her round belly and grins at him.

The moment between them seems so intimate as they stare into each other's eyes, I look away.

That. That's what I never had with Allison.

"Where's Izzy?" Tori asks, leaning over Cody to wipe his face.

"At my parents'." Brady motions over his shoulder. "We're having a date night."

Tori chuckles. "I'm coming over tomorrow, so get the 'date night' out of your system."

"Oh, my God. Stop." Kat blushes and turns her face into her husband.

"What? You're pregnant. Like it's a secret how that happened? Watch out! I'm gonna tell Mom and Dad you did the deed!"

It's funny to see how laid-back Tori is around Kat. How

much she teases her sister. Makes me realize she's still a bit buttoned up around me.

"Daddy?" Mila scrunches her nose. "What's 'the deed?'"

Tori grimaces and mouths that she's sorry.

I chuckle and tug on my daughter's pigtail. "Nothing you need to worry about for, oh, about forty years."

Everyone laughs.

After we chat, Brady and Kat meander over to the dessert window by the cash register, and Mila and Tori run to the bathroom in the back because my daughter realizes she "really, really needs to tinkle."

Logan watches the girls go, glances down at his phone, and then turns to the front of the diner.

Cody squirms in his high chair, so I clean him off and settle him on my lap.

"So what's the surprise?" I can't deny that I'm curious. Logan went on and on about it this afternoon.

I expect him to tell me he got us a new client or something work-related, but instead of being excited, he sighs. "I didn't think this through, having everyone here." He motions toward the bathrooms. "Just don't be mad."

Nothing good ever happens when he says that to me.

"How did this go from 'hey, I have a surprise for you' to 'don't be mad'?"

He shifts and looks over his shoulder again. I follow his line of vision as two blondes strut through the front door. They see Logan and wave.

"You got a date with, what, sisters? Let me guess. You're taking off for the weekend and want me to do everything we bulleted here." I tap on the mile-long to-do list we jotted down during dinner.

The blondes stop at our table, and the younger one leans down to hug Logan, while the other one smiles at me. Now that she's close, I realize she looks familiar.

"Hi, Ethan."

And she knows my name.

Logan breaks away from the woman wrapped around him to motion to the other. "Bro, this is Sandra. Remember, she has a son about Mila's age? And this is her sister Sage."

Shifting uncomfortably, I realize where this is headed. *Logan, don't do this.*

"Ladies." I'm wondering how quickly I can pack up Cody's diaper bag and toys, which are strewn across the table. "You know what? We'd better get going." I look at my brother, hoping he understands why I'm doing this. "If you want to stay, that's fine, but it's getting late."

Sandra puts her hand on my shoulder. "Your son is getting so big!"

"He eats like a horse," I joke, trying to not be a total asshole. With one hand, I hold Cody, who squirms like he has ants in his pants, while I gather his toys with the other.

Logan leans across the table and murmurs, "Let's just do this fast, okay? Before the girls get back. It'll be fine."

I'm not sure I know exactly what he's talking about, but I'm one hundred percent I don't want to find out.

Sandra leans closer. "Logan told me the good news!" She squeezes my shoulder again.

"And what would that be?"

"That your divorce is almost final, and that you wanted to go on a date with me!"

I give her an awkward smile and then shoot Logan a look.

What the fuck are you doing? He shrugs and pats the other sister on the ass.

Sage plays with his hair. "We were thinking we could do something tomorrow night, if Sandra can find a babysitter."

There's my out. I don't want to hurt Sandra's feelings. I remember her situation with her ex, and I don't want to be an ass, but I'm not interested. "Actually, ladies, I don't have a babysitter."

"I got you covered. Joey said she could babysit." Logan waggles his eyebrows.

Sandra squeals and scares Cody. "Yay! It's a date." She turns to me and bats her eyelashes. "I have to confess I've been *dying* to go out with you. I'm so glad we're doing this. I'm so glad you asked me out!"

Fucking Logan.

"Daddy." Mila's voice is a record scratch that cuts through the noise of the diner.

I close my eyes for a second before I turn to the left and see my daughter and Tori standing there. I swallow, afraid of how much they just heard.

Can this get any worse?

"Tori!" Sandra goes around our table to hug her. *Jesus, they know each other?*

Tori gives Sandra a weak smile that doesn't reach her eyes. "Hey."

"I haven't seen you since last fall. Thanks again for taking care of my son that one time."

"No worries," Tori says quietly as she helps Mila back into her chair. "How are you?"

"Better now that Ethan and I are going on a date this

weekend. He asked me out!" Sandra trots back around to my side of the table. *No, no, no.*

I try to get Tori's attention, but she's making a concerted effort to not look at me.

"That's cool. Ethan's a good guy." Tori tugs her purse over her shoulder and turns toward the front of the diner where Brady and Kat are waving bye. "You know what? I think I'm going to head home with my sister. You guys don't need me, right?"

Yes, I fucking need you.

Logan waves at her like a dipshit. "Nope, go on. Have a good weekend."

"Tori, wait." I find my voice. "Can I talk to you a sec?"

Cody starts to wail in my lap, and I look around for one of his toys, but I've already packed them at the bottom of his diaper bag. *Motherfuck.*

"Ethan, we can talk when I get back on Sunday." She pauses. "Have fun on your date."

This is not good.

But then Sandra tells her to wait.

Tori turns to her, the expression on her face a mask of indifference.

"Think you might be able to babysit for me again? For the next time Ethan and I go out?"

Oh, fuck no.

Tori looks at me. Finally.

I shake my head, wanting her to understand that I'm not gonna let this happen. That there's no way I'm going on a date with Sandra.

But Tori doesn't get my meaning. Because those hazel eyes that are usually warm and inviting glint with aloofness.

"Not a prob." Under her breath, so soft I almost don't catch it, she adds, "That's about all I'm good for. Babysitting."

"You're the best!" Sandra hugs her, and Tori laughs. It's a cold, mirthless sound that breaks my heart a little.

Then she's gone.

19

TORI

"Are you sure you don't want some pie?" my sister asks gently. "It's your favorite, pecan."

I shake my head and curl up tighter under the blanket. It's the middle of summer in Texas, but the hill country can get cold at night, and right now I have a chill I can't seem to shake. "I'm sorry I'm crashing your date. If you can get Brady's parents to babysit tomorrow, I can probably stay at Val's."

She nods, places the pie on the coffee table, and slowly lowers herself next to me on the couch. "So you're really not going to tell me what happened back there? One second you were all smiles, and the next, you were the Roadrunner, kicking up dust with your flip-flops from speeding out the diner so fast."

The words die on my lips. I'm tired of hearing myself complain about my life. So tired. I'm ready to be more, to expect more and deserve it. And if I've only been imagining that Ethan wants me, then it's time to buck the fuck up and get over it. Even if I am hurt about his date with Sandra.

My sister waits patiently, like always.

"Men confuse me," I offer lamely. "I never know if I'm coming or going, and I'm so over it." Her soft hand reaches out and holds mine in quiet solidarity.

"Things aren't working out with Ethan?"

"No, and I can't even back out of this job because I've already sublet my place in Austin. Not that I want to leave you, but you know I'm not good with conflict."

Maybe slashing Jamie's tires last summer was a tad over-the-top, but I figured he owed me for emotional distress.

Ethan doesn't make me feel that degree of lunacy. *Yet.*

Which is why I should get my heart on lockdown before I get so riled up. I'll be polite to him and eat dinner with his family, since he's already asked me to, but I'm not hanging out with him alone anymore. I need to be smart and protect myself.

She squeezes my hand. "You're just passionate. When you love someone, you give your whole heart."

"I'm tired of giving my whole heart. I want to not give a shit." I lean my head on her shoulder and close my eyes.

"Can I offer some unsolicited advice?"

I nod and wait for her to unload her big sister wisdom on me.

"Before you write off Ethan, give him a chance to explain. I don't know what happened between you guys, and I don't expect you to tell me, but men make mistakes, even when they care about you."

I can't bring myself to tell her the reality of the situation. That he's going on a date with Sandra tomorrow night. That I shouldn't care because nothing happened between us. We didn't sleep together, we didn't mess around. Hello, he never even kissed me.

But I thought... I *thought* that we were becoming friends and that maybe he liked me. That maybe he wanted more.

No, he wants more with Sandra. I'm just the nanny, someone he was probably buttering up so I'd take good care of his kids. Or maybe he thought I was someone he could fuck on the side but not get invested.

All of this makes me feel like a bigger loser, but I don't want to underscore the sad state of my nonexistent love life to my sister.

"How did you know Brady was *the one*?" I don't know where the question comes from, but I feel like a boat without a rudder, and I have no clue how to maneuver these waters.

"Hmm." A big, dopey smile lifts her lips, and her hands gravitate to her swollen tummy. "You know how in art, they say the negative space in a painting or drawing is just as important as the image itself? In fact, sometimes the negative space is an image unto itself."

"Okaaaay." *Please connect the dots for me, Kat, because I have no clue what you mean.*

"Brady is my negative space, or maybe I'm his. But the best thing about negative space is how it changes your whole perspective of the composition once you can appreciate that component. It becomes more, almost like it's breathing and changing before your very eyes. One minute you think you're seeing one image, and the next, it's different. And no matter what the images show, they always fit together perfectly."

Like those weird pics on Facebook where you can't tell if

the image is an elephant or a butterfly? I'm embarrassed to suggest it because I'm probably wrong.

I laugh awkwardly. "I'm gonna have to mull that over." This is why she's the smart sister.

Kat reaches over to the coffee table and hands me a piece of pie. "Mull it over with some pie. Pie always makes everything better."

I smile and shovel in a big bite. "This is why you're my favorite sister."

"I'm your only sister, doofus."

"And I love you the most."

20

ETHAN

THE WHOLE EVENING WEARS ON ME, LIKE THE BRAKES ON A CAR grinding.

With Allison coming tomorrow to pick up the kids, I can't keep them out late to chase after my pissed-off nanny. At least, I think she's pissed off.

I cringe when I think of her response to Sandra. *That's about all I'm good for. Babysitting.*

With a patience I don't really possess, I tuck each of my children into bed, read them their bedtime stories and cuddle, the whole time wondering how I fix this. *Tori probably thinks I played her all week. That I was trying to get in her pants. That I don't really care.*

The second the kids are asleep, I stride into the living room and yank the remote out of Logan's hand. "What the hell were you doing tonight? Why would you set me up with Sandra? In front of Mila?" I don't say the rest. *In front of Tori.*

"What?" He shrugs and returns his attention to the TV,

which I flick off. "Mila seemed fine, and you told me you'd go out with Sandra."

"The hell I did."

"Bro. For real. Week before last when I asked you about Sandra, you said you'd go out on a date."

I stare at him as I collapse on the couch, wondering if he's spent too much time in the sun.

He snaps his finger in my face. "It was that first day Tori brought you lunch."

A long minute passes. "Really?"

"Yes, dumbass, really." Groaning, I run my hand over my face. My idiot brother laughs. "Why you acting like I'm making you haul horse shit instead of thanking me for setting you up with a gorgeous woman?"

"I thought you wanted me to explore this thing with Tori."

Surprise registers on his face. "Have you fucked her?"

"Don't talk about her like that." Anger burns hot through my body, way hotter than it probably should.

"Fine." Raising his voice so he sounds like a prepubescent boy, he asks, "Have you *made love* to her?"

I smack him with my baseball cap. "No. Not that it's any of your business, but we've been hanging out."

"Is 'hanging out' code for some other sexual activity? Oral? Anal?" With a devilish grin, he adds, "You know, some girls don't consider anal to be sex."

This is why every father in a twenty-mile radius locks up his daughter when Logan Carter's around.

Undeterred by my scowl, he elbows me. "Bro, if things were moving forward with Tori, why didn't you say something to me? Every time I brought her up this week, you changed the subject. In fact, when she came home last weekend, you *told* me you weren't making a play for her."

"Have you considered that maybe I wanted to keep it to myself? That this is personal, and I don't feel like announcing shit to you so you can make light of it?" Even now I don't like talking about this. Not when everything with Tori is so new.

A beat goes by before he scratches his head. "Tori didn't seem like it was a big deal, you going out with Sandra."

"Sure she didn't," I say dryly.

He lifts his chin. "You falling for her?"

Shrugging, I lean back. "I like the girl. Isn't that enough? She's fun and sweet and beautiful, and she doesn't make me feel like an asshole for working long hours. Does that meet with your approval, Mr. Dating Expert?"

This answer doesn't appease him like I think it should because his brows pull tight.

"What about this isn't working for you, Logan? You're the one who suggested I hang out with Tori in the first place."

"I'm worried, okay?"

"Why are you worried?" I point the remote back to the TV, ready to tune him out.

"Because this sounds serious all of a sudden and you're only now getting out of a goddamn marriage. One you didn't want, I might add, and you're already diving into something else that's way too ambitious. I thought you might get up close and horizontal with Tori, not fall for her."

Now I'm getting pissed. "Why are you saying I didn't want my marriage? I busted my ass to make it work with Allison."

"Calm your tits." He waves his hand like he's trying to figure out what to say. "Can you honestly say you would've married Allison if she hadn't gotten pregnant?"

That gives me pause. I drag my palm across my chin. "It's hard to say. After graduation, she wanted to return to Dallas to be near her family, and I always planned on coming home. We hadn't discussed anything serious before Mila came along, but I always cared for her."

"That's my point. Had she not gotten pregnant, you guys would've gone your separate ways."

"Maybe." All this talk about relationships is making me anxious. I finally flip on the TV, click the DVR, and immediately regret it when the Astros game from last night flashes on the screen.

Logan clears his throat. "Sorry if I messed things up with Tori. I swear I didn't know you really had a thing for her, beyond thinking she was hot." If there's any consolation, it's that my brother is more clueless sometimes than I am. "You gonna call her?"

"Already tried. She's not picking up."

He bumps my elbow. "Try again. You know you wanna."

I do. Reaching for my back pocket, I slide out my phone and hit her name. It rings. Once. Twice.

Logan and I look at each other when we feel buzzing and then down at the couch. He reaches behind a cushion to pull out Tori's phone.

That explains why she's not picking up.

He scrolls through the messages visible on the lock screen, the nosey jerk.

"Don't snoop." I snatch it out of his hand and toss it on the coffee table.

"She's popular, bro. All her friends want her to go out this weekend." He tries to show me, but I wave him off. "I'm only saying you better get on this stat before she..."

His voice fades, and I turn to him. "Before she what?"

"Before she hooks up with someone else."

My fists ball up at my sides. "I already told you not to talk about her like that. Besides, what makes you think she's gonna run out and hook up with someone else?"

"Doesn't she think you're taking out Sandra?" He lets the question hang in the air. "Gotta talk to her before Tori writes you off. That's all I'm saying."

Well, shit. Hadn't thought about it like that.

I reach for his beer, which he lets me have without complaint. "I thought you didn't want me to date Tori."

"No, I said I was worried about you getting *serious* about Tori. I'm all for hooking up."

Rolling my eyes, I punch him in the side. "You give the worst advice, but I still love you, numbnuts."

He pretends to sniffle and wipes fake tears. "Love you, too, bro. Now how we gonna get your girl back?"

I shouldn't like how that sounds—my girl—considering I haven't even kissed her yet, but damn if I don't want to soon.

21

TORI

This bar is like so many I worked at throughout college. Dark and seedy. Smelling of spilled beer and cheap cologne.

But I like it.

Because tonight I want to blend in, which isn't hard since I don't know half of the people Vivian invited. Laughter booms behind me, and I turn to see my best friend holding court at our table, which is filled with a bevy of beautiful people.

My eyes drop to the short, pleated skirt I'm wearing, and I tug the hem, which doesn't budge. It matches the sparkly bustier-like tank top that makes guys take notice.

I'm not in the mood to have my body on display, but I had to borrow clothes because I didn't have anything nice to wear. Viv thought dressing up would cheer me up.

It doesn't.

Neither does the bluesy, heartbreaking Rihanna tune blaring through the sound system.

Viv's motto is "fuck 'til you forget," but I don't think I have that in me. I feel men's eyes on me, and it makes my skin crawl.

I toss back the rest of the mojito before leaning over the bar to order another and reluctantly rejoin Viv's table. *At least I'm not the designated driver.*

As the night wears on, the alcohol spreads through me until the smile on my face is more genuine. Until I'm not totally faking it. Until that ache I felt when I realized Ethan had a date with another woman ebbs away a little.

When I'm wondering how many more drinks it'll take before my lips go numb, Viv links her arm through mine. "Time to dance!"

I let her drag me to the back of the bar and down a dark corridor that opens up to a cavernous room where the club lights are low and the music thumps my internal organs.

Viv wraps me in a hug. "I've missed you!" she screams in my ear to be heard over the music.

"Missed you too! I'm so glad Kat had your number." *Am I ever.* "She saved it the last time I got locked out of the dorms."

Viv laughs. "Weren't you in a t-shirt and underwear?"

I shrug. "It covered my ass." Mostly.

She can't criticize me for that lapse in judgment. Her antics usually exceed mine exponentially.

We dance until we're sweaty and I'm loose-limbed, but when a remix of Twenty One Pilots' song "Stressed Out" blares though the speakers, it hits me all at once. How sad it is that I got through almost four years of college but didn't finish. That I'm a twenty-three-year-old babysitter. That the guy I'm working for was probably only hitting on me because I was convenient.

Oh, God. I've turned into one of those depressed drunks.

After trading in my mojito for ice water, I try to shake off this persistent funk, but it settles like a fog, thick and suffocating. *How much have I had to drink?*

Sticky bodies bump into us, and I'm ready to walk back to Viv's condo alone if she's not ready to go.

I turn, and almost run head first into some preppy-looking guy. He smiles, and I try to return it, but my face doesn't want to comply.

I glance around and realize Viv and I must've migrated away from each other during the last song because she's talking to someone several feet away.

Preppy leans into me. "Dance with me, pretty girl."

My first impulse is to decline, but then I remember how easy it was for Ethan to go out with another woman. "Sure."

My new friend is handsome. Tall with black hair and a cute smile that sadly does nothing for me.

Thankfully, my body moves to the music automatically, the driving rhythm animating my limbs when all I want to do is crawl into bed and veg out in my pajamas.

I'm already glistening with sweat, but I'm breathing hard by the time the beat breaks into a new song five minutes later.

As I'm twisting my long hair back and out of my face, the guy moves closer.

"I'm David," he yells as his hungry eyes take me in.

I take a step back, realizing I don't want to go down this road. Ethan might not want me, but I'm not interested in hooking up with anyone else. Eighteen-year-old me would've been delighted to kiss away bad memories, but the college-dropout me is tired of this crap.

The club lights strobe, engulfing the room in darkness

when they shift away. I scan the crowd for my friends, but I can't make out more than bodies and long shadows.

"Thanks for the dance, but I have to go."

"Wait! I thought we were having fun."

He wraps his hand around my wrist, and I shake my head. "Sorry. I can't."

I start to walk away, but he yanks me back, and I stumble into him. *What the fuck? He did* not *just grab me.*

His meaty hand slides up my arm, and I'm opening my mouth to bitch him out for touching me when he flies backward, flailing into people on the way down.

I gawk at the guy, who's sprawled on the floor.

My skin tingles, and I glance over my shoulder. Beneath the flickering strobe lights, I see him.

Ethan.

He steps closer, his brows furrowed as the music drops out, leaving the steady beat of the drum.

"You okay?" Somehow, over the din of the club, I hear his rumbling voice.

He's here.

My chest swarms with boozy-headed butterflies.

I blink, wondering if I'm imagining him. But nope, he's here.

He takes a step closer and gently grazes his fingers across my arm where David gripped me. "Tori."

The way he's looking at me, like he's worried and pissed and maybe misses me? Makes me want to snatch that kiss I never got the other night. *Yes, kissing. I definitely wanna do that with Ethan.*

Except...

Except he's probably here with Sandra.

On his date.

"I'm fine." Crossing my arms, I nod toward David, who is stomping away through the crowd. "I can take care of myself. You didn't need to do that." I work to keep my words from running all together into one incoherent strand of syllables.

Begrudgingly, I take in Ethan. It's hard not to notice how mouthwatering he looks in dark jeans and a button-up. I've never seen him in anything other than old t-shirts. *He must've made an effort to look good tonight. Dick.*

I glance away, not wanting him to see that I'm hurt. Come Monday morning when I'm taking care of his kids, I can pretend I'm cool, but right now, I still feel the hot sting of rejection.

Ethan gently lifts my chin so I'm forced to look into his eyes. "Did you want him touching you?"

Reluctantly, I shake my head, but I have to close my eyes when the room tilts one way and then the other.

He leans closer. "You sure you're okay?"

Those magnetic blue eyes stare down at me. *Why does he have to have such beautiful eyes?*

My words come out too quickly for me to temper the anger in my voice. "I'm great. You can go back to your date." I barely hold in a wince at how whiny I sound, but it's hard to sound smart when I'm buzzed.

Slowly, his hands lift to my shoulders, but he backs away until he can make eye contact. "You think I'm on a date?"

Reallllly? He wants to play games? I barely hold in a hiccup.

"Aren't you? Isn't that why you're here?" I motion toward him. "Why you're dressed up?"

His eyes crinkle, like he's keeping in a smile, before his

attention dips down my body, but I can't hear what he says because the music is too loud.

Ignoring the way I heat under his perusal, I shrug out of his hold. "By the way, it's pretty rude to check out other girls when you're here with...with..." *God, what's her name?* "With Sandra." *That's it!* "Maybe you should find her."

Except the thought of it enrages me, and I can't help but bite out the next words, which I punctuate by poking his chest. "For the record, I'm not gonna fuck you like a side piece while you date other women. If that's what you're looking for, you've got the wrong girl. And are you really getting a divorce? Or are you running around behind her back?"

That giant hand wraps around the finger I'm poking him with, and he pulls me close.

"So fucking feisty." He laughs and leans down to whisper in my ear, "My divorce goes through in less than a week. I've been separated for a year, but things between my wife and I crashed and burned long before that. And I promise I'm not on a date, sweetheart. I'm here for you."

"What?" I'm so confused.

But he doesn't answer my question. He merely takes my arms, winds them around his neck, and tugs me flush against his body. His big, hard body. *Mmm.* That deep voice rumbles in my ear. "Your sister told me where I could find you." He kisses my temple. "I came for you. To find *you.*"

Those sick, drunk butterflies are back and battle around my stomach. I peer up to find myself nose to nose with him. "You came here for me?"

He smiles.

He came here for me.

I smile back like a loser.

The music shifts to something sultry that heightens my lust-filled fog. "You're not here with Sandra?" *Because buzzed Tori needs everything to be crystal-clear.*

Ethan's eyes soften as he nestles me closer until our lips are a breath apart. "I swear that was more a misunderstanding between me and Logan. Why would I be here with another woman when you're all I've thought about since you barged into my life like a damn tornado?"

I laugh, and it feels so good. So warm. Like I've stumbled across a sliver of sunlight on a rainy day. "You must be a glutton for punishment." With Lana del Rey's "Burning Desire" swelling around us, I'm ready to scale up Ethan's delicious body.

Sweet delight pulses through me at the thought.

Until a faint voice—one that's thrashing around in my head, trying not to drown from the alcohol—cautions me against doing anything rash.

Against doing anything *naked.*

Because naked gets my heart in trouble.

Plus, don't I deserve a better explanation for what happened at the diner last night? Even buzzed, I know this.

But then his lips brush against my ear and he whispers, "I'm a glutton for anything that involves you."

Just like that, my resolve to keep some distance snaps.

22

ETHAN

Tori's smile gets me every time.

I'm not sure I even deserve it.

Soft, smooth skin greets my rough palm when I drag my hand over her slender shoulder.

"Let's get out of here," I rasp in her ear, hoping she hears me over the music.

The way those gorgeous hazel eyes heat beneath my stare makes the trek to the city worth it.

I hate clubs. Loathe them. But I'd haul my ass to Austin again to have her look at me like this. With fondness and vulnerability and desire. With the kind of intensity that makes my blood heat and my fingers itch to delve beneath the teasing hem of her skirt.

She nods but holds up a finger and motions for me to follow her through the crowd. We stop in front of a group of people, and she leans over to whisper to another girl, whose eyes dart to me. Then Tori grabs my hand and leads me to the exit.

A bouncer opens the door to let us out to the back parking lot. Warm air and the scent of barbecue and cedar hits our faces as we stroll into the dark.

"Guess I should've asked where you parked," Tori says, turning toward me.

She starts to let go of my hand, but I tighten my hold. "This way."

After having music blare in my ear for the last hour while I scanned the crowd for her, the quiet seems more amplified, making me feel like tonight, this moment, is important.

I keep stealing glances at her. She's almost too much to take in at one time. Stunning is the word that comes to mind. All that crazy hair. Those long legs. Her big, golden eyes. That playful personality.

She sneaks a peek at me and gives me a shy smile.

Damn it, I like this girl and how she's all bluster and ball-busting when she's pissed, but sweet and vulnerable at other times. Like now.

It's written all over her face. How glad she is that I came for her. And fuck, that does something to me.

Once we're along the edge of the lot, my truck comes to view.

"Darlin', how much've you had to drink?" I trace her knuckles with my thumb, not willing to let go of her.

We meander a few paces, our steps crunching on the gravel, before she answers me. "A bit."

When we arrive at my truck, I slide my gaze to her as I fiddle with my keys. "What does that mean?"

"It means I'm happily buzzed and not shit-faced." She laughs and rocks back, tucking her hands behind her. "I stopped drinking half an hour ago. Why?"

I reach around, wrapping her wrists in my palm before I crowd her against my truck. "Too buzzed to do this?"

Lowering my head, I hover near her and wait for her to ward me off, but instead her breath catches and she arches toward me. Lightly, I brush my lips against hers.

When I pull away, she exhales. "More."

I smile and lean in, except this time I graze her neck and breathe her in. Breathe in the sweet scent of coconuts and something floral.

Goosebumps break out on her skin, and I nibble the curve of her shoulder and suck.

She swallows. "Let go of my wrists."

The urgency in her voice makes me comply immediately. I'd never want to force her to do something that makes her uncomfortable.

But before I can step back, her arms wind around my neck, and she pulls me closer, lifting her leg to my hip to fit our bodies together.

I don't have time to be surprised before her hand tangles in my hair and yanks hard to line up my mouth in front of hers.

"You owe me a kiss from the other night," she whispers. A sexy-as-hell smile teases her lips before they sweep against mine.

Fuck, nothing turns me on like a woman who knows what she wants.

Her mouth opens to me on a soft sigh. My tongue slides against hers, and she moans, the sound making me rock-hard. I run my palm against her thigh, which she squeezes against me.

For a tiny thing, she has long damn legs, legs I'd like to

wrap around my face. She tastes sweet, like sugar and lime and tequila. So it pains me to stop and untangle myself from her. When the tips of my fingers reach the curve of her perfect peachy ass, I do just that.

"What's wrong?" she asks quietly.

"Just meant to kiss you, honey." Clearing my throat, I slide her leg down and fix her skirt. Even though I really want to acquaint myself with what she has going on under that particular clothing item.

As gracefully as I can, I rearrange my hard-on. "Doesn't mean I don't want to get you all kinds of naked, but not tonight. Not if you've been drinking."

She glares at me. "Seriously?"

I kiss her again. "Seriously."

Her eyes lower to my groin before she grins and palms me. "This for me?"

Her grip is perfect. So is that stroke.

Clenching my eyes, I let out a breath. *God grant me the patience to not fuck her against my Ford. Please and thank you.*

"One hundred and ten percent," I groan before taking her hand from my dick, who's cursing me out and calling me a traitor. I skim my lips over her wrist. "Besides, I wanna explain what happened last night at the diner."

Her eyes soften, and she nods and leans up to kiss me. "Your place or mine? Oh, wait, they're the same."

I chuckle, relieved, turned the fuck on, and grateful to have another chance with this woman. I hope I don't blow it this time.

∽

About an hour later, with our legs dangling off the tailgate of my pickup truck and the view of my barn looming before us, she nudges me with her elbow.

"Pancakes after a night of mojitos was the best idea ever." Tori licks her finger. "I'm sticky, though."

I ignore the dirty thoughts that spring to mind when she says the word 'sticky' and reach for my water bottle. "Glad you enjoyed it. Wasn't sure if they'd be any good."

On the way home, I pulled into an all-night truck stop and got us two orders of pancakes and bacon because I thought she might want some food to soak up that alcohol.

Needing to get this off my chest, I blurt out my apology. "I'm sorry about last night. For not clearing up the confusion with Sandra." This might've been easier when Tori was buzzed, but I like knowing she's probably not at this point.

I explain my brother's good intentions and how I must've done a decent job of keeping whatever was happening between me and Tori a secret, so Logan hadn't known I didn't want to go on any blind dates. "I called Sandra last night and cancelled our plans." Rubbing the back of my neck, I tell Tori how I hadn't wanted to embarrass the woman and back out of the date in front of everyone, but knowing how things played out, I should've done things differently.

Tori's quiet for a minute. "I understand. That was thoughtful of you. I wouldn't want you to bail on me in front of everyone either." She worries her bottom lip. "I'm sorry I stomped off." With a shrug, she glances out over the pasture. "I'm not great at communicating when I get upset. I tend to overreact, as you well know."

My heart does this trippy little thing in my chest.

"I didn't mean to hurt your feelings." My words are a

whisper, but I've never meant anything more. "I'd like to make it up to you."

Turning, she looks up at me with those big doe eyes, a smile playing on her lips. "You mean by doing more than driving to Austin in the middle of the night and feeding me pancakes?"

"A small price to pay."

I don't know what it is about Tori that makes me want to take risks when I was pretty sure getting into something with a woman was the last damn thing I'd ever want again a few weeks ago.

"Thanks for feeding me. I love pancakes." Scooting back and reclining on the thick blanket I situated before we hopped up here on the flatbed of my truck, she lets out a contented sigh. "You can make up almost any offense with a good helping of sugar and carbs."

"My pleasure. Before I forget"—I pause to reach into my back pocket—"thought you might need this."

"You found my phone."

I think she's reaching for it, but instead she grabs my wrist and pulls me down onto the blanket next to her.

Chuckling, I brace myself on my elbow. "You make me laugh," I whisper as I brush a strand of mermaid hair out of her face.

"Yeah?"

Nodding, I dip my finger down her neck and over the delicate strap of her top. "Logan says I never laugh anymore, but you make me laugh."

"I've just put you under my spell with my cooking. It's been my evil plan all along." She blinks up with playfulness tilting her lips, and I'm overwhelmed by how right this feels.

For some reason, I want to remember every detail of this moment.

How she glows in the moonlight.

How the chirp of crickets swells in the meadow around us.

How the scent of cedar and wet earth permeates the air.

And, for the first time in years, how alive I feel.

With her wild hair going every which way, her sleepy, dreamy eyes staring up at me through those thick lashes, and her skirt barely clinging to the tops of her thighs, I'm inclined to agree—this woman is wielding some powerful magic.

Clearing my throat, I lean in closer. "Whatever it is, I think I'm addicted."

She hums in the back of her throat. "I like the sound of that."

Our eyes meet. "Do you do this often? Hypnotize men with your spells?"

It's her turn to laugh. The soft, sultry sound hits me square in the chest. "I haven't had great luck in the relationship department, so my spells might need some work."

Her confession surprises me. Tori is a drop-dead beautiful woman. Feisty as all get-out and playful as sin. I'm not sure why men aren't falling at her feet, but I'm grateful for the opportunity to change her luck.

And maybe mine too.

She toys with the button on my shirt. "Have you wooed many women in the back of this truck?"

"Can't say that I have. If anything, I'm pretty rusty when it comes to all this. Been outta the dating scene for a long time."

"I thought country boys were all about seducing women with their big trucks and Southern charm."

I drag my finger along the hollow of her throat, loving the way her breath picks up. "You looking to test out my stick shift?"

Her sexy laugh draws me closer. "If you think you can handle my speed."

I'm pretty sure we're not talking about my Ford.

When my lips graze hers, I tell her the truth. "I'd love to find out."

23

TORI

Above us, ten thousand stars shine bright in the night sky. Parked in the pasture, with my arms full of this man as we make out in the bed of his truck, I'm a bundle of contradictions.

Burning hot but shivering.

Terrified but trusting.

Overwhelmed but wanting.

The stubble on his square jaw tickles my skin, and I lean into the kiss, needing to feel everything he can give me.

I don't care that the rigid steel beneath me bites through the quilt and into my back. I don't care that this thing between us could go wrong in a hundred different ways. I don't care that I could fall way too hard for him.

I'm so tired of protecting myself. I want one night, *one night* where I can feel him and touch him and let myself go and not be fearful of getting hurt.

The breeze cuts through my poor excuse for an outfit, but Ethan's warm body hovering so near heats my skin even though he's leaning over me, bracing himself a respectable distance away. Keeping himself from tumbling into me.

But his hot kisses make me desperate for more.

"Come closer," I mumble against his lips. He pauses, looking down at me with so much desire in his eyes, I could incinerate right here. "I'm not buzzed anymore, and I need you to come closer. Right now."

A smirk breaks out on his face. "Demanding little thing, aren't you?"

I let myself take him in. His disheveled hair that I've thoroughly finger-fucked. His five-o'clock shadow that scratches against my palm. Those perfectly sculpted lips, wet from my kisses.

"I'm demanding when I know what I want, and at this moment, more than anything, it's you." The relief I feel from saying those words is immediate.

I never used to be someone who held back, either with what I thought or felt, but the last year has messed with my head. Right now, though, in this dark field, wrapped in Ethan's arms, I feel safe.

And I have to take a chance.

Just one.

Leaning up, I graze his lips with mine. "I want you. So much."

He brushes his nose against mine. "Want you too, sweetness."

Emotion swells in my body, making me hope for things I probably shouldn't wish for.

One night, I remind myself. *Take a chance tonight. Don't think about tomorrow.*

Slowly, I pull back. Those blue eyes darken as he watches

my hands work the buttons on my bustier that run from between my breasts all the way down to my waist.

When I'm done, I return my hands to my sides and wait.

An eternity passes as his eyes travel down me, lingering where my top barely clings to the crests of my curves, and back up again. His deep voice breaks the silence with a raspy whisper. "You're just about the most beautiful thing I've ever seen with your clothes on. Not sure how you're gonna rock my world if I take this top off you."

A white-hot spark surges between us when I stare into his eyes.

"Maybe we should find out." I wonder if he can hear my heart beating against my ribs. "Touch me, Ethan."

He holds my stare as his rough palm wraps around my shoulder and slides down one strap of my top.

Then the other.

Until I feel the breeze on my bare skin.

When he glances down this time, his hungry groan flares the delirium burning in my veins.

"Fuck, you have an incredible body."

His fingers ghost over me, test the weight of me in one big palm, before he squeezes my breast.

God, yes.

Harder.

Like he senses what I need, he complies until his fingers almost bruise, where his hold rides that border between pleasure and pain.

Perfection.

I let out a sigh of delight and pull him closer. His powerful thigh wedges between mine, and everything pulses in me when I feel him hard and thick against my hip.

Wordlessly, I undo the buttons of his shirt because I need to feel his heat against mine. When his shirt is off, all I can do is admire his strength that doesn't come from obsessing in the gym but from long hours working on his ranch. From his dedication to his family business. And damn if that doesn't make me like him more.

Strained muscles bend and flex over me as he settles himself fully between my legs, the weight of him nearly making my eyes roll back in my head.

Which is when I realize how much larger he is than anyone I've ever been with.

Above me, his beautiful broad shoulders blot out the stars and sky. His hand stretches across the expanse of my stomach. I have to wiggle my hips to make him fit between my thighs.

Who says you can have too much of a good thing?

It's not possible.

Because Ethan feels divine.

Hard to my soft. Rough to my smooth.

I breathe in his cologne and the scent of leather that clings to his skin before our mouths connect, and I indulge in languid, deep kisses that turn fierce and desperate.

When we break apart, he dips his head to my neck and takes one long suck that has me moaning into the quiet night.

It's too much and not enough.

I writhe beneath him, out of my mind when he palms my thigh and thrusts against me. Out of my mind when he sucks my nipple into his hot mouth. Out of my mind when he reaches between my legs.

An appreciative growl rumbles in his chest.

"I love that you're so wet," he mutters against me.

Of course I'm wet. I want to tell him how much he turns me on, but my mouth can't form words.

Leaning back, he bunches my skirt at my waist and traces the damp fabric between my legs again.

When he pulls the pink lace to the side, I spread my legs more and let him look.

I want him to look.

I want him to see what he does to me.

"Love this, baby. Love that you're bare," he groans.

His eyes stay pinned to where his finger rubs me in small circles.

"Oh, my God." My breath stutters, and I reach for my breasts to pinch my nipples, wanting that bite of pain.

I'm close.

So close that when he slides a thick finger into me, I gasp.

"Yes. Yes. Yes." The word leaves my lips, increasing like a crescendo when he adds a second finger.

But it's the first swipe of his tongue that leaves me breathless.

My chant grows louder. Unintelligible. A guttural garble of pleasure and pleading.

I thread my fingers through his hair and hold him to me. Brazenly lift my hips for more. Tense and strain as I climb.

Until I'm on the edge.

The sound of him licking me seems so dirty but feels so right that I can't help but cry out when he finds that perfect rhythm—filling me deep and hard but stroking me so softly with his wet mouth.

In a burst, I come apart, the dark sky turning a brilliant white behind my clenched eyes.

It's a long minute before I can move, during which a million emotions bubble up behind my breastbone.

The most urgent one crystallizes when Ethan moves over me.

I want more.

So much more than one night.

24

ETHAN

Let me just say that when a beautiful woman comes apart in your arms, it makes you take stock of your life.

A few weeks ago, I was miserable. No two ways about it. Miserable that I hadn't been able to keep my family together. Miserable that I was working so much. Miserable that life hadn't turned out the way I planned.

Right now, though? Despite the painful erection biting into the zipper of my jeans, I feel pretty damn content.

Tori pants, laughing, the sound musical.

Wiping my mouth with my forearm, I slide down next to her and pull her close.

She nestles into me, wrapping her arm around my neck and throwing her leg over my thigh. I caress the smooth expanse of her back, enamored by her soft skin and the sweet scent of her hair.

Clearing my throat, I tell her the truth. "I'm not sure if messing around in my truck in the back pasture is the most romantic thing ever or supremely low-class."

She hums. "That's easy. Super romantic and adventurous. And I love adventures."

I chuckle, completely charmed by her free spirit. "Noted."

Tori is so unlike the women I've been with before. I wasn't lying when I told her she wasn't really my type. Why I've always dated high-maintenance women is beyond me, because being with this girl who is laid-back and fun is fucking addictive. Allison would've died twice had I suggested cuddling in the back of my truck under the stars.

Tori shivers in my arms, and I rub her shoulders to warm her. "I'm an ass. Here you are freezing to death. We should go inside."

But her immediate reaction makes me smile. "No, I love it out here. Let's stay longer."

Through the back window of the cab, I reach for another blanket, toss it over us, and pull her close. When her bare chest touches mine, I have to bite back a groan because she feels so damn good.

Completely addictive.

Threading my fingers through her thick hair, I whisper, "So I guess this means you're reconsidering that whole 'not even if you're the last man on earth' speech you gave me a few weeks ago?"

"Oh, God." She presses her lips to my chest as she snickers. "You have to know I've always thought you were hot as hell, even when we were arguing."

I like to think of myself as a fairly confident guy, but I'd be lying if I said that compliment doesn't feel good coming from her.

She glances up at me, her hair tumbling over her chest like she's my own X-rated mermaid. "If you hadn't opened your mouth that first day we met, I'm pretty sure I'd have taken you on your kitchen counter."

Smirking, I kiss her. "And if you hadn't opened *your* mouth, I'm pretty sure I'd have let you."

Crawling on me, she nibbles on my neck. Bites my ear. Licks my bottom lip.

I'm praying for some restraint when she says, "We should do this all the time. I bet we could squeeze in a quickie during the seventh-inning stretch."

Have I mentioned I love that she watches baseball?

"Baby, I'm impossibly hard right now, so I'm not sure I can handle you talking baseball and sex in the same sentence."

"Then maybe we should get to the sex."

As her hands go to my belt, I reach for her wrists to stop her. Call me old-fashioned, but when I do things with this woman, I want to do them right.

"What's wrong?" Those big eyes turn up to me.

"Nothing's wrong. Just..." *Damn, how do I say this?* "I didn't find you tonight so I could get laid." Though heaven knows I'd really enjoy it.

"Okay, but... you don't want to?"

I'm wrestling with how to say what's on my heart when she starts to pull away. But I'm too fast for her, and I wrap my arms around her tiny waist and fit her against my chest.

"Fuck, yes, I want to." I stroke her hair and press a kiss to her forehead. Clearing my throat, I blurt it out. "In exactly three days, my divorce will be finalized." Tori stops breathing, so I kiss her again. "And while I'd love nothing more than to fuck you until you can't walk straight, when we do eventually take that step, I don't want shit from my past hanging over me. Does that make sense?" *Please, let that make sense.* I barely understand why I'm turning her down right now, except I want things with Tori to be perfect.

A long, quiet minute passes, during which half of me wants to kick my own ass for not being one of those guys who can shut down the shit in his head and fuck like it's a recreational sport.

"No, I, um, I get it." Another awkward silence ensues until she pushes off me and reaches for her top. "You know, Ethan, if you didn't want to do this with me, you didn't have to. I feel stupid, like I just threw myself at you, and—"

She doesn't get to finish those words because half a second later, she's pinned underneath me.

"Honey, you feel that right now?" Looking straight into her eyes, I grind my hips into her so she can see exactly how much I want her. "You make me come undone. From the moment you strutted into my house, you have occupied most of my thoughts, half of my dreams, and at least two-thirds of my future plans, so do not for one minute think I'm not dying to be with you."

The hard look in her eyes goes hazy, and I graze her lips with mine. "When we do this, preferably in about three and a half days, I'll be one hundred percent yours to do with as you please."

That gets me a small smile before her expression turns solemn. "I'm sorry." She blows out a deep breath. "You're right. Of course we should wait." Nodding, she leans up to kiss me, but this time it's sweet and soft. "I actually really respect your decision." She looks like she wants to say something else but doesn't.

We're quiet again, and while I'm glad she understands where I'm coming from, I don't want this serious vibe to over-shadow the fun we've had tonight. So I nuzzle against her neck and nibble her soft skin. "Just so we're clear, though, you make me fucking crazy." *My cock might never forgive me for waiting.*

And then I tickle her until she's howling with laughter and the smile on her face makes my heart knock painfully against my chest.

This girl's gonna be the end of me. But I don't think I care.

25

TORI

"Morning, sweetness." Ethan's deep voice sends chills down my arms.

Unable to summon the energy to respond, I grumble against his neck and snuggle closer to the big, warm body at my side. His chest rumbles against me with barely contained laughter.

"Not a morning person, hmm?"

"Too early," I groan.

His enormous hand strokes my back, and I smile against his stubbled jaw. *Damn, it's nice waking up with him.*

After a few minutes, I blink into the bright light of day, wondering how the hell we slept through the night in the flat bed of his truck. But then I remember the half-dozen mojitos I downed before we got the pancakes, and I have my answer. Alcohol, carbs, and a mind-blowing orgasm threw me headlong into a coma.

Once I'm more awake, I'm about to tell Ethan how much I

enjoyed spending time with him, even if it meant sleeping in the truck, when Logan's grinning face pops up over the side.

"Well, well, well. What do we have here?" Logan lets out a low whistle, perks up an eyebrow, and hangs his arms over the ledge like he's just going to hang out here and shoot the shit.

Before I can register the shock of seeing him, Ethan pulls the blanket over me. "The fuck? You ever heard of privacy? Get outta here."

Logan laughs. "Pretty sure you lost the right to privacy when you guys banged like bunnies on our back lawn, bro."

"There was no banging," Ethan says gruffly.

"No? Then what's this?" I peek out the blanket and find Logan dangling my top off his index finger.

Ethan growls. "You want to lose that fucking finger?"

Boys. They get so rambunctious.

I kiss Ethan's cheek, loving that he's all up in arms about my virtue, which I'm pretty sure flew out the window of my high school boyfriend's Mustang.

Snatching my top, I pull it under the covers and wrestle it on. "We were playing naked Twister. You should try it sometime. It's really good for flexibility."

Logan laughs at my joke, but Ethan is still growly.

I'm so preoccupied with the brothers' silent back-and-forth conversation that I don't hear the car door or the female voice until the blonde steps up next to Logan.

"I needed to bring the kids back early. What's going on—"

The woman stops mid-sentence when she sees me and a shirtless Ethan.

Ohhhhhh, crap.

Allison.

I'm still buttoning my top, but it's obvious what Ethan and I were doing since his hair looks like I yanked on it all night.

While he was giving me the best oral sex of my life, for the record.

Part of me is eating him up with my eyes—those sexy tattoos, his broad chest, those sexy-AF stomach muscles—while the other part of me is a smidge terrified over what's about to go down.

And damn, did I leave that hickey on him last night? I don't remember sucking his shoulder, but I must have. He makes me bitey.

Slowly, with a piercing scowl, Allison turns to Ethan. "What the fuck is this?"

Logan chuckles. "I'm pretty sure you covered sex in health class. When a man is interested in a woman—"

"Shut the fuck up, Logan." She waves in my direction while shooting another death glare at Ethan. "This. *Her.* What's she doing here when I told you I was bringing the kids back early?"

Ethan scoffs as he snatches up his rumpled shirt and slips it over his arms. "When you texted me last night and said you were bringing them back early, I assumed that meant in the afternoon, not first thing in the morning."

Her eyes flit to me and then back to Ethan. "It's nine a.m. When was the last time you slept this late in your life? I didn't think it would be a problem."

"That's just it, Allison. You didn't think." Ethan's voice brims with frustration. "Everything's always about you. Your schedule. Your life. Your priorities. What happened to taking the kids to the zoo today?"

She rolls her eyes. "It'll still be there next month. What's the big deal? It's going to be too hot today to be outside anyway."

An unusually cool breeze blows, and I bite my tongue. *It's probably a perfect day to go to the zoo.*

I finish buttoning my top, and, as daintily as I can without flashing anyone, try to slide off the back of the truck only to find Logan there to help me. He's gallant enough to look away when I jump down.

"Thanks," I whisper, realizing my undies are probably tangled in the blankets. *Please don't fold the blankets, Ethan.*

Of course, that's exactly what he does, but not before he shakes it out, and my thong goes flying.

Noooooooo.

We all watch my undies go careening across the bed of the truck.

Eyes wide, mouth open, Allison stares at the scrap of fabric like it's a tiny terrorist.

Fuckity fuck.

It's so quiet, I can almost hear the grass growing beneath my bare feet until Logan snickers next to me. "Pink lace. I highly approve."

Allison sneers. "Shut. Up. Logan."

Ignoring her, Logan leans closer to me. "Don't worry about this. Just head on inside and grab yourself some coffee. I'll make sure they don't maim each other."

I give him a grateful smile and muster a quick glance back to Ethan, who looks like he's barely keeping his shit together.

When we make eye contact, I motion toward the house. "Do you, um, do you want me to make the kids some breakfast?"

Allison directs her glare to me, but speaks to Ethan. "Why is your skank making the kids' food?"

If her goal is to make me feel like shit, she's one to nothing. I look down at my clothes that were perfectly acceptable for a club, but now, at nine o'clock on a Sunday morning, definitely reek of the walk of shame.

Feeling the familiar burn of embarrassment in my cheeks, I suck in a breath. Memories of storming out of Jamie's house that night turn my stomach.

This isn't the same thing.

This isn't the same thing.

It just feels like the same thing.

I turn away, unable to look at Allison, because all I can do is compare myself to her. She's beautiful. Perfect blonde bob with sun-kissed streaks that probably cost a fortune to have done at a salon. Designer linen pants. Expensive perfume. Elegant diamond earrings that glint in the morning sun. I feel like a husband-stealing tart next to her, which I know isn't rational, but my emotions don't want to focus on rational right now.

"Jesus, Allison. Stop being such a..." Ethan stops midsentence and shakes his head. "Look, I'm not doing this with you."

"Not doing what? I thought we agreed we wouldn't have hookups around the kids."

He leaps off the side of the truck. "She's the nanny and a friend, okay? Lay off."

"Are you kidding me?" she shrieks, making me flinch. "How clichéd can you get? Are you seriously fucking the nanny?"

Embarrassment scorches my skin that already feels so brittle it might crack.

Logan wraps his arm around my shoulder and steers me toward the house. "You probably don't want to be around for this. It's gonna get ugly."

Understatement of the year, I think with my heart in my throat as I walk away.

Hunched over the bathroom sink, I stare at my dirty feet, wishing I'd been wearing shoes when I slunk from Ethan's truck to the house.

All those warnings from my mother come rushing back to me. *¿Quieres que te llamen una callejera?* Do you want them to call you a stray? Or the more insidious definition of *callejera,* street walker.

It's always "them" with my mom. Meaning the neighbors or my school mates. People at church. Anyone who could witness my reproachable behavior. *Them.*

She'd be mortified if she ever found out about this morning.

Braving a glance, I finally look into the mirror and cringe.

My eyes are bloodshot, that smokey makeup I applied yesterday sits like sludge beneath my lower lashes, and my hair looks like an F4 tornado blasted through it.

Awesome first impression, Victoria. No wonder Allison hates you.

As quickly as my churning stomach allows, I crawl in the shower and wash my hair, desperately trying to scrub off all traces of last night.

By the time I'm dressed in sweats and a t-shirt, the house is still eerily quiet.

With sudden clarity, the reality of what happened this morning slams into me.

Will Ethan regret last night? Will he change his mind about us?

A sad laugh escapes me. *It's too early for there to be an us.*

Despite what my silly heart wants to lament, I should be worried Allison will make Ethan fire me.

See, tontita, *this is why you don't hook up with your employer.*

The thought makes me pause because Ethan doesn't feel like my boss exactly. I mean, I work hard around here, but I like him and his family, and he really does feel like a friend at this point. And, hell yeah, I like him as more than a friend.

Standing in the doorway of my room, I force myself to bite the bullet and see what kind of fallout happened after I returned to the house.

I find Ethan leaning against the kitchen counter. Shoulders slumped, head down, he looks deep in thought. Off to the side, Mila's coloring at the table. Her eyes are puffy, and her cheeks are flushed.

"Hey. Where's Cody?" I ask softly, afraid that a loud sound will shatter whatever fragile state they're in.

I park myself next to Mila, and she immediately hops out of her seat and into my lap.

When I kiss the top of her head, it's hard to miss the fact no one brushed her hair this morning. "Hey, honey. Did you have a good time with your momma?"

She shrugs and wipes her eyes. Although Allison's Lexus was parked a decent distance from the truck—I could barely see it along the side of the house when I came in—I'm guessing Mila and her brother were still in the back seat. Based on Mila's expression, she probably heard everyone yelling.

Ethan clears his throat, still not looking at me. "Cody's with Logan. They'll be back soon."

Hugging Mila, I ask her if she's hungry, but all she does is sniffle.

When Ethan finally turns and we make eye contact, I mouth, "I'm so sorry."

God, I am. Sorry for not coming in the house last night when he suggested it. For not getting up earlier this morning. For opening my mouth around Allison.

Let's not forget the underwear.

Hot shame burns my skin as this morning replays on fast-forward through my mind.

Ethan gives me a tight-lipped shake of his head, and I'm not totally sure what it means, but I do know this family has been through too much this morning to worry about me. He might fire me as soon as he's done with his cup of coffee, and that would hurt, but I'd understand.

Right now, though, nothing is more important than cheering up the little girl in my arms, so I swallow back the thick knot of embarrassment.

"Mila, baby, how do you feel about Mickey Mouse pancakes? Someone recently reminded me that pancakes always make everything better. Think you might want to help me whip up a batch?" It takes everything in me to keep my voice light. To pretend I'm okay. To focus on her instead of my own bruised pride.

She perks up in my arms and nods. "Yeah, I can help. Can I stir the batter? I like stirring the batter."

There's my sweet girl.

Ethan gives me a half-smile.

I'll take it.

26

ETHAN

THE MORNING IS FUCKING AWKWARD. BLUE BALLS ASIDE, that is.

And while I'd love to pull Tori aside to apologize, she's getting my daughter to smile for the first time since she got home from her mother's, and I'd do almost anything to help Mila forget all the crap her mother screamed at me.

Tori's sweet voice fills the kitchen as she ignores all the embarrassing shit that went down an hour ago and makes my daughter breakfast. As they're serving it up, the front door opens, and Logan strolls in with Cody.

Pulling up a bar stool next to me, he whispers, "Medusa gone?"

I nod and sip my cold coffee before I reach for Cody. He's a mess. Dried spaghetti sauce on his chin. Crusty God-knows-what on his clothes. *Dinner from last night.*

"Hey, stinker. Want some pancakes?"

My son claps and gnaws on his fist. I'll take that as a yes.

"Tori, would you mind plating up something for Cody?"

"Coming right up."

I'm a mess of frustration and anger, but watching Tori teach my daughter how to flip pancakes dials me down a notch, especially when Mila squeals with delight when she almost misses the pan.

My brother hangs around until we put the kids down for a nap. By then, I think I've figured out what I need to do.

When I reach Tori's room, she's sitting on the bed, her hair pulled up into a messy bun.

I rap my knuckle on the door frame. "Got a second?"

Her whole body tenses, but she looks up at me and nods. Without any makeup, it's easier to see the shadows under her eyes.

You kept her up all night, asshole. And then slept out in the truck. Of course she's tired.

"May I?" I point to her bed. When she nods again, I sit next to her and rub a hand over my face. "Not sure where to start here except to thank you for cheering up Mila. You could probably tell she heard her mom and me arguing."

"No worries." She blows out a deep breath. "I feel pretty responsible for what happened, so it's the least I could do."

It takes me a second to absorb what she's saying. "You can't be serious."

"I was the reason you were out there this morning." Her slender hands twist in her lap. "Then I had to open my big mouth and ask about making the kids breakfast when I should've kept quiet." Groaning, she turns and buries her face in the comforter, mumbling something about her underwear.

Smiling, I rub her back. "You're a sweetheart, you know that? And there's nothing about last night or this morning that you should be embarrassed about. I'm the one who tracked you down at that bar and force-fed you carbs until you were putty in my hands. What can I say? I'm hard to resist when I break out the big guns."

When she peeks over at me, I lift my arms and flex.

Her shoulders shake with laughter, and she rolls over onto her side. "Pretty confident there, aren't ya, stud?"

How is it that she can look this beautiful in sweats and a t-shirt? "Just messing with you."

Those big hazel eyes study me, and she gives me a shy smile. "I sorta like when you mess with me."

Not sure why everything is so easy with this woman. I'd have never guessed this was the case when we first met.

Damn. That makes this even harder.

I look away, needing to keep my wits about me, and Tori makes it difficult to concentrate. Not to mention the sexual frustration that's had me almost crawling out of my skin since we met.

"So, I, uh... need to ask a favor."

When I glance back at her, she's nodding. "Of course."

Swallowing, I motion toward her. "Listen. I had a great time with last night."

God, I hate this.

The smile on her face fades.

"But?" she asks, her voice barely a whisper.

"But Allison leveled me with some pretty serious shit out there today. Like threatening to petition for custody of the kids when I know damn well she doesn't want them."

"Are you serious?" She sits up, her face reflecting the riot of emotions I'm feeling.

"Yeah. She wants me to fire you."

"I'm not surprised." Tori's shoulders slump. "I understand needing to make your kids a priority, and if that means you need to find another nanny, I promise I won't take it personally."

I reach for her and pull her to my side. "I'm not firing you, babe. I told Allison she'd need a court order to make me do that, so unless you really did get arrested for snorting coke off a hooker's tits back in the day, I think we're okay in that regard."

She chuckles and leans into me. "So... then?"

"So until I can see what Allison's gonna do, what she's gonna level at me on Tuesday at the courthouse and the fallout of what happened today, I think we should put what's going on between us on the back burner. I need to talk to my attorney and figure out how to deal with her demands in a way that won't set her off. I can't have her freaking out in front of the kids again."

Tori shocks me once more, wrapping her arms around my waist in a tight hug. "Whatever you need. I know Mila and Cody come first, as they should."

I kiss the top of her head, hating that I probably shouldn't even do that, but holding her is heaven, and the comfort of having her in my arms is overwhelming. "I'm so sorry," I mumble in her hair. "I want you to know I really like you. I like being with you. Hanging out."

Those words feel sorely inadequate, though I'm not sure how to phrase what this woman makes me feel.

"I like you too, Ethan." Her chest rises in another heavy sigh. "But I understand."

That's good, because I'm not sure I do.

27

TORI

CODY TUGS ON MY SHIRT, AND I NEARLY FALL OUT OF MY FLIP-flops. I don't know why I'm so jumpy. I'm not the one getting divorced today.

Poor Ethan was a wreck this morning. Spilled his coffee all over his slacks and had to change. I guess his nerves are rubbing off on me.

Since our chat on Sunday morning, we haven't had any more heart-to-hearts, nothing beyond a soft smile over dinner or a hug when I bring him lunch. Mostly, he's been working his ass off in the barn to make up for the time he and Logan had to take off today to go to court.

I can't lie—I miss the intimacy we'd started to build before Sunday morning brought everything crashing down. He's pulled back, and while he explained why he needed to do that, it's difficult not to feel a little hurt.

"Want a sandwich?" I ask Cody as I brush his blond hair off his forehead. If I cut it into small squares, he might eat it this time instead of just tearing it apart and gobbling up the lunch meat.

He blinks up at me with his daddy's blue eyes and gives me a big toothless grin. "Sammich."

"You got it, buddy." I grab the bread and a few plates. "Mila, are you hungry?"

"Yeah."

When she doesn't say more, I turn to watch her coloring at the kitchen table. She's been coloring a lot lately, ever since she heard her parents arguing Sunday morning.

Last night, Ethan mentioned that he was going to explain to her what was happening today, so I know she might be feeling emotional.

After I make the kids lunch and seat Cody in his high chair, I lean over to see what Mila's coloring.

"That's so pretty. Is it for your dad?" She's drawn a horse and an enormous butterfly.

"Yup."

"He's going to love it."

She doesn't say anything and barely touches her sandwich.

"Honey, are you sad about today? It's okay if you are."

Tears start tumbling down her cheeks, and I pull her into my lap. "Yeah, I'm sad. Re-re-realllllly sad."

My heart crumbles into a million pieces as I rock her gently. "It's okay to cry about it, to me or your dad. To your momma too. We all love you, and it's good to talk about how you're feeling with people who love you."

When Mila and Ethan spoke last night, he told me she hadn't wanted to discuss it. Just kept nodding and acting like the divorce wasn't a big deal.

It obviously is.

Mila hiccups and holds me tighter. "Momma says she doesn't want me living with Daddy any-any-anymore."

As much as I'm struggling to not voice anything derogatory about Allison, I don't think it's healthy to turn kids against their parents.

"Sweetheart, she's just upset, okay? I'm sure she'll work things out with your dad."

She nods. "I wanna st-st-stay here. With you and Daddy."

"And he wants you here. I'm sure once everything settles down, it'll be okay. Your daddy loves you so much. He'd move mountains to be with you."

"I wish it was like it used to be. Like in our pictures." She sniffles, and I grab a napkin and help her blow her nose. "Except I want you here too."

Mustering a smile, I wipe away a few of my own tears that escape. "If your momma was here, you guys wouldn't need me to help out, but I understand what you mean."

I consider the family photos on the mantel in the living room and can't help wonder what happened to Ethan and Allison to bring them to this point.

Although Allison seems like she very much wants this divorce, she sure leveled a shitload of acrimony my way when she found me with Ethan. She screamed at me like I was the other woman. Like I was responsible for breaking up her family.

Which makes me wonder if she still loves Ethan.

Or if there's a part of Ethan that still loves her.

After a few more minutes of holding Mila, I sit her in her chair. "Know what always cheers me up? Decorating cookies. Do you think you'd like to help me make some?

You can help me stir." I really shouldn't feed these kids so much sugar, but I'm at a loss for how to get her out of this funk. I make a mental note to figure out more craft projects.

"Can we do different color icing?"

"Yup. And we can do different shapes too."

"Can we make Daddy some too?" She sniffles and smiles, pausing to wipe her nose on her arm. *Okay, gross.*

"Sure can." I reach for a wet wipe to clean off the snot.

After we set up all the ingredients for the cookies, I pin her drawing to the fridge with a magnet.

When I turn back to Mila, she motions me closer. Leaning close, she points to her drawing and whispers in my ear, "You're the butterfly."

"Yeah?"

She nods. "Butterflies are my favorite."

Aww. "Thanks, babe. You and Cody are my favorite."

She whispers solemnly, "What about my daddy? Is he your favorite too?"

That's an easy answer. "Absolutely."

Probably more than I'd care to admit.

An hour later, I'm writing the directions down as quickly as possible, but Beverly's zipping through the recipe faster than I can write.

Pushing the phone higher with my shoulder, I hum into the receiver. "Wait, so you use ice water?"

"Oh, yes. The colder you get the ingredients before you

roll it, the better. Otherwise, it'll get sticky. I also roll out the ball of dough between two large sheets of plastic wrap so you don't have to peel it off a counter. Way easier."

"You're a genius. My crusts never come out right, but I'm going to try this. Baking is tougher for me, so I appreciate the tips."

"Be sure you send me a picture."

I wrinkle my nose. "Of my crust?"

"Heck, yes, girl. Gonna be checking your work."

She's snickering into the phone, and I'm shaking my head. "The pressure!" I joke. The front door opens, and my pulse kicks up. "Hey, I think Ethan's home."

When he enters the kitchen, my attention snags on how handsome he looks in a suit. *Damn, he cleans up nicely.* Except when we make eye contact, his grim expression makes my stomach clench.

"It's your mom." I motion to the phone, my heart sinking when he shakes his head because he always takes her calls.

Logan walks up behind him, slaps him on the back, and tells me they'll be in the back office.

I nod, watching the brothers disappear down the hall.

"Um, Beverly, can he call you back later?"

She's quiet. "You have my number now. Call me if you or my son need anything."

"Yes, ma'am. I sure will. We could FaceTime this week if you want so you can see the kids. They miss you."

Logan set up his mom with an iPhone before she left, but they haven't had a chance to video chat yet.

"Thanks, Tori. I appreciate it. And thank you for looking out for my son. He's told me what a great job you're doing there, taking care of the kids. Taking care of him."

"It's my pleasure." And it has been.

When we're off the phone, I do my best to keep myself busy in the kitchen even though I'm dying to know what happened today.

Is he upset his marriage is over? He doesn't seem like he's pining over Allison, but it's not like I knew them as a couple. Maybe they always argued.

It's none of your business, Tori. If Ethan wanted to tell you, he would.

My heart aches at the prospect. It's true. I'm not entitled to know anything. I'm just a babysitter. Not his girlfriend. Certainly not anyone he needs to confide in.

I'm chopping vegetables for a stew when his voice cuts through the silence.

"Hey."

I clutch my chest. "Damn, you scared me."

Ethan grabs a cup of coffee and pulls up a chair. "Sorry 'bout that."

When he sits next to me, I catch a whiff of alcohol coming off his breath. Maybe tequila.

"You okay?" I ask gently.

"No." He rubs his bloodshot eyes as his brother joins us.

Logan slides a notepad across the table to his brother. "Let's list everything. How much she invested. How much you've paid her already. The balance. How we can make up those funds and pay the bitch back."

"Stop calling her that." Ethan grabs a pen and begins scribbling on the paper. "What if Mila hears you?"

"I just can't believe her crap." Logan's grumbling trails off.

I look between the brothers, not sure what to say.

Logan must see the question in my eyes. "Allison wants us to pay back the two-hundred-thousand-dollar investment her parents made on the ranch."

"Okay." I guess that happens when people get divorced, right? They split up assets?

"In one lump sum."

"Damn." Yeah, that sucks.

"But it gets worse. She claims it's so she can be financially stable enough to petition the court for part-time custody of the kids, which"—he lowers his voice—"we all know is bull-shit because she can barely handle them four days a month. Our attorney didn't want to challenge her on that rationale because doing so might make us look bad in the eyes of the judge. He said that since Allison already agreed to let Ethan have the kids for the time being, there's no point stirring that pot."

Logan explains how Ethan provided spousal support for the last year as payment on that investment from her parents in a show of good faith. He didn't technically owe her alimony because they hadn't been married ten years, which is one of the requirements for spousal support in Texas. "But Ethan being Ethan, he wanted to help her out because he's a good guy." Logan groans and shoves his hands through his hair. "We have three weeks before we have to go back to court and settle this."

Ethan seems lost in thought. "It was the right thing to do. She's the mother of my children. I couldn't let her starve. It's not like Allison had the chance to build any kind of career while she was living here." He gets up suddenly, his chair scraping across the floor. "I know her family has money, but it's not her money."

Fists tight, shoulders rigid, he shakes his head, stalking around the kitchen before reaching for a beer in the refrigerator and slamming it shut.

All of the glass rattles.

Whoa. I'm not expecting his fierce tone or the anger radiating off him right now, especially after how Allison spoke to him on Sunday.

With a loud smack to the bottleneck of the beer to the edge of the counter, Ethan pops off the metal lid, which rolls around on the floor.

Although the bartender in me is impressed, the haunted expression that flashes on his face before he gazes out the kitchen window tugs at my heart.

I clear my throat. "Do you, uh, do you guys need some privacy? I can head to my sister's house if you want."

Logan glances at his brother, who takes a long pull before shaking his head.

"It's fine, Tori. You don't have to go." Ethan sits across the table with a beleaguered sigh.

You don't have to go.

Not *I want you to stay.*

For the next few minutes, I analyze those words. Arrange them in my head, pull them apart, and rearrange them, but no matter how I look at what he just said, his apathy came through loud and clear.

I like to think I'm not the kind of girl to make a mountain out of a mole hill, but a part of me wonders if Ethan and I are over. If whatever toll today took on him smothered his interest in me.

The guys talk quietly and debate their finances and how they're going to repay Allison, while I sit and stare at the tiny scratches on the kitchen table. Internally, I chide myself over the sadness welling up in me. I get this is just a crush, that there's no way what's going on with Ethan could be more at this point, but I was so ready to welcome more, and he's likely nowhere near that.

With a deep breath, I steel myself and return to the stew bubbling on the stove. I'm so in my head, I don't notice the guys have gotten up until Ethan's voice, low and gruff, calls to me.

I turn to find him a step away.

After a quick glance around the room, I realize we're alone.

I take in his loosened tie and how his broad shoulders fill in his button-down shirt. Since he got home, he's taken off his suit jacket, and now his sleeves are rolled up to his elbow, revealing tanned forearms and smooth, muscled skin.

"You clean up well," I whisper, needing to break the silence.

"Come here."

It's two simple words, but a sentiment I needed to hear badly.

I'm in his arms a second later, closing my eyes and breathing in his clean scent as he presses a kiss to my forehead. The relief in my chest is palpable, like the air in a balloon being let out.

"Sorry I was an asshole," he says into my hair. "I don't mean to take this out on you. You've been nothing but sweet and amazing."

Blinking back furiously against the heat stinging my eyes, I take a steadying breath because I don't want to cry on his shoulder. He's the one who's had a hellish day, and I want to be strong for him.

He feels so good in my arms. Sturdy and warm.

I have no idea when this man dug through the defenses I spent the last year building, but he's burrowed into me now, and I suspect nothing short of open-heart surgery can remove him. Foolish though it may be to have such intense emotions for someone I met this summer, I can't bring myself to shut him out.

Once my tears are on lockdown, I pull back so I can look at his handsome face. "I'm so sorry you're going through this. I wish I could take away the pain." Reflexively, I place my hand on his chest, like my touch can somehow heal him. Because it has to suck to go through a divorce. Because as much as I adore Ethan and hope that he can be mine some-day, I hate that Allison must've broken his heart.

Before he can say anything, I move my hand to caress his stubbled jaw. I know he said he needs time to deal with his divorce, but I can't help but touch him. "Do you need some ice cream therapy?"

He cracks a smile and nestles me back against his body. "I need some Tori therapy."

Best thing I've heard all day.

28

ETHAN

I may be dog-tired, but my heart rate kicks up a notch when Tori beams me a beautiful smile as I drop down onto the couch next to her.

Her eyes return to the Astros game, but she reaches over and threads her fingers through mine, and everything in me, every cell and vessel, lights up.

My life might be in chaos right now as I try to figure out how to repay my ex, but the woman sitting next to me helps me feel tethered to the ground instead of buffeted by the financial shitstorm I'm facing.

It's been almost two weeks since my divorce was finalized, and though I want nothing more than to be able to focus on what's brewing between Tori and me, the next court date looms like a dark cloud, one that keeps me up at night long after the house is still and quiet.

I've resigned myself to being satisfied with snuggling on the couch. To holding this gorgeous girl. To hugging her. To keeping things PG when all I want to do is carry her back to my bed, strip her bare, and fuck her into next week.

Not that there've been many opportunities. But that hasn't done anything to curb my craving for her, which has only grown since I've been witness to her patience with me. To her commitment to understanding where I'm coming from and being an amazing friend. To her unwavering affection for my children.

It's the bottom of the ninth when Tori yawns sleepily. "Gonna take a shower and go to bed. I'm wiped."

I pull her into a hug, careful to avoid making eye contact because it only takes one glance into those wide golden-green eyes to make me question why I'm holding out.

She wiggles closer. "Don't stay up too late. You have that client coming over tomorrow evening."

I love how much of an interest she's taken in the ranch. How much she cares. Logan and I talk shop every day with her, explaining what we do and how we train the horses. She never looks bored or annoyed. Always asks questions and perks up with curiosity when she's in the barn. We even managed to squeeze in a lesson on Stargazer. Tori was fantastic up on that horse, her obvious love of the animal a damn delight to see.

"I'm turning in soon. I promise." I breathe in her sweet scent. "Night, baby. Sleep tight."

She kisses my cheek and shuffles out of the room. I stare after her, wondering how we've somehow turned into this old married couple after skipping the part where we bone like our lives depend on it.

Not that Allison ever watched baseball with me. Or liked to snuggle.

It fills me with a strange satisfaction that Tori and I have slipped into such an easy friendship.

It's not as though our attraction has dimmed. I see how her eyes eat me up when I come in from the barn, sweaty and hot with my t-shirt stuck to my skin. How she studies the ink on my arms. How her face breaks into a sultry smile when she sees me checking her out. Which, by the way, is often.

I've probably broken my record for the number of times I've jerked off in the last few weeks.

Sitting in the dark, with longing and lust in my heart, I wait for the desire to become manageable. For the urge to charge after her and make her mine to subside.

Once I can breathe again, I reach for the remote. I've just flipped off the TV when her unmistakable voice pierces the quiet with a bloodcurdling scream.

My heart stops in my chest. *Tori.*

And then I'm in motion.

Racing to her room like my life depends on it.

I fling open the door to find it empty. Steam billows from the bathroom where the door sits ajar, but another scream has me bolting forward before I can question whether I should go darting in there.

The shower curtain is open, and her eyes widen when she sees me, but she makes no effort to hide her nudity. Water splashes off her slick body and out onto the floor. But that's not what concerns me. What has me tilting my head is that she's flailing and jumping around so much in the stall I'm afraid she's going to slip and fall.

"Spider!" she screams, smacking at her very bare, very wet skin. "Spiiiiiiiiider!"

Now that I know she's not being murdered by a serial killer, I take a deep breath, because, damn, she scared me.

That's when my lizard brain homes in on all that water sluicing down her perky, lush tits. How it runs in rivulets along her tight little body. How ethereal she looks with that wet hair and steam billowing up around her.

But before I focus on what I know is a bare expanse of skin between her thighs, I force myself to stop and look up.

She waves her hands at me. Imploring. Angry. Agitated.

"It rappelled down onto me like a goddamn ninja." Shivering, she smacks at her arms.

I let out a chuckle, one she obviously doesn't find amusing.

"Don't laugh, Ethan! How would you feel if a spider tried to terrorize you when you were wet and naked?"

That's all I can focus on. Those words. *Wet and naked.*

Swallowing, I ignore the erection in my jeans that would also love to get wet and naked.

Because there's a whole lot of naked right now.

Dutifully, I take up her cause and glance around. Up at the ceiling. Along the tiled walls. Down along the drain. All the while ignoring the naked.

Jesus, save me from temptation and the boner in my jeans.

"Babe, I think you probably killed the culprit."

Tori's breathless, her long, thick hair a tangle of wet locks cascading down her body, one I need to explore again with my mouth. Because that fumble in my truck didn't do my memory of her curves justice.

Eyes up, douchebag. Eyes up.

But the smile she gives me is a spotlight, stealing all my attention. "Really? It's gone?"

God, she's beautiful.

She stares at me from underneath damp eyelashes, the grateful expression on her face making my heart thump harder against my chest.

Leaning into the shower and ignoring the spray, I wipe away the water on her cheek with my palm and desperately try to keep my hunger for this woman at bay.

I'm about to tell her that yes, the coast is clear, when I catch a glimpse of the eight-legged suspect.

Wow. That is a big motherfucker. She's not gonna like this.

"Sweetheart, don't freak out."

Tori goes stock still, her eyes widening as I lean closer to pluck the bastard out of the hair draped across her shoulder.

"What. The. Fuck."

The look of terror on her face is punctuated by another shrill scream and more hopping, except she bumps into me as she's jumping around, and I drop the damn thing. It goes scooting over her bare foot and five hot-pink toenails on its way toward the drain.

With a pained cry, she leaps out of the shower and into my arms.

29

ETHAN

At first, I think she's laughing. Because, yeah, this whole situation is pretty crazy. I chuckle too, not caring that my clothes are drenched and I'm standing in a puddle of water the size of Canyon Lake.

I lean back toward the door and peer through her dimly lit room and into the dark hallway beyond. As loud as Tori was a few minutes ago, I think the sound machines in the kids' rooms probably kept them asleep.

After closing the bathroom door with one hand, I caress her wet hair. It's only then that I realize she's not laughing.

She's crying.

My heart seizes at the panic in her eyes and the fear fluttering her pulse at the base of her throat.

"Darlin'? Hey, it's okay." She's shivering so hard, her teeth chatter.

Worse, though? She doesn't respond. Just trembles in my arms and sniffles.

My eyes dart around the bathroom and stop on the robe

tucked through a towel rod. Grabbing it with one arm, I shake it out and drape it over her slender shoulders before I set her on the edge of the counter. When I realize how threadbare the robe is, I snatch a thick towel and wrap her in it before I tuck her icy-cold body to me.

It's a long, quiet minute before she says anything. "I'm so sorr-rr-rry."

"No need to apologize," I mutter softly in her ear, but the fear in her voice is still so stark, I realize I'd do anything to make her feel better.

With a gentle touch, I run my hand along her back. "It's not every day a beautiful woman in distress needs me to rescue her. I like to think I bring my A-game. Ethan Carter at your service, ma'am. Rascally vermin are my specialty."

That earns me a laugh, and I smile against the silky, wet skin of her neck.

I reckon a lot of people have phobias. My brother loses his shit any time a snake slithers around here. But I don't tell her that because I'm not sure if her fear extends to all creepy-crawlies or just the arachnid variety, and I'd rather not point out the wide assortment of pests native to South Texas.

Anyway, it's no hardship to hold her right now, so I can't complain.

"I'm still sorry I freaked out there." She sniffles and snuggles closer. "Thanks for not dropping me."

"I would never drop you."

Burrowing against me, she shakes her head. "I had a bad experience as a kid with spiders."

"I'm sorry, honey. What happened? I mean, if you want to talk about it. You don't have to."

"It's so stupid."

"I'm sure it's not, babe. Trauma that happens to you when you're a kid can stick with you long after the scars on your skin have faded."

She sinks into me and sighs. "I was playing with my neighbor. Her older sister babysat us while my grandmother worked, and I made the mistake of hiding in the shed along the back of the property. My friend must've gotten bored and stopped playing, so she didn't hear me yell. Didn't know I had gotten stuck and couldn't get out." Her voice is nearly a whisper when she says, "There must've been dozens of spiders in there, crawling all over me. I had bites everywhere when they finally found me late that night."

"Oh, shit. That had to be terrifying."

"I had nightmares for years. But the part that always crushed my stupid little heart was how embarrassed I was."

"Why were you embarrassed?"

Groaning, she shakes her head. "I felt so forgotten. My friend forgot me. Her sister didn't care that I had taken off. My grandmother didn't realize I wasn't at the neighbors' until several hours later, so she didn't know to look for me."

That would hurt any kid. "Where were your parents?"

Shrugging, she gives me a sad smile. "Not sure. They traveled a lot when I was young. They were migrant workers. So I'd stay with my grandmother for months at a time."

"What about your sister?"

"I'm guessing with my parents. I was probably around Mila's age, so I don't remember all the details. Just being trapped and bitten and freaked out."

The thought of my daughter being in a similar situation nearly steals my breath. A confusing mix of rage and helplessness swirls in my gut, making me wonder what I'd do if that ever happened to Mila or Cody.

Fuck, I'd wanna kill someone.

I squeeze her tighter. "I'm so sorry that happened to you, sweetness. That I couldn't be there for you."

Another sniffle escapes her. "Pretty sure if we'd been friends when we were kids, I'd have made you eat mud pies, so count yourself lucky."

And I'm pretty sure if I'd known a young Tori, I'd have been smitten from the get-go. "I love a woman who doesn't mind getting dirty." I give her my most charming smile with an innocent bat of my eyelashes.

"Lord, look at you." She presses her hand against my whole face and laughs. "You're too pretty to do that to a girl, Ethan."

Snatching her off the counter, I pretend to gobble her neck. It's the kind of thing I do with my kids. Tori's laughing and flailing, except this time it's because she's having fun.

Her towel and robe are sliding off, but I don't care. I'm not gonna steal a peek. Just want her to forget the bad stuff that happened when she was young.

"Baby, we gotta rinse you off."

In the mirror behind us, glops of shampoo and bubbles glisten in her dark strands.

"No, no, I'm fine." Her whole body stiffens as she shakes her head vehemently. "I can't... I can't get back in there tonight."

I set her back down on the counter. "Hey." I tilt her chin up and wait for her to look into my eyes. "First off, I'm not gonna make you do anything you don't want. Ever."

I caress her soft cheek with the pad of my thumb, and she relaxes in my arms and nods.

"Secondly, you have shampoo dripping down your hair, and you feel like a block of ice. While I'm more than happy to rinse out your hair in the sink, I think a hot shower would do you a world of good right now."

She gives me an owlish blink before her eyes slide over to glare suspiciously at the stall as though an army of spiders might come marching out.

"Do you want to use my shower? I can make sure the coast is clear before you jump in, and tomorrow I'll call an exterminator to inspect the house, just to be on the safe side."

I'd normally think that's a crazy length to go for one spider, but if it gives her peace of mind, I'll do it. After hearing that story, I'd do anything to help her feel safe.

With another groan, she presses her damp forehead to my chest. "Gah! I feel like such a freak right now." Her words get muffled by my t-shirt.

"If it makes you feel any better, Logan once dated this girl who got so hammered, as she leaned out of his car to puke, she peed in his passenger seat. Now, have you ever peed in someone's car while hurling chunks all over the sidewalk?"

A snort of laughter makes her shoulders shake, and she peers up at me with a huge smile.

"See. I thought not. So in the big scheme of things, I'd much rather deal with my gorgeous, naked woman leaping into my arms, than the aftermath of Logan's date."

Her smile turns shy, the vulnerability in those golden-honey eyes piercing something inside me. "Ethan?" She nibbles her bottom lip. "Am I your woman?"

I hadn't meant to convey so much just now, except it feels wrong to hide my feelings from her.

Suddenly, all that resolve to take things slow, to figure out what the hell is going on with my life before committing to this pull between me and Tori, seems foolish. Because have I ever wanted anyone more than I want her? As a friend or a lover? Never. How she's engrained herself in my life in such a short time is a mystery to me, but I'm grateful nonetheless. I'm a dumbass for not seizing this chance with her sooner.

"Darlin'." I press my mouth gently to hers, tasting her minty warm breath. "I'd love nothing more."

30

ETHAN

HER FINGERS SHIFT THROUGH MY HAIR BEFORE SHE ARCHES UP, and I kiss her earnestly. My lips slide across hers, and I yank her closer so I can breathe her in. Breathe in her sweet, warm scent that's uniquely her.

With the last thread of restraint I possess, I pause. Because I should take care of her first before I get too inspired.

Worry clouds her expression when I pull back, but I dip down to kiss her again.

"Come on."

I fold her arms through her robe and toss the towel on the floor to sop up some of the water. I'll deal with that tomorrow.

Tonight, Tori's my priority.

Threading my fingers through hers, I whisk her back to my bedroom, grateful the kids haven't budged a muscle since I tucked them in earlier.

With a flick of my wrist, the recessed lights above the walk-in shower cast a warm glow into the dim bathroom.

Turning, I reach for Tori. "Want me to wash your hair?" I run my hand over her damp locks, barely keeping back a shiver when I think of how it looks draped over her body.

Another vulnerable smile tilts her lips, but the look she gives me from beneath her lashes quickens my pulse. "Would you? Wash my hair?"

"Of course," I say, a prickle of awareness dawning in me that we're not just un-pausing our relationship tonight. We're barreling forward at full speed.

But this feels right.

With her eyes locked on mine, that shy smile fades until all I see is want.

She wants me.

And goddamn, I want her.

Everything slows down as she tugs on the thin fabric wrapped around her.

The pink robe slips down her shoulders. Over her full, pert breasts. Across the curves of her hips.

Until it's resting at her bare feet.

Her wild, dark hair marks a damp path along her olive skin. In another lifetime, she could've perched herself on a rock, sung a siren's song, and men would've gladly dashed themselves upon the craggy surface to be near her.

She shifts, and her tresses carve out a map of generous expanses I need to explore before I fucking die of hunger.

"Let me take care of you tonight, baby," I whisper, brushing my palms over her bare shoulders.

She hesitates. It's brief, but then she nods, reaching for me.

I love that this girl always goes for it. That although she has moments of shyness, she always takes a chance. Best yet? She doesn't play games.

The last six years have taught me I hate goddamn games.

Tori's a lot of things. Young. Beautiful. Feisty. Passionate. But never fickle.

It's time I met her courage straight on.

When I pull her closer and cover her lips with mine, it's with the knowledge that she and I are overdue.

And I'm looking forward to getting caught up.

31

TORI

EVERY PART OF ME FEELS FLUSHED AND HOT, LIKE I'VE RUN A race and I'm out of breath but exhilarated from the effort. Maybe it was that stupid spider scaring me out of my wits a little while ago. Or how tender Ethan's been with me tonight, coming to my rescue and listening to what happened to me as a child. Not laughing at me. Only wanting to comfort me.

Or maybe it's knowing we're about to do this for real.

Even though I've been with other guys, even though I've carelessly shared things about myself with men who didn't deserve them, I know Ethan does, and being here with him right now feels important. It feels like a first. Like I'm handing him the parts of myself I've protected as I've waited for him to come into my life.

He leans into the shower and twists knobs until a rhythmic pulsing of water hits the tiles and steam begins to rise.

A quick pulse of expectation fires in my veins when he

returns to me, finding my lips with his, and I groan into his mouth when his tongue strokes against mine.

When I pull back, I paint his mouth with my finger, wanting to memorize the feel of his skin and hue of his full lips. "I hadn't planned on you this summer."

He bites my finger, and I yelp and laugh.

"You know what they say. The best-laid plans of mice and men often go awry."

Handsome and smart. I have no clue who he quoted, but I don't really care. "Then you're my favorite mistake."

Smiling, I step back just enough to slide my hand down his t-shirt, so I can yank the offending material off his body. He laughs at my eagerness, reaching back to his collar to help me with that one-handed shirt removal guys do that looks effortlessly sexy.

He shakes out his thick, dirty-blond hair, the shirt relegated to the cold tile, and I bite my lower lip to keep myself from grinning when I'm treated to all six-foot-something of muscled man. Of broad shoulders painted with ink and shadow and shapes that contour his powerful physique.

Pushing up on my toes, I press a kiss to his sternum and run my fingers through his smattering of chest hair. Like I'm following a treasure map, I let the trail lead me lower. He smells so good—like soap and leather and man. His hair is still damp and curling at the ends from a shower he took earlier this evening, but I don't remind him that he's already clean.

His gunmetal-blue eyes stay pinned on mine as I unbutton his jeans and shove off the denim. I look down to find his bulge straining against his boxer briefs.

And what a beautiful bulge it is.

With a held breath, I skate my finger along the thick curve, but before I make it to the tip, he catches my wrist in his big palm.

"No dessert before dinner," he chides.

I laugh and dart into the shower, letting out a squeal when he smacks my ass.

Why is he so much fun? He works tirelessly every day, his brow furrowed as he slaves in the barn, only to be this flirty, sweet guy when he comes home.

Home.

My heart warms at that word and how I've come to associate it with Ethan and his family.

He joins me a moment later—stark naked—and my girly parts spasm at the sight. The man is built like one of his horses. Sleek, smooth, strong.

And very hung.

He wraps me in his arms, my back to his chest. Like this, his impressive erection thumps against my rear, and I expect him to ravish me, but instead, he nibbles my neck.

"Let's wash your hair."

And he does. Working in the shampoo until I'm covered in bubbles and a lovely grapefruit scent.

The feeling of his strong hands massaging my scalp has me wanting to purr and curl up at his feet like his pet.

After rinsing it out, he repeats the motions with conditioner.

I'm a wrung-out mass of relaxed muscle by the time he's done. My eyelids droop, my breath is a slow, labored effort, and my entire body feels boneless.

"How are you so good at this?" I cringe at my question,

because do I really want to know about his experiences with his ex-wife or former girlfriends? *Yeah, no.*

The thought of him with other women is enough to send a sharp shard of jealousy through me. Even though that's ridiculous. We're only starting out. Barely becoming a *we.* I can't become a crazy jealous lover if we're hardly even lovers.

I brace myself, just in case, but the effort is unnecessary.

"I have two kids, remember?" But then he kisses my neck and murmurs, "I'm glad you're enjoying this, though, because I've never washed a woman's hair before."

All that anxiety melts away like a thunderstorm dissolving into the horizon.

How was he married and yet this is the first time? Isn't this something a husband does for his wife from time to time?

Because, yeah, if Ethan were my husband, I'd want the deluxe package. Hair-washing, conditioning, and steamy shower sex. On the regular.

My heart does a happy skip in my chest at the thought of Ethan being mine in a permanent kind of way.

Calm down, crazy. He hasn't asked you to pick out wedding invitations.

His big hands land on my hips and slowly turn me, and I'm smiling from all of his attention. From knowing I'm the first woman he's touched like this.

Standing in the shower, with water pulsing down and warm, amber lights shimmering from above, I'm overwhelmed by him. By the stubble across his strong jaw. By the electricity in his eyes. By the sleek strength of his body.

"I've never had a guy wash my hair." I'm not sure why, but

I feel shy and stare at his chest when I say this. "You're going to spoil me."

I swallow. The barest parts of me just beneath my skin feel so thirsty, like I've survived a long drought waiting for the rain. Waiting for him.

With one finger, he tilts my head so I have to look up at his beautiful face.

He smiles and leans down to brush his lips against mine. "Good. Because thinking about some other guy touching you like this makes me insane." One more kiss, this time to my shoulder. "And I'd gladly wash your hair every day, sweetness."

This is too fast. Too crazy. Too soon, a voice in my head screams, my limbs going weak.

Closing my eyes, I try not to get overwhelmed.

No, I want this. I've wanted this all summer, if I'm being honest with myself.

Aren't the best things in life about taking chances? At least that's how I used to feel when I was younger. It's not fair to deny Ethan my full heart because I've made mistakes in the past. Carpe the fucking diem and all that, right?

I'm doing this, I decide. *I'm all in.* Because I don't want to look back on my life and realize I screwed this up or lost out on a great man because I was too chickenshit to try.

His hot breath is in my ear when I pull his body closer, wrapping my arms around his neck, his sizable erection thumping against my stomach.

We slide together, and the moment our mouths connect again, we both groan. Those rough hands move down to my ass. Stroke along my thighs. Squeeze my breasts.

"You sure about this, baby?" he asks between deep, drugging kisses.

I'm over my internal crisis. Everything in me is slanted toward him like a field of wheat pointed toward the sun. "Fuck, yes."

I grip his wet hair and hold his mouth to mine, which gets me another groan rumbling from his chest.

A moment later, and my back is against the wall. Wedged against the corner, where he picks me up by the back of my legs like I weigh nothing and settles me on his thick thighs so that my core is nestled perfectly against his erection.

We both look down at how he spears my flesh, the sight obscenely beautiful.

My thighs tighten and I try to move, but he won't let me. For a second, his rough hands merely smooth over me, over my back and breasts and stomach until I'm a writhing mess. Slick and swollen and ready for him to fill me.

He doesn't though. Not yet.

My heart is a heavy beat between my legs when he slides his wide cock against my skin. Quick jolts surge though me as his thick crown notches against my clit. Over and over and over again.

"You feel so good. So wet," he murmurs against me. His shoulders and neck and forearms pull taut from holding me. From holding back and working me over.

I'm wordless. A free-fall of want and need and drive to finish.

My head falls back—mouth open, breath caught—as every part of me tenses, but then he's sucking on my neck. Licking behind my ear. Biting my shoulder.

Unintelligible words fall from my lips, but they're all a

mixture of how good he makes me feel and how close I am and dear God, don't stop.

But when his mouth closes around my nipple, I come apart, flailing. Flying. Shocking jolts of pleasure shuddering up my body.

I'm wrapped around him with my face pressed to his neck, panting and shivering with the euphoric surge of that orgasm.

Though he's pressing sweet, soothing kisses to my shoulder as though we have all the time in the world to love and fuck, he's still very hard and very thick between my legs.

The thought of that urges me out of my stupor and down to my knees. Because now it's his turn to fall apart.

32

ETHAN

My gorgeous mermaid slides down to her knees, the sight of which jerks my cock in anticipation.

"Do you have a condom?" she asks softly as she wraps her slender hand around my length and kisses the tip.

I watch her pink tongue dart out to taste me, to lick off the bead of cum weeping out of me.

Breathe.

Don't blow all over her pretty face.

That would be rude.

And anti-climactic.

Her eyes shift up, and I remember she asked a question. "Yeah." I clear my throat. "I do."

Mentally, I thank my brother for being a nosy son-of-a-bitch and bringing me a box when it was clear I had it bad for this girl.

At first, she licks around the crown with teasing sucks and hungry noises that's better than any spank bank material I've ever had. Because she *is* the fantasy. Long, wet hair tumbles over her shoulder, and I reach down to squeeze her ripe breasts that are flushed and full.

Mist rises around us, and my beautiful woman is kneeling before me, giving me the blow job of my life.

She strokes me with long pulls, all the while lavishing me with tantalizing licks, pausing once to glance up at me.

She's such a vision. Eyes bright and vulnerable. Cheeks glowing and pink. Lips wet and swollen.

It's only a moment, but that look is almost better than the blow job. Because it tells me she cares. That she's invested. That she wants me as much as I want her.

Leaning back down, she welcomes me into her mouth again, the sensation so intense, I have to balance against the shower wall.

Fuck. She feels good.

Wet warmth envelops me while her fingers score my thigh like she's trying to get closer. The sight of her stretched wide, sucking my crown before taking me down her throat, sends heat searing through my body. Instinctively, I wrap her long hair in my hand, a little moan escaping her when I fist it tight.

I don't mean to do it, to pull, but then her hooded eyes lift to mine, and I realize she likes it, so I do it again, harder this time, yanking her down on me, the groan vibrating out of her tightening my balls.

"Jesus. Yes. Take it, baby. You feel amazing, letting me fuck your mouth."

Words spill out of me, shit I've never said in my life, because I was raised to respect women, but for some reason, Tori makes me want to own her in every filthy way imaginable. Based on the smile in her eyes and the care in her touch, she very much likes the praise. Likes the way I thrust into her and swell against her tongue.

Because when I let go of her hair, her hands dig into my thighs and she holds me down the back of her throat. *Goddamn.*

It's too much. Too raw. Too carnal. With a pained groan, I close my eyes so I don't explode like a geyser.

As gently as I can, I pull her off and run my thumb along her swollen lips. "You okay? I didn't mean to be so rough."

She blinks, sending droplets of water to her cheeks, and nods slowly, but I can see the worry in her eyes when she quietly asks, "Did you... did you not like it?"

Leaning down, I pick her up, needing to feel her against me. "Fucking loved every moment of it." Which I underscore with a ravenous kiss. "But I don't want to end this with the world's best blow job."

Her airy laugh fills the room as I stalk out of the shower, reaching into the cabinet and fumbling with the condoms until I have one in hand. All the while she clings to me. Naked and pliant and so fucking exquisite, she steals the breath right out of my lungs.

The cold air makes her nipples tighten, and I can barely focus on putting one foot in front of the other to get us back under the warm jets. The moment I do, she wiggles out of my arms, plucks the condom from my hand, and rips it open with her teeth. A second later, she reaches between us to roll it on.

Perfect fucking woman.

I scoop her up again, two seconds from spearing her on my cock, but manners.

"Can you take me like this?" Not trying to brag, but I'm a big guy, and she's, what, five foot three? Maybe?

But she's nodding and kissing me and telling me to hurry and when my fingers sink into her warm center from behind, finding her even wetter than when she came against my mouth, I can't hold back any longer.

Leaning her back against the tile, with one hand on her curvy ass and one hand on my length, I prod against her opening. It takes a second to work my way in, the torturously erotic strain of it all making me throb harder.

Her eyes flutter closed and her mouth parts in a moan that tells me this feels as good for her as it does for me. Seeing her like this, thighs parted on mine, breasts heaving, nipples tight, it almost does me in.

"Tori, baby," I groan into her hair, blissed-out of my mind to be with her like this. "You're so beautiful. You feel so fucking good." It's been a long time since I've been with anyone. My whole body sizzles in expectation of delving deeper.

Her legs tighten around me, but then she hooks her feet against my thighs so she can lift herself, just an inch, before she settles down again, and I have to watch every mesmerizing second. Watch where we connect. Watch how she swallows me up. How she squirms and moans and shivers in my arms as she sinks lower.

I grab her ass with both hands to help her. Then we're kissing, and she's yanking on my hair, and I'm so goddamn deep I bottom out with a grunt.

And though my balls are tight and I'm really fucking close to coming, a gentleman always puts a lady first.

With her thighs plastered to mine and her wetness

coating my cock, I snake a hand between us to rub that sweet nub until she's bucking and crying out. Until she's pulsing on me and grinding down so hard, I explode too, emptying into her with such force, I have to wrap my arms around her and lean against the wall so we don't collapse to the ground.

Has it ever been that good before?

We shudder on each other, aftershocks working their way through our connected bodies. Like fault lines after an earthquake, the ground shifts, the scenery rearranges, but the pieces fit back together.

In this case, the aftermath is better because Tori is in my arms, blinking up at me with heat and sweetness in her eyes.

Maybe she's what I've needed all along.

I dry her off and wrap her in a huge towel, while those drowsy hazel eyes stare up at me.

This—her, me, *us*—this feels right, and I'm smiling like a fool when I toss on a pair of boxers to check on the kids, who are still asleep.

Breathing a sigh of relief that my kids are conked out, I turn in the hall and nearly bump into Tori, who's now wrapped in her thin pink robe. I take my time admiring her long lean legs and the way the robe drapes over her hips and breasts, ignoring the twitch in my groin.

"Where you going?" I whisper.

Because it looks like she's headed to her room.

Her soft voice is so low, I have to strain to hear her.

"Thought you'd want to get to bed. Want your space. I know you have to get up early."

I almost laugh. With my lips grazing her ear, I ask, "Is that really what you want? To sleep in your room? If it is, that's fine, but I'd rather have you in my bed."

She smiles against my shoulder. "Yeah?"

I pull back just far enough to look her in the eye. "Sweetness, you're mine now, right?"

That smile tugs up further. "Yes."

"And what happened back there..." I hook my thumb over my shoulder. "That wasn't a late-night booty call. That was us taking the next step, which means I definitely want you in my bed."

Every.

Damn.

Night.

33

TORI

GOOSEBUMPS LINE MY SKIN EVEN THOUGH I'M NOT COLD. HOW can I be cold? Ethan's naked body is wrapped around me— arm slung over my hips, face nuzzled against my breasts.

I stare down at his huge form nestled around me and grin.

He called me his woman.

Yeah, I'm still thinking about that, hours later in the dark.

A wave of euphoria washes over me as I let myself relish being with him like this.

In my head, I'm ticking off all the boxes...

He's self-employed and smart and ridiculously handsome.

He adores his kids and treats his momma well.

He likes my cooking and makes me laugh.

Not to mention, he's a rock star when it comes to sex.

Who comes twice the first time they sleep with a man? No one I know. Most of my friends fake it, go home, and ride the vibe alone.

That silly saying comes to mind: *Save a horse. Ride a cowboy.*

I am so down with this.

I'm blushing when I think of his obscenely large but magnificent package.

And he wields it well, as the steady ache between my thighs indicates.

Then he cuddled me, whispering sweet words and stroking my back until I passed out.

Holy fucking boyfriend lottery.

He didn't even make me feel like an idiot for freaking out over that spider. I should've been embarrassed. Screaming and flailing around naked and looking like a fool. But he was so considerate and gentle, I want to cry about it now.

Here I was, thinking my sister had found the husband of the century, and I'd be shit out of luck. Yes, cognitively, I realize that luck is not preordained. It isn't meted out at birth like tickets to a carnival ride. *Ten for you and none for you, you little loser.*

But if love makes you stronger, helps you feel optimistic and hopeful, pain is dysmorphic, magnifying your weaknesses and pointing out your faults. And last year was so gut-wrenching, so insistent on reminding me that I was a big, fat dumbass who failed out of college and dated other big, fat dumbasses, and I couldn't help but wonder if my sister had been born with all the lucky genes.

It's probably the residual hormones from those orgasms making me high—I mean, hello, I had two!—but I haven't felt this at peace with myself in a while.

Sure, the feminist voice in the back of my head quirks an eyebrow and asks, *Girlfriend, did you really need a man to feel better about yourself?* But I don't view Ethan as my savior. He's more like the really handsome guy who gave me a ride out of my pity party.

In this fantasy, though, we're riding a horse, and Ethan is shirtless and sweaty.

It's my fantasy. Don't judge.

I'm staring up at the dark ceiling, running my fingers through his thick hair, all the while ignoring how turned on I'm getting.

It's hard not to with his warm breath brushing over my nipple and that massive redwood jutting against my leg.

The hot shower and sex relaxed me into a boneless state, but I jerked awake a few minutes ago, afraid Ethan had let me sleep in and the kids would find me in his bed.

I watch the clock, all of a sudden anxious about what happens when it goes off. You can never tell what sex is going to do a couple's dynamic. I'm laughing to myself, thinking about some of Viv's morning-afters.

Once, she woke up in a guy's bed, realized he never washed his sheets because they smelled like dirty feet, and she raced out of there, never to give him the time of day again.

On an impulse, I turn my head and take a whiff of Ethan's pillow.

Yum. *Clean man and dryer sheets.*

When the alarm goes off, I smile at the growly sound that rumbles through him. He leans over and smacks the clock into silence and then pulls me back to him, fitting my back to his chest.

"I haven't slept that well in years." His voice, thick with sleep, sends another wave of chills down my arms.

"You hardly slept." Maybe four hours?

"I go for quality, not quantity."

I laugh and arch my back against the erection pressing against my ass. "That's a shame. I was about to ask if you wanted a quickie before work, but I know you must be exhausted."

He makes a thoughtful noise as though we're debating global warming. "It's *possible* you might be able to persuade me as to the benefits of a quickie. I'm not *that* tired."

Smiling, I close my eyes when his big hand kneads my breast. "You do have a stressful job, and morning quickies are like taking your vitamins."

"Are you suggesting that since vitamins are daily, quickies should be too?" His hips flex against mine, slowly driving me crazy.

"We do want you to be healthy, right?"

"Yes, health first."

He's nibbling on my shoulder when I fit him between my thighs so his length runs flat against my core. "I'm a big advocate of health. Big, huge advocate."

"Christ, you're wet." He groans appreciatively and nuzzles my neck.

"We slept naked with your face pressed to my tits, and your morning wood's been saluting me for twenty minutes, so yeah, I'm ready to go."

He snickers, and I'm smiling, thinking this has to be the best morning after ever.

A few minutes later, after reaching for a condom, he slides into me from behind and reaches down to rub my clit. I'm half ready to sing a hallelujah chorus from how good he makes me feel.

I go off in an embarrassingly short amount of time.

I'm throbbing around him when he grunts, "Holy shit. Did you just come?"

"That's why it's called a quickie." Though, to be honest, I'm stunned it took all of sixty seconds to get to O-Town.

"Goddamn, that's the hottest thing ever." His hips buck faster, and I ignore my soreness and tighten my legs to make it extra snug for him. "Oh, fuck. What are you doing? That feels too good."

I toss my arm behind me and fist his hair, arching my back to send him deeper. "That's the point. Wanna make the taco a happy place for you."

"Shit. Don't make me laugh." He's swelling and jerking inside me and laughing at the same time.

We stay connected for a few minutes, catching our breath and snuggling close. A quiet contentedness fills me from head to toe.

Then he whispers, "You're the best time I've ever had."

I feel the exact same way.

34

ETHAN

"Why are you smiling so much today?"

I shrug like I haven't a clue what Logan's talking about and try to focus on the bills in front of me.

"Nah, don't give me that. Hmm." He rubs his chin like he has wisdom to spare and looks me over. "Let's see. You didn't yell at me for being late or accidentally spilling coffee on your desk. And I caught you whistling this morning." A smirk spreads on his face. "If you ask me, you look like a man who finally got laid."

"Good thing I didn't ask."

That smirk widens. "And you didn't deny it."

"What are we, in high school? You wanna compare dick sizes now? We got shit to do. Stop being an ass and get to work."

He snorts. "We both know I'd win in the dick compartment."

"In your pea-head dreams, bro." Laughing, I shake my head and reach for a pen on my messy desk.

A soft knock on the door makes me look up. Tori peeks in my office, and I have to force myself to not charge toward her and pin her to the wall for a kiss. "Hey, honey. What's up?"

She gives me one of those smiles that sends prickles of heat all over my body. "Just wondering if y'all wanted some dinner. I know you're waiting for that client, but I made some stew. I can bring it in here if you want."

God, this woman.

Logan taps a pencil on the desk. "Actually, can you come in here a sec? I wanna ask a favor."

Sighing, I sit back in my chair, wary of whatever hare-brained idea my brother's concocted.

"Sure." She smiles hesitantly and sits in one of the chairs opposite my desk, next to my brother.

He motions toward the kitchen. "Joey's still here, right?"

She nods, and he darts out of the room for a second and then returns, settling back into the chair. "Joey's gonna watch the kids for a sec. Okay, so you see this mess?" He waves at the mountain of paperwork in front of me and the files behind me, stacked in precarious piles on the cabinet. "Think you can help us get organized in here?"

What the fuck? "Logan, really? What did we *just* talk about the other day?" I specifically told him he's not allowed to ask her to do any more around here.

He jabs a finger on a pile of bills. "I said I wouldn't give her more work on her current salary, and I'm not. I mean, not really. Hear me out."

Turning back to Tori, he breaks out one of his flirty smiles that makes me want to punch him in his pretty face. "I was thinking that Ethan and I are great with the horses but shitty with organizing all of this, and we really need to get our act together before that court date this week. I've gathered our tax returns and supporting docs for our attorney, but we've been so overwhelmed with that and our clients, I'm afraid we're gonna miss paying one of our vendors or a tax bill or the vet. Who knows? We have a million things we're not on top of right now, and I generally leave all of this to Ethan, but he's working at max capacity right now."

Internally, I cringe, because he's right. If I'm being honest, I could cut out the few hours of baseball Tori and I watch. Except, fuck, when will I ever get a break? Even after enjoying a few innings, I head back to the barn to get all the horses to bed if I haven't yet. Yes, even horses get tucked in too. Some require blinders. Others might need blankets if it's raining. All of them like a little soothing talk. A few scratches behind the ear. Some TLC.

She nods sympathetically. "Makes sense. You guys have your hands full. What would you need me to do?"

Logan practically wags his tail, he's so pleased with himself. "You worked at a law firm for a while in college, right? You probably have some office experience we could use here."

Her face is blank, and she licks her lips. "Yeah, I mean, I didn't work there long, but I can organize your bills if that's all you need."

"Cool. Your sister mentioned it when she first brought up you working here, and I thought maybe some of those office skills might be handy right about now."

"Oh." She seems to breathe a sigh of relief but then furrows her brow and looks down at her hands. She swallows. "I, uh, I should tell you that I got fired from that job."

Logan and I look at each other, and he lifts an eyebrow. *Shit.*

I rub my forehead again. This is what happens when I let my brother run the background check. *Half-assed as usual.*

Not that I'd change anything. Tori is amazing with the kids, and I'm pretty damn fond of her myself. She's done nothing to make me question her character. Even that one argument we had when we met isn't really her fault. I *was* being an asshole.

I almost smile at the memory. Her all feisty and pissed. I love her fiery side. It's different than Allison's rage, which is always mean and manipulative.

No, unless Tori stabbed a coworker with a letter-opener, I don't care that they fired her. It's their loss.

He clears his throat. "Mind if I ask why?"

She gives me a sheepish smile. "I told off my boss."

I laugh. "Did he deserve it?"

"Of course. I think in legal speak it's called sexual harassment, but everyone ignored his behavior. Boys will be boys and all that."

"He harassed you?" I don't disguise the anger in my voice. The thought of some fuckhead being disrespectful toward Tori makes me want to kick that loser's ass.

"No, thank God. He was perving on his secretary who put up with his behavior. I called him out on it one day, and he had me fired for insubordination and a lack of professionalism." Her eyes tilt down again, and pink tints her cheeks. "I was just a college student, and I couldn't afford the kind of expensive clothes they expected me to wear. He used that against me. Said I didn't uphold their standards, and since I was a lowly paper-pusher and he was a senior partner, no one cared what I had to say about any of it. But the real kick in the head is the secretary I stood up for denied anything shady happened because she was afraid of losing her job."

"Oh, darlin', I'm so sorry."

Another shrug. "Anyway, I wanted to be honest about my level of experience. I'm probably better at mixing drinks than anything requiring a suit and heels, but I can try my best. When do you want me to get started?"

I'm curious about this myself since, aside from a few hours of baseball a week, we've been working around the clock lately.

Logan gives her a big, charming smile that makes me roll my eyes. "I was wondering if I could pay you extra to stay this weekend and get a jump start."

I let out an unamused laugh. "What do you plan on paying her with? Pizza and beer? Come on, Logan. Get serious. She works enough, going above and beyond every day. Now you want her to give up the time she spends with her sister? That's not fair."

"Chill, man." He scowls like I've insulted him. "I have my own money, you know. I've been saving. Besides, Joey said she might be able to help us watch the kids this weekend, so it's the perfect time."

"So you're planning to pay Joey too?"

He scoffs. "No, she's helping because she loves me. Duh."

Swear to God, my brother is such a dipshit sometimes. He means well, but it's like he's operating on a half-tank of gas.

Tori tries to hide a smile. "How about this?" she replies gently. "I'll grab breakfast with Kat Saturday morning, but I'll be back by noon to organize your office, and I'll split whatever you wanted to pay me with Joey."

This girl is too cool. I give her a big, dumb smile, because yeah, she's awesome. She stares back at me with those beautiful eyes, and I swear my heart skips a beat.

Logan clears his throat again. "You guys done eye-fucking?"

I reach over and punch him in the arm. "Have some respect."

He chuckles and rubs his arm. "After this weekend, I figure we could get you some time occasionally to help manage the chaos in the office. Maybe when the kids nap. Not sure what we're gonna do at the end of the summer when you head back to Austin, but I guess we'll cross that bridge when we get there."

His words toss a bucket of ice water on me, and I look up to find Tori with the same disconcerted expression that's probably on my face.

Silence hangs in the air, thick and uncomfortable. She shakes her head. "I, uh, I guess I don't know what I'll be doing this fall." Her eyes shift away. "Your mom will be back soon, and I'm guessing y'all won't need me around then."

I don't know what to say. I don't want her to go, that's for sure, but I have no idea what my mother's plans are once she returns, or if it's financially feasible for me to keep Tori on staff once Mila's in school.

If Tori heads back to Austin, will I ever see her again? Brady got her car running again, but it's a piece of crap, and I still can't get her to drive my truck. If we do long-distance, it's not fair to ask her to do all the mileage. I'm just not sure how I'd be able to get to Austin more than every other weekend when the kids are with their mom.

The idea of going from seeing Tori daily to twice a month wrecks me.

I shoot Logan a pained look. Couldn't he let me be happy and blissfully ignorant for one fucking day? Because I don't have the goddamn answers.

For all I know, next Wednesday the judge is gonna make me sell this place to pay back my ex-wife. Although my attorney said that's highly unlikely, he couldn't rule it out entirely, especially since Allison's counsel already requested it. She swore up and down after the hearing that wasn't her idea, that she was surprised by how aggressive her attorney was being, but I was too shell-shocked to process her words.

Since then, I've thought of little else. The only thing that's brought me any reprieve is Tori.

And I might be losing her too at the end of the summer.

My brother glances back and forth between us and laughs awkwardly. "Sorry. Didn't mean to open a whole can of worms here. Especially since you guys are in this ooey-gooey phase that makes me want to hurl."

Leaning on my desk, I groan and drop my face into my hands, needing to block out everything for two minutes. A steady pounding beats in my temples, but I don't have the energy to hunt down pain relievers.

There's some shuffling of feet, and I'm guessing Logan just hightailed it outta here.

"Hey."

I look up and find Tori standing next to me. She slides into my lap and presses her face into my neck. I pull her legs up over mine, wrap my arms around her and stick my nose into her hair.

How did she know I needed this?

"We'll figure this out, okay?" Her soft words settle over me and soothe all the anxiety riffling through my nerves. She might be younger, but I swear she's an old soul. "I'm here as long as you need me."

Always. I'll always need you.

I'm shocked at how fiercely that sentiment resonates in me, all the way down to my work boots. Have I ever felt this way about another woman? Never. Not even Allison.

Part of me is shouting this is insane, to fall for this girl when I'm barely out of my marriage.

While I can list a million reasons why Tori and I work as a couple, none of them negate the issues my brother brought up or the fact that I can't afford to keep her on staff come this fall.

Squeezing her tight, I decide I need to find a way to make this happen. She's too important to let go. I've lived with enough regrets in my life. Tori won't be one of them.

35

TORI

TOTALLY UNFAIR.

My sister is so pregnant, she can barely dress herself, but she's never been more beautiful. I'd look like a constipated hippo if I were that pregnant.

I sit on one end of the couch in her living room and pat my lap. "Come on. Kick up those hobbit feet so we can do this pedicure."

"Don't call them hobbit feet, brat."

I snicker and help her shift her legs up one at a time. "Just giving you a hard time. You're gorgeous, preggers."

Since Ethan needed me to work this afternoon, I spent last night with my sister, forgoing my Friday night TV routine of baseball and ice cream with my sexy BB—boss and boyfriend—and I'm hoping to pamper Kat before I head back to the ranch in a bit.

Izzy skips through the room with her dad trailing behind. She sees me break out the nail polish, and she pouts.

"Tori, will you do my nails later? Pretty, pretty please?" She presses her hands together like a little beggar.

"I'm not going to be here when you get back, but maybe I can sneak over in a few days to do them."

Jutting out her lower lip, she frowns. *Ugh. How can I say no to that face?*

Brady shakes his head. "Don't give your aunt a guilt trip, kid. I'll do your nails later if you want."

"Really?" She grins up at him like he just bought her a pony, but then she quirks a saucy eyebrow like my sister. "Can I do your nails too?"

He lets out a comical sigh. "Sure, but I get to pick the color this time. No pink." He turns to us. "This child's obsessed with pink. Pretty sure she'd spray paint her room the color of Pepto-Bismol if we let her."

My brother-in-law is awesome. I love that he lets Izzy paint his nails.

With his keys in hand, Brady leans over and kisses my sister, and she lets out a swoony sigh that would make Scarlett O'Hara proud. *Oh, man.* Do I look like her when Ethan's around? No wonder Logan makes gagging sounds.

Ethan and I have kept everything under wraps around the kids since we thought Mila needed time to process the divorce. No need to push our relationship in her face or upset Allison while Ethan still has his finances all wrapped up in hers. Rocking that boat seems stupid, like kicking a hornet's nest.

So when Ethan's alarm goes off at three or four in the morning—yes, he gets up at an insane hour—I sneak back to my bedroom. It's not a perfect situation, but at least I'm just trudging down the hall and not having to trek back to Austin.

I've been thinking long and hard about the concerns Logan brought up the other day. Their mom is returning. Mila's starting school. I don't have to be a genius to know they won't need my help anymore. It's not as if there are an abundance of well-paying jobs out here in the sticks, and I have a ton of bills. School loans for a degree I didn't get. Bills from frivolous crap in college I couldn't afford. Some insufferably bad decisions. Too many mistakes to list, really.

It's easy to forget those mistakes when I'm at Ethan's. Pretend I've got my shit together. Pretend I'm the upstanding adult my sister seems to think I am despite the facts.

Brady breaks into my pity party. "Watch out for my girl while I'm gone."

"Of course. Good seeing you."

"You too, squirt." He leans down to give me a hug, making sure to mess up my hair when he lets go. I've always wanted a big brother, and when Brady married my sister, I definitely got one.

Especially when he nears the door and turns back at the last minute to say, "Tell Ethan I said hi," in a saccharine-sweet, sing-songy voice.

Jerking her dad to a stop, Izzy tells me, "Have fun kissing!" And she smacks her lips together to make smooching sounds.

Brady, Kat, and I look at each other, frozen, and Izzy shrugs. "What? Mr. Ethan's cute!"

I hold up my hand, and she runs over to high-five me. With a pained groan, Brady clutches his chest.

"That's what you guys get for talking about this!" I quip with an evil laugh. "As you often like to remind me, kids have big ears."

"She's seven. She's not supposed to think boys are cute

yet." Brady turns his daughter toward him and musters the biggest frown I've ever seen. "Child, I want to remind you that there is to be no kissing until you're thirty. Maybe forty."

"Awww, Dad!"

Izzy is just as boy-crazy as I was at that age. Lord help Kat and Brady.

I'm still snickering when my sister wiggles as much as her giant belly lets her and claps her hands. "I can't wait anymore. Let's talk about Ethan! I want all the details!"

"That's my cue to leave," Brady says, taking his daughter's hand and heading out the door.

He can act disinterested, but I know for a fact Kat tells him everything. They're the worst matchmakers I know.

I can't feel embarrassed. Why bother? They've seen me at my lowest. Dating Ethan is awesome, and I'm not going to pretend otherwise.

I already told Kat about the night we spent in his truck and that there was plenty brewing between us, but I haven't told her about the recent developments and the spider from hell that dropped down onto my unsuspecting naked ass.

So I fill her in on some of the juicy details. Nothing too graphic. Don't want to upset her delicate sensibilities.

When I'm done, she smacks me in the shoulder. "How could you not call me immediately and give me the scoop?"

It crossed my mind, but I wasn't ready to share it with anyone. "I guess I wanted to see how things went. If he really meant what he said about us being official."

A *teeny* part of me was afraid he'd wake up the next day and regret it. Or that he'd want to backtrack. Reel things in before they got too serious.

Typical man reasons.

Not that he's given me reasons to doubt him, but I worried the stress of his pending court date would affect how he'd view us. Like maybe he'd see me as another kind of pressure.

She nods knowingly and grabs my hand. "You've dated some huge jerks, but Ethan is the real deal. When he says something, he means it." With a sniffle, she pulls me into a hug. "I'm so sorry I wasn't there that day."

I laugh and hug her back. "That's okay. I'm pretty sure I prefer Ethan saving me from that shower spider than you, no offense."

"That's not what I mean."

Oh. She means the first time I had a run-in with spiders.

Lamely, I pat her shoulder. "Wasn't your fault you couldn't be there."

"I hate that I missed out so much when you were little. I never thought much about it until recently, but it had to suck to not have Mom and Dad around like I did. And then *Abuelita* died, and I know she meant the world to you."

At the mention of my grandmother, I tear up and decide we cannot continue talking about this. There's no need to make her feel worse when she was a kid herself at the time. "Don't beat yourself up, *hermana*. You're already my hero." Truly, she's everything I want to be when I grow up some day.

Wanting to change the subject, I blurt out something that's been on my mind before we both need therapy for our childhood.

"Can we get back to Ethan?" I can't believe I haven't asked her this before. "What was he like with his wife? Did you know Allison?"

She sits back and hums thoughtfully. "Not well. They came over a couple of times when we had our farmers' fair, but she was always distant. Even with him. Definitely with the children. She never struck me as being particularly maternal. Not that someone can't grow into the role of being a mom, but she always looked so irritated. Made me sad for Ethan and the kids. But when we'd invite them for dinner, he came by himself. And you could see he was trying to make her happy, but nothing seemed to please that woman."

Twin vines of relief and jealousy sprout in me. Not that I wish Ethan or his children any pain, but it's hard to think of him with his wife. Though it's silly of me to want any of his firsts. He married her first. Had kids with her first. Lived his life with her first. *Loved her first.* My heart wallows in that thought.

If there's any silver lining, it's that they didn't complement each other well. "So you weren't surprised they were getting a divorce?"

"No way. I thought the writing was on the wall long before he told us she left him."

Wait. What?

Hold up. Hold the fuck up.

She left him?

Why was I thinking *he* had filed for divorce? Especially after how she treated him?

"Are you sure? *She* left him?"

"Oh, yeah. He tried to get her to reconsider for months. Maybe that's why it took so long to finalize the divorce."

That shouldn't change anything. Shouldn't make me question what Ethan and I have developed, but my delicate heart doesn't like this revelation one bit.

My sister must see the apprehension in my eyes because she shakes her head. "Do not freak out about Allison. She's history, but since you asked, I wanted you to know that Ethan is the kind of guy who isn't going to jerk you around. Look at how hard he tried to make his horrible marriage work."

Okay, she makes a good point.

But something about the morning Allison found us in the truck niggles in the back of my mind.

For a woman who seemed apathetic during her marriage, she sure lost her shit to see her ex had moved on.

And that has me worried.

My sister conks out on the couch in a puddle of drool as soon as I'm done with her pedicure, but I don't want to leave before she wakes up, so I cover her with a light blanket, do a load of her laundry, and fold a million adorable green and yellow infant outfits. She's such a wench to make me wait to find out the sex of her baby!

I'm still folding clothes when two fuzzy arms wrap around my legs, and I whirl around with a muffled scream.

"Bandit, you scared the shit out of me!" I whisper-yell.

My sister's pet raccoon holds up his little arms like a toddler even though he's ancient in raccoon years.

"You are so spoiled." I pick him up, settle in the rocking chair, and pat his fat butt while he snuggles against me. "Have you been a good boy? Hmm? I don't think you'll be allowed in the nursery once the baby arrives."

Sighing, I mull over everything my sister told me this morning about Allison even though I know I should put it out of my mind. But how can I? I want to analyze it from every angle so I know what I'm getting myself into. Though it's not like I can backpedal. I'm already in too deep, which is all the more reason to guard myself against that woman. How could Allison leave Ethan and those two precious children? I want to throttle her on their behalf.

Kat waddles into the doorway and smiles sleepily. "Sorry I passed out, *manita*."

"No worries. You're gestating. You need rest."

"Want some lunch? I'm starving."

I don't point out that we ate not two hours ago. "No, I should probably get going soon, but I'll be back tomorrow so we can shop for the nursery. Want me to make you a sandwich before I go?"

A huge smile lights her face. "You're my favorite sister."

"I'm your only sister," I say, smiling at our familiar lines.

One second she's laughing and then she's hunched over in pain.

"What's wrong?" I shoo Bandit off me and fly across the room.

"Just Braxton Hicks contractions. Nothing to worry about."

I lead her over to the rocking chair and help her sit. "What can I get you? Some water? A heating pad? Should I call Brady?" Like a splash of cold water in my face, I feel like an idiot for not knowing more about her pregnancy. For not having researched all the potential problems or complications. She asked me to be close this summer for the baby, and all this time I've been obsessing over my own love life.

With a grimace, she waves me off. "No, no. Don't bother

him. He hasn't seen his parents all week. Let them have their time."

My sister is the most selfless person I know. If she could have this baby in her bathroom without putting anyone out, she would. I'll text Brady just in case. He'd want me to. I also make a mental note to read up on the ins and outs of what my sister can expect during the last few weeks of her pregnancy.

I stay with her for a bit, rubbing her back to make sure she's comfortable.

"Hey, speaking of parents, have you heard from ours?" I ask, because I haven't in ages. I'd wanted to ask earlier today but since we got emotional, I figured I should table the topic.

"I swear they call me every other day. They're so excited about this child." She laughs and rubs her belly that undulates under her floral muumuu. "Oh! The baby is moving. Feel it." Grabbing my hand, she places it on her tummy, and I smile even though I'm still bummed out about our parents.

Sure, at the beginning of the summer, I was reluctant to talk to them because I was afraid I'd get the usual lecture about not screwing up a new job, but when they never called, I can't deny I was disappointed.

Deep down, I get this is all residual psychological bullshit from my childhood. My parents took Kat—not me—and left South Texas for months at a time while they did their best to get whatever migrant farm jobs they could. It may be irrational, but every now and again I feel like the kid they forgot about. Granted, they eventually found permanent jobs in Corpus, and we were able to settle down, but that doesn't erase those early memories.

When Mila cries on my shoulder at night, telling me she misses her mom, I get it. I *so* get it.

"They never call me," I tell my sister, feeling like an ass for bringing it up. I'm so bad at adulting. Sometimes life is like riding a bike with two shaky wheels that eventually fall off. It's only a matter of when. Because if the past is any indication, my wheels *always* fall off.

"Seriously?" She frowns.

"Nope. Not since I moved to the ranch."

"That's weird. Are you sure?"

"Why would I lie?" I bite my nail, feeling like a petulant kid for not letting this go. "I think they're still mad."

"They're not still mad." She tilts her head like she's reconsidering it. "Well, they can't be *that* mad."

I give her a look, the one that says, *Come on.* "It's bad enough that they were so embarrassed by me growing up that they told everyone I had gotten a scholarship to St. Mary's when we all know I could never swing those kind of grades."

"You didn't get a scholarship?" Her look of confusion is almost funny.

"You know I sucked at school. Do you really think I had the scores for a scholarship? It was need-based. Not for smarts. You got all those genes, brainiac."

She scoffs, insisting I'm smart, but she has to say that. She's a consoler. She wants to make me feel better. I finish biting my thumbnail.

When she's done insisting I'm not a *tontita*, a stupid girl, I continue. "When I failed out of UT, Dad was livid, reminding me of all the sacrifices they made for me. How I was ungrateful. How all I did was get in trouble. How they should've sent you the little bit of money they had and not me."

She gasps and covers her mouth. "They did not say that!"

"Swear to God they did. Ask them."

"Oh, Tor." Big tears well in her eyes. *No, don't cry.* "They were just mad. I know they love you so much, and you mean the world to me."

Those tears hurdle over her lids and career down her cheeks, and I sniffle, feeling like I want to sob right along with her.

"Love you too, Kitty Kat."

We hug, and she pats my head like she did when we were young and she'd pretend I was her life-sized doll.

"If it makes you feel any better, Tori, I'm proud of you. So proud of you. Of the way you regrouped after that jerk broke your heart last year. For the way you've worked your butt off on the ranch this summer. Babysitting kids is hard work, and not only do you do a great job taking care of them, those children adore you. And with the divorce, that's even more important."

Her baby kicks us both, and we jerk apart, laughing.

"I think that's my hint that I should get going before we start crying again." I motion toward the door. "But you're going to let me plan your baby shower, right?" It's getting late in the game, but my family is strangely superstitious and doesn't want to jinx anything. I'm sure my mother has nearly burned down the church lighting candles for this child.

Kat fidgets, tugging on her top. "Um..."

"What do you mean, *um*? Didn't I do a great job with your bachelorette party?" I rocked that shit like a badass.

She rolls her eyes. "I think my in-laws are still traumatized by those presents."

Scoffing, I get up. "*Pfft.* You know that was an honest mistake. Anyway, who will ever forget that Christmas? Just think of all those special holiday memories!" It really was a mistake. Totally not my fault.

"Tor, I don't think Nipple Nibblers sex cream screams 'special holiday memories'."

"You can use that as a lipgloss. Says right there on the package." I give her my sweetest smile. "But you're going to let me plan the baby shower, right?"

36

ETHAN

A LONE SLIVER OF LIGHT CUTS THROUGH THE DARKNESS AT THE bottom of the closet door. I'm so tired, I might fall asleep if the kids don't find me soon, but I will my eyes to stay open.

"Ready or not, here we come!" my daughter belts from the other room.

Little feet go pounding down the hall, this way, then that, before Mila confers with her brother, who yells, "Daa-dee! We find Daa-dee!"

I smile. My kids are so stinkin' cute.

A minute later, when the closet door swings open, I jump out with a roar, and my kids scream bloody murder and attack me with hugs and tickles.

With one child under each arm, I stomp into the living room, pretending to be a troll like that show they watch. "Who dares to cross my bridge?"

They giggle and squirm and screech until Logan and Joey run in from the other room and stab me with swords made out of old paper towel tubes and duct tape. Not sure when this game became 'let's hop on Ethan and beat the crap outta him,' but we end up in a body pile on the floor with Cody wrapped around my head like an octopus, Logan giving me a wedgie from hell, and my daughter jamming her finger up my nose.

"I give up!" I'm laughing so hard, my gut hurts.

Suddenly, everyone stops and, like a family of meerkats, turns simultaneously toward the front door, where Tori stands staring at us with amusement.

"Tori!" My children release me and careen across the room, where they smash into her and take her down to the floor. Oh shit.

"Ohhhh, Toh-wee! Meees you," Cody announces proudly as he sits on her. *Aww, my little dude is telling her he missed her.*

The woman left yesterday evening, but by their welcome, you'd think she's been gone a week.

I trot over and help her up, so taken by her when our eyes connect, I almost forget we're not doing any PDA in front of the kids. When did it become so hard to keep myself from kissing her?

"Guys, be gentle. Tori's not your personal jungle gym." She's *my* personal jungle gym. Or maybe I'm hers. Doesn't really matter how you break it down.

Once she's standing and dusted off, I give her a wink. "How's your sister?"

"Pregnant and emotional, which makes me *not* pregnant *but* emotional." She leans back down to wipe something sticky off Cody's face.

Funny how the thought of Tori being pregnant doesn't shoot terror through my bones. Always thought after Mila and Cody, I wouldn't want any more, but the idea of having babies with Tori makes me strangely open to the idea. If I can ever afford it, that is.

Tori would make a fantastic mother. She's patient and kind. Loving and open-minded. Tender but passionate.

The idea of seeing her swollen with my child does something crazy to my heart.

Take it easy. You just started dating.

"Thanks for coming back to help us out. I'll make it up to you. I promise."

My children bounce around us like a pack of wolves raised them, and she gives me that secret smile, the one that promises late-night touches and out-of-this-world sex.

Clearing my throat, I ask Joey and Logan to keep an eye on my tribe while I show Tori how the filing cabinet is organized in our office.

Logan snorts. "Sure, bro. 'Show her around.' Show her *all* the ins and outs back there."

Joey smacks him in the gut and smiles sweetly at me and Tori. "We got it covered. Take your time."

As soon as we're in the office, I pin her up against the closed door. Her hands are in my hair. Mine are on her curvy ass. Our mouths connect, and somewhere in the distance, fireworks go off.

"Missed you." I fist her hair and taste her neck. The curve of her shoulder. The sweet spot behind her ear. She smells like sunshine and flowers. Sweet and sexy and warm.

"Missed you too. So much."

I pull back so I can see her expression, and she gives me that breathtaking smile that makes me feel like a goddamn king.

"If my kids weren't awake in the other room..." I groan, hating that I need to stop.

"I know." She heaves out a pained sigh as I put her down, but before I can drop my hands, she pushes up on her tiptoes and whispers against my lips, "But I'll let you tuck me in bed tonight."

"Promises, promises." I smack her ass as I move past her. God, she's fun. With her around, I almost don't mind having to organize this pigsty.

∼

"Do you want me to add this to your federal tax folder or do you have a separate place for your property tax bills?"

I look up from my desk and study Tori, who's tied up her hair on top of her head with a number two pencil. She's so sexy, I want to fuck her right now on my desk.

After a quick adjustment to my jeans, I motion for the bill.

"There should be a separate folder for this somewhere." Rubbing my chin, I smile sheepishly. "Not sure where it is, though. Maybe check the second drawer?"

I've been feeling stretched so thin lately, the office was the first to fall into disarray. Because it's not like I can ignore my children, or the horses, or my employees. But having Tori here to help me get this under control has made such a huge difference, I feel a weight lifting off my shoulders.

Logan strolls in, drops onto the couch, and covers his face with his forearm. "Your kids exhaust me."

I ignore his whiny ass and continue paying bills. We've worked through the bulk of the mess. Tori rearranged the filing cabinet so it's easy to find the business bills versus the house bills.

Eventually, the fatigue of working my butt off all damn week catches up to me, and I close my eyes, wishing I could sleep into next year, but as soon as the sun goes down, I need to get back out to the barn to finish up in there.

"You guys ready for Friday?" Tori asks quietly as she walks behind me, pausing to massage my shoulders.

Jesus, that feels good.

Grunting, I let my head hang down while she works her magic. Would rather forget about Friday, and this back massage is the perfect way to do that.

"I can't do this for long." She whispers in my ear, "You have big muscles."

I smile to myself, feeling like a puffed up peacock.

"So Logan, I have a question for you," she says, still working over my shoulders. "Are you and Joey... you know?"

This I have to see. I crack my eyes and swing my head to the side. My mother has always wanted those two to end up together.

He's shaking his head, confusion written all over his face. "Just friends."

Tori snickers. "Like '*just friends* with bennies' or '*just friends* but you wanna bang' or '*just friends* and you're both in denial'?"

I laugh, reaching back to scoop her into my lap. "So many options."

"Right? I've been trying to figure them out because Joey is

really pretty, and she obviously cares about him, but I'm thinking he's in denial."

"Like the river in Egypt."

"I'm right here," Logan points out. "And I swear Joey and I are really and truly platonic. Nothing has ever happened between us. She's like a little sister. I would never corrupt her. I mean, we grew up together, so she knows what I'm like."

Joey is kinda sheltered. I can understand my brother's reluctance on some level. He loves to play the field, but he'd have to be ready to settle down to consider doing anything with Joey.

"Maybe she wants to be corrupted." Tori coughs. "Just saying."

"No way, dude." Logan rubs the back of his neck. "She might read too many romance novels, but she knows we're only buds."

Tori makes this sound of disbelief. "So you're totally cool with her dating someone else? Her being 'corrupted' by someone else?" The blood drains from Logan's face, and Tori's voice softens. "Maybe you should think about that before you dismiss her as someone you could be interested in."

She's right. One day Joey is gonna wake up and stop trailing behind my brother.

Tori gives Logan a sympathetic smile. "I don't mean to hurt your feelings. I think you're a good guy, but sometimes it's hard to appreciate something that's been staring you in the face for so long, and I don't want you to lose out on a great woman because you're worried it's complicated."

I love that she's a straight shooter. She's just expressed everything my family has always wondered about Joey and Logan's non-relationship relationship.

He doesn't say anything, which is surprising since he always has something to say about everything. After a few quiet minutes, Tori twists in my lap. "Are you feeling good about court this week?"

Groaning, I rest my head against her shoulder. "Not really, but there's not much I can do. We've already submitted all of the financial docs the judge requested, which is why the office looked like a tornado had blasted through here." Gave me a heart attack, trying to hunt down the tax returns while my brother pieced together our profit-and-loss statements for the year.

The thought of what might happen on Friday makes a cold sweat break out on my neck. "I'm hoping for the best. For the judge to see we're maxed out already. For him to accept the verbal agreement I had with Allison before she decided she was out for blood."

I glare at the giant file folder on the corner of my desk that has copies of everything we gave to our attorney, more than a little resentful I have to drag my family's private business through court because of my mistakes.

"Can I ask a dumb question?"

I'm learning that Tori never asks dumb questions. "You can always ask me anything."

"Do you guys ever compete in these?"

She reaches into the trash and, like a magnifying glass straight to my heart, pulls out a flyer for the Triple Crown Futurity, which is the premier cutting horse competition that takes place each year in Fort Worth.

"Nope." That's the easy answer. The other answer pains me too much to voice.

Logan stalks off the couch and snatches the flyer out of

her hand. "You'd think with the four-million-dollar purse, we'd consider it, right?"

"You know that's divided up a hundred ways for different events. One person doesn't win all that."

"But one person could win a big chunk, bro."

"Why don't y'all compete? I'm assuming your horses are at the top of their game, right?" She looks between me and my brother.

I scratch the stubble on my chin. "Yeah, they're well trained. Some of our riders compete."

"But... you don't?" she asks.

Now that she's redirected her attention from Logan's dating to my lackluster life goals, I'm not as eager to see where this goes.

I stand, needing some space, and slide her off my lap.

Logan answers in my silence. "He used to. That's how he's licensed to train cutters now, and Dad thought Ethan would compete after college. That was the plan, at least."

"Plans go to shit. Dad died. Allison got pregnant. We couldn't afford to send you to college." I don't mean to bark at him, but I'm tired of revisiting these old wounds.

"Don't take that on too," he argues. "I didn't want to go to college. Not my scene. And to answer your question, Tori, if we want to stay competitive in this business, we *should* be entering the Futurity."

A bitter laugh bursts out of me. "Yeah? With what time? I'm already busting my ass from dusk till dawn. Sure, we might win some money, but who's gonna pay for all that travel? For the number of cattle we need to increase the training? For the new trailer we'd need to haul our asses all the way to Fort Worth? For the entry fees? They're a goddamn fortune."

"Why do you need more cattle?" Tori asks, propping herself on my desk like she owns the place, which, despite my irritation, I kinda like.

I rub my face, wishing she hadn't brought up this topic, which only reminds me of all the ways I'm letting down my father.

Fortunately, Logan answers again. "We use cattle from a neighboring ranch to train our horses, but to compete on a bigger scale, we'd need a larger lot of animals because, after a while, those cows get used to the horses and stop responding the way they will in the arena. They get sour and don't wanna play."

She laughs and picks up the flyer again. "It's funny to think of cows playing."

"I don't know if they enjoy it," I add with a chuckle. "They just wanna get away from the big bossy horse in front of them, but the horses are definitely playing. The good ones, the ones who have cutting in their blood, they're playing from the minute they enter the pen. You can feel it in the saddle and the way they move. They love it."

"But the cows don't get hurt, right?" The look of concern on Tori makes me want to kiss her.

"No, honey. They don't get hurt. Cutting ain't like the shit you see at some rodeos. No one is tying down any animals. There's no steer wrestling or calf roping or chute dogging. In fact, some of the horses we train are used to help injured cattle. Say you have an animal that gets hurt in the middle of a herd. How do you get her away from the others? A ranch hand can't wander in there, but a cutting horse can get the animal maneuvered away from the others quickly so she can see the vet. Competitions are just extensions of those same skills."

Logan nods. "All packed into the best two and a half minutes of your life."

"Then you're not doing something right on your Saturday nights." I can't help but bust his balls. "You of all people know there's at least one thing better than competing." I eye Tori appreciatively in her cutoffs and tank top, and her eyes ignite under my perusal. "And I sure as hell hope *that* takes longer than two and a half minutes."

He slaps me on the back with a hearty laugh. "I forgot what you were like when you had a sense of humor."

"Fuck off. I'm plenty humorous."

"Thanks to Tori."

Looking down at my work boots, I smile at his assessment, because he's right about that.

37

TORI

Cold, soapy water runs down my arms in rivulets, the contrast to the sweat streaking along the back of my tank top making me shiver in the oppressive heat. *What an odd sensation.*

The barn is stifling hot even though the sun is starting to set. I don't know how Ethan does this day in and day out. I'd die from heat stroke.

Since it's Sunday, none of his ranch hands are here, so the barn is still and serene except for the occasional stomp or whinny from the animals residing in the stalls. Dust motes float lazily in the air, which is thick with the scent of hay and sawdust.

Leaning up on my toes, I strain to reach the top of Stargazer, a handsome dappled grey horse Ethan needed to groom this weekend.

"You really didn't need to help me out here," Ethan says from the other side of the animal. "You did enough this afternoon in the office."

When he explained he had to groom a few horses this evening so he could stay on schedule, the exhaustion in his eyes did me in. I couldn't let him do this by himself, especially since Logan didn't look like he was going to budge from the couch in the living room where the kids were watching a movie.

"I don't mind." Honestly, I don't. "Kind of wanted to keep you company."

I lean up again and catch him smiling. "I love the company. Maybe tomorrow you can sleep in and I'll take the kids out for breakfast. We'll bring you some pancakes."

Ethan Carter is such a sweetheart. I catch myself sighing.

It's funny how the moment I walked in his house this afternoon and he whisked me into the office for a quick makeout sesh, all of those reservations that crept into my mind about him and Allison this morning melted away. Whatever happened between them is the past, and we're here. Together. Now.

"That sounds wonderful, but when do you get to sleep in?" Even as the words slip out, I already know the answer.

"Never."

I want to laugh, to make a joke out of it, but I know he's telling the truth, and it hurts me to see how he's running himself ragged.

We finish up with Stargazer and then start on Tiny Dancer.

"There's nothing tiny about you, huh?" I scratch the huge butter-colored horse behind her ear, and she turns her head into me.

I love these animals and their gentle strength. Her soulful eyes almost do me in.

Ethan is quiet the whole time we work, and my heart is heavy with thoughts of what will happen to his amazing ranch if the judge doesn't side with him and his brother.

If I'm this concerned about it, Ethan must be sick with worry.

Peeking over at him, I take in his tight shoulders and serious expression. The tension in his jaw. The furrow of his brow.

He's in his own world. Quiet and troubled.

I wish... I wish there was something I could do to ease his burdens. To help him make sense of his life. To help him make the most of his business, so he can repay Allison without gutting the ranch. He and Logan have discussed the possibility of selling off some of their land, selling Logan's house, or auctioning two of their stallions, but each of those prospects will affect their ability to maintain the income they so badly need.

We're almost done with the last horse when he strips off his wet t-shirt.

He doesn't notice me staring, or that I shiver for a reason totally unconnected to the cold water that splashes me as I scrub down Tiny Dancer.

He's in his head, washing the horse. Focused on his task.

With two big strides, he heads to the giant sink in the corner and begins to clean up. Rinsing out the sponges. Scrubbing his hands. Washing his face. Water and soap go everywhere. Down his abs and low-slung jeans that fit him snug around the thighs and ass, making my girlie parts tingle.

He's hot and glistening with sweat, his face ruddy, his brow furrowed in concentration.

I should leave him alone. Let him work.

But he's so incredibly beautiful. So utterly masculine. So intense with those taut muscles all strained with exertion.

On a whim, I reach for the hose, spike the pressure, sneak across the stall and call his name.

Then I shoot him with the water.

"What the—" He whirls around, his mouth open and shock in his eyes.

At first, anger radiates off him, which only makes me redouble my efforts, accidentally spraying him in the face. *Whoops!*

"That's it," he sputters, a laugh bursting out of him.

Thank God, he's amused.

"You're in trouble, little girl," he yells, wiping his face with his one arm and chucking a huge sponge at me with the other. It lands with a wet plop across my thin white tank top and slides down.

I gasp. It's fucking freezing. Goosebumps break out along my arms, my nipples pebble, and I shiver again.

But I don't get a chance to retaliate because he snatches the hose out of my hands and shoves it down the front of my shirt.

"That'll teach you," he says in my ear, pressing my back to his chest.

"OH, MY GOD!" I squirm. Fight. Fling my arms. Screech with laughter while the frigid water shoots down my shirt, through my shorts, and along my legs, puddling at my feet.

The whole time, he holds me to his hard body while I flail.

Tiny Dancer glances back at us with a bored expression while I freak out and squeal.

"You are a *very* bad girl." His voice rolls through me, singeing the parts of my skin that brush against him.

"You should definitely punish me." I can barely get out the words because I'm laughing and out of breath and so turned on, I might burst.

I try to wiggle out of his hold, but his grip tightens as he lifts me up, and despite the blast of water tunneling down my clothes, when my ass grazes the huge erection in his jeans, I groan and thrust back.

Need fires through my veins, and just like that, we're a tangle of eager hands.

I don't have to tell him how I feel. He knows.

The hose drops to the ground and we stumble to the side of the stall, where he pins me to the smooth beige wall.

"Wanna fuck you so hard," he groans against my ear, his voice gravelly.

"Do it." *Please, God, do it.*

One hand dives under my shirt and bra, palming my sensitive skin, kneading and pinching, making me gasp in delight at his roughness. The other snakes under the leg of my shorts.

The rumble of his chest tells me he likes what he finds when he slicks a finger against my skin—me swollen and wet and so ready.

Back and forth he teases while he seals his mouth to my neck. He sucks and licks and bites me, all the while grinding his cock against my ass.

We've had amazing sex. Sweet sex. Sultry sex.

But this is different.

This feels out of control.

Desperate.

Impulsive and wild.

His breath is ragged and his fingers dig into my skin, and he's telling me how he can't wait to fuck my pussy. How I make him so hard. How I'm the only woman who's ever made him this crazy.

"Hurry," I gasp, needing to feel him.

He releases me, and I whip off my tank and shove down my shorts. The clink of his belt hitting the floor is the last thing I hear before he's on me again.

My damp back makes a slick sound when he yanks me to his sweaty chest, but the feeling of his hot erection, full and thick against my thigh, makes me arch my spine.

"Hold on to this. Don't let go," he commands.

Bracing my hands on a bar just above my head, he explores my nipples and my waist and the wet valley between my thighs. All while I hold on to the warm metal.

But the sweltering heat of the barn makes it hard to breathe, and watching his movements along my body makes it harder still. Watching his hand move under my panties. Seeing his forearm flex and contract while he works me over, the pounding of my heart resonating from somewhere beneath the pad of his coarse fingers.

He knocks my legs farther apart so he can breach my opening. I'm already so close to the edge, his touch has me crying out.

"Remember, don't let go." His voice is tight.

I'm nodding even though I'm confused why he's stepping away, but when he dips to his knees in front of me and grabs my ass, pulling my thighs to his face, all I can do is moan and writhe.

From this angle, I can see every movement of his tongue

as it parts my lips and licks up my center. The erotic movement of my hips as I ride his face. The searing pleasure in his eyes as he watches me come apart.

My body is still twitching with delirium when he positions himself behind me, slides himself against my folds—once, twice, three times—and drives into me with one epic thrust.

Fuck me standing. It feels too good, too intense, and my knees quake.

"Hold. On."

And then he's hoisting my thighs over his, and I tilt forward, barely clinging to the bar. Except I don't want him to stop. Don't want him to put me down. My knuckles are turning white, but I won't let go.

I feel like we're doing some crazy acrobatic move I read in *Cosmo* once, maybe the Wheelbarrow or the Superwoman? But my torso is more upright, and at this angle, my thighs are snug against his hips as he tunnels in and out of me, and that tension, all that delicious pressure that has me strung tight, makes my core clench and strain against his huge intrusion.

But before I can analyze how I'm feeling so good, so euphoric even though my arms are *this close* to slipping off the bar, I'm coming again and screaming, shuddering around him.

"Oh, fuck, baby." He grunts as his cock swells and jerks inside me.

Gasping and panting, we barely keep from tumbling to the ground. Just as my hands slip, he hugs my torso tight, leaning me against the wall. Gently, he puts my legs down, and with a wicked smile, I realize he's still twitching inside of me, so I nuzzle back and let him finish.

"Tiny Dancer got an eyeful," I joke, loving how he's nestled against me, arm slung around my chest, his face tucked into my neck.

When he doesn't respond, I reach back and thread my fingers through his hair, but I'm met with silence.

With a groan, he slides out of me, and I wince at the bite of pain between my legs, but hell, I'd take being sore any day if it means sex that hot.

I watch as he takes care of the rubber I didn't even realize he'd slid on earlier. I'm on the pill, and he knows that, but he's been meticulous about using condoms.

We're quietly putting on our soggy clothes, and I'm wondering why he hasn't said anything, when he reaches for me and clears his throat. "Are you okay, baby? Was I too rough?"

Smiling, I reach up to stroke his face. "I love every kind of sex you have to give me. Feral happens to be my favorite."

A chuckle vibrates his chest. "I love having you here. You and my kids are the best part of my day."

My stomach quivers, every part of me lighting up from what he just said as he leans down to kiss me.

It's sweet and soft and a complete one-eighty from what we just did, but it makes me want to take an emotional snapshot of this moment. Of us and his gentle touches in the half-lit barn. Of the tender look in his eyes that tells me more than any words he's uttered. Of the full-bodied wave of affection welling up in me for this man.

For once in my life, I'm not afraid of the future or my place in this world. Because Ethan brings me hope that maybe my past happened for a reason. That it brought me to this place with him. And I wouldn't change that for anything.

38

ETHAN

EXHAUSTION WEIGHS MY BONES, AND I SINK DEEPER INTO THE couch. Next to me, Cody snuggles on Tori's lap, and I smile to myself as I watch him gingerly stroke the tendrils that cascade over her shoulder. He's obsessed with her hair. *Like father, like son.*

I reach over and grab a long lock from her other shoulder and twist it in my fingers. *So soft.*

She smiles at me from under those thick lashes, and even though I got up at four this morning and baked all day outside in ninety-five-degree Texas heat, that one glance gives me a kick of adrenaline.

I can't stop thinking about what we did in the barn last weekend. How she let me take her hard and desperate, like a goddamn animal rutting away to release. I've never been that rough with a woman before, and as soon as we were done, I felt a pang of shame for not being more delicate with her. Even more shocking, though, was the playful look in her eyes when she told me how much she enjoyed it. How she likes it "feral" and wild. If the scratches on my back from last night are any indication, she's not lying.

That I have any energy at all to do more than fall face first into bed each night is a miracle, but Tori seems to give me superpowers.

"Daddy, can I have one more?" Mila is kneeling in front of the coffee table, reaching for the last slice of pizza.

"Sure thing."

I probably shouldn't be ordering pizza for dinner—I should be counting every penny and praying the judge doesn't dismantle my ranch this week—but with how hard Tori's been working alongside me this week, I couldn't let her cook one more meal, and I barely had the energy to drag myself in from the barn.

She's been a lifesaver. An angel. But the girl is running herself ragged, looking after the kids, helping me with the office, cooking for us. You'd think she'd be cranky as fuck—I am—but she does it all with the sweetest smile. Makes me want to lavish her with love and affection.

"Daddy?"

"Hmm?"

"Is Tori your girlfriend?"

Alarmed, I look at my daughter, whose attention is darting between me and Tori, and I realize we're sitting side by side on the couch, with Tori in a corner and me right next to her even though there's a good three feet on my right side. And some time in the last few minutes, I put my arm around her shoulders.

Sitting up and resting my elbows on my knees, I rub the scruff on my chin, wishing I had planned for how I was gonna explain this new development in our lives. Because I know whatever happens between me and Tori affects Mila and Cody too.

A quick glance to Tori tells me she's worried about how this will go down, and she gently shakes her head at me, which I know is because we've already agreed to keep things quiet for a few months. To see where things go. To ease the kids through the divorce. But I don't need more time to know what I want. I had years with my ex-wife and couldn't get a good reading about where we were headed sometimes, but with Tori, it's clear as day. I want this to last. I want something permanent, and I'm ready to invest my heart and soul into making our relationship work.

As for the divorce, I've been honest with Mila from the beginning, and I don't want to backtrack now. I'm not sure where she's learned about girlfriends and dating, but my guess is Logan talks too much about his social life.

"Honey, how would you feel if I said I liked Tori and wanted her to be my girlfriend?" No need to tell her she already is. Anything I can do to ease her shock is worth stretching the truth a bit.

The huge smile on her Mila's face is an instant relief. "I'd say YAY!" She jumps around like I just told her Santa was about to shoot his happy ass down our chimney.

I chuckle and pull my daughter onto my lap where I give her a big hug. "Listen. Tori and I are really good friends, okay? That's where this starts, being boyfriend and girlfriend. This summer, she's become my best friend. I like having her around. She makes me smile, and I think she makes you and your brother happy too, right?"

My daughter is nodding emphatically, the excitement and joy in her face so sweet to see after I'd worried she might have a difficult time with this transition. But nope. She's as happy as a clam. All of this makes sense. Since Tori came to the ranch, Mila's nightmares have almost disappeared.

A sniffle next to me makes me turn my head in time to catch Tori wiping a tear. Man, she kills me. "Come here." I pull my two girls close, with my son giggling in the middle of our group hug. Squeezing them tight, I press a kiss to the top of Mila's head.

But my son steals the show because he wiggles and squirms in Tori's lap, a gleeful smile spreading on his face as he points to his crotch. "I go pee pee, Daa-deee! Yay! Pee pee!"

We choke back laughter and high-five my boy like he hit a grand slam. Tori's been talking to him about letting her know when he has to go, so she can get him to the john in time. At the very least, she wants him to gain an awareness of it to set the groundwork for potty training. Just one more thing I've been too busy to think about.

It's a small victory at the end of a very long day. I'll take it.

39

TORI

A FREAKING AMBUSH. THAT'S WHAT I'D CALL THIS.

Sighing, I glance around the Lone Star Station. The diner is pretty empty, but then again, it's mid-morning on a week day.

My sister bats her eyelashes at me, a huge, self-pleased grin plastered on her face. *Traitor.*

"*Mija,*" my mother says, reaching for the cream, "your father and I were concerned."

Here we go.

They don't call me all summer and now *they're concerned.*

I shoot my sister a dirty look across the table, but she avoids my glare and rubs her ginormous stomach.

My parents sit on either side of me at a small four-top table, right next to the table I sat at with Ethan and Logan that one time. God, that seems ages ago.

"And why is that, Mom?"

She gives me that look, that *you know what you did* look.

I give her one in return. *Seriously, I have no clue.*

Crossing my arms over my chest, I wait her out. She likes the buildup. The drama. My Mexican mother is where I get all my crazy, so I know how this goes.

"We called you, Tori. Your sister says we haven't called, but we have." I start to shake my head, but she cuts me off. "*¿Por qué me dices que no?*"

Why do you tell me I haven't?

I pull out my phone and wave it around. "Maybe because I have this thing called a phone, and it never rings with calls from you. Either of you."

Not sure why being around them makes me whine like a teenager, but two minutes at this table with them has me crawling out of my skin with anxiety. At Ethan's, I'm all cool, calm, and collected, but seated next to my parents and sister, I'm the fucking basket case everyone thinks I am.

I'm twenty-three. I shouldn't care that my parents don't call me. I *sooo* get that. But I care. More than I want to admit.

"You guys didn't really drive from Corpus to argue about this, did you?" I shift in my seat, wondering why today of all days they're here.

"No," my dad interjects. "We wanted to make sure Katherine's nursery was all set up."

A part of me is disappointed they're not here for me, but I nod. I get it. They adore my sister. Hell, I adore my sister. She's why I considered working for Ethan in the first place. It makes sense my parents would want to check on Kat since she's so pregnant.

My mom digs into her purse. I sit back, knowing it could take a while before she ever finds what she's looking for in there. Toothpicks, antacids, a sewing kit, an extra shoe lace, mints. All shit she lines up on the table in her search at the bottom of the faux leather bag.

Then she waves her tiny red flip phone. "*Mira. Aquí.*" *Look. Here.* With the speed of a turtle, she opens it, turns it on, and waits for the device to light up. Finally, she holds it to my face. Like, right to my face so I have to lean back to actually read the screen.

I see my name and my number.

I blink a few times.

Huh.

"Um. Mom. That's my old number."

She makes a face. It's the *See, I'm right. As usual* face.

"What? I told you I changed it last spring." She lifts an eyebrow that warns me I'm going to hell if I lie to my *santa madre.* "I left you guys a message. Swear to God."

"Don't swear." She crosses herself, likely making a mental note to say a rosary for her heathen daughter this Sunday at church.

My sister snickers across the table, and we all turn to her.

"Aww, you guys! I'm just so happy we're together. We should do this more often. I love having you in one place." Tears well in her eyes. *Oh, Jesus. No.*

I sigh, feeling too wrung out to get emotional right now. Ethan's court date is the day after tomorrow, and I'm on pins and needles for him. I can't get all worked up in my family's version of a telenovela.

Needing to switch gears, I blurt out an apology. "You're right, Mom. I'm sorry I said you didn't call. You obviously did."

All three heads swivel around, their eyes wide as they

stare at me like I'm a monkey in a zoo exhibit, scratching its ass, about to throw a turd.

I shrug, wanting this weird moment over so we can get back to talking about how my cousins are spoiled or my aunts are gossips or whatever. Anything but this. "You're right. I could've called you guys too. I probably should have." I'm a brat. I know this. But I'm the baby of the family, and sometimes I need love too, damn it. "So yeah. Sorry."

After a long minute, my mom blinks a satisfied smile, and my dad leans over to hug me. "You look good, *chiquita*."

Smiling at my childhood nickname, Little One, I hug him back. "You too, Pops." I pat his round stomach. "Enjoying Mom's cooking, I see."

He chuckles. "How's the farm? Your sister tells me you're working for a nice family."

My eyes catch Kat's and I tilt my head, wondering at my father's meaning of the word 'family.' Does he think I'm working for a married couple or does he know it's a single dad? I figured my sister would've told him all the details.

"It's a *great* family." I sound like the freaking Frosted Flakes tiger, but why spill the beans now if they're under the wrong assumption?

Is this why Kat picked me up this morning and told our parents we'd meet them at the diner? She wanted to avoid them meeting Ethan? Avoid them seeing my living situation?

"¿*Y la esposa*?" My mother sips her coffee, her expression not giving me a hint of what she wants to know.

Is the wife... what?

I look to Kat for a clue here, but she's too busy gorging on the omelet the waitress set down in front of her to notice my distress.

Come on, Kat!

She's chowing down, making these hungry sounds like she's starving to death.

Meanwhile, my stomach gurgles, from acid reflux or some kind of ulcer, and I press a sweaty palm to my belly.

Fuck it. Might as well rip off the Band-Aid.

I glance between my parents. "You know they're divorced, right? That I work for a single dad and his brother?"

Based on the shock on my dad's face and the horror on my mother's, they did not know.

Folding my hands in front of me, I wait for the apocalypse to rain down on my head. It's a position I'm used to in my family. Because this is what I do. I screw up.

Kat finally pauses in her race to fend off starvation and waves a fork at us.

"Ethan is awesome. I told you guys," she says around a mouth full of food. "He's good friends with Brady, and he pays his taxes, and he's an awesome dad."

That's your argument? That he pays his taxes?

Where has my sister gone? The one who could argue the devil out of his due?

The bell over the front door jingles, and goosebumps break out on my arms. It's the most insane thing ever that as I look up, I already know Ethan is here. He's strolling up with his daughter.

My first reaction is the one I always have when I see him. Elation. The same feeling I got as a kid when I'd daydream one day my parents would win the Lotto and buy me a pony.

When our eyes connect and his lips tilt up, I swear I hear that old time-y song my parents love by Frank Sinatra about flying to the moon.

Or maybe it's playing on the overhead speakers. Whatever. The important thing is Ethan Carter is mine, and booyeah, baby, I'm fucking psyched!

But then I remember we're not alone.

That soaring sensation of being batshit crazy about him takes a steep nosedive as I quickly tabulate all the things that can go wrong when he meets my family.

Sweet Jesus. I'm so sorry I haven't been to church in ten thousand years!

A gurgle bubbles up in my gut.

What is it they say? When it rains, it pours? Here comes the deluge. I brace myself for my parents to lose their shit. At least our brunch will be memorable despite the hole in my stomach lining.

When my sister called this morning and asked if I could join her for an hour, Ethan said he and Logan could watch the kids, that I'd earned a reprieve from the ranch. I hadn't known my parents were lurking to ambush me, just that Kat wanted to grab something to eat.

Had I *known*, I might've mentioned *something* to prepare him in case he randomly decided he needed to come to the Lone Star diner in the middle of a work day.

He's holding Mila's hand as she skips toward us. They're so freaking cute together. Pretty sure the people next to us hear my ovaries explode and splat on the floor.

"Hey, babe." The smile on his face makes my insides somersault. I smile back, likely looking dumb and in love, but he gives me all the damn feels. What am I supposed to do? Be a robot?

My parents look slowly between us, like they're trying to

gauge, one, if Ethan is a serial killer; two, if he really pays his taxes; and three, if we're sleeping together.

No, yes, and definitely.

When my father's searching gaze reaches mine, my smile fades, and I cough. "Mom, Dad, this is Ethan Carter. My, um... my, uh, boss."

God, that doesn't sound right, though technically it is. But I can't exactly put an asterisk by that statement and add he makes me want to spawn and have his babies. That's not brunch-appropriate.

I've never brought a guy home to meet my parents. *Never ever.* I saw how they gave Brady the nth degree when he was trying to get Kat on the love lockdown. I didn't want any part of that drama.

Ethan glances down at his shoes, a brief but shy smile on his face like he knows I have no clue how to do this, and then he reaches over and gives each of my parents a friendly handshake.

In my head, I'm yelling for him to ignore everything we say at this table. *Every. Thing. We. Say.* And that he should run far, far away before this conversation goes to shit. Because it will.

My father is in the middle of taking a drink of his coffee when Mila leans up on the table, gives us a wide grin, and declares, "Tori is Daddy's girlfriend. They have sex."

Oh, holy fuckadoodle.

Well, that was fast.

40

ETHAN

THERE COMES A TIME IN EVERY MAN'S LIFE WHERE YOU THINK you can't be easily embarrassed anymore. That you're grown up enough to withstand whatever trivial things life might throw your way.

Your baby puking on you? No biggie.

Your son peeing in your face during a diaper change? Gross, but not the end of the world.

Your child pooping straight through his diaper and your jeans too? Survivable.

But your kid saying whatever crazy thing enters her brain at any given moment? That I had not taken into account.

For instance, take my child, the cute one with the delighted smile on her face. My tiny intercontinental ballistic missile dressed in pink is one hundred percent clueless that she just detonated the fuck outta any chance I had to get Tori's parents to like me.

I didn't realize that was who she was meeting up with this morning when her sister picked her up. Wasn't even thinking this was where they went for breakfast or brunch or whatever this is. But Mila heard that Tori was going out to eat and asked if we could too. She looked up at me with those sad, puppy-dog eyes, and I couldn't say no.

With how much I've been working lately, I thought some father-daughter time might be good. I wanted to make sure Mila was still feeling okay about what we'd talked about last night when I explained that Tori and I were dating.

Pretty sure this new topic takes precedence.

I wait until Mr. Duran's done choking on his coffee to address my daughter.

Squatting down next to her so that we're eye to eye, I lower my voice. "Honey, where did you learn that word?" Her blank expression tells me she has no clue what I'm talking about.

Mr. and Mrs. Duran's laser-point stares burn holes through my body. *Christ. Was I ever this nervous with Allison's parents?* They weren't my biggest fans either, but I can safely say I never cared this much.

I clear my throat. "Mila, where did you learn the word 'sex'?"

She shrugs. "Uncle Logan."

Of course. Gonna kill that brother of mine.

"And what do you know about it?" Please, God, I will do anything if she thinks sex is an island in the Pacific.

She shrugs. "Just that he likes to have sex with his girl-friends. Like *all* the time." She tilts her head. "Is it a game? Like Monopoly?"

I laugh awkwardly and glance up at Tori's parents, whose stony expressions freak me out. Turning back to my daughter, I shake my head. "It's an adult word, okay? Kids shouldn't be talking about it, but no, it's not like Monopoly."

In my head, I put two and two together. She heard my brother use the word 'girlfriend' and 'sex,' and she equated them. *Fucking Logan.*

She scrunches her nose, my answer clearly not satisfying her curiosity. *Fuck my life.* Why don't I know how to answer this?

Tori reaches over and takes Mila's other hand, her soft voice immediately soothing to my frayed nerves. "It's how babies are made, but you don't have to worry about that for a long, long time."

For a second, I'm worried Mila's gonna ask if Logan is trying to have babies with *all* of his girlfriends—*again, please, God, no*—but instead, she shrugs again, the concern in her eyes disappearing.

"Can I have some pancakes, Daddy?" she asks, and I nod, relieved to have this conversation over.

Standing, I direct her away from the table. "Mr. and Mrs. Duran, it was nice to meet you. I certainly enjoyed this little exercise in mortification. I hope y'all have a good lunch."

Kat snickers. "Ethan, you're the sweetest thing ever. At least that's what my sister tells me."

Pretty sure I'm blushing. A grown man. Blushing.

I run my hand over my face and blow out a breath. When my eyes connect with Tori's, though, the crazy swirl of affection I have for this woman almost overwhelms me. "Take your time here today. Enjoy the visit with your parents."

For a second, it's just the two of us, like some scene out of a movie where all the ambient sound fades, and she comes into sharp focus, knocking my heart rate up a few notches with her secret smile.

Yup, pretty sure I'm head over heels for this girl. I give her a wink and quickly nod to her scary parents before I scoop up my daughter and head for the counter to order her some pancakes in a to-go box.

Because we need to go. ASAP.

"*What* happened?" Logan's laughing so hard, he snorts, and I shove him off the living room couch. He lands on the carpet with a loud thump and rolls onto his back.

He clutches his stomach, tears streaming down his face as he relishes one of the most awkward moments of my life.

"Mila said *what*?" he asks again, more for dramatic effect than the need to have me repeat it.

"Get off the fucking floor."

"Oh, my God. That's hysterical." With a quick swipe of his palm, he wipes one eye and then the other. "Bro."

I can't make out what else he mutters because blood is pulsing in my ears. Taking a deep breath, I try to calm down before I choke my sibling.

Once I'm confident I won't stroke out from anger, I try to put into words how utterly embarrassing this situation was.

My eyes dart to the hallway, ensuring my kids are still taking their afternoon naps, before I jab a finger in his direction. "What do I always tell you? Mila isn't window dressing. She fucking hears you talk about your dating life, dumbass. Thanks for her first lesson on sex, for traumatizing me, Tori, her parents. Fuck, her parents. You should've seen their expressions. Like I was an ax murderer. Like I had defiled their daughter and then told my kid about it."

With my hand to my forehead, I try to focus on the silver lining. "'Course, Tori came to my rescue. As always."

"Love that girl." Logan pats himself on the back. Literally. "Pretty sure you have me to thank for planting her cute little ass in your life."

"Don't talk about her ass," I growl, even though I know he doesn't think of her that way. He'd better not be jerking it to thoughts of Tori.

"Just saying you can't be too angry at me since I'm the reason she's here in the first place. And hey, have you even thought about our court appointment this week since all this happened?"

I still. Then scratch my chin.

My silence is the only answer he needs, and his trademark smirk spreads on his face. I hate when he's right. I've been a mess of nerves, and while informing Tori's parents that I've fucked their daughter is not exactly the reprieve I was looking for, it has rewired my headspace.

Now that I'm home, though, now that I've had some time to mull it over, there are a million things I wish I'd told Mr. and Mrs. Duran. Like how much I adore their daughter. That she's one of the most capable people I've ever met. That they raised a brilliant, passionate woman who's an amazing example for my kids.

Did I say any of that? No. I stumbled through a terrible description of sex, one that only confused Mila, and then hightailed it out of there. *What the fuck is wrong with me?*

I groan, dropping my head into my hands.

Never again. Tori deserves better.

The front door opens and shuts with a soft click. Tori drops her bag in the front hall, traipses across the living room, and plunks herself on my lap.

Before I can begin to figure out how to apologize for this morning, she beats me to it after planting a soft kiss on my lips.

"I'm so sorry you got ambushed. I didn't realize Kat was meeting up with our parents." She shudders. "I'd never drag you into something like that on purpose."

Having her in my arms immediately puts me at ease. "Nothing to apologize for, honey. I'm sorry I didn't handle it better."

She nibbles on her bottom lip. "I feel bad. You guys have a lot going on this week. You don't need more stress."

Logan, who's still on the floor, groans. "Shit. Guess I need to wear a suit on Friday, right?"

My suit is ready to go. In fact, every morning when I see it hanging in my closet, it gives me a little heartburn, knowing why I need it ready. "That's probably a good idea. We can't show up looking like bums."

"Speaking of." Tori tugs on my t-shirt. "I've been thinking about your situation."

I lift an eyebrow.

"Why you don't compete anymore in those cutting horse competitions."

All of my muscles tense, and I lean back, trying to put some space between me and Tori even though she's sitting on my lap. Not sure why this puts me on edge, but it does.

She must sense my anxiety because she pats my chest. "I get that there's a cashflow problem. That the competitions are expensive. But the purses are fairly substantial, and a few years of doing the cutting circuit could get you out of debt with Allison."

All shit I've debated and analyzed this summer, except I don't see how we can make it happen.

"What's the biggest expense if you wanted to compete?" she asks. "The guy who provides the cattle?"

I scoot out from under her and stand up. This whole discussion makes my skin itch. "Yeah. That eats up a bulk of our budget."

"And you pay him outright?"

Nodding, I wonder where she's headed with this.

"This morning my parents were talking about this farming collective they'd heard about from one of their friends." Tori turns to Logan to explain her parents used to be migrant farmers. "The families all share in the cost and prof-its, you know, pooling their resources. It got me thinking that maybe you could ask the guy who provides the cattle to do it for a reduced rate for a cut of the profit. That way you're offsetting the cost. And maybe, if you can get him on board, I wonder if Allison would be open to getting paid that way too. So rather than taking an immediate payout on the ranch, she could view that money as an investment with different terms, say a payout within five years or whatever you guys decide."

Logan and I look at each other, and that glimmer in his eyes makes me want to put on the brakes.

With a sigh, I yank off my baseball cap and scrub my hand through my hair. "I'd say this plan has potential, but there's one colossal variable." Leaning back against the fire-place mantel, I restrain myself from listing all the ways this could go wrong.

Tori gets up and wanders over to me, beaming that luminescent smile, the one that makes me consider jumping off high dives like this one. "Yeah." She nods, stopping right between my legs. "It assumes you win. That you go to Fort Worth and kick ass." Her eyes cut to Logan. "Can Ethan do this? Can he go and be the best right out of the gate? Or is he just there to make his Wranglers look good?"

I chuckle and reach for her. I can't help it. Kinda want to spank her for all that sass. Except she'd like it.

I wait for my brother to say something sarcastic, but his attention drills into me. "Ethan's the best. I'd bet on him to win. Our daddy always said he was a natural. That he had cutting in his blood like one of the horses. Now, he'd have to qualify with enough points in earlier competitions and we're already midway through the season, but if anyone could do it, he could."

Aww, bro.

Feeling a little sentimental, I shrug and struggle to find something to say, but Tori fills the silence. "I wasn't thinking that you'd have to compete right away, just set the groundwork for it this fall, get your investors on board, and then go for it in the new year so you can have a good shot at qualifying for the Futurity."

Twisting her in my arms so I can see her face, I smile. "Have you been researching all of this?"

"Maybe." She bats her eyelashes at me, and I belt out a laugh. "Though I might've fallen asleep reading the contest rulebook online."

I kiss her forehead, feeling cautiously optimistic. But no matter what happens, I'm grateful for this girl in my arms. So fucking grateful.

Logan strides over and smacks me on the back. "Tori's made some great points. I think we should go for it. Figure shit out along the way. She's right—you could win the big enchilada in a year or two, and that would take our ranch to a whole new level. If you wanna do this, bro, I got your back. I know Mom will too when she gets back from Chicago."

We grin at each other like assholes, and Tori coos at us. "You guys are adorable. I always wanted brothers to look out for me the way you two do with each other."

With a smile on my lips, I pull her closer and whisper, "Baby, I can assure you I do *not* think of you as my sister."

Not even a little bit.

41

TORI

"Like this?" Mila asks, her face a mask of seriousness.

"Yes, ma'am. You're doing great."

We're sitting in the family room with a mountain of art and craft supplies. I'm showing her how to make dolls with some artificial flowers, wire, and yarn I found in the sewing room. I made her one the other day, and she loved it, so I thought we could do them together this afternoon to take her mind off her parents, who have that court date to settle their finances.

I didn't think Ethan told Mila he was going before a judge again today, but when she saw him wearing a suit and tie this morning, I got the feeling she understood he was headed to another serious adult meeting. Kids are so smart. They always sense what's going on, even if they're not told.

Making dolls is a great distraction for me too because whenever I think about what today could mean for Ethan, I want to hurl. Ethan talked to Allison for an hour on the phone yesterday, trying to get her to consider the co-op plan I suggested. I could hear bits and pieces from the kitchen, and as much as I tried not to let it bother me, by the end of the convo when Ethan was laughing and sweet, where I could tell she had chilled out and they were getting along, a hot streak of jealousy shot through me.

Deep down, I don't want them to argue. For the sake of the kids and Ethan's sanity, I can appreciate how much better their lives will be if everyone gets along.

But there's a teeny, tiny part that wants Ethan and Allison to stay far, far away from each other.

Like maybe on different continents.

Squinting out the big picture window, I don't see the giant oak or the rolling hills beyond the ranch's sprawling front yard. The sounds of the children fade away, replaced with Jamie's private conversations over a year ago. The ones he'd dart into the other room to take, talking in hushed tones. His muffled laughter making me realize only after the fact that he was never talking to contractors or his parents or friends. I was just too naive and stupid to see the truth.

Thanks for fucking with my head, douchebag.

But I've learned from my mistakes.

The biggest mistake was letting that breakup *break me*. Letting it derail me so much that I failed out of school. How on God's green planet did I give another person so much control over my life?

Maybe it's all this fresh air and country living or being away from Austin and the scene of the crime, but it's so obvious to me that I was too trusting. Worse, though? I didn't trust myself afterward.

There's one thing I really need to do for myself right now. If Ethan can go through this horrid divorce and come out in one piece with this awesome business and his amazing family, what the hell is holding me back from finishing my degree? I have *two* classes—not rocket science telemetry or neurosurgery or decoding hieroglyphs. Surely I can handle two freaking undergrad courses. I've saved up enough money this summer to afford them, so I really have no excuse.

I decide right here and now.

This fall, come hell or high water, I'm getting my degree. For myself. Not because my parents are nagging me to do it or because I've disappointed my sister or because my boyfriend might be embarrassed that I failed out. For me. To have something I've completed that I'm proud of.

Cody pops his head up over the coffee table. "Wook, Toh-wi. Ahhh cuh-lah good."

God, I love this kid. I hold up my hand for a high five.

"You sure do color good, bud." I'm delighted that Cody's talking to me more now. It took a while because even though I knew he liked me, he was a bit shy. "Is that Thomas?" This child is obsessed with trains.

"Yup!"

"Is that what you want for your birthday? A train theme?" Cody's birthday is in a few weeks, and his dad kissed the hell out of me the other day when I told him I could plan Cody's party for him.

I'm sure Cody hasn't a clue what I'm talking about other than we're discussing trains, which gets me a happy, drooly nod.

Hopefully, my sister will see what an outstanding job I can do with a two-year-old's birthday party since I'm not allowed to plan her baby shower. Our cousin is coordinating it. *Cousin!* Where's the loyalty? No wonder she didn't want to talk about it or the fact it's next weekend. Kat claims it's because I'm already working so hard on Ethan's ranch. *Pfft.* I might have to stick a red sock in her whites the next time I do her laundry.

I made one teeny mistake with those bachelorette gifts years ago and I'm still banned from coordinating the festivities. It's not like I was planning to whip up a dildo cake or anything. *Though that would be funny. We could celebrate the fertilization. My parents would die.* I laugh to myself.

Kat doesn't know it yet, but I am totally planning her kid's first birthday party. It'll be so much fun, her kid will be farting fairy dust by the end of it.

Mila holds out the small wire figure. "I'm ready for the next part."

"Awesome. Now keep it still, okay? This is tricky, but I think you can handle it." I stretch over to the end of the coffee table and retrieve the hot glue gun. "Careful, okay? I'll put the glue on, but don't touch it because it's really hot."

She gives me a serious nod, and I wait for her to settle the materials in front of me. Leaning forward, I lay down a strip of oozy clear gel. "This will be the prettiest doll ever." She hands me the flower, and I adhere it to the wire frame, pinching it tight.

When she doesn't chirp back with her usual enthusiasm, I nudge her with my elbow. "What's going on in your big brain?" The kid's obviously thinking really hard over there.

"Um. Nothing." I wait her out. Finally, she sighs. "Just, I was wondering..." I give her an encouraging smile. Mila could ask me for almost anything, and I'd try to make it happen. "Could we maybe give this one to my mommy?"

"Of course." I might have my differences with Allison, but

I want Mila to feel loved and appreciated, and if that means playing nice with her mother, I'll gladly do it, even if that woman makes me want to punch her in the throat sometimes. A lopsided grin spreads on her face, and I wrap her in a hug. "You're the most thoughtful girl ever."

"You're the bestest babysitter ever."

I smile, knowing she means that in the most complimentary way possible even though the word 'babysitter' feels as good as rolling around in a bed of pinecones.

Because it's so transitory. Temporary. Babysitters come and go, and I hope I end up meaning more to these kids than a blurry memory from when they were young.

Ugh, I must be PMSing. *Take a chill pill, Tori.*

My cell buzzes on the table. Vivian's name pops up, and I send it to voice mail.

"Aren't you gonna answer?" Mila scrunches her brows.

"Nah. I'll call her back tonight."

"Why?"

"Because I want to give you and Cody all of my attention during the day." I boink her on her nose, expecting a laugh but getting a sigh instead.

"Mommy talks on the phone. Like all weekend."

Ah, my little tattletale. "Maybe they're important calls? Like to your grandparents?" *Who I've heard are assholes, but again, not my business.*

That gets me a shrug.

My phone buzzes with a text message from Viv. *Call me back asap!*

Six texts later, including one that screams, *911! I NEED TO TALK TO YOU NOW,* I finally give in.

"It's about fucking time," she yells into the phone.

"Dude, I'm working. I can't talk. Are you dead or dying or in danger of dying? Is this a legit emergency?"

"Yes, it's a love life emergency."

Lord help me. "You don't have a love life." Viv is a serial dater. She's more of a "love the one you're with" kind of girl.

"I'm reconsidering getting back with David, but I can't decide, and I need to figure this out before he marries that ginger twatwaffle."

I laugh and hand Mila something to color while I wrap up this call. Cody is on his fifth train design. It looks like the slug that ate New York is crawling across the paper, complete with one blob that might be a smeared booger.

Turning my head and lowering my voice, I tell Viv I can talk for two minutes, so she'd better hurry.

She dives right into the story. "Do you remember David? Tall, dark, and delicious? My only hesitation is he always has to be on top, and you know I like reverse cowgirl. Oh, and he was boring, but built like a god."

"I thought you didn't like him because he's a mouth-breather."

"I can get over it. He makes six figures, drives a new BMW, and gets in to all the best clubs. Plus, I hate seeing him with this girl."

Oh, Viv. "You know as well as I do that those aren't good reasons for falling in love. The fact that you need a pro-con list should give you your answer."

"Who says we're talking about love?" She chuckles. "I can't help wanting David back now that he's with someone else. It's making me reevaluate the things that bugged me about him. Maybe I can get over his mouth-breathing or get him a subscription to some brainy magazine to jumpstart his personality. So," she adds with a snort, "now that you're ga-ga for that farm boy, you're the expert? Let me ask you this. Are *you* in love with this guy?"

My heart does a pirouette in my chest, the Julie Andrews arms-wide whirl from *Sound of Music*, at the thought of Ethan. "Yeah," I whisper, my answer as easy to recognize as a rainbow in the sky after a storm. "I kind of think I am."

An ear-piercing shriek next to me makes me drop my phone. Mila is wildly shaking her hand, big tears tumbling down her cheeks. "It hurts! Owie! Owie! Owie!"

I uncurl her clenched hand and find an angry red burn and the start of a blister. *Damn it.* While I was shooting the shit about totally inconsequential things—because, let's get real, David is not Viv's long-term paramour on this planet or any other—my sweet Mila burned her hand on the glue gun.

"I'm so sorry, Mila. I should've put that dumb thing away." I yank the offending device out of the wall plug and place it high on the mantel where the kids can't get it. Leaning over, I scoop her into my arms and rush her to the bathroom where I clean it up.

42

ETHAN

Closing the door to Mila's bedroom, I shuffle down the hall in search of Tori. We should be celebrating tonight, but Mila burned her hand, and Tori was so bummed my daughter got hurt during her watch, she retreated to her room after dinner. But now that the kids are in bed, I want to check on Tori.

Knocking gently on the door, I wait for her to respond before I enter.

I find Tori curled up on her bed. Tears streaking down her face. Cheeks splotchy. "Babe, what's wrong?"

She sniffles and shakes her head. "Just emotional."

I kick off my boots and slide in behind her, wrapping her in my arms, taking a second to breathe in the sweet scent of her hair, damp from a shower. "It's not nothing if it has you in tears." Reaching back, I pull the comforter over us to warm her up because she's shivering.

"It's stupid."

"You're a smart woman. Whatever's making you cry can't be stupid."

Her voice, thick with emotion, guts me. "I'm really upset by what happened with Mila—that she burned herself so badly—but I'm also on my period, and that's why I can't stop crying. Because what if something worse had happened?"

"Shh." I kiss her neck. "The fact that we've only had that one injury all summer speaks to the great job you've been doing looking out for my troublemakers. Mila will be okay. I promise. No need to beat yourself up about it." By the time I got home, Tori had already cleaned and dressed the wound. "If it makes you feel any better, when I was a kid, I accidentally tripped Logan, and he flew into the coffee table and knocked out his front two teeth. They were baby teeth, so they grew back, thank God, or my momma never would've forgiven me. Baby, you gotta look at the bright side—at least my kids have their teeth." Cody is still mostly slobber, but he's damn proud of his three tiny chompers.

Turning in my arms, she gives me a watery smile and burrows into my chest. "I'm really sorry, though. I want you to know that."

"Tell you what." I run my fingers through her damp hair. "You can make it up to me."

Her head pops up, the earnestness in her eyes doing me in. "Okay. Yeah, whatever you want."

"Go out with me next weekend."

Her lips tug up in the corners. "How is this me making it up to you?"

I stroke her back and pull her over me so she straddles my waist. "We're pretty far into this relationship, and I've never taken you on a date. Doesn't seem right." The night I tracked her down at the club doesn't count.

Deep down, I'm big on grand gestures, and Tori makes me want to pull out all the stops.

Tears pool in her eyes again. "Really?"

Not that I want to know about the men she's dated in the past, but if her expression is any indication, they've been shitheads.

"Yes, ma'am." With my thumb, I wipe her cheek. "We should be celebrating. Allison agreed to reconsider the payout, and the judge approved our interim proposal since Allison was amenable. That's due to you. Who knows what could've happened if you hadn't suggested the co-op? I was already maxed out on alimony payments. You saved the day, darlin'. So no more tears, okay? My kid is tough. She'll be fine."

That gets me the smile I'm looking for. And another sniffle.

"C'mere." I smooth my hand over the back of her neck and bring her lips to mine. They taste like tears and chapstick.

A curtain of silky hair blocks out the dim nightstand light until she's all I can see. I lick her bottom lip and she opens for me with a soft moan. With her curvy ass swaying on my lap, my cock is already digging into the zipper of my jeans, but I don't want this to be about me or sex or getting off. Just making her feel better.

Rolling her over until we're on our sides, I slide her thigh over mine and trail my hand along her shoulders. "We don't have to do anything tonight, sweetness. I know you're not feeling well." Otherwise, I'd be rubbing that peachy ass in those tiny sleep shorts.

"I'm so bloated, and I have the worst cramps." Tucking her head against my chest, she groans.

"If you hadn't told me you had your period, I'd never know. You're so beautiful to me, you could be prancing around in a paper sack and I'm pretty sure I'd still have stars in my eyes." I tilt up her chin, her shy smile so fucking radiant I finally get why those Greeks fought for Helen of Troy.

In this moment, in our quiet bubble, all the heartache of the last few years is worth it. The divorce. The self-doubt. The loneliness. I'd do it again. Because it brought me to this place with this incredible girl.

I drag my lips against her shoulder. "I've heard sex can make you feel better. All those endorphins get released into your body."

She arches into me, pulling me closer. "Shark Week sex kinda grosses me out, but now that you're touching me, I'm really turned on."

A chuckle rumbles in my chest. *Shark Week.*

"So let me make you feel good." I suck on that tender spot on her neck, loving that I can feel her nipples harden through her thin tank top. "We don't have to be traditional about it. I can just get you off. Make you feel good."

"Mmm." Her eyes flutter closed, her minty breath on my lips. "Okay, but we both have to come."

No objections here.

With gentle movements, I kiss her lips, wanting her to feel how much she means to me. Wanting her to know how grateful I am to have her in my life. She's turned everything around. My outlook. My attitude. My expectations for my family.

When she opens to me on a pleasured sigh, I stroke her slick tongue with mine until her whole body relaxes against me.

"This is for you," I mumble against her swollen lips. "If you want me to stop at any point or you're not feeling well, just say the word. I'm not squeamish, so I don't want you to worry about that."

Her moan is my answer as I caress her breasts.

"These sore?" Luscious curves fill my hands, and I give them a careful squeeze.

Nodding, she gasps. "But that feels good. And, um... I just took a shower, so I'm, you know, clean."

Wouldn't really care one way or another, as long as she's comfortable. "You smell delicious, and I'm as hard as a lamp post"—which I underscore with a thrust between her legs—"but we can take another shower if things get messy."

Her lips twist, and I rub her lower lip with my thumb.

"I have a tampon in right now." The tension in her body ratchets up again, and she shakes her head. "Am I grossing you out? I am, aren't I?"

On a ranch, you grow up learning about reproduction at an early age. Even my brother, who has the maturity of a monkey at times, can handle the topic.

I chuckle, and rub out the knot in her shoulder, which makes her collapse against me with a pleasured sigh. "If a man can put his dick in a woman, he sure as hell should be able to talk about her cycle. And no, I'm not grossed out."

That seems to do the trick, and her lips tilt up. "You're one of a kind, you know that?" Her hand delves into my hair, and this time she kisses me back like her life depends on it, using her foot to pull my hips tighter to hers.

I roll her onto her back, my body cradled by her welcoming arms and legs. Our tongues tangle with that deliberate slide and thrust that mimic all the things I want to do to her tonight. Even if we have to modify it a bit so she's comfortable.

When her breath stutters and her chest heaves against me in a pant, I lick down the long column of her throat. Across her clavicle. Down the valley between her ample breasts.

With a few quick tugs, I remove her tank and my t-shirt and resume my exploration of her body. First with a few soft sucks of her tantalizing nipples, which makes her squirm breathlessly beneath me. Then with a tug of my teeth that lifts her hips off the bed.

Her skin smells like coconuts, the delicate scent that I've come to associate with Tori making me unbearably hard.

When I slip off her tiny sleep shorts, I do it slowly, so she can stop me if this is going too far, but she doesn't.

Tiny pink lace panties greet me, and her satiny skin peeks through, making my mouth water. But tonight requires patience, so even though I want to rip off the dainty fabric with a hard yank and a growl, I don't.

She reaches for the button on my jeans, and I watch her lick her lips as she releases my cock from the confines of my clothes.

But as she's reaching for me, I catch her wrist.

"Don't move," I instruct as I grab a dark towel from her bathroom and the lube I tossed in her nightstand last week. After I slide the towel beneath us and kick off my jeans and boxer briefs, I flip open the bottle and drizzle the clear liquid over my length before snapping it shut and tossing the container on the bed.

Eyes wide, pouty lips wet, she watches me palm my length and spread the lube. Squeezing from root to tip, I curve around the swollen head and back, the pace languid. Because it's for her.

A deep flush paints her cheeks and tints her plump, pert breasts. "You're making me crazy right now," she whispers before licking two fingers and dipping her hand into her panties.

A groan catches in my throat.

Is there anything hotter than watching a stunning woman touch herself? Fuck, no. And especially not my woman.

My cock swells in appreciation of the quick motion of her hand underneath the lace. Of the way her other hand pinches her nipple with a hard tweak. Of her ravenous stare.

"I could watch you do this all night." It's true. Tori's a vision. A goddamn goddess. Hair tangled around her, tits high and flushed, slender hips gyrating to a tempo I can feel, a heavy thumping bass that extends all the way down my hips.

With a squeeze to my balls, I edge back before I embarrass myself.

Her sultry voice zings through me. "Ethan, touch me."

She swallows when I caress her legs, from the back of her knee to where her thigh reaches her ass. My fingers dig into that sweet dip between the two until they meet in the middle and she's out of breath.

"Gonna take these off"—I finger the lace scrap adorning her pretty pussy—"and then you're gonna come."

She nods on a pant that has me palming myself again.

Her eyes are hazy with lust, but beneath the desire, beneath the craving, I see something I've never had in any other relationship. Absolute trust.

And it makes me fall that much harder for this girl.

Keeping my eyes pinned to hers, I guide her panties down until they're out of my way, and then I kneel between her open thighs. Pulling my length up, I let my cock slap against her swollen mound, and she gasps, arching toward me and telling me yes. My girl likes it rough sometimes, though tonight, I want to take it easy on her. Mostly.

With a leisurely thrust, I glide against her. Notching through her folds. Knocking the head of my cock against that sensitive nub.

Slow, I remind myself.

But then she parts herself so I can fit even closer, and my balls draw up tight.

"Goddamn, baby."

A gasp escapes her at the sensation, and she pulls her knees to her chest, the sight enough to send me right back to the edge again.

Really and truly, I want to thank Jesus right now for the honor of fucking this beautiful woman.

My thrusts make her tits bounce, delighting the caveman in me, who wants to carry her to my lair and fuck her into the next ice age.

Nearly mindless with desire, I squeeze her pussy lips that cradle me, tightening her around me, and when she gazes down at my slick crown parting her, that's all it takes for her to come with a muffled cry.

Head thrown back, body tight and arched, her body heaving, Tori's still shuddering when light dots my vision and that tidal wave of pleasure barrels through me.

My body quakes as I shoot my release on her stomach, the sensation so intense, I catch myself on one arm before I almost crush her.

So. Fucking. Good. How does it get better every time?

When I can finally breathe again, I laugh. "Sorry, sweetness. Didn't mean to make a mess on you."

She gives me a sleepy, sexy smile and yanks me closer. Guess we might need that shower after all.

43

TORI

For the record, Ethan was totally right about the endorphins. I feel freaking fabulous.

With a contented sigh, I push my nose into his neck, loving how he smells. I could stay in this bed with him for the next year if left to my own devices.

I've never even contemplated getting naked with a guy when Aunt Flo was visiting. Jamie wouldn't touch me with a ten-foot pole. I thought all men were like that. Even though, really, most of what Ethan and I did was in the shower, so there wasn't a mess. I'd never consider it unless I really trusted a guy, but Ethan makes me want to open up to him. I mean, I'd have to trust him to let him run the red light.

His palm brushes over my stomach, an area I'm less than pleased with this time of the month, but given how we just jumped each other in the shower, I'm too boneless and hopped up on sex to care.

"What time do you need to get up in the morning?" My voice is hoarse from sex. For real, that's a thing I never really got until this summer. Thank God I don't share a bedroom wall with the kids.

"Around four thirty."

With a strained effort, I crack open my eyes to check the clock on my nightstand. "It's almost midnight. Don't you need more sleep?" The man has to be exhausted. I don't know where he gets his stamina.

"Gonna be too hot this week to work in the afternoons, so I'll need to get more done at night. The upshot is maybe I can grab a nap during the day."

"Let me know what you need me to do, how I can help you."

"You do enough, baby."

Rolling over to use him as a body pillow, I toss my leg over his. We're both wearing underwear, but our chests are skin to skin, and he's so warm, I wanna purr.

"Don't tell anyone, but I'll be your sex slave," I admit. "It's a rough job, but someone has to do it."

The rumble of laughter in his chest makes me smile. "I happen to have an opening."

"Lucky me."

He kisses the top of my head. "I'd say lucky me."

We lie in silence, the moon casting long shadows through the curtains at the edge of my room.

Drawing circles on his chest, I let out a sigh of relief for how today went. "I'm so glad the judge approved your proposal."

"God, me too. The guy who provides the livestock is on board, and we've worked out that contract. I just hope negotiations with Allison go as smoothly. We spent a lot of time arguing last year, but I thought things were beginning to chill out."

Hmm. I have a theory.

"I'm sure her finding us half-naked in the back of your truck didn't help much."

He heaves a frustrated sigh. "You're probably right."

"Sometimes it's hard for people to move on." I think back to Vivian's situation with her ex David, whom she tossed away like a used tissue. When we spoke earlier today, though, you'd think he was the love of her life.

"The only thing I'm concerned about is Allison's willingness to be a silent partner. She's never taken an interest in the horses or the business, so that bodes well for us, but having an ex as a partner is not ideal. Logan just wants me to compete again, and he's willing to do anything to make that happen, even put up with her."

My hand stills on his chest. Yeah, when I came up with the brilliant plan, I wasn't really thinking about how that would connect Ethan to Allison even more long-term. This is why I should stick to things like cooking and crafts and bartending.

But I don't want to compound Ethan's worry. "Maybe you guys need time for the dust to settle."

"I hope so, babe." Turning me in his arms, he lets out a laugh. "I feel like you know my dirty laundry. Please tell me you have a crazy ex story too."

That's one topic I haven't shared this summer, but it's probably not fair that I know so much about his life, and he doesn't know this huge thing that happened to me last year.

"I do. In fact, I could probably top your crazy."

"Really?"

"Oh, yeah." I nibble on my lip, hating this subject but wanting to have this conversation out of the way. "I dated someone my last year at UT. I guess I thought we were getting serious only to find out the guy lied the entire time we dated. Pretended to be devoted. Pretended he cared. Made all kinds of promises. Until the day I found out the bastard was married."

"Are you fucking serious?" Ethan's whole body stiffens, and he shifts us so he can see my face. "What happened? Please tell me his wife caught his sorry ass."

Shame washes over me, and I sit up, pulling the sheet up and tucking it around me. "Not exactly." Part of me hates that I never ratted him out to his wife.

Leaning up, he pulls me to his chest. "I'm so sorry he hurt you, baby."

"That was the reason I didn't want to work for you. After Jamie, I didn't date anyone for over a year, until I moved in with you. I felt like I couldn't trust my judgment anymore because he had me so fooled. When I interviewed with you, I think I was such a bitch that day because you scared me."

"I scared you?"

I nod, glad he can't see the heat traveling up my face. "There you were, this really handsome, intense guy." Closing my eyes, I can see him that day. The way those stormy blue eyes pierced through me. The way our chemistry pulsed in the air like a live current. "You were dripping wet from washing off in the kitchen sink, flashing those abs and tattoos. A girl would have to be dead, dumb, or decapitated not to be attracted to you."

His quiet chuckle makes me shift around to face him.

"You think this is funny? That I thought you were so hot, I

probably subconsciously sabotaged the interview because I didn't want to work for someone I was into? That, deep down, I *liked* the fact that you were pissed off that day? That I couldn't decide if I wanted to slap you silly or ride you next to your commercial range oven?"

He groans. "Option number two, please."

"Shut up. You made me break my man diet." I laugh and smack his arm, but he catches my wrist and pulls me down until I'm resting on his chest. "Do I win? Does my ex's crazy trump Allison's?"

"You definitely win."

The way he kisses me makes me grateful I couldn't stay away from him.

Maybe the worst is behind me and the best is yet to come. If Ethan is a part of my life, I'm becoming more optimistic about those odds.

44

TORI

I'm folding a green jumper embroidered with tiny frogs when my Aunt Imelda sits primly next to me and folds her hands.

"Isn't this a lovely shower?" she asks, her intention as obvious as the gun-toting, hooded thief who screams, *This is a robbery!*

"Yes, *tía*. It's perfect." No dildo cakes. No mis-gifted sex toys. No embarrassing games. My mother must be delighted. Although... my cousin Natalia melted chocolate candies in diapers and made everyone sniff them to guess the candy. That's gross, right?

Forcing myself to smile, I try to be grateful. *My sister got a beautiful shower. She was happy, and that's all that matters. I won't retaliate with laundry hijinks.*

My feelings are still a wee bit hurt, but I'm an adult. I can be mature. Isn't this what people call a "learning experience"? And today, I've learned you have to get to the front of the line for the cake because that shit goes fast.

Aunt Imelda elbows me while her unibrow wiggles like an angry caterpillar. "So when are you going to settle down and marry a good man? You're not getting any younger." She points to the corners of my eyes like I'm an old hag.

Jeeesus. "As soon as I pay off my attorney bill from that time I almost got a felony."

My mom chokes on her sparkling soda.

What? If I give Imelda a civilized answer, I'm giving her positive reinforcement to be an asshole.

I don't think my mom hears my internal dialogue because she gives me scary eyes, the ones that make me grateful I'm out of reach.

Ugh, I need to get out of here. I always revert to a teenager when I'm around my family.

Of course, it takes ten years to clean up after the party —*thanks, cuz, for not helping with that*—hug everyone, and trudge to my car.

By the time I reach Ethan's gravel driveway, I'm in desperate need of an alcoholic beverage, preferably something so strong you can light it on fire, especially when I see Allison's sleek black Lexus parked in front of the house.

Motherfuckity.

I consider backing out, but she's standing on the porch with Ethan and the kids, and they see me.

When I catch the time on the dashboard clock, I let out a curse. Why didn't I realize I might run into her? It's Sunday evening, the time I usually hide from the harpy.

When they shift around, probably as bewildered why I'm showing up now as I am, I'm startled by how much they look like a family. All beautiful and tan with dirty-blonde hair and big, blue eyes, the kind of perfect people you see glossing the covers of magazines in the grocery store.

Reluctantly, I park my junker next to her import, and it rushes through me—how much I hate this comparison. I'll never be Allison with her designer clothes and French manicures. I know Ethan doesn't care about that stuff, but it's hard to feel confident next to someone who looks like his ex does.

With a quick glance in the rearview mirror to make sure I don't have raccoon eyes, I smooth down my sundress and slide out of the car. *Hey,* I tell myself. *At least this time I'm wearing underwear, and I'm not half-naked and hungover in the back of Ethan's truck.*

Ah, gallows humor.

Ethan's attention zeroes in on me like a shaft of sunlight. His eyes connect with mine, travel down my dress, pausing on my cleavage, dip down to my legs, and make a slow lift back to my face. I can't help but smile at him.

"Hey, guys."

The kids immediately grab my legs and try to scale me like a mountain.

Allison huffs, ignoring me altogether. "Can I invite my parents or not?"

Ethan shifts awkwardly, running a hand over his scruffy chin. "Didn't think y'all would want to come, honestly."

Her chest heaves. "You thought I'd miss my own kid's birthday party?"

"I thought you'd do something for Cody with your family." His voice is calm despite the hellishly awkward vibe in the air.

"That's stupid, Ethan. I should bring my parents here for your party. There's no point in doing separate events for a two-year-old who won't even remember it. They could use something cheerful since my grandfather just passed. "

Her shrill voice makes Mila's bottom lip tremble.

I hate interjecting, but Mila's two seconds from crying, and if she cries, Cody might join her, especially since he's tired and rubbing his eyes. "Can I take the kids inside?"

"No. You cannot take *my* kids inside," Allison barks.

Ethan places a gentle hand on my shoulder. "Actually, hon, do me a favor and take the kids to the diner for some ice cream." He pulls out his wallet and hands me a twenty-dollar bill.

It's obvious he doesn't want Mila and Cody to witness the showdown happening here. I've already told Ethan I'm not comfortable driving his truck, but this is probably his way of not contradicting Allison while still protecting the children. *He's such a good guy. He tries so hard.* I barely refrain from shooting Allison a dirty look. *How could she not want this man?*

"I don't have car seats in my—" I motion toward my rust heap, and I swear Allison's eye twitches.

"Take the truck." He's reaching for his keys, and I'm shaking my head no, and Mila's yanking on my dress.

No, no, no. I can't explain *why* I shouldn't drive them in front of Allison, not when she's looking at me like I might infect her with the plague.

But Ethan opens my palm and makes me take the keys. "Please."

One word.

That's all he has to say for my resolve to wane, but I have a sinking suspicion his conversation with Allison was going fine until I showed up, so I want to help him however I can.

"Sure. Yeah."

I just hope he's not upset with me when I tell him I can't keep doing this.

~

Forty-five minutes later, Logan strolls through the door of the Lone Star, pausing briefly to flirt with one of the waitresses, before sliding into our booth. Cody is asleep in my arms, his ice cream melted into a puddle in his bowl, and Mila clings to my other side, stressed out from watching her parents argue.

"Hey, little darlins," Logan drawls.

I'm too tired to do more than lift my hand.

I don't ask why he's here and Ethan's not, but something about that pisses me off more than being in the middle of everything. But damn it, it hurts to hear Mila cry over her parents and how she's worried they're mad at her. Just thinking about it makes my eyes sting and my belly burn with frustration.

I want to protect these kids, but they're not mine to protect. I want to protect Ethan, but sometimes he doesn't feel like he's mine either. Like on that porch earlier this evening, I had zero control about anything.

And really, who am I to have any say here? I'm the nanny. Not their mom.

Logan taps a finger on his cell. "Heard you guys had a rough time at the ranch. I'm supposed to bring you home as soon as I get a text."

The meaning is clear. When Allison is gone, we can return.

She's still there? Jealousy tears through me at the thought of her being alone with Ethan.

Get used to it, genius. You did suggest they remain a team for the sake of the ranch. Plus, it was her house first.

Fuck me sideways, this sucks.

My emotions must be clear as day because Logan gives me a sympathetic smile. I hate that look. I know it well. It's the one all my friends gave me when they found out I'd been unknowingly dating a married man. "This will all work out. I know my brother."

I nod, fear making me wonder, *Work out for whom?*

His phone vibrates, and he smiles as if this is proof of our impending happiness.

But I have a bad feeling about this. All of this.

Logan scoops up Cody, and I help him get the kids situated in his truck before I follow them back to the ranch.

The familiar sounds of baseball make me smile when we walk through the front door, but my sprig of optimism is quickly dashed.

Ethan is sound asleep on the couch. In front of him is an open bottle of wine and two glasses.

Ethan drinks beer.

I look at Logan, but he just shrugs and helps me carry the kids to bed. He does me a favor and doesn't try to bullshit me and try to make me feel better, and I don't bother to pretend I'm in a good mood.

When the kids are asleep, I go to my room and close my door, hoping to have some perspective in the morning. Because right now, I don't have a good perspective. Not at all.

45

ETHAN

A HARD KICK TO MY LEG JARS ME AWAKE.

"What the fuck?" I snarl at my brother, who's hovering over me with an eat-shit-and-die expression.

My heart races from the shock to my system, and I realize I've been dozing in the living room. The game is over, and it's dark outside. Shit.

"How long have I been out?" My throat feels like a dusty Texas road after a heat wave. Rubbing the sleep out of my eyes, I try to shake myself out of this lethargy.

"Long enough."

"Where are the kids?"

"In bed asleep."

Like the slow flicker of a movie reel through a camera, I remember what happened earlier. The scene on the porch. The look on Mila's face as she watched me argue with her mother. Tori's imploring expression when I sent her away. All the arguing. "Fuck."

"Fuck is right, asshole. What happened here?" He points to the half-empty wine glasses.

The mess in front of me looks like something I need to clean up, but that can't be what has his panties in a twist.

"Why are you looking at me like that?" His glare, the kind reserved for men who beat their wives and other scum of the earth, prickles my skin. "I tried to talk Allison off the ledge."

"With wine?" He paces in front of me. "And candles?"

What the fuck is he talking about? "Christ, it's not what you think. I asked her what she wanted to drink, and she helped herself to shit in the kitchen. It's her wine. She bought it and left it here. What's weird about it? And those candles were there before." Weren't they? It's not like we lit them.

"Wow, and everyone thinks you're the smart one," he mutters. Crossing his arms, he leans back against the fireplace.

"What are we even talking about right now? You're mad because I let Allison drink her own wine?"

"No, asshole. I'm not. I could care less if Allison drank every fucking bottle in the house, but did you bother to consider how this"—he swirls a finger at the stemware on the coffee table—"might appear to your current girlfriend? The one who looked like someone'd kicked her puppy when I found her comforting your children at the diner?"

My gut reaction is to scoff. Surely Tori knows my heart by now. That I would never hurt her or cheat on her. Much less with my ex. That's a one-way trip to the loony bin. I've never cheated on anyone and don't plan to tarnish that track record. Only lowlifes cheat on their women.

But judging by the seriousness in Logan's tone—and, let's face it, my brother is rarely serious except when he's about to level me with something I genuinely need to know—I shouldn't dismiss his concerns.

"Are Mila and Cody okay?" I rasp, finding it hard to say the words with the giant knot in my throat. I want to ask about Tori too, but one thing at a time.

"I think so. Mila looked a little worse for wear, but she knocked out as soon as we got home. Cody fell asleep in Tori's arms at the restaurant." The flare of his nostrils tells me what he's gonna say before he says it. "You shoulda been the one to go to the diner."

Nodding, I close my eyes. *I know.* For my kids. For Tori.

"Did Tori say something?" A whole host of things come to mind, most of which I probably deserve for not taking her feelings into consideration before shoving my keys in her face and making her take the kids.

"Nope. Not a word. Just...silence."

Damn. That's not good. Tori's not one to hide her feelings.

Logan lifts his brow. "I wasn't the one she wanted to see tonight. Shoulda been you."

The more he says that, the more frustrated I grow.

He sits next to me, the weight of everything suddenly suffocating. Doesn't he know I'm doing my best? The divorce, the bills, children who need love and attention constantly, Allison's demands, the horses in my stable, my employees. It feels like I'm juggling fifty balls at once and about to drop the one thing that makes them all collapse to the ground.

I don't know what to say except to start at the beginning where all this started.

Resting my elbows on my knees, I run my hands through my hair, feeling more exhausted than before I fell asleep. "Allison was dropping off the kids. She brought up Cody's birthday and how she wanted to bring her parents and some friends to the party."

"How did she know about it?" He rubs his chin.

"My guess is Mila spilled the beans."

He laughs. "That kid."

We've done this before. Back when Dad died. I sat in this here spot and poured my heart out to my brother, who was only a teenager at the time. Told him my girlfriend was pregnant, and I didn't know which way was up or down. Wasn't sure what I should do.

The house was a lot smaller then. Logan's the one who suggested adding on the extra rooms, so Mom could stay here and help with the baby when she arrived, which would've been great except Allison never did get along with my mother.

He sinks back into the couch and kicks one ankle over the other. "So Allison decided to invite herself? Did she even give a shit about the kids' birthdays last year?"

I shake my head, but he already knows that answer. "We were disagreeing, but it wasn't contentious. Well, until..." I don't want to say it.

"Until Tori showed up?" he adds helpfully. "And now Allison wants to come to the shindig Tori's planning for our family? *Fuck.*"

"What do I do? I can't tell Tori she can't come to the party. I want her there. She's important to me. But I can't exactly tell Allison she's not invited. Not when we're in the middle of negotiating that contract."

His head dips back to the back of the couch with a groan. "You sure know how to get yourself in a mess. See, this is why bachelor life is great. Wanna bang a hot new chick? No prob.

Wanna fuck two cocktail waitresses at the same time? Someone hand me the lube. But this?" He shivers dramatically. "This I can't handle. I know I said I was on board with the co-op and having silent investors, but the operative word there is *silent*."

"Look at you with the big words."

He socks me in the shoulder. "I'm just saying, are you sure you want to be tied to Allison for another four or five years? Because if we do this deal, you're on the hook. We both are."

Frustration, hot and fierce, fires up in my gut. "What am I supposed to do? Refinance the ranch again? Leave Mom nothing for retirement? She doesn't even have Dad's life insurance because those bastards never paid out." The damn life insurance company argued that he had a preexisting health condition he failed to disclose and denied Mom's claim.

Blowing out a breath, I break it down for Logan. "You heard our attorney as plainly as I did. People in our situation can either refinance to pay off the other spouse or sell assets." I spread my arms. "Which assets you wanna sell? Your house? Some farmland, which ain't worth shit except for our houses and barns? The horses, which is where we get our income from? Please spell it out for me."

The pained groan that rumbles out of him tells me he's as worked up as I am, and for a minute, we sit there, silent, muddling through our thoughts, with the recap of the Astros game on in the background.

Shifting on the couch, I try to explain it better. "All I did tonight was talk some sense into Allison. Sat her down, let her relax with a glass of wine, so she'd stop yappin', and made sure she understood that our disagreements over shit had better start and stop with the kids. That if we sign the co-op contract, she's a silent partner when it comes to the business." With a palm over my mouth, I mumble the rest. "I might've offered a bigger percentage for her to promise she wouldn't contest custody of the kids."

I cringe, knowing my brother might be pissed, but when we make eye contact, all I see is acceptance.

"Mila and Cody are yours, and I'll go down fighting to make sure it stays that way. Hate that she's getting more outta this deal, but I can't say I blame you for trying. If those kids were mine, I'd do the same thing."

I'm so relieved, I could cry. Instead, I squeeze his arm. "Thanks for having my back, brother."

He ruffles my hair like I'm a kid. "Always. Now go explain this shit to Tori. Make sure she gets where you're coming from and doesn't think you were wining and dining your ex-wife."

My attention returns to glasses in front of me. To the red lipstick on the stemware. To the half-empty bottle of Pinot.

Goddamn it.

I have to believe she knows me better than that.

The hard thud of my heart in my chest is all I hear as I tap on Tori's bedroom door, but there's no answer. With a twist of the handle, it opens, and I'm relieved, so fucking relieved, she didn't lock me out.

"Tor?" Her petite outline curled up on the bed sends a bittersweet ache through me.

What would she and I be like without all the drama? If we were just two singles in Austin bumping into each other on a Friday evening over drinks in a bar? I'd ask her out in a second. I'd spare no expense to make her feel special.

Instead, tonight, I asked her to whisk away the kids while I dealt with my ex-wife.

How long will Tori deal with that kind of baggage? In my head, I consider all the reasons this would've been easier if we hadn't gotten involved. If we'd kept things professional. Because the boss in me feels like I'm taking advantage of her by asking her to do me personal favors, like watch my kids on a Sunday night.

But the boyfriend in me? Yeah, he's grateful as hell to be able to trust her with my children. To know when they're in her care, I don't have to worry like I would with a stranger. Save for my brother and Mom, there's no one who adores Mila and Cody more.

Does she have any idea how much she means to me? How grateful I've been for our friendship and all the nights she's let me wrap myself around her in bed?

I toss my t-shirt and jeans on the ground next to the bed and crawl in behind her.

Her breathing is slow and deep, and though I'm relieved we don't have to talk about all the shit that went down tonight because I'm beat, I hate letting unresolved issues linger. I did that with Allison, allowed too many unspoken things go, and I don't want to make that mistake again.

"Baby," I whisper as I hug her to me.

She's not a terribly deep sleeper, but tonight she's out. I almost forgot she had her sister's shower today. Tori must be worn out.

And when she got home, you made her babysit. Nice job, asshole.

Wishing I could wake her and apologize, tell her how sorry I am to put her in that position, I settle for whispering it to her and hoping we get time tomorrow to have this conversation face to face.

If tonight has clarified anything for me, it's that I can't do this—life, the ranch, the business—without her help.

But more than that, I don't want to do it without her.

46

TORI

THE INGREDIENTS SEEM TO WEIGH A MILLION POUNDS AS I MIX in the mayo for a new potato salad recipe I'm testing for Cody's birthday party next week. My mind snags on Logan and Ethan's argument last night, their voices animated enough to swell through my closed bedroom door as I was dozing off, drained from my sister's shower and the Allison drama.

Was it arguing?

All I remember is Ethan saying, "It's not what you think."

Those words send chills down my arms.

Because cheaters say those kind of things, my heart warns.

No. No, *tontita.*

Ethan is not Jamie. It's a mantra I've reminded myself of all summer. Just because Ethan and Allison talked over a glass of wine does *not* mean anything happened. Rationally, I understand this. Rationally, I don't have a problem with the two of them needing to calm down to discuss the plan for Cody's birthday.

But Loony Tunes Tori? The one who fails out of school when she's too depressed to get out of bed and attend class when her boyfriend cheated on her with his *wife*? Yeah, she needs help stepping away from the ledge. Because she's screaming I'm being naive.

My stomach knots at the thought that I might come out the loser again.

Maybe I should take a step back. Maybe Ethan isn't ready for more. Maybe the kids need time to adjust to everything that happened this summer.

Basically everything Ethan told me after Allison found us that Sunday morning in the back of his truck comes rushing back to me like a dark tide after a storm.

I cannot believe I fell asleep before I could talk to him last night.

With a wipe of my elbow across my clammy forehead, I sigh and taste the mixture before reaching for the mustard.

Sometimes I wonder if I should've confronted Jamie about what he did last year instead of shutting him out. Sure, I slashed his tires like a fucking psycho, and that felt amazing in the moment, but it didn't do anything to help me deal with the emotional turmoil he'd unleashed on my life. Never mind that it was stupid as hell. What if he'd called the cops? It's not like I can afford to get in trouble again.

Between my sister not wanting me to plan her baby shower and Ethan's cozy chat with Allison, that kernel of worry snowballs, making me question if this is the right place for me.

Maybe I should be trying to carve out my own life in Austin after all. Ethan and I could take things slow and see each other when Allison has the kids. I've never done slow in my life, as my driving record indicates, but if that's what this family needs to move forward, I'm willing to take a step back.

My hands drop to my sides, mashed potatoes sliding off the wooden spoon and landing on the floor with a wet plop.

It would break my heart to leave the ranch. Already, I feel the cracks forming at the thought, like fissures of ice on the sidewalk when it freezes, making it hard to breathe. I've been so intimate with Ethan, opened up to him in ways I've never opened up to any man before, but can I really afford to go any further if I'm some kind of rebound from Allison?

I look up at the ceiling and blink away the heat building in my eyes.

Please, Ethan. Please don't jerk me around.

When I woke up this morning, I could've sworn I was going to roll over and find Ethan, but the sun was up, which meant he was already in the barn, and I couldn't figure out if I'd only dreamt him wrapping his arms around me last night or if we'd really slept in the same bed.

The kids' voices bring me back to the present where they're sitting at the kitchen table with a million crayons, coloring Paw Patrol images I printed off the internet. Back to apple slices and story time and dress-up—simple things that bring so much joy to my life.

No more crazy, I decide, mentally boxing up all of this emotional crap until I can deal with it later. Because I have a job to do. I can't very well take care of these children if I'm an emotional wreck, and they deserve my best. But more than any job or expectation, I love Mila and Cody, and I always want to be in the moment with them instead of staring off into space like a lunatic.

I clear my throat and try to sniffle quietly.

Their jubilant laughter makes me break out into a watery smile. They're such a bright spot, always cheerful and loving and sweet. Truly, no one deserves happiness more than my tiny tikes.

I turn around and... *Oh, holy shit.*

Sputtering, I'm caught with my mouth hanging open at the sight before me—Cody's head coated in butter, his mischievous eyes peeking up at me through the pale yellow slime.

The condiment tub, gaping and empty, sits on the floor. Next to it, Cody-sized hand prints decorate the hardwood floor like an art exhibit gone wrong.

What just happened?

He giggles. "Rawr! Scawwwwwwyyyyy!" Waving his hands, he grins up at me.

Mila shields her smile with her hand like she's embarrassed. "He's a ghost. For Halloween."

Internally, I'm yelling at myself for not paying better attention.

Because like everything else, this is my fault too.

47

ETHAN

With a haughty flick of her wrist, Mallory Mathers shoves a lock of red hair over her shoulder. All the better to glare at me.

I glare back. "You need to lean back more. If you're sitting up that high in the saddle, your ass is gonna go flying off that new filly of yours faster than you can blink."

"Maybe we should call it a day."

"It's your dollar. You wanna quit twenty minutes early, be my guest." I'm in a foul mood, and Mallory's piss-poor attitude is gnawing on my last nerve. All I want to do is head into the house, hug my kids and kiss my girlfriend. Make sure they're okay after last night. But no. I'm sweating my balls off while I deal with this spoiled princess.

Mallory's eyes narrow like she's mentally murdering me, and I force a smile. No sense in actually being murdered. "Cool off your horse. You know the routine. And put your saddle in the right place this time."

Last week, she left it in the stall instead of in the tack room. Almost had a hemorrhage when I saw the damn thing. She's off her rocker if she thinks I'm gonna clean up after her again.

It's barely ten a.m., but the heat is unforgiving. Sweat barrels down me like I just hopped out of the shower. As soon as my client is gone, I can take a break. I'm gonna have to or I might pass out.

I glance at the clock on the back wall. Where the hell is Logan? He was supposed to be here hours ago.

Trudging toward the giant sink in the grooming stable, I swivel on the cold water and wash my face. The water is tepid at best, but I'll take anything right now.

I'm wiping the salt out of my eyes when her voice makes me turn.

"I won't be in next week since I'm headed to the Bahamas for a few days, but I'll be back for the party."

"What party?" I tilt my head. Surely, she can't mean...

"Your son's birthday." She looks at me like I'm an idiot. "Allison called me about it yesterday. You really should give people more notice."

Let me get this straight. My ex-wife invited my client to Cody's birthday party? Before she even talked to me? What the fresh hell?

As soon as Mallory's gone, I stomp toward the house, needing to sit down for this conversation I plan to have with Allison. She is out of her goddamn mind.

I'm kicking off my filthy boots and hopping on one foot when I catch a glimpse in the kitchen where all hell has broken loose.

Cody is covered in... *butter*? And Mila is sliding and

twirling on the mess like a nutty ballerina. They're both giggling uncontrollably.

Where's Tori?

Stepping closer, I finally let out a sigh of relief when I spot her bent over—face down, ass up—reaching for something that must've rolled under the stove.

The corner of my mouth lifts. *That is a beautiful ass.*

A chuckle escapes me at the insanity in this kitchen. The kids spot me and run full-out, laughing and sliding toward me.

"Whoa, there." Jesus, I sound like I'm talking to one of my horses.

They ignore me and go crashing into my legs. We end up in a buttery pile on the floor.

Holy crap, that hurt.

"I can explain!" Tori shouts as she shuffles toward us.

"Watch out." From this angle, it's easy to see the oil slick on the floor that my kids dragged along the wood.

It happens in slow motion, Tori wiping out. Arms windmilling. Legs flying out from under her. The yelp she cries before she hits the ground.

I feel helpless under a pile of sticky children. *Shit.*

"Babe, you okay?" I grunt as I slowly peel Mila and Cody off me.

Tori moans, slowly reaching around to rub her elbow, then her ass. Speaking of ass, mine hurts like the dickens. That floor is harder than it looks.

I'm limping toward her when the front door closes and my brother's voice rings out. "Holy shit. What happened here?"

But it's the gasp that follows that has me looking up.

"Good lord, boy. I didn't raise y'all in a barn." My mother chuckles at her joke.

"GRANDMA!" my kids shout and scramble toward her, but I snag the backs of their t-shirts, stopping them in their buttery tracks.

"Nope. Bath time first. Then you two miscreants can hug your grandma."

My mother looks tickled to find her brood in such a disarray. "Need some help?"

I blow out a breath and send up a prayer of thanks. "You have no idea."

48

TORI

IT COMES AT THE PERFECT TIME.

I stare at the text message, wondering if I've somehow willed it into existence.

Kat: *Can you help me this week? Please? I'm desperate. I'm behind on a ton of orders, but I'm too big and too tired to do this on my own. I'll owe you!*

When I don't respond because I'm too busy re-reading the message, another one pops up.

Kat: *Want my truck? You can have it.*

She must really need my help.

Kat: *Stay with me. Maybe a week or two? I'll pay you! More than the sisterly wage of love and tacos.*

I chuckle. She knows I'd do anything for her for free.

A wave of relief settles over me. At least this way I can leave on my own terms instead of having Ethan let me go.

But when I tell him my plan, he looks confused.

He's paying bills in his office, and I'm sitting in front of him. It's a very boss-employee moment, which is weird since we haven't had this kind of vibe since he peeled off my panties in the back of his truck.

His eyebrows pull together. "What are you talking about? Don't you wanna stay?" A hurt expression flashes on his face, but then it's gone. Did I imagine it?

I nod. "Of course I want to stay, but where do you suggest I bunk? With your mom?"

We were all surprised Beverly returned early, but she was homesick. She's staying here for now because Logan needs "a few days to clean his house," which probably means he needs to clear out ten million pizza boxes and trash cans full of condoms. Gross.

Ethan has a spacious house, but it has limitations. Where's Beverly supposed to sleep? With Mila, the human octopus? Beverly should have my room. I could sleep on the couch or on the floor in the sewing room, but I can't bring myself to suggest it.

The idea of sleeping on the floor reeks of desperation, and that embarrasses me. Nothing used to embarrass me, but I'm starting to think it's because I didn't know better.

In any case, I'm not shacking up with Ethan while his mom is here.

He doesn't say anything, and I shift in my seat.

"Look, Ethan, I know you can't afford me, and since your mom is home, I figured you'd want to save the money."

When I was in here cleaning his office, I caught a glimpse of his bank statements and bills, including the one from his attorney, which almost made me lose my lunch. No wonder the man is stressed out. I may not have much to my name, but I don't have nearly the overhead that he does.

He motions behind me. "Close the door and come here."

My eyes widen. "What?"

"You heard me."

It takes a second to un-freeze, and I make sure the hallway is empty before I close the door. As I stride toward him, I shake my head. "I'm not having sex with you when your mom in the other room."

That's another reason I need to go. I can see it now, Ethan sneaking into my room, his mother hearing us, me dying of embarrassment. I want his mom to like me, and she won't if she hears me riding her son into oblivion. It's a small miracle we haven't traumatized the kids with our nighttime activities.

But when I reach his side of the desk, he tugs me into his lap and gives me a slow, sweet kiss. "Don't want you to go."

His voice makes me shiver. It's almost enough to over-shadow the throb on my hip from the giant bruise I got this morning when I wiped out on the butter.

I almost say it. Almost tell him I love him. It's right there on my lips, but something holds me back.

Ask me to stay.

I run my finger along the A&M logo on his t-shirt. "I don't want to go either, but I think the writing's on the wall." My eyes sting, the reality of what I'm doing hitting sharp and deep, like I've impaled myself, but the momentum is gaining ground, and I can't stop.

"Kat needs help, and you don't," I choke out. Doesn't he see I'm obviously sucking at my job? First Mila burns her hand, and then the kids run wild with the butter, right under my nose? What if something worse had happened? I wouldn't be able to live with myself if the kids got hurt because I was distracted.

In the silence, I start to chicken out when the reality of what I'm doing sinks in. Because I don't want to go. If I give him space, will Allison dig her claws deeper? Will that client he had this morning get a shot with him? Will he question why he's with me?

My heart is pounding. Can he feel it? I swallow and wait for him to say something.

Tell me to stay.

As your girlfriend, not as an employee.

Tell me you love me.

He doesn't.

A big, calloused hand cups my face. "Is this about last night?" He sighs. "I wanted to talk about that. I..."

Driving up to the ranch while he and Allison argued on the porch feels like a lifetime ago.

I shake my head. "No." I sniffle. "Not really." Though it is about how he probably needs time to figure out what he wants. It might not be me.

Don't fucking cry, Tori.

In the hallway, the thump of children's feet tells me we're out of time.

"You're still my girl, right?" He tilts my chin up, so I have to look at him.

Even through my tears, his stormy blue eyes captivate me. "Yeah."

A question wells up in my heart: *But are you still my guy?*

A mockingbird tweets cheerfully in the tree outside Kat's

kitchen. The sun shines bright and high in the sky. Everything belies the misery in my bones. It should be raining and gray and cold like my sad little soul.

My sister side-eyes me again. "Are you sure you're okay? It's been days, and you've barely said a word. Are you mad at me?"

"No, of course I'm not mad at you. Stop talking to me or I'll screw up your recipe." Food is forgiving. Her bath and body supplies? Not so much.

I'm making a batch of bath salts for her lavender company, and I always misread the ingredients when she's talking to me. It's the reason I didn't ask her to hire me instead of working for Ethan earlier this summer. I screwed up a huge order for her last year, and it was an expensive mistake. Really, I shouldn't be measuring anything when my head is such a mess, but I can't let my pregnant sister do this herself. I'm sure Brady could manage, but he has one more week at the tattoo parlor before he takes off on maternity leave. What's it called for dudes? Paternity leave?

My sister tugs on my shirt. "Come on, *manita*. Please talk to me. I know something is wrong. You haven't tried to embarrass me all week."

"Oh, my God. Fine. I miss Ethan and the kids."

She tugs a lock of hair. "I'm surprised you haven't gone over to see them."

I would've, had he asked me.

But I don't say that.

Clearing my throat, I shrug. "We've texted a bit. Had two awkward phone calls. He's up early and exhausted by the time he's ready to crash. Not super-conducive to being chatty on the phone."

My big plan to keep this relationship going while I'm back in Austin is slowly withering away. Ethan's not big on the phone. He's clearly not comfortable texting. Those are required criteria for living in different towns, even though they're not terribly far apart.

The whole thing makes me irritable. I'm trying to be optimistic. He called *me*. Twice. He says he misses me. That's something. But I won't bang down his door while he has so much going on.

I have one small bright spot. He said once we wrap up the party, he wants to take me out on that date.

Hopefully we'll be able to talk for real. To find some time to connect. Because right now, he feels like a stranger.

But first I have to get through the party with Allison and her friends.

Kat wipes the counter. "You still doing the food for Cody's birthday?"

"Yup." Beverly gave me the head count yesterday, and I almost choked on my spit. Sixty-five people and rising. *Thank you for inviting the entire county, Allison.* "Bev said I could hire a caterer, to save the bill, and they'd reimburse me."

"That's a relief."

I roll my eyes. "Ethan can't afford a caterer. Except for the cake, I'm going to make everything." She gasps, and I look at her sharply. "You think I can't pull it off?"

"No, of course you can. It's just a lot of work."

"Newsflash. I'm a hard worker." I might mess up once in a while, but I always give my whole heart. This way, Ethan only has to pay for the ingredients.

"Of course you are. I'm not suggesting you're not."

"I'll keep it simple."

I have to pray I don't screw up for once and hope that Allison and I can stay out of each other's way at the party.

I might need a miracle.

49

ETHAN

"You need help bringing everything over?" With one shoulder, I hold the phone to my ear while I button my jeans.

Tori pauses on the other end. "I can manage, but thanks."

"I can't believe you made all that food. You're a stubborn woman, you know that?" She laughs, and it sounds so goddamn good. It makes me realize I don't know the last time I heard her laugh, and that's wrong.

"I've been told that once or twice," she says softly.

"Listen, I know you were trying to save me some money, which I appreciate, but I want to pay you for the time you spent cooking. I'm sure you've busted your ass on this like you do with everything, so I'm not taking no for an answer."

"I wasn't doing this because I wanted to get paid, Ethan."

I smile at the fierceness in her voice. My girl is balls to the wall. Love that about her. "Darlin', I didn't say you were."

She huffs. "I'm doing this because—"

"Because you're awesome and you love Cody. I get it. I'm still paying you." She might be my girlfriend, but there's no way I'm gonna take advantage of her time or good intentions. "Now get your ass over here. I fucking miss you."

Can't believe I haven't seen her in almost two weeks. This shit ends now. I'd gotten the impression she wanted space, that maybe the kids and I had overwhelmed her. After Cody took a bath in butter, Tori looked like she'd had enough of our antics and needed a break. God knows my children and I are a handful, but time's up. She's mine, and she belongs here with me.

If she'll have me.

～

The sound of tires along the gravel in front of my house is music to my ears. Peeking out the front blinds, I spot Tori hopping out of Kat's truck.

So she'll drive her sister's truck but doesn't wanna drive mine? What's that about?

"Logan," I call out. "Keep an eye on the kids. Gonna help Tori unload."

That's a mistake because they hear me.

My two daredevils come tearing down the hall screaming my girlfriend's name, and I smile. They miss her too.

I was hoping to have a minute with Tori to kiss her until she begged to stay tonight. I'll have to drag her away during the party at some point to make that happen.

"All right." I open the front door and hoist my son into my arms. "C'mere, bud." He's too excited. With my luck, he'll take a tumble and land face first. That's no way to start a birthday party.

Tori is a vision in jeans and a white tank. Hair blowing in the wind. All that beautiful golden skin. And fuck me, that smile.

"Hey, babe." I kiss her forehead, and she grins up at me while hugging my daughter, who's attached herself to Tori's leg. "We've missed you around here."

"Yeah?" Her eyes widen. The vulnerability coming off her makes my stomach tighten. Why does she seem surprised?

"So much."

Doesn't she know that? How much we want her here?

Fuck, haven't I told her how much I need her? I hadn't wanted to overwhelm her, but now I'm wondering if she's been waiting for me.

Jesus, I'm dense sometimes.

"Can we chat later?" I whisper in her ear. Her eyebrows furrow. "It's all good, I promise." I kiss her lips. It's quick 'cause my kids are with us, but it's obvious she and I need some time alone to talk this out.

We get all the food set up buffet-style on picnic tables my brother set up in the back yard under an enormous white tent Allison's parents loaned us. They "entertain" often and offered it to us, probably so they don't melt under the sun.

"This looks amazing." My stomach rumbles as I check out the spread. Homemade potato salad, chicken salad, fruit salad, barbecue chicken, different kinds of dips. My woman outdid herself. "Pretty sure that's gonna taste better than anything we could've gotten catered."

"Hells yeah." Logan leans over and grabs a chunk of watermelon.

My mom smacks it out of his hand. "Manners! Wait until the guests finish arriving." She turns and pulls Tori into a hug. "This looks delicious, dear. I knew you were a keeper the moment I met you."

A smile lifts my lips. Mom is one hundred percent Team Tori. She apologized the other night for barging in on us, surprising us with her return, but that's nonsense. We'll figure out how to make everything work. It'll be better now that Mom's moved back in with my brother, though he's less excited now that he has no place to sex up his lady friends.

"You know, some people might be vegan." Allison saunters up, a scowl on her face. How was I ever attracted to this woman? Was she always this mean?

I open my mouth to respond, but Mom beats me to it. "This is Texas, Allison. Finicky guests can eat the fruit salad or suck on some hay."

Allison rolls her eyes and then glares at Tori. "Don't you want to change?" Of course, Allison is gussied up in overpriced designer threads.

"Be nice," I growl under my breath. "I'm not fucking kidding." We've had it out, and I've warned her that Tori is important to me.

I can't really make heads or tails of Allison's behavior. One minute, she's irate and throwing temper tantrums, the next, she's all smiles. She's making me dizzy with her back and forth.

Tori shrugs, looking uncomfortable. "I wasn't planning to change. This is what I wear."

"Whatever." Turning to me, Allison motions across the yard. "Remember that the Harrisons want a trainer, and the Dumonts are looking for help breeding their mare." For a woman who had zero interest in the ranch when we were married, she sure has pulled a turnabout. Half of these people are friends of her parents, and Allison says I should schmooze.

Yeah, I don't schmooze.

But I'm trying not to be a dick because I suppose this is her way of supporting the ranch. It's true we can always use new clients, but I underestimated how annoyed I'd be having to deal with my ex-wife. I keep telling myself it's worth it if I get the kids. I'll give every last penny in my pocket to make that happen.

When Allison heads for her parents, I grab Tori's hand and pull her off to the side. "We just gotta get through today." I lower my voice. "My lawyer is finalizing the terms of the contract. Pretty sure after this weekend, things will change around here." I fucking hope so because I can't stand Allison's bullshit any longer.

Tori nods and gives me a hesitant smile. She's about to say something when banging on the other side of the tent starts up again.

"What's going on?"

I motion behind me. "My friend James is putting the finishing touches on a new swing set for the kids."

"They're gonna love it!" Her brilliant smile wanes. "I hope it wasn't too expensive, though."

"I got a great deal since I helped him a while back when he was having trouble with his marriage. He kinda owes me."

She puts her hand on my arm. "Mila and Cody will be so excited."

"I hope so. This summer has been tough on them, and I wanted to do something extra special." I lean in closer. "Wanna do something special for you too. Can you stay over tonight?"

Before she answers, Mila tugs on her arm. I'm smiling down at my two favorite girls when my buddy smacks me on the back. "We're all set, Ethan." James flashes that smile that's always gotten all the girls. It's gotten him in trouble once or twice with his wife too. Glad he's changed it all around.

He catches a glimpse of Tori and does a double-take.

I joke with him under my breath, "Don't even think of flirting with my woman, asshole."

A streak of jealousy rises in me when I consider James laying that charm on Tori.

With a quick shake of my head, I shrug off that idea. He'd never do anything to threaten his marriage again or our friendship.

50

TORI

I'M GLAD I'M NEAR THE GROUND, KNEELING NEXT TO MILA, because that voice would've knocked me over if I were standing. With a trembling hand, I balance myself against the ground beneath me and take a shallow breath.

What is he doing here?

I must've been a bad person in a prior life because why else does this shit happen to me?

I'm frozen, like a deer trapped on a long stretch of highway traffic. The only movement is my pounding heart that I can practically see thumping through my tank top.

I peer around Mila, wondering if I'm experiencing some kind of psychotic break. How else can I explain why Jamie—Jamie, my cheating douchebag ex—is standing a few feet away?

He and Ethan are chatting it up like old friends, but I can't make sense of what they're saying because blood is rushing through my ears.

"Babe. Want you to meet someone." Ethan turns and smiles down at me. That smile pierces my heart.

Will he look at me the same way once he knows what happened? And that it happened with *his friend*?

Oh, God, I slept with one of Ethan's friends. I told Ethan the broad strokes of what went down with my ex, but not *how* I found out Jamie was married and certainly not how my life imploded afterward. *Fuck, fuck, fuck.*

I take the doll Mila was trying to hand me, and she bolts for her friends who are surrounding the swing set. The one Jamie just set up.

Dusting off my shins, I slowly stand on unsteady legs. I feel all knobby-kneed and light-headed. Maybe I'll pass out or die from a heat stroke and spare myself this conversation.

Swallowing, I let Ethan take my clammy hand.

"James, this is my girlfriend Tori."

I steel myself and look at the dirtbag, who seems almost as shocked as I am to see him.

He's hulkier than when we were together, which is silly because he was already a big guy. Now he reminds me of a beefed-up bulldog, all bulky mass punctuated with a tiny head.

"James, is it?" I ask, not bothering to hide the venom in my voice. "Not Jamie?" Asshole was full of lies. I'm not surprised he goes by a different name.

He laughs uneasily and shifts back and forth. "Tori. Jesus Christ, girl. It's been a while."

Ah, the fucker is going to admit he knows me? This should be fun.

Nausea is swirling in my gut, acid thick in the back of my

throat. "Not since your birthday last summer," I add helpfully.

Ethan looks back and forth between us. "You guys know each other?"

I open my mouth to spew forth all the ways *James* can go to hell when he laughs.

"Yeah, I know Tori. She used to bartend at this place in Austin my buddies and I used to go to sometimes, but it's been a while." He gives me a pointed look to keep my mouth shut.

That's how you're going to play it?

Ethan wraps his arm around my shoulder. I'm so grateful to have him next to me, I could cry.

James's eyes narrow as he watches us together, the cool smile spreading on his face making me more anxious. "I thought you were trying to get Allison back. It's a shame you spent all last year wanting to make it work, hoping to win her back."

Fuck my life, he did not just say that.

Ethan coughs. "We went south a long time ago. Not sure there was anything to work out."

"Huh. That's weird. Pretty sure I just heard her tell Felicia that you guys might reconcile." He points his chin to the other side of the tent where Allison is talking to a woman with long black hair. *Jamie's wife.* Yes, I remember her naked ass as she blew her husband. Isn't this a festive party?

"No, man." Ethan squeezes my shoulder. "You must've misheard."

I'm going to hurl. Would it be wrong to shank Jamie—I mean *James*—first?

Beverly waves everyone over to the buffet table, and I skirt out of the way, a potent mixture of shame and contempt rounding the curves of my heart like a raging river.

"Tori, dear," Beverly whispers, "can you do me a favor and grab more napkins out of the kitchen?"

I've never moved so fast in my life.

～

Except for the cake cutting, I manage to hide out in the kitchen. Whipping up more fruit salad or dip. Washing dishes. Making sure the kids make it to the potty in time. I eventually fall into the familiar routine of making a few guests mixed drinks.

When Beverly asks if I'm okay, I tell her I have a headache, and she pats my hand sweetly and offers pain relievers. When Ethan asks if I'd like to join him outside, I use the same excuse, even though lying to him makes me feel guilty. But there's no telling what I might say to Jamie right now, and I won't let myself make a scene at Cody's birthday party. Not with so many of Ethan's business associates here.

This is where my sister would tell me to lock down the crazy. That it's not worth the repercussions of being unfiltered.

I'll tell Ethan the truth after the guests have left.

Not here, though.

Not now.

Through the back window, the sounds of the party waft up through the late afternoon and early evening. Children laughing. Women gossiping. Men talking about horses and beer and cigars. The scent of barbecue and cedar floating in the air.

On a typical day, I'd love this kind of party. I'd be playing with the kids on the new swing set. Joking and mingling and having a blast. Taking Ethan's hand so we could dance to the Rolling Stones drifting from the sound system.

Wild Horses, I think with a smile. Logan must've made the playlist.

Instead, I'm hiding and confused and hurt.

Because it pains me to see Allison planted next to Ethan at the picnic table with her parents and his mom. It hurts to see the easy way they laugh, and the picture-perfect way they look when Cody climbs onto his dad's lap, and Mila wanders over to her mom's side.

But what can I do?

Nothing.

Because they were a family long before I arrived on the ranch.

Allison is obviously on her best behavior, and I feel murderous when she places her hand on Ethan's shoulder and leans toward him to whisper something.

"You're in over your head, sugar plum." Jamie's voice in my ear makes me jerk away. "She's a done deal. You think Ethan can resist that beautiful woman and her family's money?"

He trails a finger over my shoulder, and I slap it away. "Don't fucking touch me, *Jamie.*" My breath is a harsh pant, that light-headed feeling back with vengeance.

"I just hate seeing you get hurt, is all. Don't want you caught up in this mess."

"That's rich coming from you. I'm sure your great sense of

altruism is at the heart of your advice." I step around the island, needing to put space between us. He follows two steps behind like a predator.

"Honestly, I think you probably saved their marriage. Ethan might deny it to you, but I know for a fact they've been talking every day."

The air in my lungs stalls when I look for some hint that he's lying, but he stares me straight in the eye.

In my head, the comparison is quick. I've barely spoken to Ethan during the last two weeks, but he's been talking to Allison daily?

The corner of his mouth tilts up and he continues his assault to my heart. "Want to hear the ironic part here?" He lifts his thumb over his shoulder. "Ethan's the one who talked me into staying with Felicia. Said the side chick I was seeing wasn't worth my time. Wasn't worth my marriage. That marriage was sacred and worth any sacrifice. Wise words. Ones I'm guessing he'll probably heed once Allison tells him she's reconsidered the divorce and wants to come home. I think she saw the hot piece of ass Ethan was fucking and had a change of heart, and she has you to thank for showing her how good she had it. See. I told you. Ironic."

He laughs, the sound scraping over my skin like white-hot coals.

A boulder of emotion builds in my chest, and I shake my head. "You're lying." Isn't he?

"Sugar plum, I've lied about a lot of things in my life, but I'm not now." With one hand on the counter, he leans back, cool and collected.

He's telling the truth. At least in part. But which part?

Shoving his hands in his pockets, he lowers his voice.

"Why are you with Ethan anyway? I thought you and I had a good thing."

Laughter, shrill and maniacal, sweeps out of me. "You can't be serious." Why does this asshole care?

His spicy cologne and smug smile take me back to the days and weeks after that dreadful day at his house. The messages he left on my phone. Those stupid bouquets of carnations. How he kept trying to track me down at work.

"Are you jealous I'm with Ethan?"

He scoffs, but there's that weird tick in his jaw. "Just saying when it goes to hell here, you know who you can turn to."

Yeaaah, no.

Outside the window, guests are leaving. A steady stream of voices leads around the side of the house to the cars parked out front.

Thank God. Let this day end.

The back door opens and several sets of footsteps echo closer. My heart is in my throat when I see that it's Ethan, Allison, and Felicia.

Jamie's wife watches me warily as she strides up to her husband and wraps her arm around his waist. "Boo, Allison and I were saying we should go on a double date while we're still in town. For old times' sake."

Jamie's thousand-watt full-of-bullshit smile lights up. "Definitely."

Needing to see his reaction despite the dread building in my belly, I glance at Allison and Ethan across the island. She tugs on his arm and stares up at him. "Wouldn't that be fun?"

Confusion etches across Ethan's face, and he removes her hand. "Allison, I don't think that's—"

Her other hand slithers up his chest, and a pout forms on her lips as she leans closer to him.

My vision hazes red like that elevator scene from *The Shining.*

"Get your fucking hands off him." The words are out of my mouth before I can think better of it. And now that I've started, I can't stop. "You had your chance with him, and you walked away from him and your kids, you selfish bitch."

Everyone stares at me, mouths open, eyes wide. Let them stare.

It takes a second for her to gather herself, and I can almost see her talons extend, but I also see victory in her eyes.

She wants this. She's been waiting to strike like a viper.

"Guess what, you slut, now that I'm a partner on this ranch, you're fired, so get your shit and your trampy ass out of my house. This is my kitchen. Those are my kids. This is *my* husband."

Ethan rears back like someone slapped him. "Allison, what the fuck is wrong with you?"

Little feet come padding down the hall, interrupting him. Mila immediately hugs Allison. "What's wrong, Mommy?"

With a dramatic sniffle, Allison wipes her eyes. "I'm just trying to make Daddy see how much I love you guys." *Oh, my God. This woman has no limits.* I've never seen her extend one compassionate gesture to her kids or husband in private. Allison turns to Ethan. "Didn't you tell me you'd do *anything* to have me back? That you'd do *anything* for their kids to have their mommy home? Didn't you say they cry at night because they miss me so much? We could end all of that right now."

Ethan glances down at his daughter, a pained expression on his face.

The tick tock of the clock on the wall swells in my ears as he stands still and I silently beg him to say something. Anything.

Chuckling, Jamie smirks at me and stretches an arm around his wife. "Gotta say, man, I'm kinda surprised you hired Tori. What with her record and all. Hope you didn't let her drive the kids anywhere."

"What?" My voice is fragile, like spun glass. One misstep and I'll break apart.

Why would he bring that up? He knew how mortified I was about that time in my life.

His wife sneers like she just stepped in a steamy pile of horse shit. "I thought you needed certain standards to hold this kind of job."

"Sorry, Tori," Jamie says as though the man feels even a hint of remorse. "Want to make sure my friends know the real you. Know that they're getting a college dropout who partied so hard, she nearly killed a car-load of her friends when they were out joyriding. Not sure that's the kind of woman I'd hire to watch my children."

The gasp I hear is mine.

Because that's a version of the truth, but it's distorted and ugly. It's my life, the blood and guts of it all smeared and inside out, like some victim of a horror movie.

For a second, I can't breathe.

I'm underwater.

Sinking. Sucking in water. Suffocating.

I open my mouth, but nothing comes out.

I don't know how to explain what really happened. How

to untangle the thread of truth from the ball of lies Jamie just threw in my face.

Absurdly, my thoughts go to that astronomy course I nearly failed. Of the way planets collide so powerfully, they rip apart time, gnawing it open with their jaws.

I wonder if this is how it feels to be trapped in that kind of wreckage. Like noiseless, dark energy sparking out of existence.

Ethan's voice slices through the overwhelming silence in the room. But it's not the voice of my boyfriend. It's the man who interviewed me months ago. Harsh. Demanding. Angry. "What's he talking about, Tori?"

My eyes dart between everyone in the room.

Ethan, who's pissed and confused, whose eyes beseech me to tell him that Jamie's lying, that beg me to tell him he knows the real me.

Allison, who's triumphant and conniving and likely planning my slow death.

And Jamie, who's arrogant and so fucking pleased with himself he's practically levitating off the ground.

It's his haughty smirk that pushes me over the edge.

I'm a car skidding off a cliff. Tires squealing. Dirt flying. Engine roaring.

I'm that girl.

Again.

The one who loses control and veers off the road.

Untethered and unmoored.

Reckless.

But if I'm going down, I'm taking that asshole with me.

51

TORI

Flushed and feverish, I kneel down in front of Mila. "Honey, go find Uncle Logan. Stay with him, okay?" I don't understand how I channel a gentle tone with Mila when the storm of emotion whipping through me is cresting.

She nods and skips off, completely ignoring Allison when she tells her to stay.

As I stand, I point to the path Mila took out the back door. "That's what happens when you ignore your kids, Allison. They ignore you." My voice gains strength. "And you can sweep in here and pretend like you're mother of the year for all your friends, but let's get one thing straight. I know you're a shitty parent, but worse? So do Mila and Cody, and they're the only ones who matter."

It's her turn to sputter, but I ignore her and turn to Ethan.

The distance in his eyes is devastating, but when he doesn't come to Allison's defense, I take that as a small victory and plow forward. Deep down, though, I'm preparing for the death blow to my heart when he learns the truth. "The question you should be asking is how Jamie knows so much about me."

His attention shifts to his friend, and I continue, my anger rising. "The question you should be asking is why Jamie cares. By the way, I'm calling him Jamie because that's what he told me to call him during the six months we dated." Ethan's eyes cut back to mine, his nostrils flaring. "I didn't know he was married. I didn't know he had children. I didn't know because he lied. About everything."

Behind me, Felicia gasps, he and his wife shouting I'm a liar and a whore and a cunt, but I ignore them. This isn't about them. This is about Ethan understanding.

"Remember when I told you about my ex?" I remind him. "Yes, part of what he told you about my past is true, which is why I never drove your kids anywhere except the one time you insisted."

"She's lying," Felicia screeches. "James has never cheated on me."

Looking over my shoulder, I shrug. Jamie's pale as I tell his wife the truth. "Then ask him how I know you have a tattoo of a fairy on your lower back, just above the dimple on your ass. Ask him how I know he bought *you* tickets to a Rangers game for *his* birthday last year. Ask him about how you came home early that day. How he shoved me in your bedroom closet so he could protect his dirty secret. Why he nearly choked you on his dick when I walked out to confront him."

I'd felt unhinged when I finally gathered myself and stormed out of that closet ready to tear into him, his marriage be damned. But one look at their naked bodies before me, closer this time, with his wife in his lap, taking him down her throat, and I was rendered speechless.

I'd thought, *That could be me. Completely clueless.*

The dirtbag had moaned loudly, shoving her down hard to distract her from my presence. In the moment, my rage deflated, and all I felt was resignation. He was an asshole. Her asshole. And she was welcome to have him.

In the two seconds I stood there, all of the crazy I'd planned to unleash fell by the wayside. I didn't need anymore problems.

But that didn't stop me from slashing his tires.

I clear my throat. "If he did that with me, how many other times has he cheated?"

"Motherfucker," Ethan growls behind me, and my skin prickles.

"You little psycho," Felicia wails. "You're the one who vandalized his car!"

"Guilty as charged." I hold up my hands and return my focus to Ethan. "I'm a lot of messed-up things, but I always cop to what I've done. I'm sorry I didn't tell you about my driving record. At first, I thought you hadn't done my background check because I was only supposed to be here temporarily while you found a real nanny through an agency. Then I hoped my sister had warned you. Because she does that. She cleans up my messes and gets me jobs."

I swallow, knowing how badly I've screwed up. "But when you kept offering me your truck, when you told me to drive the kids, I got too afraid to ask what you knew. Too much time had gone by. Too many opportunities to tell you about my past." *Too many intimate moments.* Tears burn in my eyes, and I swipe at them with the back of my hand. "I can't explain how you looked at me, but for the first time, I wasn't a screw-up. You didn't see me the way my family does. A mess. A flunky. A basketcase. And I didn't want to mess this up too. You and Mila and Cody were too important to me."

Ethan's expression is blank. "So tell me now. Tell me what happened."

"Are you serious?" Allison blows out a breath. "She's endangered the lives of our children."

"No, I didn't endanger your kids. I drove them once. *Once*. Under the speed limit for all of two miles, and Logan drove them home." Angrily, I wipe at another tear. "Here's the truth. I got a DUI my freshman year of college for driving my friends with open containers in the car. We drag-raced through some back roads we thought were empty, and they were empty, except for that state trooper who pulled me over. No one was injured, though." Even though Jamie made it seem like I had run over a busload of kids.

Awkwardly, I shift on my feet. "I had a few beers that night, but the breathalyzer showed that I was point zero five over the drinking limit. Plus, I was underage and drag-racing. All stupid shit on my part. I spent a night in jail. Lost my license for a while. Let my life fall apart. Wasn't the last time, either." I glare at Jamie.

I wish freshman year had taught me a lesson. While I never drove under the influence again, I partied away most of college like an idiot. Partied and worked to pay off my attorney bills. You'd think one night in county would teach me, but it took getting screwed over by Jamie for me to take a long, hard look at my life and try to make some lasting changes.

Allison moves close to Ethan before she narrows her eyes at me. "You need to leave. Now."

Ethan looks shell-shocked. Like the news of me having an affair with his friend and my arrest have shattered his impression of me.

With a trembling hand, I touch his chest. I keep my eyes pinned to the collar of his t-shirt. "I never meant to keep any of this from you, and I'm sorry if you feel like I've lied. That was never my intention." Finally, I brave a glance in his raging blue eyes. They're the color of the sky during a storm. "But I would suffer through all of that humiliation again if it brought me back to you."

Tell me you love me.

Tell me we're okay.

That we'll get through this.

That you forgive me.

He clears his throat and reaches for me, his touch gentle on my shoulder. "Tori, I—"

"Daaaaaddy!" Mila's wailing, frantic, as she skids into the kitchen. "Daddy! Cody fell. He's hurt re-re-real bad. Logan says it's an emer-emer-gency."

One minute Ethan's staring at me with so much emotion in his eyes, I want to weep. The next, he's gone, picking up his daughter and racing out the back door.

I watch it slam shut.

When I make sense of what just happened, that the baby is injured, I start to follow, but Allison grips my arm, digging her nails into my skin.

Her voice, toxic and bloodthirsty, is in my ear. "Get the fuck out of my house before I call the police. Unless you'd like another arrest on your record." She rattles off things she could lie about. That I stole jewelry or hurt the children or did drugs.

I'm standing there in stunned silence when two large hands grab me from behind and drag me down the hallway where I'm shoved out the front door.

I land on my ass and gasp for breath because the wind gets knocked out of me.

White spots dot my vision as I stare up at Jamie's furious face, but I'm scrambling back toward my car. Ignoring the voices. Ignoring the yelling.

Although everything in me is screaming to check on Cody, he's with his dad, and Ethan will know what to do. There's no one better to take care of the baby.

Jamie reaches again for me, his hulking figure something straight from my nightmares, and I stumble for my car.

I have to get away before he does something worse than push me.

I need the one person who's always had my back.

My sister.

52

TORI

"Does it hurt?" Kat's sweet voice washes over me.

I'm too weary to sugarcoat it tonight. "Yeah." My sister looks weepy as she stares at the angry purple bruises painting both of my biceps. I don't tell her about the one on my ass. "But I'm okay." Physically, at least.

I'm sprawled out on the couch in her living room, and Brady is pacing back and forth in front of us. "That goddamn asshole. I'm gonna rip his arms off his fucking body."

Brady didn't take any of this well, especially not the part where Jamie picked me up and physically threw me out of the house.

"I appreciate the sentiment, but you will do no such thing." I motion to Kat's enormous belly. "Stork alert. We got a baby about to land over here. You ending up in jail is not the way to kick things off. And we both know you're the one who bails *me* out. Not the other way around."

Neither of us laugh at my lame joke. I have to keep Brady

out of trouble, though. He's been there for me too many times over the years to let him get tangled up in my mess.

The mention of babies has me thinking about Cody, and I blink back the heat in my eyes. I hope he's okay. That whatever happened tonight wasn't too serious.

"Have you called Ethan?" my sister asks.

I shake my head, hot tears stinging my cheeks. The truth is I've been too scared to call. I know I should be brave, but I'm tired. So fucking tired. I don't have the heart to chase after Ethan. I've laid it on the line, and if he wants me, he knows where to find me.

But he doesn't call.

My phone sits still on the coffee table, its black screen taunting me.

Eventually, I stop checking it.

Kat lets me cry on her shoulder, and tonight I don't hold back.

Tonight, it's a dark torrent, this love. Full and unyielding. Crashing through me and carving out the last tender parts of my heart.

I let it cut.

Because when it's done, I won't wallow.

I won't let myself fall apart over another man.

Not again.

Not ever.

With a final click of the mouse, I force myself to smile. *This is good*, I remind myself. It doesn't matter that I feel like death because I'm moving forward. I've registered for my classes this fall, and that's positive.

Yes, I'm utterly heartbroken that Ethan and I are probably over, and while I'd love to curl up in a ball for the next week and eat my weight in ice cream, I won't let myself go that route.

Ignoring my swollen, itchy eyes, I set Kat's laptop on the kitchen table and reach for her hand. "Thanks," I whisper. "For everything."

"Anytime. I mean that."

She looks exhausted, and I feel guilty for bawling all over her last night, but that's what sisters are for, right? "I know you do. That's why you're my favorite sister."

We smile at each other like fools.

"Morning." Brady comes stomping in and pauses when he sees us.

I wave him in. "I'm done crying. You can do whatever you have to do."

He tells Kat he needs to pick up his check at the tattoo parlor in Austin, and then he'll get Izzy from his parents' house. "It shouldn't take longer than two hours." Worry knits his brows. "But maybe I should ask one of the guys to drop off the check."

I squeeze my sister's hand. "I've got Kat. If anything happens, I'm right here." He frowns, and I mock being offended. "What? I watch all those medical shows. *Grey's Anatomy*, reruns of *ER*, *House*. I got you, bro." Plus, my parents are driving up later today. They want to be here the moment this baby arrives.

Still frowning, he kisses his wife's forehead. "You're sure you're okay? You moaned all night."

"Oh my God, you guys." I cover my ears. "Too much information!"

Brady snickers and shakes his head. "She was moaning because she's so pregnant, doofus. Not because I was giving her the midnight express."

"LOL." Thank God.

My sister laughs. "I don't think you're supposed to say LOL in person."

"Says who? I do things my way. You do it yours." I'm difficult, but she knows this.

Brady eventually leaves after we assure him—again—that Kat's fine.

The first half hour alone goes well. We drink this weird ginger pregnancy tea, and I make my sister some scrambled eggs.

But then my luck goes south.

Really south.

Because her water breaks.

~

Kat looks at me like I'm crazy. "Let's just wait for Brady."

"He's probably in Austin right now, and your contractions are five minutes apart. *Five.* Why didn't you tell me your back hurt *all night*?"

"I didn't think they were contractions!" Her voice is wheezy since she's trying to breathe through the pain.

"Look, I'm driving you to the hospital. It'll be fine. If we hurry, we'll beat the noon rush. Bet you can pop out this baby before dinner. I'm a speed demon when I want to be, remember? We can drag-race on the way there."

Her death grip on my hand makes me pause. "Stop trying to be funny."

"I'm not *trying*. I'm naturally funny. Now get your ass in the truck. Come on, I'll help you waddle." In the meanwhile, hopefully Brady will get my messages and haul himself back here.

Except, shit. Now we're headed to the hospital. Whatever. One crisis at a time.

We only make it to the Lone Star diner when I have to pull over because Kat says she has to push.

All I know is that's bad.

I run into the packed restaurant screaming like a crazy person. "I need a doctor! A nurse! A paramedic! Someone who knows more than McDreamy references." Everyone stares at me.

Fuck my life, nothing ever works like it does in the movies.

Rounding the truck, I open the passenger door. "How you doing?"

Sweat beads her forehead, and she reaches for me with a clammy hand. "Baby's coming. Like, now."

Can't freak out.

Can't.

Cannot.

"Everything's gonna be okay." I don't recognize my voice because inside I'm losing my shit. "Ambulance is on its way."

The Texas heat sears into me as I bounce on my toes with nervous energy and yank my hair into a massive bun on top of my head.

Why did I tell Brady to go? Why?

A small audience gathers behind me. Patrons from the restaurant and some neighbors. Scanning the faces, I spot one of the waitresses. "Get me some clean towels and some hot water. Maybe a glass of ice water too. Oh, and a clean turkey baster!"

She nods like this makes perfect sense, and I ignore the strange look on my sister's face. No need to tell her what that last item is for.

"Let's get you more comfortable." I release the lever for Kat's seat and shift the whole contraption back as slowly as possible before I recline her. "Better?"

"Yeah." Her pasty, pale complexion freaks me out. She might be the one in labor, but I have to remind myself to breathe too.

I feel bad that she's sitting here with a towel under her ass like a diaper and half of our town is watching this go down. *Ugh, the indignity of childbirth.*

Please, don't poop, Kat. I know you'll never forgive me for dropping a deuce in front of so many people.

The waitress runs up to me with the supplies I asked her for, and I lean over my sister and set everything on the driver's seat except for the ice water, which I offer to Kat to drink.

"Tori!"

Goosebumps race up and down my arms. That voice.

When I see Ethan stalking toward me, weaving through the crowd, my knees almost buckle.

It takes two seconds to shake myself out of it.

Fuck that.

I don't have time to deal with him right now even though my heart can't decide if I'm elated to see him or so fucking mad, I wanna sock him in the nuts.

"What's going on?" he asks over my shoulder.

I snort. "What does it look like? Kat's having her baby." *Duh.* I roll my eyes.

As discreetly as possible, I reach for the container of hand sanitizer and squirt it all over myself.

When Kat sees what I'm doing, her eyes widen. "Why do you need that?"

"In the event you pop out a living, breathing human before the paramedics arrive, I thought I should have clean hands. So I can catch him. Or her." Damn it, why didn't I bring any blankets? "I used to play basketball in high school. I got you, babe."

I don't remind her that I sucked at basketball and all that dribbling. I'm not good with big balls.

I'm too freaked out to mentally snicker at my dirty joke.

When her next contraction overwhelms her, a war-like shriek breaks from her lips, making me jump, but Ethan places a warm hand on my shoulder.

I clench my eyes shut and say a prayer for Kat and this baby. That they're okay. That I can get them through this.

We can do this.

Behind me, I tell everyone behind me to back off, because I need to protect the sanctity of my sister's vag, and Ethan helps me, making sure no one can see into the cab of the truck.

I hoist up Kat's butt so I can push down her soggy underwear, which is tough to do standing outside the passenger side, leaning in, but it's not like there's an easier way. She lifts her swollen legs, balancing her feet on the edge of her seat, and grunts.

"Where's Brady?" She's crying and trembling.

Ethan leans over my shoulder. "He's coming. I just talked to him."

Holding her hand, I start spouting nonsense to distract her. "I can't believe you didn't tell me you lost your mucus plug. I thought sisters were supposed to tell each other everything."

She sniffles in between contractions. "How do you know about mucus plugs?"

"Google. I told you I was studying up on pregnancy. You're my big sister. My only sister. You think I'm going to let you pass a beach ball through your hoo-ha and not research it? *Hello*. I'm true blue."

Ethan mumbles something behind me that sounds like, "You are," but I don't have time to figure it out because my sister is pushing and bawling and sweating. So much sweating.

"Do you want to squat? I hear squatting is a thing. It's all natural and helps get more oxygen to the baby. And, like, women drop trou in the Amazon, squat, and squirt out their babies, but you know, without the actual squirting. Hopefully." *Please, Jesus, no squirting.*

"Stop making me laugh." She smacks me, and I flinch because she nailed that bruise on my arm, but she probably doesn't know it because my t-shirt has three-quarter sleeves. "Yes, I want to squat. Help me."

It's a tough squeeze because she's carrying a Goliath-sized

child, but I help her plant her feet on the floor and wedge her body between the seat and the dash.

Pausing, she pulls me close until we're eye to eye. Damn, she's strong for a pregnant lady. "Catch. The. Baby. Or. Else."

"On my life, I'll catch this baby." Truer words were never spoken.

Reaching underneath her, I ignore the weird gush of fluid and hope I don't catch a turd instead of a child.

Holy shit. I'm really doing this.

Another contraction makes Kat wobble, but Ethan reaches over my shoulder and steadies her. She eyes me warily. "Sorry this is so gross."

"It is gross, but it's okay. I love you. Just don't forget to name the baby after me."

"No more jokes."

"I can't help it."

Her face goes red with another contraction. More screaming and crying.

And then... a wet, squelching plop.

I fumble, but only a smidge.

Because I promised my sister.

Checking between the baby's legs, I smile through my tears—I have a niece!

And I caught her with a prayer and my bare hands like a freaking wide receiver.

I am officially a badass.

"And then Tori sucked the fluid out of the baby's mouth with a turkey baster!" my sister exclaims while she snuggles baby Annabelle Victoria Shepherd to her chest. "She was amazing!"

Everyone in the hospital room stares at me. Brady, his parents, my parents, Ethan.

I avert my teary eyes.

My mother crosses herself. "*Gracias a Dios que estabas con tu hermana, Victoria.*"

She thanks God I was with my sister.

"Yes, *mija*. We're so glad you were there." Dad gives me a weird side hug. "If anyone could do this, it's you. You were always the brave one. Always so bold and strong."

Wait. Whaaaat?

Dad smiles at Ethan. "But you know you have your hands full with this one, right?"

I look away, not wanting to see Ethan's expression. It's still too painful.

My parents don't know we broke up. I mean, I guess we broke up. Ethan never came to see me last night, and now that the adrenaline from the live birth experience is waning, all the reasons why I'm pissed at him are falling into place like a game of Tetris.

So I'm shocked—stunned—when Ethan pulls me to his chest and kisses my forehead. "Well, I love her, so I'll gladly take whatever she's offering."

I shove him away. "*Now*? You tell me that *now*?"

My dad laughs and pats him on the back. "Good luck with my little fireball."

"We need to talk." Angrily, I poke Ethan in the chest, and everyone behind me chuckles except Brady. I'm pretty sure if he weren't about to cradle his baby, he'd be in Ethan's face right now for letting Jamie treat me like shit.

I give my brother-in-law a look.

I got this.

53

ETHAN

Tori marches out of the hospital room and into the hall, breathing flames of fury and looking so damn beautiful, she takes my breath away. Even with God knows what on her t-shirt and her half-skewed hair bun.

My heart's been in my throat all morning. I need to talk to her. Want to wrap my arms around her and explain.

I was frantic to find her, racing back to her sister's house only to spot Kat's truck in the parking lot of the diner. Since then, well, Kat giving birth took precedence.

In the hall, I pause at the nurse's station to swipe an extra set of scrubs. "Tori, wait."

Reluctantly, she slows down, but doesn't turn to look at me.

I get it. I fucked up last night. Just... I need to explain.

Jogging, I catch up to her and drag her into an empty room and close the door behind us. It's quiet here on the maternity ward, and I don't bother turning on the lights. I'm half-afraid they'll be too harsh and startle her.

"Here." I hand her the scrubs and wave to her top. "You, uh, you got some blood on you. Thought you might want to change." Her nostrils flare, and I smile. "Don't be stubborn. Take it."

"Don't tell me what to do."

I love this. Her fierceness.

My smile widens when she snatches it outta my hand. She doesn't bother turning around. Just whips off her t-shirt and is halfway into the scrubs when she steps into the sliver of sunlight peeking through the window blinds.

Just like that, my humor dries up.

"What the fuck is this?" I run my finger over the purple marks on her arm. *It looks like a hand wrapped around her.* Slowly, I turn her to the other side where I find a matching bruise. "Is this from—" I should've killed him last night instead of breaking his nose.

She shrugs out of my hold, and though her stance is strong—legs apart, chin up—her voice wavers. "When you went out back to check on Cody, your wife and Jamie threw me out of the house."

"She's not my wife." I stalk closer, backing her up against the wall, and cup her face. "Baby, he touched you?" It pains me to say those words. She tries to look away, but I tilt her chin up. "Don't hide from me." I take a breath. "Did he touch you?"

The scrubs wrap around the front of her chest and fore-arms. Slender pink straps from her bra peek up over her shoulders. She's so vulnerable like this. Bare and half-clothed. The thought of James hurting her makes me want to punch a hole through the drywall.

Those big hazel eyes water, so much emotion brimming

between us. A single tear spills over her lashes. "Yes. He dragged me out of the house. Threw me down on the ground."

I'm almost grateful I don't have my shotgun because at this very moment, I'm tempted to use it on that asshole.

"*Motherfucker.*" I take a breath to calm down before leaning closer. "I'm so sorry he hurt you and that I wasn't there to stop him." If I ever see that lowlife again, I will end him.

Like a dam that breaks, her choked sob nearly does me in, and I whisper more apologies. Whisper how much she means to me. How much I love her.

"Then why didn't you say anything last night?" She's wiping her cheeks and I stop her. I deserve to see each drop fall. To feel every bit of her pain. "Why didn't you call me afterward? Or come over? Or something? I felt so stupid watching my phone, thinking you'd call."

Misery overwhelms me to know I did this to her. "God, I'm sorry. Cody broke his arm and—"

"*What?*" Her small fists land on my shoulders, her eyes huge saucers.

Remembering what happened, seeing my son crumpled on the ground, hits me with a wave of helplessness. "He fell off the swing set, and we weren't sure if he also lost consciousness. After the doctors set his arm in a cast, they wanted to keep him here for observation overnight. My phone died, but as soon as he was discharged this morning, I got him comfortable at home and came to find you." By the time my cell charged in my truck, I was almost home and wanted to talk face-to-face with Tori. "My mom's with him now."

A trembling hand covers her mouth. "Oh, my God. Is he okay?"

"He was pretty shaken. Hell, I was too." The last twenty-four hours have been pure madness. From nearly breaking my hand on James's face to carrying Cody into the ER and watching Tori deliver Kat's baby, my emotions are wrung out.

She hugs me, and I close my eyes. I know she still has to be hurt from what happened last night, but here she is, comforting me. So with my nose in her silky hair, I tell her what's been eating at me, gnawing at me. "I should've said something last night. I wish I could rewind the whole evening and do it differently. At first, I was pissed that James knew so much about you that I didn't. I was straight-up jealous." Insanely jealous. Out-of-my-mind jealous.

I trace her shoulder with my lips. Up her slender neck. Behind the soft lobe of her ear. "I hated the idea of him touching you, baby. Being with you. Loving you." Even now, I have to close my eyes to stave off the anger.

This possessiveness is new to me. I've never been a jealous guy or felt the need to mark my territory. But I'm different with Tori. I want her in a way I've never wanted another woman.

I need her to forgive me for my missteps last night, but I have to know. "Why didn't you tell me? About that shit in college? About the way James screwed you over?" That monster threw her in a goddamn closet while his wife gave him head. No wonder Tori gave me the hairy eyeball at the beginning of the summer. I'd have trust issues too after that experience.

Her tears wet her flushed cheeks, and I kiss them away. One by one.

"I felt ashamed, Ethan." She hiccups and shakes her head. "It was all so humiliating. Jamie turned into such a creeper after we broke up, stalking me. Sending me flowers. Trying to talk to my friends about me. I let what happened with him suck me into a downward spiral that I never really recovered from. Failed out of school. Couldn't get my shit together. It's one of the reasons I wanted to be near my sister. To regroup."

Fuck, it hurts to hear all the ways he tormented her. "Last night I was reeling from shock that this friend I looked up to and respected had not only cheated on his wife, but was a scumbag to you. He had me completely fooled." I'd known James through Felicia since she and Allison grew up together, but he and I became tight when he helped me renovate my house. At the time, I'd thought he was someone to admire. Someone I should emulate. What a fucking joke.

Years later, when he told me he was "struggling with temptation," he made it sound like he'd only been flirting around, not cheating. Not that I condone either behavior, but clearly he was sugarcoating the truth.

Tori chews on her nail. "Why didn't you know about my driving record? Didn't you do a background check?"

"That was Logan's doing. He said he had it covered and that you were cool. I should totally kick his ass for lying to me, but I can guess what he was thinking. That he liked you as a person and knew Kat and Brady and trusted them."

"I'm sorry. I should've said something when he brought up my internship at the law firm." Her lips twist, and her eyes cast down. "All of this stuff in my past was so embarrassing, and I didn't want you to see me differently or think I couldn't handle watching Cody and Mila. Didn't want you to see me the way my family does."

That gives me pause. "What are you talking about? They love you. Did you see the same woman I did today? Delivering Kat's baby in a pick-up with nothing but towels from a diner, hand sanitizer, and a turkey baster? You're a hero, honey. I'm not sure I would've been so even-keeled, and I've delivered a dozen foals over the years."

She laughs through her tears, the realization of what she did shining in her eyes. "I did do that, huh?"

"You kicked ass. I'm so fucking proud of you." I drag my lips against hers, moaning when she opens to me. I'm ready to make all kinds of promises to this girl when the door bangs open, and we pop apart.

A nurse wheeling in a very pregnant woman glares at us, and I laugh as I help Tori put on her scrubs. "Sorry 'bout that, ma'am." Grabbing Tori's hand, I drag her out, because we need more time to talk.

54

ETHAN

THE WINDSHIELD WIPERS THUMP NOISILY BACK AND FORTH ON my truck, barely swiping away the rain before my visibility drops to zero again.

"This is crazy," Tori murmurs next to me.

"Nothing like a summer storm." This one blew in out of nowhere, darkening the afternoon sky and backing up traffic.

Tori wanted to love up on Cody before she returned to her sister's to prepare for the baby's arrival, so I said I'd drive her. Told her I didn't mind dropping her back off at the hospital tomorrow either. Life is hectic for both of us right now, but if I have to play chauffeur to see her a few minutes each day, then so be it. Because I need to be with my girl.

Despite our talk at the hospital, she's been quiet on the drive to the ranch. I'm about to ask her if she's okay when the rain gets so intense, I have to pull off down an access ramp. I'd rather wait out the storm for ten minutes than get in an accident.

We take the first exit, winding along an isolated road, and

end up in a parking lot behind a deserted warehouse. I shift my truck into park.

"Whatcha thinking about over there?" I thread my fingers through hers. "Lay it on me."

Her thumb slides back and forth across my hand. "How is this supposed to work?" With a sad sigh, she pulls away. "I understand everything that happened with Jamie, and I totally get where you were coming from and what happened last night with him. But what I can't reconcile is where I stand with you and Allison. Jamie told me you guys were talking on the phone every day, and you have photos of her all over the house—"

"Let me clear this up." *Tori is jealous. Glad I'm not the only one who loses it over this kind of thing.* "Allison called *me* every day. Left messages. To ask about stupid shit or tell me she had invited someone else to the party. Since you left to your sister's, I've only talked to her once on the phone." I reach for her hand again. "As for the photos, I never wanted Mila to miss her momma. She started having nightmares, and I thought keeping pics of our family might help her, but she stopped having those a few weeks after you moved in with us, so maybe it's time to tuck them away."

That wrinkle in her forehead smooths for a second, but then reappears. "Oh. No." She shakes her head. "The kids should have the photos. That makes sense. *Ugh.* I sound crazy."

"No, you don't." I kiss her wrist. "What else? Tell me what else happened last night."

Her shoulders slump. "It was bad." She swallows. "She threw me out of your house, Ethan. She threatened to call the cops for a whole host of made-up reasons."

She fills me in on how Allison told her off after I ran to check on Cody, and my blood starts to boil all over again, making me even more confident in my decision. "Baby, I don't want you to worry. There is no me and Allison."

"How can you say that? You guys are signing that co-op deal this week, and she made it clear she intends to reconcile with you."

"Trust me when I say it won't be a problem." That gets me an eye roll. She huffs and turns toward the window, which is fogged over. Unclicking my seatbelt and then hers, I scoop her out of her seat and into my lap. That gets me a glare.

"Seriously?"

I shrug. "What? I want to make sure you're hearing me when I say this. Are you listening?"

After another eye roll, she nods and settles in my arms.

"This is simple. I'm not going through with the co-op. Not with her at least."

"What are you talking about? How do you plan to pay her back that money?"

I rest my hand on her thigh. "Logan and I talked about it in the ER last night."

"After I told Logan what happened in the kitchen, he and I decided we're not moving forward with Allison as a partner." I've never been more grateful than last night to have my brother by my side. Once he knew Cody would be okay at the hospital, he got a ride home from a friend so he could get back to Mila, who was with our mom.

"We love the co-op idea, though, so we're spending the next few weeks trying to find an investor or two, just not Allison." I run my thumb along the hem of Tori's scrubs. "She showed her true colors yesterday, and I plan to fight for sole custody with no shared visitations if she threatens me."

"Oh, wow."

"I haven't wanted to play dirty, to drag her through the mud, but I will if she pushes me. I'm tired of her shit and disgusted with the way she treated you. The way she treats the kids, like they're an afterthought. The idea of getting back with her is so fucking insane, I'm still shocked she went there."

Allison didn't even bother to come to the hospital last night. After she saw our son wailing and hurt and crying for her, she left with Felicia. That's all I need to know about where her loyalties lie.

I tangle my fingers in Tori's hair and move her closer. "I feel like crap I wasn't there to protect you. My house is your home too, and I want you to be comfortable there."

Her eyes get misty. "Thanks. That means a lot to me."

"You mean a lot to me. You mean everything." I stroke her soft cheek. "I love you, Tori. So much."

"I love you too." Her eyes shift down, and an embarrassed smile tilts her lips. "I've sort of had it bad for you for a while now."

"Oh, yeah?" I kiss her neck, and she shivers in my arms. "You cold, baby?"

She nods and turns her face toward me. "But I'm thinking you could warm me up."

That's an idea I can get behind.

Glad we're parked off the beaten path, I scoot her around so she can straddle my lap, except my hand gets trapped between her and the door, and I wince.

"What's wrong?" she asks. I tilt her toward the passenger

seat so I can slide my hand free. When she sees the bruises, she gasps. "Did I do that just now?" She takes my hand in hers.

"No, it's from last night. From breaking James's nose."

Her mouth drops open. "Are you serious?"

"Dead serious, and had I known what he'd done to you in my own damn house, I would've given him a bigger ass-beating."

Christ. *He must've gone after Tori before he and I got into it.*

I had gotten Cody situated in the back of my truck with Logan so we could take him to the ER, and as I rounded the front of the vehicle, James got in my face to trash talk Tori. I'm not usually a man to break out a left hook, but between the vile things he was spouting about my girlfriend and my son's injury, my emotions were running high. Now that I know he basically stalked Tori after she found out he was married, I think the shithead was jealous.

Concern fills her eyes. "Are you okay? Does it hurt?"

"Yeah. A lot actually." I glance out the window that's still blurry with rain and condensation to mask my smile. "But you know, if you kiss it, I might feel better."

Out of the corner of my eye, I see the worry in her expression slowly morph into a sultry smirk. "Oh, yeah?"

"Definitely. Could help with the swelling."

Speaking of... I shift underneath her to make more room. With another flick of my wrist, I slide my seat back and recline a bit. *Better.*

Those pouty lips dust over my knuckles before she whispers, "What else hurts? What else can I make feel better?" She rocks in my lap, and I groan. Reaching up, I untie her bun and all that hair tumbles over us.

Setting aside the jokes, I tell her the truth. "Without you, everything hurts."

Her eyes turn hazy, those lips parting with a deep breath, electricity and love and some crazy goddamn chemistry sparking between us.

Our mouths crash together.

Somewhere in the universe, stars collide.

We scramble to get closer. To get skin to skin. I'm so hard, my groin aches.

Her shirt goes flying. Then mine. Until my gorgeous woman is only wearing that sheer pink bra and mesh shorts, so I know she can feel how hot I am for her as she thrusts against me.

I'm ravenous. Biting her neck. Sucking on her tight little nipples through the lace. Squeezing her luscious ass. Sliding my hand into her underwear and reveling at how wet she is for me.

Her hands fumble with my fly until she's pulling me out and stroking my cock that juts out to greet her. With a grunt, I shove my jeans down to make more room and then I'm tugging her shorts and underwear to the side so we can rub, without any barriers.

The feel of her, hot and slick, makes me clench my eyes shut. "Baby, you feel so good."

"You're about to feel better."

I'm reaching for my wallet when it hits me. "Damn it. I don't have any condoms." I gave the last one in my wallet to my brother the other night when he had a date.

Tori and I are panting and out of breath, but then she caresses my face. "You know I'm on the pill, but on a scale of one to ten, if I were to get pregnant, how freaked out would you be? Not that I'm looking to make this happen. Just asking as a barometer."

An automatic smile stretches across my face. That's an easy answer. "I wouldn't be freaked out at all. I'd love to have babies with you some day." God's honest truth. Never thought I'd be in a place to make long-term plans with another woman again, but when I look at Tori, I see my future stretched out before me, and I want it all with her.

Her eyes get shiny, and she gives me a soft kiss. "And you love me, right?"

"So damn much."

"Then maybe we don't have to use condoms." She studies me, her words cautious. "It would be a first for me, but I want to feel you."

"Fuck, yes." The idea of taking her bare is too intense, and I can't hold back.

Like an explosion of light and energy, we slam back together. Kissing and biting and grinding against each other like we might die if this doesn't happen.

Sweat builds along my back and chest, the steam from our bodies making the windows opaque against the rainstorm outside.

Reaching between us, she guides me into her tight heat, sliding her hips back and forth and wedging me in. It's a snug fit because I haven't done much to prepare her, but based on her moans, she's loving this as much as I am.

"Ethan. Oh, my God."

"I know, baby. You feel so good."

Finally, her ass hits my thighs, and she grabs on to the roof handle with one hand and my knee with the other. I shove her bra down so her swollen tits spill over and suck her nipples to the same rhythm she's using to impale herself on my cock. I help her glide up and down, the friction so insane, I'm outta my mind for her. For this.

"Need you to come," I grit out, pushing my hand into her panties and rubbing her clit in those tight circles I know she loves.

I make the mistake of looking down, of seeing how we're connected, her bare mound moving over my glistening length, taking me in, and I almost lose control.

Dragging my other hand into her hair, I pull her face to mine and kiss her. Bliss is sizzling at my spine, and I'm so damn close that when she starts to contract around me, I can't hold back any longer. My orgasm barrels through me like a cannonball. Pretty sure I curse or yell, but for the life of me, I can't make sense of the words coming out of my mouth because I'm coming so hard.

Tori's whole body arches, and I tuck my forehead to her chest as we pulse together, her body milking mine until she collapses against me.

Dear Jesus, that was awesome.

Drowsy and near delirious with endorphins, I hold her to me and try to catch my breath.

"Think I died and went to heaven," I pant with a laugh.

She makes a sleepy, contented sound against the crook of my neck. "Let's just stay here like this and not move."

"M'kay." Pretty sure we're making a mess all over our clothes, but I can't bring myself to care. I run my palm along her back. "Love you, baby."

Her lips tilt into a smile along my skin. "Love you too."

She snuggles on top of me, and I let my eyes fall closed, too content to move. "Got any plans this weekend? Been wanting to take you on that date." My voice is dry and a bit hoarse. "Sorry I've done everything ass-backwards, but I'd like to take you out." *And make you mine. Permanently.*

"I'd like that." She kisses my neck. "Will it be chaperoned, Mr. Carter?"

"Mmm." I rub her round bottom. "Not sure you can control yourself around me, huh?" I give her a hip thrust, seeing how I'm still nestled deep inside her.

A half-moan, half-giggle escapes her. "Where you're concerned, definitely not."

"Darlin', that makes two of us."

EPILOGUE

TORI
One year & four months later

THERE ARE A LOT OF SHOULD'VES IN THIS WORLD.

Like...

I *should've* studied harder in school.

I *should've* listened to my parents more growing up.

I *should've* partied less in college.

But I wouldn't change any mistake in my past because they've brought me here, to this point, with the people I love the most in this world.

"Guys, squish in closer," the photographer yells.

My family jostles together, my mom shivering in the chilly air. I wanted to do official family photos for the holidays, and since everyone loved the idea, we've all trekked down to San Antonio to do a special shoot at the River Walk. It's lit up with twinkle lights for the holidays. Every branch of every cypress tree that lines the sleepy waterway is glowing bright. The festive air grows as the late afternoon sky turns to dusk and more tourists bustle along the cobblestone footpath.

Brady's parents and Ethan's brood stand off to the side, watching my sister and me pose with our mom and dad in an alcove that extends over the water. Behind us, another tourist barge floats by, the sound of laughter and merriment spilling over.

The flash goes off. *Holy crap, that's bright.*

Ethan winks at me, and I smile a big, goofy grin, my heart doing a twirly-whirl in my chest.

He and I have been going strong since the summer I took that nanny job. After Cody's disastrous birthday party, even though Ethan and I were on the same page about moving forward in our relationship, we also decided we needed to take things slower. For the sake of the kids. For the sake of his divorce. For my own sanity.

Anyway, I thought it would be easier for him to fight for custody if he didn't have his new girlfriend shacking up with him. So I stayed with my sister and helped her with baby Annie and Izzy and took classes two days a week in Austin for a semester to finish my degree.

Living with my sister had its advantages. Besides being able to spoil my nieces, Kat tutored me, and I totally aced my classes. She also taught me how to balance the books for her lavender business, and with the right training, I found I was pretty decent at it.

When Ethan heard I was doing my sister's accounting, he wanted to hire me to do the same for Carter Cutting Horses. *Tori Duran, decent at math? Who knew?* I sure as hell didn't. But since bookkeeping is largely done on the computer, I'm not taxing my big brain too much.

Working for him also gave me an excellent reason to be at the ranch several days a week.

But Ethan was serious about taking me on dates. About wooing me like some hero in an old black-and-white movie. Even if some weeks he was so tired all he did was make me dinner, he made me feel special.

My favorite nights, though, are the ones where he wraps me in a blanket under the stars.

Our first "big" date was here, actually, at the River Walk, so today, as I look around this beautiful setting, all I can think about is how he kissed me right in this very spot and told me how much he loved me. It's pretty sweet that he suggested we take our photos here.

"Great! Let's switch things around." The photographer motions for Brady and his family to move in, so he and Kat can get their family's pic.

I'm stepping out of the shot when Brady calls my name. "Where you going? Get back in here, doofus." He's holding a slobbery Annie in one arm, and Izzy with the other. "We can't do a family portrait without my little sister." I smile like an idiot and squish back in.

Nerves twist in my stomach. Ethan's family is up next. Will they want me in their photo? Logan is hugging his mom to keep her warm, and Joey is holding everyone's coats when they step into the photo, poor girl. I'm really hoping Logan offers to take a pic with her because if he just brought Joey along to be our bellhop, I'll throttle him.

Next to them, Cody is climbing up his dad. Cody's almost

three and a half now, all rough-and-tumble boy, and still one hundred percent adorable. His arm healed well, thank God.

Mila smiles at me over her cup of hot chocolate. She and her brother have had a tough time with their mom, who finally admitted to Ethan she stood to gain a substantial inheritance from her late grandfather, but the stipulation in the will required her to be married. Which explains why Allison wanted to reconcile with her ex-husband all of a sudden that summer.

Ethan didn't have to rake her through the mud to maintain sole custody of the children. She met a guy, got married —probably to inherit that money—and lost what little interest she had in her kids.

As for the money Ethan owed her, since she had her grandfather's inheritance, she was less dogged about the situation. Ultimately, she agreed to getting repaid within three to five years, which meant she and Ethan would save the massive fees they were forking over to their attorneys because they didn't drag it out in court.

The day that was settled, Ethan asked me to move in with him, which I did in a heartbeat. My parents weren't thrilled, but where's the fun if I'm not keeping them on their toes? They do love Ethan and his kids, though, so they've been supportive and not too judgy.

The photographer claps and motions for Ethan's crew to move in. I step out with my family, but a hand wraps around mine and tugs me back.

"C'mon, sweetness." Ethan's voice, low and raspy in my ear, sends chills down my arms. "You know you belong in this one. You're my family too."

If there was snow on the ground, I'd be making snow

angels. Instead, I bite my lip to contain my smile a smidge, but he's laughing, so I know he sees it.

He's exhausted from his trip to Fort Worth, but you'd never know it by how chatty he's been today with my family. I guess it helped that he did so well at the Futurity, nabbing first place in his division. It's been a team effort to help him and his brother attend the contests, and I have to be honest— I like being on a team. Especially his team.

Between his winnings and how business is booming on the ranch, Ethan has been able to hire more help. That means we always have time to take the kids to the zoo or enjoy a late-night baseball game on TV.

After several more pics, the photographer tells us we're done, but Ethan waves at her. "I'd like to get a group shot of all of us if that's okay."

It's a tight fit, but Brady, Kat, and their kids stand on one side, both sets of parents on the other. Then Ethan's clan all get on their knees in the front. I start to move down too, but my sister tugs on my hand.

"What? Should I stand?"

She gives me the strangest smile. "Yes, I think you're supposed to stand for this part."

But I'm in the middle of the front row. Won't it be weird?

Except...

I look down and...

Whoa.

The flash goes off.

Ethan is on one knee holding up a small, velvet box.

"Oh, my God!" I jump up and down. *"YES!"*

Our families laugh, and Ethan gives me a wide smile. "Baby, I think you're supposed to wait until I ask."

I laugh, my pulse racing. *I can be quiet. I think.*

Taking my hand in his, he clears his throat. "Tori, in such a short time, you've become everything to me. My best friend, my soulmate, my confidante. Thank you for bringing me back to life. For showing me how to take challenges in stride. For believing in me. I love you like I've never loved anyone one else, and it would be my greatest honor if you'd be my wife."

That sound? That's the sound of my heart melting all over the pavement. "I love you too, Ethan." He blurs through my tears. "Can I say yes now?" I whisper. When he nods, I tackle him in a hug. "YES!"

The flash keeps going off, and there's a crowd of tourists oohing and awwing, and I'm crying all the tears.

His strong arms wrap around me, and he sits me on his knee. "You might want to see the ring before you say yes," he jokes.

I grab his handsome face in my hands. "You could give me a trinket out of a vending machine, and I'd still say yes." Truth.

Those baby-blue eyes on my rugged man mist a little. "But my girl deserves diamonds." He opens the velvet box and pulls out a blinding ring with a stunning rock in the middle and a gazillion small diamonds all around. "It's an eternity setting because that's how long I plan to love you."

Sniffling, I tuck my face into his neck because I'm overwhelmed. "Love you too. So, so much." I breathe him in and take a minute to count my blessings. "Does this mean we get to ride off into the sunset?"

Gently, he lifts my face to his and wipes away the tears.

"Absolutely. You'll be mine," he whispers. "Always and forever."

I smile against his kiss. "Always and forever."

Once upon a time, I didn't believe in fairy tales.

But then I found my prince.

And we saved each other.

TO MY READERS

Thanks for picking up *Reckless*! If you enjoyed Tori and Ethan's story, I hope you'll leave a review on Goodreads and the vendor where you purchased it. I try to read them all.

If Kat and Brady's story piqued your interest, be sure to check out *Shameless*!

Want to stay connected? Head over to my website, www.lexmartinwrites.com, and subscribe to my newsletter. You'll get new release alerts and access to exclusive giveaways, like signed paperbacks.

Want to read about Tori's bachelorette gifts for Kat accidentally landing in the wrong hands? You can get it here: http://BookHip.com/FGWSLB

Would you like a book for Logan? Let me know!

ACKNOWLEDGMENTS

I used my experiences growing up in Texas and my own family as inspiration for Tori's cultural background. Is Tori representative of every Hispanic female in South Texas? No, nor is she intended to be. She's simply the little rebel I wanted to hang out with for a few months while I drafted her story. I hope you enjoyed it because Tori was, hands-down, one of my favorite characters to write.

I have several people to thank for helping me make this book a reality...

My husband and daughters are endlessly supportive and love me even when I'm a cranky ass. If I've ever made you laugh or swoon as a reader, it's because my husband is amazing, and when I can't deal with life, he's the one who dusts me off and helps me figure it out. I'm a lucky girl.

My family probably blushes when confronted with my covers or blurbs, but they're the first to brag about my writing. Without my parents' many sacrifices growing up, I'd never have the bravery or skills to do this.

Kimberly Brower is the best agent ever, and I'm so grateful she stumbled across my little book three years ago.

Lauren Perry never ceases to amaze me with her gorgeous cover photos, and Najla Qamber always designs me stunning covers. I'm in awe of their talent.

Stacy Kestwick is the sprinkler of fairy dust. She makes my stories so much better with her critical eye and suggestions. I need her tough love.

RJ Locksley squeezes me in at the last minute for editing and doesn't yell at me when I'm late. I hope I can cross the pond some day and hug her. Speaking of last minute, Alison Evans-Maxwell, Becky Grover, and Jerica MacMillan are life-savers when it comes to proofing.

Serena McDonald is my magical unicorn and an amazing friend. I honestly don't know what I'd do without her. She admins Wildcats and is someone I lean on daily. (Hourly?) Plus, she always loves my early drafts and cheers me on until I'm done with each book. Everyone needs a Serena in their lives.

Ray generously took so much time to help me understand cutting horse competitions and training. Hanging out on his farm with his daughter years ago inspired Carter Cutting Horses. I'm so grateful to have stayed in touch with Ray's lovely family all this time. Plus, he has the best Southern accent, and I could listen to him talk all day.

A huge thanks to the four attorneys who helped me figure out the legalities of Ethan's divorce, dividing the family's estate, custody issues, and Tori's underaged drinking dilemma. My BFF Angela, Rob, Shea, and my writing partner, Leslie—I appreciate all of your patience with me and my ten million questions! I have y'all on speed dial. Just so you know. ;)

Leslie McAdam gets double thanks because I made her read *Reckless* three times. I owe her a big bottle of booze and a manicure. I'm so excited to work on another book with her!

Whitney Barbetti is my person, and she doesn't mind my 3 a.m. texts. I'm trying to talk her into moving with me back to Texas so we can be neighbors. C'mon, Whitney!

KL Grayson is always there when I need advice or help with a blurb. Kirby, thanks for all of your help with my drafts!

A huge hug to my beta readers. Bella Love, Amy Vox Libris, Erika Christofferson, Dora Ruiz Davalos, Lisa Marie Barrera, Natalie Léger Liebl, and Ella James— thanks for your critical eye, horse expertise, or Spanish proofing skills.

My sweet Aunt Judy creates the dolls Tori made with Mila. Judy sent them to my daughters, and I decided I had to include them in a book because they are such treasures. I'll post them on my Instagram so you can see what they look like.

Wildcats, you guys kick ass, and I love you.

Readers, thank you for taking the time to pick up my books. I'm endlessly grateful for your support.

Bloggers, I see all of your posts and book love. You're amazing. I appreciate every like, comment, and review so damn much.

Should we continue these Texas stories with something angsty and delicious for Logan? Let me know!

xo,

Lex

ALSO BY LEX MARTIN

All of my books can be read as standalones. Each one features a different couple.

Shameless

The Dearest Series:

Dearest Clementine

Finding Dandelion

Kissing Madeline

All About the D

(cowritten with Leslie McAdam)

ABOUT THE AUTHOR

Lex Martin is the *USA Today* bestselling author of *Shameless*, the *Dearest* series, and *All About the D*, books she hopes her readers love but her parents avoid. To stay up-to-date with her releases, head to her website and subscribe to her news-letter, or join her Facebook group, Lex Martin's Wildcats.

www.lexmartinwrites.com